JACOB'S ROOM

&

THE WAVES

BOOKS BY VIRGINIA WOOLF

VIRGINIA WOOLF

JACOB'S ROOM

THE WAVES

HARCOURT, BRACE & WORLD, INC. · NEW YORK

A HARVEST BOOK

B.6.61

JACOB'S ROOM

o of course," wrote Betty Flanders, pressing her heels rather deeper in the sand, "there was nothing for it but to leave."

Slowly welling from the point of her gold nib, pale blue ink dissolved the full stop; for there her pen stuck; her eyes fixed, and tears slowly filled them. The entire bay quivered; the lighthouse wobbled; and she had the illusion that the mast of Mr. Connor's little yacht was bending like a wax candle in the sun. She winked quickly. Accidents were awful things. She winked again. The mast was straight; the waves were regular; the lighthouse was upright; but the blot had spread.

". . . nothing for it but to leave," she read.

"Well, if Jacob doesn't want to play" (the shadow of Archer, her eldest son, fell across the notepaper and looked blue on the sand, and she felt chilly—it was the third of September already), "if Jacob doesn't want to play"—what a horrid blot! It must be getting late.

"Where *is* that tiresome little boy?" she said. "I don't see him. Run and find him. Tell him to come at once." ". . . but mercifully," she scribbled, ignoring the full stop, "everything seems satisfactorily arranged, packed though we are like herrings in a barrel, and forced to stand the perambulator which the landlady quite naturally won't allow. . . ."

Such were Betty Flanders's letters to Captain Barfoot—many-paged, tear-stained. Scarborough is seven hundred miles from Cornwall: Captain Barfoot is in Scarborough: Seabrook is dead. Tears made all the dahlias in her garden undulate in red waves and flashed the glass house in her eyes, and spangled the kitchen with bright knives, and made Mrs. Jarvis, the rector's wife, think at church, while the hymn-tune played and Mrs. Flanders bent low over her little boys' heads, that marriage is a fortress and widows stray solitary in the open fields, picking up stones, gleaning a few golden straws, lonely, unprotected, poor creatures. Mrs. Flanders had been a widow for these two years.

"Ja—cob! Ja—cob!" Archer shouted.

"Scarborough," Mrs. Flanders wrote on the envelope, and dashed a bold line beneath; it was her native town; the hub of the universe. But a stamp? She ferreted in her bag; then held it up mouth downwards; then fumbled in her lap, all so vigorously that Charles Steele in the Panama hat suspended his paint-brush.

Like the antennae of some irritable insect it positively trembled. Here was that woman moving—actually going to get up —confound her! He struck the canvas a hasty violet-black dab. For the landscape needed it. It was too pale—greys flowing into lavenders, and one star or a white gull suspended just so—too pale as usual. The critics would say it was too pale, for he was an unknown man exhibiting obscurely, a favourite with his landladies' children, wearing a cross on his watch chain, and much gratified if his landladies liked his pictures—which they often did.

"Ja—cob! Ja—cob!" Archer shouted.

Exasperated by the noise, yet loving children, Steele picked nervously at the dark little coils on his palette.

"I saw your brother—I saw your brother," he said, nodding his head, as Archer lagged past him, trailing his spade, and scowling at the old gentleman in spectacles.

"Over there—by the rock," Steele muttered, with his brush between his teeth, squeezing out raw sienna, and keeping his eyes fixed on Betty Flanders's back.

"Ja—cob! Ja—cob!" shouted Archer, lagging on after a second.

The voice had an extraordinary sadness. Pure from all body.

pure from all passion, going out into the world, solitary, unanswered, breaking against rocks—so it sounded.

Steele frowned; but was pleased by the effect of the black—it was just *that* note which brought the rest together. "Ah, one may learn to paint at fifty! There's Titian . . ." and so, having found the right tint, up he looked and saw to his horror a cloud over the bay.

Mrs. Flanders rose, slapped her coat this side and that to get the sand off, and picked up her black parasol.

The rock was one of those tremendously solid brown, or rather black, rocks which emerge from the sand like something primitive. Rough with crinkled limpet shells and sparsely strewn with locks of dry seaweed, a small boy has to stretch his legs far apart, and indeed to feel rather heroic, before he gets to the top.

But there, on the very top, is a hollow full of water, with a sandy bottom; with a blob of jelly stuck to the side, and some mussels. A fish darts across. The fringe of yellow-brown seaweed flutters, and out pushes an opal-shelled crab——

"Oh, a huge crab," Jacob murmured——

and begins his journey on weakly legs on the sandy bottom. Now! Jacob plunged his hand. The crab was cool and very light. But the water was thick with sand, and so, scrambling down, Jacob was about to jump, holding his bucket in front of him, when he saw, stretched entirely rigid, side by side, their faces very red, an enormous man and woman.

An enormous man and woman (it was early-closing day) were stretched motionless, with their heads on pocket-handkerchiefs, side by side, within a few feet of the sea, while two or three gulls gracefully skirted the incoming waves, and settled near their boots.

The large red faces lying on the bandanna handkerchiefs stared up at Jacob. Jacob stared down at them. Holding his bucket very carefully, Jacob then jumped deliberately and trotted away very nonchalantly at first, but faster and faster as the waves came creaming up to him and he had to swerve to avoid them, and the gulls rose in front of him and floated out and settled again a little farther on. A large black woman was sitting on the sand. He ran towards her.

"Nanny! Nanny!" he cried, sobbing the words out on the crest of each gasping breath.

The waves came round her. She was a rock. She was covered with the seaweed which pops when it is pressed. He was lost.

There he stood. His face composed itself. He was about to roar when, lying among the black sticks and straw under the cliff, he saw a whole skull—perhaps a cow's skull, a skull, perhaps, with the teeth in it. Sobbing, but absent-mindedly, he ran farther and farther away until he held the skull in his arms.

"There he is!" cried Mrs. Flanders, coming round the rock and covering the whole space of the beach in a few seconds. "What has he got hold of? Put it down, Jacob! Drop it this moment! Something horrid, I know. Why didn't you stay with us? Naughty little boy! Now put it down. Now come along both of you," and she swept round, holding Archer by one hand and fumbling for Jacob's arm with the other. But he ducked down and picked up the sheep's jaw, which was loose.

Swinging her bag, clutching her parasol, holding Archer's hand, and telling the story of the gunpowder explosion in which poor Mr. Curnow had lost his eye, Mrs. Flanders hurried up the steep lane, aware all the time in the depths of her mind of some buried discomfort.

There on the sand not far from the lovers lay the old sheep's skull without its jaw. Clean, white, wind-swept, sand-rubbed, a more unpolluted piece of bone existed nowhere on the coast of Cornwall. The sea holly would grow through the eye-sockets; it would turn to powder, or some golfer, hitting his ball one fine day, would disperse a little dust—No, but not in lodgings, thought Mrs. Flanders. It's a great experiment coming so far with young children. There's no man to help with the perambulator. And Jacob is such a handful; so obstinate already.

"Throw it away, dear, do," she said, as they got into the road; but Jacob squirmed away from her; and the wind rising, she took out her bonnet-pin, looked at the sea, and stuck it in afresh. The wind was rising. The waves showed that uneasiness, like something alive, restive, expecting the whip, of waves before a storm. The fishing-boats were leaning to the water's brim. A pale yellow light shot across the purple sea; and shut. The lighthouse was lit. "Come along," said Betty Flanders. The sun blazed in their faces and gilded the great blackberries trembling out from the hedge which Archer tried to strip as they passed.

"Don't lag, boys. You've got nothing to change into," said Betty, pulling them along, and looking with uneasy emotion at the earth displayed so luridly, with sudden sparks of light from greenhouses in gardens, with a sort of yellow and black mutability, against this blazing sunset, this astonishing agitation and vitality of colour, which stirred Betty Flanders and made her think of responsibility and danger. She gripped Archer's hand. On she plodded up the hill.

"What did I ask you to remember?" she said.

"I don't know," said Archer.

"Well, I don't know either," said Betty, humorously and simply, and who shall deny that this blankness of mind, when combined with profusion, mother wit, old wives' tales, haphazard ways, moments of astonishing daring, humour, and sentimentality—who shall deny that in these respects every woman is nicer than any man?

Well, Betty Flanders, to begin with.

She had her hand upon the garden gate.

"The meat!" she exclaimed, striking the latch down.

She had forgotten the meat.

There was Rebecca at the window.

The bareness of Mrs. Pearce's front room was fully displayed at ten o'clock at night when a powerful oil lamp stood on the middle of the table. The harsh light fell on the garden; cut straight across the lawn; lit up a child's bucket and a purple aster and reached the hedge. Mrs. Flanders had left her sewing on the table. There were her large reels of white cotton and her steel spectacles; her needle-case; her brown wool wound round an old postcard. There were the bulrushes and the *Strand* magazines; and the linoleum sandy from the boys' boots. A daddy-long-legs shot from corner to corner and hit the lamp globe. The wind blew straight dashes of rain across the window, which flashed silver as they passed through the light. A single leaf tapped hurriedly, persistently, upon the glass. There was a hurricane out at sea.

Archer could not sleep.

Mrs. Flanders stooped over him. "Think of the fairies," said Betty Flanders. "Think of the lovely, lovely birds settling down on their nests. Now shut your eyes and see the old mother bird with a worm in her beak. Now turn and shut your eyes," she murmured, "and shut your eyes."

The lodging-house seemed full of gurgling and rushing; the cistern overflowing; water bubbling and squeaking and running along the pipes and streaming down the windows.

"What's all that water rushing in?" murmured Archer.

"It's only the bath water running away," said Mrs. Flanders.

Something snapped out of doors.

"I say, won't that steamer sink?" said Archer, opening his eyes.

"Of course it won't," said Mrs. Flanders. "The Captain's in bed long ago. Shut your eyes, and think of the fairies, fast asleep, under the flowers."

"I thought he'd never get off—such a hurricane," she whispered to Rebecca, who was bending over a spirit-lamp in the small room next door. The wind rushed outside, but the small flame of the spirit-lamp burnt quietly, shaded from the cot by a book stood on edge.

"Did he take his bottle well?" Mrs. Flanders whispered, and Rebecca nodded and went to the cot and turned down the quilt, and Mrs. Flanders bent over and looked anxiously at the baby, asleep, but frowning. The window shook, and Rebecca stole like a cat and wedged it. The two women murmured over the spirit-lamp, plotting the eternal conspiracy of hush and clean bottles while the wind raged and gave a sudden wrench at the cheap fastenings.

Both looked round at the cot. Their lips were pursed. Mrs. Flanders crossed over to the cot.

"Asleep?" whispered Rebecca, looking at the cot.

Mrs. Flanders nodded.

"Good-night, Rebecca," Mrs. Flanders murmured, and Rebecca called her ma'm, though they were conspirators plotting the eternal conspiracy of hush and clean bottles.

Mrs. Flanders had left the lamp burning in the front room. There were her spectacles, her sewing; and a letter with the Scarborough postmark. She had not drawn the curtains either.

The light blazed out across the patch of grass; fell on the child's green bucket with the gold line round it, and upon the aster which trembled violently beside it. For the wind was tearing across the coast, hurling itself at the hills, and leaping, in sudden gusts, on top of its own back. How it spread over the town in the hollow! How the lights seemed to wink and quiver in its fury, lights in the harbour, lights in bedroom windows high up! And rolling dark waves before it, it raced over the Atlantic, jerking the stars above the ships this way and that.

There was a click in the front sitting-room. Mr. Pearce had extinguished the lamp. The garden went out. It was but a dark patch. Every inch was rained upon. Every blade of grass was bent by rain. Eyelids would have been fastened down by the rain. Lying on one's back one would have seen nothing but muddle and confusion—clouds turning and turning, and something yellow-tinted and sulphurous in the darkness.

The little boys in the front bedroom had thrown off their blankets and lay under the sheets. It was hot; rather sticky and steamy. Archer lay spread out, with one arm striking across the pillow. He was flushed; and when the heavy curtain blew out a little he turned and half-opened his eyes. The wind actually stirred the cloth on the chest of drawers, and let in a little light, so that the sharp edge of the chest of drawers was visible, running straight up, until a white shape bulged out; and a silver streak showed in the looking-glass.

In the other bed by the door Jacob lay asleep, fast asleep, profoundly unconscious. The sheep's jaw with the big yellow teeth in it lay at his feet. He had kicked it against the iron bed-rail.

Outside the rain poured down more directly and powerfully as the wind fell in the early hours of the morning. The aster was beaten to the earth. The child's bucket was half-full of rainwater; and the opal-shelled crab slowly circled round the bottom, trying with its weakly legs to climb the steep side; trying again and falling back, and trying again and again.

rs. Flanders"—"Poor Betty Flanders"—"Dear Betty"—"She's very attractive still"—"Odd she don't marry again!" "There's Captain Barfoot to be sure—calls every Wednesday as regular as clockwork, and never brings his wife."

"But that's Ellen Barfoot's fault," the ladies of Scarborough said. "She don't put herself out for no one."

"A man likes to have a son—that we know."

"Some tumours have to be cut; but the sort my mother had you bear with for years and years, and never even have a cup of tea brought up to you in bed."

(Mrs. Barfoot was an invalid.)

Elizabeth Flanders, of whom this and much more than this had been said and would be said, was, of course, a widow in her prime. She was half-way between forty and fifty. Years and sorrow between them; the death of Seabrook, her husband; three boys; poverty; a house on the outskirts of Scarborough; her brother, poor Morty's, downfall and possible demise—for where was he? what was he? Shading her eyes, she looked along the road for Captain Barfoot—yes, there he was, punctual as ever; the attentions of the Captain—all ripened Betty Flanders, enlarged her figure, tinged her face with jollity, and flooded her eyes for no reason that any one could see perhaps three times a day.

True, there's no harm in crying for one's husband, and the tombstone, though plain, was a solid piece of work, and on summer's days when the widow brought her boys to stand there one felt kindly towards her. Hats were raised higher than usual; wives tugged their husbands' arms. Seabrook lay six foot beneath, dead these many years; enclosed in three shells; the crevices sealed with lead, so that, had earth and wood been glass, doubtless his very face lay visible beneath, the face of a young man whiskered, shapely, who had gone out duck-shooting and refused to change his boots.

"Merchant of this city," the tombstone said; though why Betty Flanders had chosen so to call him when, as many still remembered, he had only sat behind an office window for three months, and before that had broken horses, ridden to hounds, farmed a few fields, and run a little wild—well, she had to call him something. An example for the boys.

Had he, then, been nothing? An unanswerable question, since even if it weren't the habit of the undertaker to close the eyes, the light so soon goes out of them. At first, part of herself; now one of a company, he had merged in the grass, the sloping hillside, the thousand white stones, some slanting, others upright, the decayed wreaths, the crosses of green tin, the narrow yellow paths, and the lilacs that drooped in April, with a scent like that of an invalid's bedroom, over the churchyard wall. Seabrook was now all that; and when, with her skirt hitched up, feeding the chickens, she heard the bell for service or funeral, that was Seabrook's voice—the voice of the dead.

The rooster had been known to fly on her shoulder and peck her neck, so that now she carried a stick or took one of the children with her when she went to feed the fowls.

"Wouldn't you like my knife, mother?" said Archer.

Sounding at the same moment as the bell, her son's voice mixed life and death inextricably, exhilaratingly.

"What a big knife for a small boy!" she said. She took it to please him. Then the rooster flew out of the hen-house, and, shouting to Archer to shut the door into the kitchen garden, Mrs. Flanders set her meal down, clucked for the hens, went bustling about the orchard, and was seen from over the way by Mrs. Cranch, who, beating her mat against the wall, held it for a moment suspended while she observed to Mrs. Page next door that Mrs. Flanders was in the orchard with the chickens.

Mrs. Page, Mrs. Cranch, and Mrs. Garfit could see Mrs. Flanders in the orchard because the orchard was a piece of Dods Hill enclosed; and Dods Hill dominated the village. No words can exaggerate the importance of Dods Hill. It was the earth; the world against the sky; the horizon of how many glances can best be computed by those who have lived all their lives in the same village, only leaving it once to fight in the Crimea, like old George Garfit, leaning over his garden gate smoking his pipe. The progress of the sun was measured by it; the tint of the day laid against it to be judged.

"Now she's going up the hill with little John," said Mrs. Cranch to Mrs. Garfit, shaking her mat for the last time, and bustling indoors.

Opening the orchard gate, Mrs. Flanders walked to the top of Dods Hill, holding John by the hand. Archer and Jacob ran in front or lagged behind; but they were in the Roman fortress when she came there, and shouting out what ships were to be seen in the bay. For there was a magnificent view—moors behind, sea in front, and the whole of Scarborough from one end to the other laid out flat like a puzzle. Mrs. Flanders, who was growing stout, sat down in the fortress and looked about her.

The entire gamut of the view's changes should have been known to her; its winter aspect, spring, summer and autumn; how storms came up from the sea; how the moors shuddered and brightened as the clouds went over; she should have noted the red spot where the villas were building; and the criss-cross of lines where the allotments were cut; and the diamond flash of little glass houses in the sun. Or, if details like these escaped her, she might have let her fancy play upon the gold tint of the sea at sunset, and thought how it lapped in coins of gold upon the shingle. Little pleasure boats shoved out into it; the black arm of the pier hoarded it up. The whole city was pink and gold;

domed; mist-wreathed; resonant; strident. Banjoes strummed; the parade smelt of tar which stuck to the heels; goats suddenly cantered their carriages through crowds. It was observed how well the Corporation had laid out the flower-beds. Sometimes a straw hat was blown away. Tulips burnt in the sun. Numbers of sponge-bag trousers were stretched in rows. Purple bonnets fringed soft, pink, querulous faces on pillows in bath chairs. Triangular hoardings were wheeled along by men in white coats. Captain George Boase had caught a monster shark. One side of the triangular hoarding said so in red, blue, and yellow letters; and each line ended with three differently coloured notes of exclamation.

So that was a reason for going down into the Aquarium, where the sallow blinds, the stale smell of spirits of salt, the bamboo chairs, the tables with ash-trays, the revolving fish, the attendant knitting behind six or seven chocolate boxes (often she was quite alone with the fish for hours at a time) remained in the mind as part of the monster shark, he himself being only a flabby yellow receptacle, like an empty Gladstone bag in a tank. No one had ever been cheered by the Aquarium; but the faces of those emerging quickly lost their dim, chilled expression when they perceived that it was only by standing in a queue that one could be admitted to the pier. Once through the turnstiles, every one walked for a yard or two very briskly; some flagged at this stall; others at that. But it was the band that drew them all to it finally; even the fishermen on the lower pier taking up their pitch within its range.

The band played in the Moorish kiosk. Number nine went up on the board. It was a waltz tune. The pale girls, the old widow lady, the three Jews lodging in the same boarding-house, the dandy, the major, the horse-dealer, and the gentleman of independent means, all wore the same blurred, drugged expression, and through the chinks in the planks at their feet they could see the green summer waves, peacefully, amiably, swaying round the iron pillars of the pier.

But there was a time when none of this had any existence (thought the young man leaning against the railings). Fix your eyes upon the lady's skirt; the grey one will do—above the pink silk stockings. It changes; drapes her ankles—the nineties; then it amplifies—the seventies; now it's burnished red and stretched above a crinoline—the sixties; a tiny black foot wearing a white cotton stocking peeps out. Still sitting there? Yes—she's still on the pier. The silk now is sprigged with roses, but somehow one no longer sees so clearly. There's no pier beneath us. The heavy chariot may swing along the turnpike road, but there's no pier for it to stop at, and how grey and turbulent the sea is in the seventeenth century! Let's to the museum. Cannon-balls; arrow-heads; Roman glass and a forceps green with verdigris. The Rev. Jaspar Floyd dug them up at his own expense early in the forties in the Roman camp on Dods Hill—see the little ticket with the faded writing on it.

And now, what's the next thing to see in Scarborough?

Mrs. Flanders sat on the raised circle of the Roman camp, patching Jacob's breeches; only looking up as she sucked the end of her cotton, or when some insect dashed at her, boomed in her ear, and was gone.

John kept trotting up and slapping down in her lap grass or dead leaves which he called "tea," and she arranged them methodically but absent-mindedly, laying the flowery heads of the grasses together, thinking how Archer had been awake again last night; the church clock was ten or thirteen minutes fast; she wished she could buy Garfit's acre.

"That's an orchid leaf, Johnny. Look at the little brown spots. Come, my dear. We must go home. Ar—cher! Ja—cob!"

"Ar—cher—Ja—cob!" Johnny piped after her, pivoting round on his heel, and strewing the grass and leaves in his hands as if he were sowing seed. Archer and Jacob jumped up from behind the mound where they had been crouching with the intention of springing upon their mother unexpectedly, and they all began to walk slowly home.

"Who is that?" said Mrs. Flanders, shading her eyes.

"That old man in the road?" said Archer, looking below.

"He's not an old man," said Mrs. Flanders. "He's—no, he's not—I thought it was the Captain, but it's Mr. Floyd. Come along, boys."

"Oh, bother Mr. Floyd!" said Jacob, switching off a thistle's head, for he knew already that Mr. Floyd was going to teach them Latin, as indeed he did for three years in his spare time, out of kindness, for there was no other gentleman in the neighbourhood whom Mrs. Flanders could have asked to do such a thing, and the elder boys were getting beyond her, and must be got ready for school, and it was more than most clergymen would have done, coming round after tea, or having them in his own room—as he could fit it in—for the parish was a very large one, and Mr. Floyd, like his father before him, visited cottages miles away on the moors, and, like old Mr. Floyd, was a great scholar, which made it so unlikely—she had never dreamt of such a thing. Ought she to have guessed? But let alone being a scholar he was eight years younger than she was. She knew his mother—old Mrs. Floyd. She had tea there. And it was that very evening when she came back from having tea with old Mrs. Floyd that she found the note in the hall and took it into the kitchen with her when she went to give Rebecca the fish, thinking it must be something about the boys.

"Mr. Floyd brought it himself, did he?—I think the cheese must be in the parcel in the hall—oh, in the hall——" for she was reading. No, it was not about the boys.

"Yes, enough for fish-cakes to-morrow certainly— Perhaps Captain Barfoot——" she had come to the word "love." She went into the garden and read, leaning against the walnut tree to steady herself. Up and down went her breast. Seabrook came so vividly before her. She shook her head and was looking through her tears at the little shifting leaves against the yellow sky when three geese, half-running, half-flying, scuttled across the lawn with Johnny behind them, brandishing a stick.

Mrs. Flanders flushed with anger.

"How many times have I told you?" she cried, and seized him and snatched his stick away from him.

"But they'd escaped!" he cried, struggling to get free.

"You're a very naughty boy. If I've told you once, I've told you a thousand times. I won't *have* you chasing the geese!" she said, and crumpling Mr. Floyd's letter in her hand, she held Johnny fast and herded the geese back into the orchard.

"How could I think of marriage!" she said to herself bitterly, as she fastened the gate with a piece of wire. She had always disliked red hair in men, she thought, thinking of Mr. Floyd's appearance, that night when the boys had gone to bed. And pushing her work-box away, she drew the blotting-paper towards her, and read Mr. Floyd's letter again, and her breast went up and down when she came to the word "love," but not so fast this time, for she saw Johnny chasing the geese, and knew that it was impossible for her to marry any one—let alone Mr. Floyd, who was so much younger than she was, but what a nice man—and such a scholar too.

"Dear Mr. Floyd," she wrote.—"Did I forget about the cheese?" she wondered, laying down her pen. No, she had told Rebecca that the cheese was in the hall. "I am much surprised . . ." she wrote.

But the letter which Mr. Floyd found on the table when he got up early next morning did not begin "I am much surprised," and it was such a motherly, respectful, inconsequent, regretful letter that he kept it for many years; long after his marriage with Miss Wimbush, of Andover; long after he had left the village. For he asked for a parish in Sheffield, which was given him; and, sending for Archer, Jacob, and John to say good-bye, he told them to choose whatever they liked in his study to remember him by. Archer chose a paper-knife, because he did not like to choose anything too good; Jacob chose the works of

Byron in one volume; John, who was still too young to make a proper choice, chose Mr. Floyd's kitten, which his brothers thought an absurd choice, but Mr. Floyd upheld him when he said: "It has fur like you." Then Mr. Floyd spoke about the King's Navy (to which Archer was going); and about Rugby (to which Jacob was going); and next day he received a silver salver and went—first to Sheffield, where he met Miss Wimbush, who was on a visit to her uncle, then to Hackney— then to Maresfield House, of which he became the principal, and finally, becoming editor of a well-known series of Ecclesiastical Biographies, he retired to Hampstead with his wife and daughter, and is often to be seen feeding the ducks on Leg of Mutton Pond. As for Mrs. Flanders's letter—when he looked for it the other day he could not find it, and did not like to ask his wife whether she had put it away. Meeting Jacob in Piccadilly lately, he recognized him after three seconds. But Jacob had grown such a fine young man that Mr. Floyd did not like to stop him in the street.

"Dear me," said Mrs. Flanders, when she read in the *Scarborough and Harrogate Courier* that the Rev. Andrew Floyd, etc., etc., had been made Principal of Maresfield House, "that must be our Mr. Floyd."

A slight gloom fell upon the table. Jacob was helping himself to jam; the postman was talking to Rebecca in the kitchen; there was a bee humming at the yellow flower which nodded at the open window. They were all alive, that is to say, while poor Mr. Floyd was becoming Principal of Maresfield House.

Mrs. Flanders got up and went over to the fender and stroked Topaz on the neck behind the ears.

"Poor Topaz," she said (for Mr. Floyd's kitten was now a very old cat, a little mangy behind the ears, and one of these days would have to be killed).

"Poor old Topaz," said Mrs. Flanders, as he stretched himself out in the sun, and she smiled, thinking how she had had him gelded, and how she did not like red hair in men. Smiling, she went into the kitchen.

Jacob drew rather a dirty pocket-handkerchief across his face. He went upstairs to his room.

The stag-beetle dies slowly (it was John who collected the beetles). Even on the second day its legs were supple. But the butterflies were dead. A whiff of rotten eggs had vanquished the pale clouded yellows which came pelting across the orchard and up Dods Hill and away on to the moor, now lost behind a furze bush, then off again helter-skelter in a broiling sun. A fritillary basked on a white stone in the Roman camp. From the valley came the sound of church bells. They were all eating roast beef in Scarborough; for it was Sunday when Jacob caught the pale clouded yellows in the clover field, eight miles from home.

Rebecca had caught the death's-head moth in the kitchen.

A strong smell of camphor came from the butterfly boxes.

Mixed with the smell of camphor was the unmistakable smell of seaweed. Tawny ribbons hung on the door. The sun beat straight upon them.

The upper wings of the moth which Jacob held were undoubtedly marked with kidney-shaped spots of a fulvous hue. But there was no crescent upon the underwing. The tree had fallen the night he caught it. There had been a volley of pistol-shots suddenly in the depths of the wood. And his mother had taken him for a burglar when he came home late. The only one of her sons who never obeyed her, she said.

Morris called it "an extremely local insect found in damp or marshy places." But Morris is sometimes wrong. Sometimes Jacob, choosing a very fine pen, made a correction in the margin.

The tree had fallen, though it was a windless night, and the lantern, stood upon the ground, had lit up the still green leaves and the dead beech leaves. It was a dry place. A toad was there. And the red underwing had circled round the light and flashed and gone. The red underwing had never come back, though

Jacob had waited. It was after twelve when he crossed the lawn and saw his mother in the bright room, playing patience, sitting up.

"How you frightened me!" she had cried. She thought something dreadful had happened. And he woke Rebecca, who had to be up so early.

There he stood pale, come out of the depths of darkness, in the hot room, blinking at the light.

No, it could not be a straw-bordered underwing.

The mowing-machine always wanted oiling. Barnet turned it under Jacob's window, and it creaked—creaked, and rattled across the lawn and creaked again.

Now it was clouding over.

Back came the sun, dazzlingly.

It fell like an eye upon the stirrups, and then suddenly and yet very gently rested upon the bed, upon the alarum clock, and upon the butterfly box stood open. The pale clouded yellows had pelted over the moor; they had zigzagged across the purple clover. The fritillaries flaunted along the hedgerows. The blues settled on little bones lying on the turf with the sun beating on them, and the painted ladies and the peacocks feasted upon bloody entrails dropped by a hawk. Miles away from home, in a hollow among teasles beneath a ruin, he had found the commas. He had seen a white admiral circling higher and higher round an oak tree, but he had never caught it. An old cottage woman living alone, high up, had told him of a purple butterfly which came every summer to her garden. The fox cubs played in the gorse in the early morning, she told him. And if you looked out at dawn you could always see two badgers. Sometimes they knocked each other over like two boys fighting, she said.

"You won't go far this afternoon, Jacob," said his mother, popping her head in at the door, "for the Captain's coming to say good-bye." It was the last day of the Easter holidays.

Wednesday was Captain Barfoot's day. He dressed himself

very neatly in blue serge, took his rubber-shod stick—for he was lame and wanted two fingers on the left hand, having served his country—and set out from the house with the flagstaff precisely at four o'clock in the afternoon.

At three Mr. Dickens, the bath-chair man, had called for Mrs. Barfoot.

"Move me," she would say to Mr. Dickens, after sitting on the esplanade for fifteen minutes. And again, "That'll do, thank you, Mr. Dickens." At the first command he would seek the sun; at the second he would stay the chair there in the bright strip.

An old inhabitant himself, he had much in common with Mrs. Barfoot—James Coppard's daughter. The drinking-fountain, where West Street joins Broad Street, is the gift of James Coppard, who was mayor at the time of Queen Victoria's jubilee, and Coppard is painted upon municipal watering-carts and over shop windows, and upon the zinc blinds of solicitors' consulting-room windows. But Ellen Barfoot never visited the Aquarium (though she had known Captain Boase who had caught the shark quite well), and when the men came by with the posters she eyed them superciliously, for she knew that she would never see the Pierrots, or the brothers Zeno, or Daisy Budd and her troupe of performing seals. For Ellen Barfoot in her bath-chair on the esplanade was a prisoner—civilization's prisoner— all the bars of her cage falling across the esplanade on sunny days when the town hall, the drapery stores, the swimming-bath, and the memorial hall striped the ground with shadow.

An old inhabitant himself, Mr. Dickens would stand a little behind her, smoking his pipe. She would ask him questions—who people were—who now kept Mr. Jones's shop—then about the season—and had Mrs. Dickens tried, whatever it might be—the words issuing from her lips like crumbs of dry biscuit.

She closed her eyes. Mr. Dickens took a turn. The feelings of a man had not altogether deserted him, though as you saw him coming towards you, you noticed how one knobbed black boot swung tremulously in front of the other; how there was a shadow between his waistcoat and his trousers; how he leant forward unsteadily, like an old horse who finds himself suddenly out of the shafts drawing no cart. But as Mr. Dickens sucked in the smoke and puffed it out again, the feelings of a man were perceptible in his eyes. He was thinking how Captain Barfoot was now on his way to Mount Pleasant; Captain Barfoot, his master. For at home in the little sitting-room above the mews, with the canary in the window, and the girls at the sewing-machine, and Mrs. Dickens huddled up with the rheumatics—at home where he was made little of, the thought of being in the employ of Captain Barfoot supported him. He liked to think that while he chatted with Mrs. Barfoot on the front, he helped the Captain on his way to Mrs. Flanders. He, a man, was in charge of Mrs. Barfoot, a woman.

Turning, he saw that she was chatting with Mrs. Rogers. Turning again, he saw that Mrs. Rogers had moved on. So he came back to the bath-chair, and Mrs. Barfoot asked him the time, and he took out his great silver watch and told her the time very obligingly, as if he knew a great deal more about the time and everything than she did. But Mrs. Barfoot knew that Captain Barfoot was on his way to Mrs. Flanders.

Indeed he was well on his way there, having left the tram, and seeing Dods Hill to the south-east, green against a blue sky that was suffused with dust colour on the horizon. He was marching up the hill. In spite of his lameness there was something military in his approach. Mrs. Jarvis, as she came out of the Rectory gate, saw him coming, and her Newfoundland dog, Nero, slowly swept his tail from side to side.

"Oh, Captain Barfoot!" Mrs. Jarvis exclaimed.

"Good-day, Mrs. Jarvis," said the Captain.

They walked on together, and when they reached Mrs. Flanders's gate Captain Barfoot took off his tweed cap, and said, bowing very courteously:

"Good-day to you, Mrs. Jarvis."

And Mrs. Jarvis walked on alone.

She was going to walk on the moor. Had she again been pacing her lawn late at night? Had she again tapped on the study window and cried: "Look at the moon, look at the moon, Herbert!"

And Herbert looked at the moon.

Mrs. Jarvis walked on the moor when she was unhappy, going as far as a certain saucer-shaped hollow, though she always meant to go to a more distant ridge; and there she sat down, and took out the little book hidden beneath her cloak and read a few lines of poetry, and looked about her. She was not very unhappy, and, seeing that she was forty-five, never perhaps would be very unhappy, desperately unhappy that is, and leave her husband, and ruin a good man's career, as she sometimes threatened.

Still there is no need to say what risks a clergyman's wife runs when she walks on the moor. Short, dark, with kindling eyes, a pheasant's feather in her hat, Mrs. Jarvis was just the sort of woman to lose her faith upon the moors—to confound her God with the universal that is—but she did not lose her faith, did not leave her husband, never read her poem through, and went on walking the moors, looking at the moon behind the elm trees, and feeling as she sat on the grass high above Scarborough . . . Yes, yes, when the lark soars; when the sheep, moving a step or two onwards, crop the turf, and at the same time set their bells tinkling; when the breeze first blows, then dies down, leaving the cheek kissed; when the ships on the sea below seem to cross each other and pass on as if drawn by an invisible hand; when there are distant concussions in the air and phantom horsemen galloping, ceasing; when the horizon swims blue, green, emotional—then Mrs. Jarvis, heaving a sigh, thinks to herself, "If only some one could give me . . . if I could give some one. . . ." But she does not know what she wants to give, nor who could give it her.

"Mrs. Flanders stepped out only five minutes ago, Captain," said Rebecca. Captain Barfoot sat him down in the arm-chair to wait. Resting his elbows on the arms, putting one hand over the other, sticking his lame leg straight out, and placing the stick with the rubber ferrule beside it, he sat perfectly still. There was something rigid about him. Did he think? Probably the same thoughts again and again. But were they "nice" thoughts, interesting thoughts? He was a man with a temper; tenacious, faithful. Women would have felt, "Here is law. Here is order. Therefore we must cherish this man. He is on the Bridge at night," and, handing him his cup, or whatever it might be, would run on to visions of shipwreck and disaster, in which all the passengers come tumbling from their cabins, and there is the captain, buttoned in his pea-jacket matched with the storm, vanquished by it but by none other. "Yet I have a soul," Mrs. Jarvis would bethink her, as Captain Barfoot suddenly blew his nose in a great red bandanna handkerchief, "and it's the man's stupidity that's the cause of this, and the storm's my storm as well as his" . . . so Mrs. Jarvis would bethink her when the Captain dropped in to see them and found Herbert out, and spent two or three hours, almost silent, sitting in the arm-chair. But Betty Flanders thought nothing of the kind.

"Oh, Captain," said Mrs. Flanders, bursting into the drawing-room, "I had to run after Barker's man . . . I hope Rebecca . . . I hope Jacob . . ."

She was very much out of breath, yet not at all upset, and as she put down the hearth-brush which she had bought of the oil-man, she said it was hot, flung the window further open, straightened a cover, picked up a book, as if she were very confident, very fond of the Captain, and a great many years younger than he was. Indeed, in her blue apron she did not look more than thirty-five. He was well over fifty.

She moved her hands about the table; the Captain moved his head from side to side, and made little sounds, as Betty went on chattering, completely at his ease—after twenty years.

"Well," he said at length, "I've heard from Mr. Polegate."

He had heard from Mr. Polegate that he could advise nothing better than to send a boy to one of the universities.

"Mr. Floyd was at Cambridge . . . no, at Oxford . . . well, at one or the other," said Mrs. Flanders.

She looked out of the window. Little windows, and the lilac and green of the garden were reflected in her eyes.

"Archer is doing very well," she said. "I have a very nice report from Captain Maxwell."

"I will leave you the letter to show Jacob," said the Captain, putting it clumsily back in its envelope.

"Jacob is after his butterflies as usual," said Mrs. Flanders irritably, but was surprised by a sudden afterthought, "Cricket begins this week, of course."

"Edward Jenkinson has handed in his resignation," said Captain Barfoot.

"Then you will stand for the Council?" Mrs. Flanders exclaimed, looking the Captain full in the face.

"Well, about that," Captain Barfoot began, settling himself rather deeper in his chair.

Jacob Flanders, therefore, went up to Cambridge in October, 1906.

his is not a smoking-carriage,"
Mrs. Norman protested, nervously but very feebly, as the door
swung open and a powerfully built young man jumped in. He
seemed not to hear her. The train did not stop before it reached
Cambridge, and here she was shut up alone, in a railway carriage,
with a young man.

She touched the spring of her dressing-case, and ascertained
that the scent-bottle and a novel from Mudie's were both handy
(the young man was standing up with his back to her, putting
his bag in the rack). She would throw the scent-bottle with her
right hand, she decided, and tug the communication cord with
her left. She was fifty years of age, and had a son at college. Nevertheless, it is a fact that men are dangerous. She read
half a column of her newspaper; then stealthily looked over the
edge to decide the question of safety by the infallible test of appearance. . . . She would like to offer him her paper. But
do young men read the *Morning Post?* She looked to see what
he was reading—the *Daily Telegraph.*

Taking note of socks (loose), of tie (shabby), she once more
reached his face. She dwelt upon his mouth. The lips were shut.
The eyes bent down, since he was reading. All was firm, yet
youthful, indifferent, unconscious—as for knocking one down!
No, no, no! She looked out of the window, smiling slightly
now, and then came back again, for he didn't notice her. Grave,
unconscious . . . now he looked up, past her . . . he seemed so
out of place, somehow, alone with an elderly lady . . . then he
fixed his eyes—which were blue—on the landscape. He had not
realized her presence, she thought. Yet it was none of *her* fault
that this was not a smoking-carriage—if that was what he meant.

Nobody sees any one as he is, let alone an elderly lady sitting opposite a strange young man in a railway carriage. They see a whole—they see all sorts of things—they see themselves. . . . Mrs. Norman now read three pages of one of Mr. Norris's novels. Should she say to the young man (and after all he was just the same age as her own boy): "If you want to smoke, don't mind me"? No: he seemed absolutely indifferent to her presence . . . she did not wish to interrupt.

But since, even at her age, she noted his indifference, presumably he was in some way or other—to her at least—nice, handsome, interesting, distinguished, well built, like her own boy? One must do the best one can with her report. Anyhow, this was Jacob Flanders, aged nineteen. It is no use trying to sum people up. One must follow hints, not exactly what is said, nor yet entirely what is done—for instance, when the train drew into the station, Mr. Flanders burst open the door, and put the lady's dressing-case out for her, saying, or rather mumbling: "Let me" very shyly; indeed he was rather clumsy about it.

"Who . . ." said the lady, meeting her son; but as there was a great crowd on the platform and Jacob had already gone, she did not finish her sentence. As this was Cambridge, as she was staying there for the week-end, as she saw nothing but young men all day long, in streets and round tables, this sight of her fellow-traveller was completely lost in her mind, as the crooked pin dropped by a child into the wishing-well twirls in the water and disappears for ever.

They say the sky is the same everywhere. Travellers, the ship-wrecked, exiles, and the dying draw comfort from the thought, and no doubt if you are of a mystical tendency, consolation, and even explanation, shower down from the unbroken surface. But above Cambridge—anyhow above the roof of King's College Chapel—there is a difference. Out at sea a great city will cast a brightness into the night. Is it fanciful to suppose the sky, washed into the crevices of King's College Chapel, lighter, thin-

ner, more sparkling than the sky elsewhere? Does Cambridge
burn not only into the night, but into the day?

Look, as they pass into service, how airily the gowns blow out,
as though nothing dense and corporeal were within. What sculptured faces, what certainty, authority controlled by piety, although great boots march under the gowns. In what orderly
procession they advance. Thick wax candles stand upright;
young men rise in white gowns; while the subservient eagle
bears up for inspection the great white book.

An inclined plane of light comes accurately through each window, purple and yellow even in its most diffused dust, while,
where it breaks upon stone, that stone is softly chalked red, yellow, and purple. Neither snow nor greenery, winter nor summer, has power over the old stained glass. As the sides of a
lantern protect the flame so that it burns steady even in the wildest night—burns steady and gravely illumines the tree-trunks—
so inside the Chapel all was orderly. Gravely sounded the voices;
wisely the organ replied, as if buttressing human faith with the
assent of the elements. The white-robed figures crossed from side
to side; now mounted steps, now descended, all very orderly.

. . . If you stand a lantern under a tree every insect in the forest creeps up to it—a curious assembly, since though they scram-
ble and swing and knock their heads against the glass, they seem
to have no purpose—something senseless inspires them. One gets
tired of watching them, as they amble round the lantern and
blindly tap as if for admittance, one large toad being the most be-
sotted of any and shouldering his way through the rest. Ah, but
what's that? A terrifying volley of pistol-shots rings out—cracks
sharply; ripples spread—silence laps smooth over sound. A tree—
a tree has fallen, a sort of death in the forest. After that, the wind
in the trees sounds melancholy.

But this service in King's College Chapel—why allow women
to take part in it? Surely, if the mind wanders (and Jacob looked
extraordinarily vacant, his head thrown back, his hymn-book
open at the wrong place), if the mind wanders it is because sev-

eral hat shops and cupboards upon cupboards of coloured dresses are displayed upon rush-bottomed chairs. Though heads and bodies may be devout enough, one has a sense of individuals —some like blue, others brown; some feathers, others pansies and forget-me-nots. No one would think of bringing a dog into church. For though a dog is all very well on a gravel path, and shows no disrespect to flowers, the way he wanders down an aisle, looking, lifting a paw, and approaching a pillar with a purpose that makes the blood run cold with horror (should you be one of a congregation—alone, shyness is out of the question), a dog destroys the service completely. So do these women— though separately devout, distinguished, and vouched for by the theology, mathematics, Latin, and Greek of their husbands. Heaven knows why it is. For one thing, thought Jacob, they're as ugly as sin.

Now there was a scraping and murmuring. He caught Timmy Durrant's eye; looked very sternly at him; and then, very solemnly, winked.

"Waverley," the villa on the road to Girton was called, not that Mr. Plumer admired Scott or would have chosen any name at all, but names are useful when you have to entertain undergraduates, and as they sat waiting for the fourth undergraduate, on Sunday at lunch-time, there was talk of names upon gates.

"How tiresome," Mrs. Plumer interrupted impulsively. "Does anybody know Mr. Flanders?"

Mr. Durrant knew him; and therefore blushed slightly, and said, awkwardly, something about being sure—looking at Mr. Plumer and hitching the right leg of his trouser as he spoke. Mr. Plumer got up and stood in front of the fireplace. Mrs. Plumer laughed like a straightforward friendly fellow. In short, anything more horrible than the scene, the setting, the prospect, even the May garden being afflicted with chill sterility and a cloud choosing that moment to cross the sun, cannot be imagined. There was the garden, of course. Every one at the same moment looked at it. Owing to the cloud, the leaves ruffled grey, and the sparrows—there were two sparrows.

"I think," said Mrs. Plumer, taking advantage of the momentary respite, while the young men stared at the garden, to look at her husband, and he, not accepting full responsibility for the act, nevertheless touched the bell.

There can be no excuse for this outrage upon one hour of human life, save the reflection which occurred to Mr. Plumer as he carved the mutton, that if no don ever gave a luncheon party, if Sunday after Sunday passed, if men went down, became lawyers, doctors, members of Parliament, business men —if no don ever gave a luncheon party——

"Now, does lamb make the mint sauce, or mint sauce make the lamb?" he asked the young man next him, to break a silence which had already lasted five minutes and a half.

"I don't know, sir," said the young man, blushing very vividly.

At this moment in came Mr. Flanders. He had mistaken the time.

Now, though they had finished their meat, Mrs. Plumer took a second helping of cabbage. Jacob determined, of course, that he would eat his meat in the time it took her to finish her cabbage, looking once or twice to measure his speed—only he was infernally hungry. Seeing this, Mrs. Plumer said that she was sure Mr. Flanders would not mind—and the tart was brought in. Nodding in a peculiar way, she directed the maid to give Mr. Flanders a second helping of mutton. She glanced at the mutton. Not much of the leg would be left for luncheon.

It was none of her fault—since how could she control her father begetting her forty years ago in the suburbs of Manchester? and once begotten, how could she do other than grow up cheese-paring, ambitious, with an instinctively accurate notion of the rungs of the ladder and an ant-like assiduity in pushing George Plumer ahead of her to the top of the ladder? What was at the top of the ladder? A sense that all the rungs were beneath one apparently; since by the time that George Plumer became Professor of Physics, or whatever it might be, Mrs. Plumer could only be in a condition to cling tight to her eminence, peer down at the ground, and goad her two plain daughters to climb the rungs of the ladder.

"I was down at the races yesterday," she said, "with my two little girls."

It was none of *their* fault either. In they came to the drawing-room, in white frocks and blue sashes. They handed the cigarettes. Rhoda had inherited her father's cold grey eyes. Cold grey eyes George Plumer had, but in them was an abstract light. He could talk about Persia and the Trade winds, the Reform Bill and the cycle of the harvests. Books were on his shelves by Wells and Shaw; on the table serious sixpenny weeklies written by pale men in muddy boots—the weekly creak and screech of brains rinsed in cold water and wrung dry—melancholy papers.

"I don't feel that I know the truth about anything till I've read them both!" said Mrs. Plumer brightly, tapping the table of contents with her bare red hand, upon which the ring looked so incongruous.

"Oh God, oh God, oh God!" exclaimed Jacob, as the four undergraduates left the house. "Oh, my God!"

"Bloody beastly!" he said, scanning the street for lilac or bicycle—anything to restore his sense of freedom.

"Bloody beastly," he said to Timmy Durrant, summing up his discomfort at the world shown him at lunch-time, a world capable of existing—there was no doubt about that—but so unnecessary, such a thing to believe in—Shaw and Wells and the serious sixpenny weeklies! What were they after, scrubbing and demolishing, these elderly people? Had they never read Homer, Shakespeare, the Elizabethans? He saw it clearly outlined against the feelings he drew from youth and natural inclination. The poor devils had rigged up this meagre object. Yet something of pity was in him. Those wretched little girls——

The extent to which he was disturbed proves that he was al-

ready agog. Insolent he was and inexperienced, but sure enough
the cities which the elderly of the race have built upon the skyline showed like brick suburbs, barracks, and places of discipline
against a red and yellow flame. He was impressionable; but the
word is contradicted by the composure with which he hollowed
his hand to screen a match. He was a young man of substance.

Anyhow, whether undergraduate or shop boy, man or woman,
it must come as a shock about the age of twenty—the world of
the elderly—thrown up in such black outline upon what we are;
upon the reality; the moors and Byron; the sea and the lighthouse; the sheep's jaw with the yellow teeth in it; upon the obstinate irrepressible conviction which makes youth so intolerably
disagreeable—"I am what I am, and intend to be it," for which
there will be no form in the world unless Jacob makes one for
himself. The Plumers will try to prevent him from making it.
Wells and Shaw and the serious sixpenny weeklies will sit on its
head. Every time he lunches out on Sunday—at dinner parties
and tea parties—there will be this same shock—horror—discomfort—then pleasure, for he draws into him at every step as he
walks by the river such steady certainty, such reassurance from
all sides, the trees bowing, the grey spires soft in the blue, voices
blowing and seeming suspended in the air, the springy air of
May, the elastic air with its particles—chestnut bloom, pollen,
whatever it is that gives the May air its potency, blurring the
trees, gumming the buds, daubing the green. And the river too
runs past, not at flood, nor swiftly, but cloying the oar that dips
in it and drops white drops from the blade, swimming green
and deep over the bowed rushes, as if lavishly caressing them.

Where they moored their boat the trees showered down, so that
their topmost leaves trailed in the ripples and the green wedge
that lay in the water being made of leaves shifted in leaf-breadths
as the real leaves shifted. Now there was a shiver of wind—instantly an edge of sky; and as Durrant ate cherries he dropped
the stunted yellow cherries through the green wedge of leaves,
their stalks twinkling as they wriggled in and out, and some-

times one half-bitten cherry would go down red into the green. The meadow was on a level with Jacob's eyes as he lay back; gilt with buttercups, but the grass did not run like the thin green water of the graveyard grass about to overflow the tombstones, but stood juicy and thick. Looking up, backwards, he saw the legs of children deep in the grass, and the legs of cows. Munch, munch, he heard; then a short step through the grass; then again munch, munch, munch, as they tore the grass short at the roots. In front of him two white butterflies circled higher and higher round the elm tree.

"Jacob's off," thought Durrant, looking up from his novel. He kept reading a few pages and then looking up in a curiously methodical manner, and each time he looked up he took a few cherries out of the bag and ate them abstractedly. Other boats passed them, crossing the backwater from side to side to avoid each other, for many were now moored, and there were now white dresses and a flaw in the column of air between two trees, round which curled a thread of blue—Lady Miller's picnic party. Still more boats kept coming, and Durrant, without getting up, shoved their boat closer to the bank.

"Oh-h-h-h," groaned Jacob, as the boat rocked, and the trees rocked, and the white dresses and the white flannel trousers drew out long and wavering up the bank.

"Oh-h-h-h!" He sat up, and felt as if a piece of elastic had snapped in his face.

"They're friends of my mother's," said Durrant. "So old Bow took no end of trouble about the boat."

And this boat had gone from Falmouth to St. Ives Bay, all round the coast. A larger boat, a ten-ton yacht, about the twentieth of June, properly fitted out, Durrant said . . .

"There's the cash difficulty," said Jacob.

"My people'll see to that," said Durrant (the son of a banker, deceased).

"I intend to preserve my economic independence," said Jacob stiffly. (He was getting excited.)

"My mother said something about going to Harrogate," he said with a little annoyance, feeling the pocket where he kept his letters.

"Was that true about your uncle becoming a Mohammedan?" asked Timmy Durrant.

Jacob had told the story of his Uncle Morty in Durrant's room the night before.

"I expect he's feeding the sharks, if the truth were known," said Jacob. "I say, Durrant, there's none left!" he exclaimed, crumpling the bag which had held the cherries, and throwing it into the river. He saw Lady Miller's picnic party on the island as he threw the bag into the river.

A sort of awkwardness, grumpiness, gloom came into his eyes.

"Shall we move on . . . this beastly crowd . . ." he said.

So up they went, past the island.

The feathery white moon never let the sky grow dark; all night the chestnut blossoms were white in the green; dim was the cow-parsley in the meadows.

The waiters at Trinity must have been shuffling china plates like cards, from the clatter that could be heard in the Great Court. Jacob's rooms, however, were in Neville's Court; at the top; so that reaching his door one went in a little out of breath; but he wasn't there. Dining in Hall, presumably. It will be quite dark in Neville's Court long before midnight, only the pillars opposite will always be white, and the fountains. A curious effect the gate has, like lace upon pale green. Even in the window you hear the plates; a hum of talk, too, from the diners; the Hall lit up, and the swing-doors opening and shutting with a soft thud. Some are late.

Jacob's room had a round table and two low chairs. There were yellow flags in a jar on the mantelpiece; a photograph of his mother; cards from societies with little raised crescents, coats of arms, and initials; notes and pipes; on the table lay paper ruled with a red margin—an essay, no doubt—"Does History consist of the Biographies of Great Men?" There were books enough; very few French books; but then any one who's worth anything reads just what he likes, as the mood takes him, with extravagant enthusiasm. Lives of the Duke of Wellington, for example; Spinoza; the works of Dickens; the *Faery Queen;* a Greek dictionary with the petals of poppies pressed to silk between the pages; all the Elizabethans. His slippers were incredibly shabby, like boats burnt to the water's rim. Then there were photographs from the Greeks, and a mezzotint from Sir Joshua—all very English. The works of Jane Austen, too, in deference, perhaps, to some one else's standard. Carlyle was a prize. There were books upon the Italian painters of the Renaissance, a *Manual of the Diseases of the Horse,* and all the usual text-books. Listless is the air in an empty room, just swelling the curtain; the flowers in the jar shift. One fibre in the wicker arm-chair creaks, though no one sits there.

Coming down the steps a little sideways [Jacob sat on the window-seat talking to Durrant; he smoked, and Durrant looked at the map], the old man, with his hands locked behind him, his gown floating black, lurched, unsteadily, near the wall; then, upstairs he went into his room. Then another, who raised his hand and praised the columns, the gate, the sky; another, tripping and smug. Each went up a staircase; three lights were lit in the dark windows.

If any light burns above Cambridge, it must be from three such rooms; Greek burns here; science there; philosophy on the ground floor. Poor old Huxtable can't walk straight;—Sopwith, too, has praised the sky any night these twenty years; and Cowan still chuckles at the same stories. It is not simple, or pure, or wholly splendid, the lamp of learning, since if you see them there under its light (whether Rossetti's on the wall, or Van

Goch reproduced, whether there are lilacs in the bowl or rusty pipes), how priestly they look! How like a suburb where you go to see a view and eat a special cake! "We are the sole purveyors of this cake." Back you go to London; for the treat is over.

Old Professor Huxtable, performing with the method of a clock his change of dress, let himself down into his chair; filled his pipe; chose his paper; crossed his feet; and extracted his glasses. The whole flesh of his face then fell into folds as if props were removed. Yet strip a whole seat of an underground railway carriage of its heads and old Huxtable's head will hold them all. Now, as his eye goes down the print, what a procession tramps through the corridors of his brain, orderly, quick-stepping, and reinforced, as the march goes on, by fresh runnels, till the whole hall, dome, whatever one calls it, is populous with ideas. Such a muster takes place in no other brain. Yet sometimes there he'll sit for hours together, gripping the arm of the chair, like a man holding fast because stranded, and then, just because his corn twinges, or it may be the gout, what execrations, and, dear me, to hear him talk of money, taking out his leather purse and grudging even the smallest silver coin, secretive and suspicious as an old peasant woman with all her lies. Strange paralysis and constriction—marvellous illumination. Serene over it all rides the great full brow, and sometimes asleep or in the quiet spaces of the night you might fancy that on a pillow of stone he lay triumphant.

Sopwith, meanwhile, advancing with a curious trip from the fireplace, cut the chocolate cake into segments. Until midnight or later there would be undergraduates in his room, sometimes as many as twelve, sometimes three or four; but nobody got up when they went or when they came; Sopwith went on talking. Talking, talking, talking—as if everything could be talked—the soul itself slipped through the lips in thin silver disks which dissolve in young men's minds like silver, like moonlight. Oh, far away they'd remember it, and deep in dulness gaze back on it, and come to refresh themselves again.

"Well, I never. That's old Chucky. My dear boy, how's the world treating you?" And in came poor little Chucky, the unsuccessful provincial, Stenhouse his real name, but of course Sopwith brought back by using the other everything, everything, "all I could never be"—yes, though next day, buying his newspaper and catching the early train, it all seemed to him childish, absurd; the chocolate cake, the young men; Sopwith summing things up; no, not all; he would send his son there. He would save every penny to send his son there. Sopwith went on talking; twining stiff fibres of awkward speech—things young men blurted out—plaiting them round his own smooth garland, making the bright side show, the vivid greens, the sharp thorns, manliness. He loved it. Indeed to Sopwith a man could say anything, until perhaps he'd grown old, or gone under, gone deep, when the silver disks would tinkle hollow, and the inscription read a little too simple, and the old stamp look too pure, and the impress always the same—a Greek boy's head. But he would respect still. A woman, divining the priest, would, involuntarily, despise.

Cowan, Erasmus Cowan, sipped his port alone, or with one rosy little man, whose memory held precisely the same span of time; sipped his port, and told his stories, and without book before him intoned Latin, Virgil and Catullus, as if language were wine upon his lips. Only—sometimes it will come over one— what if the poet strode in? "*This* my image?" he might ask, pointing to the chubby man, whose brain is, after all, Virgil's representative among us, though the body gluttonize, and as for arms, bees, or even the plough, Cowan takes his trips abroad with a French novel in his pocket, a rug about his knees, and is thankful to be home again in his place, in his line, holding up in his snug little mirror the image of Virgil, all rayed

round with good stories of the dons of Trinity and red beams of
port. But language is wine upon his lips. Nowhere else would
Virgil hear the like. And though, as she goes sauntering along
the Backs, old Miss Umphelby sings him melodiously enough,
accurately too, she is always brought up by this question as she
reaches Clare Bridge: "But if I met him, what should I wear?"—
and then, taking her way up the avenue towards Newnham, she
lets her fancy play upon other details of men's meeting with
women which have never got into print. Her lectures, therefore,
are not half so well attended as those of Cowan, and the thing
she might have said in elucidation of the text for ever left out. In
short, face a teacher with the image of the taught and the mirror
breaks. But Cowan sipped his port, his exaltation over, no
longer the representative of Virgil. No, the builder, assessor, sur-
veyor, rather; ruling lines between names, hanging lists above
doors. Such is the fabric through which the light must shine, if
shine it can—the light of all these languages, Chinese and Russian, Persian and Arabic, of symbols and figures, of history, of
things that are known and things that are about to be known.
So that if at night, far out at sea over the tumbling waves, one
saw a haze on the waters, a city illuminated, a whiteness even in
the sky, such as that now over the Hall of Trinity where they're
still dining, or washing up plates, that would be the light burning there—the light of Cambridge.

"Let's go round to Simeon's room," said Jacob, and they rolled
up the map, having got the whole thing settled.

All the lights were coming out round the court, and falling on
the cobbles, picking out dark patches of grass and single daisies.
The young men were now back in their rooms. Heaven knows
what they were doing. What was it that could *drop* like
that? And leaning down over a foaming window-box, one
stopped another hurrying past, and upstairs they went and down
they went, until a sort of fulness settled on the court, the hive

full of bees, the bees home thick with gold, drowsy, humming, suddenly vocal; the Moonlight Sonata answered by a waltz.

The Moonlight Sonata tinkled away; the waltz crashed. Although young men still went in and out, they walked as if keeping engagements. Now and then there was a thud, as if some heavy piece of furniture had fallen, unexpectedly, of its own accord, not in the general stir of life after dinner. One supposed that young men raised their eyes from their books as the furniture fell. Were they reading? Certainly there was a sense of concentration in the air. Behind the grey walls sat so many young men, some undoubtedly reading, magazines, shilling shockers, no doubt; legs, perhaps, over the arms of chairs; smoking; sprawling over tables, and writing while their heads went round in a circle as the pen moved—simple young men, these, who would—but there is no need to think of them grown old; others eating sweets; here they boxed; and, well, Mr. Hawkins must have been mad suddenly to throw up his window and bawl: "Jo—seph! Jo—seph!" and then he ran as hard as ever he could across the court, while an elderly man, in a green apron, carrying an immense pile of tin covers, hesitated, balanced, and then went on. But this was a diversion. There were young men who read, lying in shallow arm-chairs, holding their books as if they had hold in their hands of something that would see them through; they being all in a torment, coming from midland towns, clergymen's sons. Others read Keats. And those long histories in many volumes—surely some one was now beginning at the beginning in order to understand the Holy Roman Empire, as one must. That was part of the concentration, though it would be dangerous on a hot spring night—dangerous, perhaps, to concentrate too much upon single books, actual chapters, when at any moment the door opened and Jacob appeared; or Richard Bonamy, reading Keats no longer, began making long pink spills from an old newspaper, bending forward, and looking

eager and contented no more, but almost fierce. Why? Only perhaps that Keats died young—one wants to write poetry too and
to love—oh, the brutes! It's damnably difficult. But, after all, not
so difficult if on the next staircase, in the large room, there are
two, three, five young men all convinced of this—of brutality,
that is, and the clear division between right and wrong. There
was a sofa, chairs, a square table, and the window being open,
one could see how they sat—legs issuing here, one there crumpled in a corner of the sofa; and, presumably, for you could not
see him, somebody stood by the fender, talking. Anyhow, Jacob,
who sat astride a chair and ate dates from a long box, burst out
laughing. The answer came from the sofa corner; for his pipe
was held in the air, then replaced. Jacob wheeled round. He had
something to say to *that,* though the sturdy red-haired boy at
the table seemed to deny it, wagging his head slowly from side
to side; and then, taking out his penknife, he dug the point of it
again and again into a knot in the table, as if affirming that the
voice from the fender spoke the truth—which Jacob could not
deny. Possibly, when he had done arranging the date-stones, he
might find something to say to it—indeed his lips opened—only
then there broke out a roar of laughter.

The laughter died in the air. The sound of it could scarcely
have reached any one standing by the Chapel, which stretched
along the opposite side of the court. The laughter died out, and
only gestures of arms, movements of bodies, could be seen shap-
ing something in the room. Was it an argument? A bet on the
boat races? Was it nothing of the sort? What was shaped by
the arms and bodies moving in the twilight room?

A step or two beyond the window there was nothing at all,
except the enclosing buildings—chimneys upright, roofs hori-
zontal; too much brick and building for a May night, perhaps.
And then before one's eyes would come the bare hills of Turkey
—sharp lines, dry earth, coloured flowers, and colour on the
shoulders of the women, standing naked-legged in the stream to
beat linen on the stones. The stream made loops of water round

their ankles. But none of that could show clearly through the swaddlings and blanketings of the Cambridge night. The stroke of the clock even was muffled; as if intoned by somebody reverent from a pulpit; as if generations of learned men heard the last hour go rolling through their ranks and issued it, already smooth and time-worn, with their blessing, for the use of the living.

Was it to receive this gift from the past that the young man came to the window and stood there, looking out across the court? It was Jacob. He stood smoking his pipe while the last stroke of the clock purred softly round him. Perhaps there had been an argument. He looked satisfied; indeed masterly; which expression changed slightly as he stood there, the sound of the clock conveying to him (it may be) a sense of old buildings and time; and himself the inheritor; and then to-morrow; and friends; at the thought of whom, in sheer confidence and pleasure, it seemed, he yawned and stretched himself.

Meanwhile behind him the shape they had made, whether by argument or not, the spiritual shape, hard yet ephemeral, as of glass compared with the dark stone of the Chapel, was dashed to splinters, young men rising from chairs and sofa corners, buzzing and barging about the room, one driving another against the bedroom door, which giving way, in they fell. Then Jacob was left there, in the shallow arm-chair, alone with Masham? Anderson? Simeon? Oh, it was Simeon. The others had all gone.

". . . Julian the Apostate. . . ." Which of them said that and the other words murmured round it? But about midnight there sometimes rises, like a veiled figure suddenly woken, a heavy wind; and this now flapping through Trinity lifted unseen leaves and blurred everything. "Julian the Apostate"—and then the wind. Up go the elm branches, out blow the sails, the old schooners rear and plunge, the grey waves in the hot Indian Ocean tumble sultrily, and then all falls flat again.

So, if the veiled lady stepped through the Courts of Trinity, she now drowsed once more, all her draperies about her, her head against a pillar.

"Somehow it seems to matter."

The low voice was Simeon's.

The voice was even lower that answered him. The sharp tap of a pipe on the mantelpiece cancelled the words. And perhaps Jacob only said "hum," or said nothing at all. True, the words were inaudible. It was the intimacy, a sort of spiritual suppleness, when mind prints upon mind indelibly.

"Well, you seem to have studied the subject," said Jacob, rising and standing over Simeon's chair. He balanced himself; he swayed a little. He appeared extraordinarily happy, as if his pleasure would brim and spill down the sides if Simeon spoke.

Simeon said nothing. Jacob remained standing. But intimacy —the room was full of it, still, deep, like a pool. Without need of movement or speech it rose softly and washed over everything, mollifying, kindling, and coating the mind with the lustre of pearl, so that if you talk of a light, of Cambridge burning, it's not languages only. It's Julian the Apostate.

But Jacob moved. He murmured good-night. He went out into the court. He buttoned his jacket across his chest. He went back to his rooms, and being the only man who walked at that moment back to his rooms, his footsteps rang out, his figure loomed large. Back from the Chapel, back from the Hall, back from the Library, came the sound of his footsteps, as if the old stone echoed with magisterial authority: "The young man— the young man—the young man—back to his rooms."

hat's the use of trying to read Shakespeare, especially in one of those little thin paper editions whose pages get ruffled, or stuck together with sea-water? Although the plays of Shakespeare had frequently been praised, even quoted, and placed higher than the Greek, never since they started had Jacob managed to read one through. Yet what an opportunity!

For the Scilly Isles had been sighted by Timmy Durrant lying like mountain-tops almost a-wash in precisely the right place. His calculations had worked perfectly, and really the sight of him sitting there, with his hand on the tiller, rosy gilled, with a sprout of beard, looking sternly at the stars, then at a compass, spelling out quite correctly his page of the eternal lesson-book, would have moved a woman. Jacob, of course, was not a woman. The sight of Timmy Durrant was no sight for him, nothing to set against the sky and worship; far from it. They had quarrelled. Why the right way to open a tin of beef, with Shakespeare on board, under conditions of such splendour, should have turned them to sulky schoolboys, none can tell. Tinned beef is cold eating, though; and salt water spoils biscuits; and the waves tumble and lollop much the same hour after hour—tumble and lollop all across the horizon. Now a spray of seaweed floats past —now a log of wood. Ships have been wrecked here. One or two go past, keeping their own side of the road. Timmy knew where they were bound, what their cargoes were, and, by looking through his glass, could tell the name of the line, and even guess what dividends it paid its shareholders. Yet that was no reason for Jacob to turn sulky.

The Scilly Isles had the look of mountain-tops almost a-wash. . . . Unfortunately, Jacob broke the pin of the Primus stove.

The Scilly Isles might well be obliterated by a roller sweeping straight across.

But one must give young men the credit of admitting that, though breakfast eaten under these circumstances is grim, it is sincere enough. No need to make conversation. They got out their pipes.

Timmy wrote up some scientific observations; and—what was the question that broke the silence—the exact time or the day of the month? anyhow, it was spoken without the least awkwardness; in the most matter-of-fact way in the world; and then Jacob began to unbutton his clothes and sat naked, save for his shirt, intending, apparently, to bathe.

The Scilly Isles were turning bluish; and suddenly blue, purple, and green flushed the sea; left it grey; struck a stripe which vanished; but when Jacob had got his shirt over his head the whole floor of the waves was blue and white, rippling and crisp, though now and again a broad purple mark appeared, like a bruise; or there floated an entire emerald tinged with yellow. He plunged. He gulped in water, spat it out, struck with his right arm, struck with his left, was towed by a rope, gasped, splashed, and was hauled on board.

The seat in the boat was positively hot, and the sun warmed his back as he sat naked with a towel in his hand, looking at the Scilly Isles which—confound it! the sail flapped. Shakespeare was knocked overboard. There you could see him floating merrily away, with all his pages ruffling innumerably; and then he went under.

Strangely enough, you could smell violets, or if violets were impossible in July, they must grow something very pungent on the mainland then. The mainland, not so very far off—you could see clefts in the cliffs, white cottages, smoke going up—wore an extraordinary look of calm, of sunny peace, as if wisdom and piety had descended upon the dwellers there. Now a cry sounded, as of a man calling pilchards in a main street. It wore an extraordinary look of piety and peace, as if old men smoked by the door, and girls stood, hands on hips, at the well, and horses stood; as if the end of the world had come, and cabbage fields and stone walls, and coast-guard stations, and, above all, the white sand bays with the waves breaking unseen by any one, rose to heaven in a kind of ecstasy.

But imperceptibly the cottage smoke droops, has the look of a mourning emblem, a flag floating its caress over a grave. The gulls, making their broad flight and then riding at peace, seem to mark the grave.

No doubt if this were Italy, Greece, or even the shores of Spain, sadness would be routed by strangeness and excitement and the nudge of a classical education. But the Cornish hills have stark chimneys standing on them; and, somehow or other, loveliness is infernally sad. Yes, the chimneys and the coast-guard stations and the little bays with the waves breaking unseen by any one make one remember the overpowering sorrow. And what can this sorrow be?

It is brewed by the earth itself. It comes from the houses on the coast. We start transparent, and then the cloud thickens. All history backs our pane of glass. To escape is vain.

But whether this is the right interpretation of Jacob's gloom as he sat naked, in the sun, looking at the Land's End, it is impossible to say; for he never spoke a word. Timmy sometimes wondered (only for a second) whether his people bothered him. . . . No matter. There are things that can't be said. Let's shake it off. Let's dry ourselves, and take up the first thing that comes handy. . . . Timmy Durrant's notebook of scientific observations.

"Now . . ." said Jacob.

It is a tremendous argument.

Some people can follow every step of the way, and even take a little one, six inches long, by themselves at the end; others remain observant of the external signs.

The eyes fix themselves upon the poker; the right hand takes the poker and lifts it; turns it slowly round, and then, very accurately, replaces it. The left hand, which lies on the knee, plays some stately but intermittent piece of march music. A deep breath is taken; but allowed to evaporate unused. The cat marches across the hearth-rug. No one observes her.

"That's about as near as I can get to it," Durrant wound up. The next minute is quiet as the grave.

"It follows . . ." said Jacob.

Only half a sentence followed; but these half-sentences are like flags set on tops of buildings to the observer of external sights down below. What was the coast of Cornwall, with its violet scents, and mourning emblems, and tranquil piety, but a screen happening to hang straight behind as his mind marched up?

"It follows . . ." said Jacob.

"Yes," said Timmy, after reflection. "That is so."

Now Jacob began plunging about, half to stretch himself, half in a kind of jollity, no doubt, for the strangest sound issued from his lips as he furled the sail, rubbed the plates—gruff, tuneless—a sort of pæan, for having grasped the argument, for being master of the situation, sunburnt, unshaven, capable into the bargain of sailing round the world in a ten-ton yacht, which, very likely, he would do one of these days instead of settling down in a lawyer's office, and wearing spats.

"Our friend Masham," said Timmy Durrant, "would rather not be seen in our company as we are now." His buttons had come off.

"D'you know Masham's aunt?" said Jacob.

"Never knew he had one," said Timmy.

"Masham has millions of aunts," said Jacob.

"Masham is mentioned in Domesday Book," said Timmy.

"So are his aunts," said Jacob.

"His sister," said Timmy, "is a very pretty girl."

"That's what'll happen to you, Timmy," said Jacob.

"It'll happen to you first," said Timmy.

"But this woman I was telling you about—Masham's aunt——"

"Oh, do get on," said Timmy, for Jacob was laughing so much that he could not speak.

"Masham's aunt . . ."

Timmy laughed so much that he could not speak.

"Masham's aunt . . ."

"What is there about Masham that makes one laugh?" said Timmy.

"Hang it all—a man who swallows his tie-pin," said Jacob.

"Lord Chancellor before he's fifty," said Timmy.

"He's a gentleman," said Jacob.

"The Duke of Wellington was a gentleman," said Timmy.

"Keats wasn't."

"Lord Salisbury was."

"And what about God?" said Jacob.

The Scilly Isles now appeared as if directly pointed at by a golden finger issuing from a cloud; and everybody knows how portentous that sight is, and how these broad rays, whether they light upon the Scilly Isles or upon the tombs of crusaders in cathedrals, always shake the very foundations of scepticism and lead to jokes about God.

"Abide with me:
Fast falls the eventide;
The shadows deepen;
Lord, with me abide,"

sang Timmy Durrant.

"At my place we used to have a hymn which began

Great God, what do I see and hear?"

said Jacob.

Gulls rode gently swaying in little companies of two or three quite near the boat; the cormorant, as if following his long strained neck in eternal pursuit, skimmed an inch above the water to the next rock; and the drone of the tide in the caves came across the water, low, monotonous, like the voice of some one talking to himself.

"Rock of Ages, cleft for me,
Let me hide myself in thee,"

sang Jacob.

Like the blunt tooth of some monster, a rock broke the surface; brown; overflown with perpetual waterfalls.

"Rock of Ages,"

Jacob sang, lying on his back, looking up into the sky at midday, from which every shred of cloud had been withdrawn, so that it was like something permanently displayed with the cover off.

By six o'clock a breeze blew in off an icefield; and by seven the water was more purple than blue; and by half-past seven there was a patch of rough gold-beater's skin round the Scilly Isles, and Durrant's face, as he sat steering, was of the colour of a red lacquer box polished for generations. By nine all the fire and confusion had gone out of the sky, leaving wedges of apple-green and plates of pale yellow; and by ten the lanterns on the boat were making twisted colours upon the waves, elongated or squat, as the waves stretched or humped themselves. The beam from the lighthouse strode rapidly across the water. Infinite millions of miles away powdered stars twinkled; but the waves slapped the boat, and crashed, with regular and appalling solemnity, against the rocks.

Although it would be possible to knock at the cottage door and ask for a glass of milk, it is only thirst that would compel the intrusion. Yet perhaps Mrs. Pascoe would welcome it. The summer's day may be wearing heavy. Washing in her little scullery, she may hear the cheap clock on the mantelpiece tick, tick, tick . . . tick, tick, tick. She is alone in the house. Her husband is out helping Farmer Hosken; her daughter married and gone to America. Her elder son is married too, but she does not agree with his wife. The Wesleyan minister came along and took the younger boy. She is alone in the house. A steamer, probably bound for Cardiff, now crosses the horizon, while near at hand one bell of a foxglove swings to and fro with a bumble-bee for clapper.

These white Cornish cottages are built on the edge of the cliff; the garden grows gorse more readily than cabbages; and for hedge, some primeval man has piled granite boulders. In one of these, to hold, an historian conjectures, the victim's blood, a basin has been hollowed, but in our time it serves more tamely to seat those tourists who wish for an uninterrupted view of the Gurnard's Head. Not that any one objects to a blue print dress and a white apron in a cottage garden.

"Look—she has to draw her water from a well in the garden."

"Very lonely it must be in winter, with the wind sweeping over those hills, and the waves dashing on the rocks."

Even on a summer's day you hear them murmuring.

Having drawn her water, Mrs. Pascoe went in. The tourists regretted that they had brought no glasses, so that they might have read the name of the tramp steamer. Indeed, it was such a fine day that there was no saying what a pair of field-glasses might not have fetched into view. Two fishing luggers, presumably from St. Ives Bay, were now sailing in an opposite direction from the steamer, and the floor of the sea became alternately clear and opaque. As for the bee, having sucked its fill of honey, it visited the teasle and thence made a straight line to Mrs. Pascoe's patch, once more directing the tourists' gaze to the old woman's print dress and white apron, for she had come to the door of the cottage and was standing there.

There she stood, shading her eyes and looking out to sea.

For the millionth time, perhaps, she looked at the sea. A peacock butterfly now spread himself upon the teasle, fresh and newly emerged, as the blue and chocolate down on his wings testified. Mrs. Pascoe went indoors, fetched a cream pan, came out, and stood scouring it. Her face was assuredly not soft, sensual, or lecherous, but hard, wise, wholesome rather, signifying in a room full of sophisticated people the flesh and blood of life. She would tell a lie, though, as soon as the truth. Behind her on the wall hung a large dried skate. Shut up in the parlour she prized mats, china mugs, and photographs, though the mouldy little room was saved from the salt breeze only by the depth of a brick, and between lace curtains you saw the gannet drop like a stone, and on stormy days the gulls came shuddering through the air, and the steamers' lights were now high, now deep. Melancholy were the sounds on a winter's night.

The picture papers were delivered punctually on Sunday, and she pored long over Lady Cynthia's wedding at the Abbey. She, too, would have liked to ride in a carriage with springs. The soft, swift syllables of educated speech often shamed her few rude ones. And then all night to hear the grinding of the Atlantic upon the rocks instead of hansom cabs and footmen whistling for motor cars. . . . So she may have dreamed, scouring her cream pan. But the talkative, nimble-witted people have taken themselves to towns. Like a miser, she has hoarded her feelings within her own breast. Not a penny piece has she changed all these years, and, watching her enviously, it seems as if all within must be pure gold.

The wise old woman, having fixed her eyes upon the sea, once more withdrew. The tourists decided that it was time to move on to the Gurnard's Head.

Three seconds later Mrs. Durrant rapped upon the door.

"Mrs. Pascoe?" she said.

Rather haughtily, she watched the tourists cross the field path. She came of a Highland race, famous for its chieftains.

Mrs. Pascoe appeared.

"I envy you that bush, Mrs. Pascoe," said Mrs. Durrant, pointing the parasol with which she had rapped on the door at the

fine clump of St. John's wort that grew beside it. Mrs. Pascoe
looked at the bush deprecatingly.

"I expect my son in a day or two," said Mrs. Durrant. "Sailing
from Falmouth with a friend in a little boat. . . . Any news of
Lizzie yet, Mrs. Pascoe?"

Her long-tailed ponies stood twitching their ears on the road
twenty yards away. The boy, Curnow, flicked flies off them occasionally. He saw his mistress go into the cottage; come out
again; and pass, talking energetically to judge by the movements
of her hands, round the vegetable plot in front of the cottage.
Mrs. Pascoe was his aunt. Both women surveyed a bush. Mrs.
Durrant stooped and picked a sprig from it. Next she pointed
(her movements were peremptory; she held herself very upright) at the potatoes. They had the blight. All potatoes that
year had the blight. Mrs. Durrant showed Mrs. Pascoe how bad
the blight was on her potatoes. Mrs. Durrant talked energetically; Mrs. Pascoe listened submissively. The boy Curnow
knew that Mrs. Durrant was saying that it is perfectly simple;
you mix the powder in a gallon of water; "I have done it with
my own hands in my own garden," Mrs. Durrant was saying.

"You won't have a potato left—you won't have a potato left,"
Mrs. Durrant was saying in her emphatic voice as they reached
the gate. The boy Curnow became as immobile as stone.

Mrs. Durrant took the reins in her hands and settled herself on
the driver's seat.

"Take care of that leg, or I shall send the doctor to you," she
called back over her shoulder; touched the ponies; and the carriage started forward. The boy Curnow had only just time to
swing himself up by the toe of his boot. The boy Curnow, sitting
in the middle of the back seat, looked at his aunt.

Mrs. Pascoe stood at the gate looking after them; stood at the
gate till the trap was round the corner; stood at the gate, looking
now to the right, now to the left; then went back to her cottage.

Soon the ponies attacked the swelling moor road with striving
forelegs. Mrs. Durrant let the reins fall slackly, and leant back-

wards. Her vivacity had left her. Her hawk nose was thin as a bleached bone through which you almost see the light. Her hands, lying on the reins in her lap, were firm even in repose. The upper lip was cut so short that it raised itself almost in a sneer from the front teeth. Her mind skimmed leagues where Mrs. Pascoe's mind adhered to its solitary patch. Her mind skimmed leagues as the ponies climbed the hill road. Forwards and backwards she cast her mind, as if the roofless cottages, mounds of slag, and cottage gardens overgrown with foxglove and bramble cast shade upon her mind. Arrived at the summit, she stopped the carriage. The pale hills were round her, each scattered with ancient stones; beneath was the sea, variable as a southern sea; she herself sat there looking from hill to sea, upright, aquiline, equally poised between gloom and laughter. Suddenly she flicked the ponies so that the boy Curnow had to swing himself up by the toe of his boot.

The rooks settled; the rooks rose. The trees which they touched so capriciously seemed insufficient to lodge their numbers. The tree-tops sang with the breeze in them; the branches creaked audibly and dropped now and then, though the season was midsummer, husks or twigs. Up went the rooks and down again, rising in lesser numbers each time as the sager birds made ready to settle, for the evening was already spent enough to make the air inside the wood almost dark. The moss was soft; the tree-trunks spectral. Beyond them lay a silvery meadow. The pampas grass raised its feathery spears from mounds of green at the end of the meadow. A breadth of water gleamed. Already the convolvulus moth was spinning over the flowers. Orange and purple, nasturtium and cherry pie, were washed into the twilight, but the tobacco plant and the passion flower, over which the great moth spun, were white as china. The rooks creaked their wings together on the tree-tops, and were settling down for sleep when, far off, a familiar sound shook and trembled—increased—

fairly dinned in their ears—scared sleepy wings into the air again —the dinner bell at the house.

After six days of salt wind, rain, and sun, Jacob Flanders had put on a dinner jacket. The discreet black object had made its appearance now and then in the boat among tins, pickles, preserved meats, and as the voyage went on had become more and more irrelevant, hardly to be believed in. And now, the world being stable, lit by candle-light, the dinner jacket alone preserved him. He could not be sufficiently thankful. Even so his neck, wrists, and face were exposed without cover, and his whole person, whether exposed or not, tingled and glowed so as to make even black cloth an imperfect screen. He drew back the great red hand that lay on the table-cloth. Surreptitiously it closed upon slim glasses and curved silver forks. The bones of the cutlets were decorated with pink frills—and yesterday he had gnawn ham from the bone! Opposite him were hazy, semi-transparent shapes of yellow and blue. Behind them, again, was the grey-green garden, and among the pear-shaped leaves of the escallonia fishing-boats seemed caught and suspended. A sailing ship slowly drew past the women's backs. Two or three figures crossed the terrace hastily in the dusk. The door opened and shut. Nothing settled or stayed unbroken. Like oars rowing now this side, now that, were the sentences that came now here, now there, from either side of the table.

"Oh, Clara, Clara!" exclaimed Mrs. Durrant, and Timothy Durrant adding, "Clara, Clara," Jacob named the shape in yellow gauze Timothy's sister, Clara. The girl sat smiling and flushed. With her brother's dark eyes, she was vaguer and softer than he was. When the laugh died down she said: "But, mother, it was true. He said so, didn't he? Miss Eliot agreed with us. . . ."

But Miss Eliot, tall, grey-headed, was making room beside her for the old man who had come in from the terrace. The dinner would never end, Jacob thought, and he did not wish it to end, though the ship had sailed from one corner of the window-frame to the other, and a light marked the end of the pier. He saw Mrs. Durrant gaze at the light. She turned to him.

"Did you take command, or Timothy?" she said. "Forgive me if I call you Jacob. I've heard so much of you." Then her eyes went back to the sea. Her eyes glazed as she looked at the view.

"A little village once," she said, "and now grown. . . ." She rose, taking her napkin with her, and stood by the window.

"Did you quarrel with Timothy?" Clara asked shyly. "I should have."

Mrs. Durrant came back from the window.

"It gets later and later," she said, sitting upright, and looking down the table. "You ought to be ashamed—all of you. Mr. Clutterbuck, you ought to be ashamed." She raised her voice, for Mr. Clutterbuck was deaf.

"We *are* ashamed," said a girl. But the old man with the beard went on eating plum tart. Mrs. Durrant laughed and leant back in her chair, as if indulging him.

"We put it to you, Mrs. Durrant," said a young man with thick spectacles and a fiery moustache. "I say the conditions were fulfilled. She owes me a sovereign."

"Not *before* the fish—*with* it, Mrs. Durrant," said Charlotte Wilding.

"That was the bet; with the fish," said Clara seriously. "Begonias, mother. To eat them with his fish."

"Oh dear," said Mrs. Durrant.

"Charlotte won't pay you," said Timothy.

"How dare you . . ." said Charlotte.

"That privilege will be mine," said the courtly Mr. Wortley, producing a silver case primed with sovereigns and slipping one coin on to the table. Then Mrs. Durrant got up and passed down the room, holding herself very straight, and the girls in yellow and blue and silver gauze followed her, and elderly Miss Eliot in her velvet; and a little rosy woman, hesitating at the door, clean, scrupulous, probably a governess. All passed out at the open door.

"When you are as old as I am, Charlotte," said Mrs. Durrant, drawing the girl's arm within hers as they paced up and down the terrace.

"Why are you so sad?" Charlotte asked impulsively.

"Do I seem to you sad? I hope not," said Mrs. Durrant.

"Well, just now. You're *not* old."

"Old enough to be Timothy's mother." They stopped. Miss Eliot was looking through Mr. Clutterbuck's telescope at the edge of the terrace. The deaf old man stood beside her, fondling his beard, and reciting the names of the constellations: "Andromeda, Bootes, Sidonia, Cassiopeia. . . ."

"Andromeda," murmured Miss Eliot, shifting the telescope slightly.

Mrs. Durrant and Charlotte looked along the barrel of the instrument pointed at the skies.

"There are *millions* of stars," said Charlotte with conviction. Miss Eliot turned away from the telescope. The young men laughed suddenly in the dining-room.

"Let *me* look," said Charlotte eagerly.

"The stars bore me," said Mrs. Durrant, walking down the terrace with Julia Eliot. "I read a book once about the stars. . . . What are they saying?" She stopped in front of the dining-room window. "Timothy," she noted.

"The silent young man," said Miss Eliot.

"Yes, Jacob Flanders," said Mrs. Durrant.

"Oh, mother! I didn't recognize you!" exclaimed Clara Durrant, coming from the opposite direction with Elsbeth. "How delicious," she breathed, crushing a verbena leaf.

Mrs. Durrant turned and walked away by herself.

"Clara!" she called. Clara went to her.

"How unlike they are!" said Miss Eliot.

Mr. Wortley passed them, smoking a cigar.

"Every day I live I find myself agreeing . . ." he said as he passed them.

"It's so interesting to guess . . ." murmured Julia Eliot.

"When first we came out we could see the flowers in that bed," said Elsbeth.

"We see very little now," said Miss Eliot.

"She must have been so beautiful, and everybody loved her, of course," said Charlotte. "I suppose Mr. Wortley . . ." she paused.

"Edward's death was a tragedy," said Miss Eliot decidedly.

Here Mr. Erskine joined them.

"There's no such thing as silence," he said positively. "I can hear twenty different sounds on a night like this without counting your voices."

"Make a bet of it?" said Charlotte.

"Done," said Mr. Erskine. "One, the sea; two, the wind; three, a dog; four . . ."

The others passed on.

"Poor Timothy," said Elsbeth.

"A very fine night," shouted Miss Eliot into Mr. Clutterbuck's ear.

"Like to look at the stars?" said the old man, turning the telescope towards Elsbeth.

"Doesn't it make you melancholy—looking at the stars?" shouted Miss Eliot.

"Dear me no, dear me no," Mr. Clutterbuck chuckled when he understood her. "Why should it make me melancholy? Not for a moment—dear me no."

"Thank you, Timothy, but I'm coming in," said Miss Eliot. "Elsbeth, here's a shawl."

"I'm coming in," Elsbeth murmured with her eye to the telescope. "Cassiopeia," she murmured. "Where are you all?" she asked, taking her eye away from the telescope. "How dark it is!"

Mrs. Durrant sat in the drawing-room by a lamp winding a ball

of wool. Mr. Clutterbuck read the *Times*. In the distance stood a
second lamp, and round it sat the young ladies, flashing scissors
over silver-spangled stuff for private theatricals. Mr. Wortley read
a book.

"Yes; he is perfectly right," said Mrs. Durrant, drawing herself
up and ceasing to wind her wool. And while Mr. Clutterbuck
read the rest of Lord Lansdowne's speech she sat upright, without
touching her ball.

"Ah, Mr. Flanders," she said, speaking proudly, as if to Lord
Lansdowne himself. Then she sighed and began to wind her
wool again.

"Sit *there*," she said.

Jacob came out from the dark place by the window where he
had hovered. The light poured over him, illuminating every
cranny of his skin; but not a muscle of his face moved as he sat
looking out into the garden.

"I want to hear about your voyage," said Mrs. Durrant.

"Yes," he said.

"Twenty years ago we did the same thing."

"Yes," he said. She looked at him sharply.

"He is extraordinarily awkward," she thought, noticing how
he fingered his socks. "Yet so distinguished-looking."

"In those days . . ." she resumed, and told him how they
had sailed . . . "my husband, who knew a good deal about sailing, for he kept a yacht before we married" . . . and then how
rashly they had defied the fishermen, "almost paid for it with our
lives, but so proud of ourselves!" She flung the hand out that held
the ball of wool.

"Shall I hold your wool?" Jacob asked stiffly.

"You do that for your mother," said Mrs. Durrant, looking at
him again keenly, as she transferred the skein. "Yes, it goes
much better."

He smiled; but said nothing.

Elsbeth Siddons hovered behind them with something silver on
her arm.

"We want," she said. . . . "I've come . . ." she paused.

"Poor Jacob," said Mrs. Durrant, quietly, as if she had known him all his life. "They're going to make you act in their play."

"How I love you!" said Elsbeth, kneeling beside Mrs. Durrant's chair.

"Give me the wool," said Mrs. Durrant.

"He's come—he's come!" cried Charlotte Wilding. "I've won my bet!"

"There's another bunch higher up," murmured Clara Durrant, mounting another step of the ladder. Jacob held the ladder as she stretched out to reach the grapes high up on the vine.

"There!" she said, cutting through the stalk. She looked semi-transparent, pale, wonderfully beautiful up there among the vine leaves and the yellow and purple bunches, the lights swimming over her in coloured islands. Geraniums and begonias stood in pots along planks; tomatoes climbed the walls.

"The leaves really want thinning," she considered, and one green one, spread like the palm of a hand, circled down past Jacob's head.

"I have more than I can eat already," he said, looking up.

"It does seem absurd . . ." Clara began, "going back to London. . . ."

"Ridiculous," said Jacob, firmly.

"Then . . ." said Clara, "you must come next year, properly," she said, snipping another vine leaf, rather at random.

"If . . . if . . ."

A child ran past the greenhouse shouting. Clara slowly descended the ladder with her basket of grapes.

"One bunch of white, and two of purple," she said, and she placed two great leaves over them where they lay curled warm in the basket.

"I have enjoyed myself," said Jacob, looking down the greenhouse.

"Yes, it's been delightful," she said vaguely.

"Oh, Miss Durrant," he said, taking the basket of grapes; but she walked past him towards the door of the greenhouse.

"You're too good—too good," she thought, thinking of Jacob, thinking that he must not say that he loved her. No, no, no.

The children were whirling past the door, throwing things high into the air.

"Little demons!" she cried. "What have they got?" she asked Jacob.

"Onions, I think," said Jacob. He looked at them without moving.

"Next August, remember, Jacob," said Mrs. Durrant, shaking hands with him on the terrace where the fuchsia hung, like a scarlet ear-ring, behind her head. Mr. Wortley came out of the window in yellow slippers, trailing the *Times* and holding out his hand very cordially.

"Good-bye," said Jacob. "Good-bye," he repeated. "Good-bye," he said once more. Charlotte Wilding flung up her bedroom window and cried out: "Good-bye, Mr. Jacob!"

"Mr. Flanders!" cried Mr. Clutterbuck, trying to extricate himself from his beehive chair. "Jacob Flanders!"

"Too late, Joseph," said Mrs. Durrant.

"Not to sit for me," said Miss Eliot, planting her tripod upon the lawn.

rather think," said Jacob, taking his pipe from his mouth, "it's in Virgil," and pushing back his chair, he went to the window.

The rashest drivers in the world are, certainly, the drivers of post-office vans. Swinging down Lamb's Conduit Street, the scarlet van rounded the corner by the pillar box in such a way as to graze the kerb and make the little girl who was standing on tiptoe to post a letter look up, half frightened, half curious. She paused with her hand in the mouth of the box; then dropped her letter and ran away. It is seldom only that we see a child on tiptoe with pity—more often a dim discomfort, a grain of sand in the shoe which it's scarcely worth while to remove—that's our feeling, and so—Jacob turned to the bookcase.

Long ago great people lived here, and coming back from Court past midnight stood, huddling their satin skirts, under the carved door-posts while the footman roused himself from his mattress on the floor, hurriedly fastened the lower buttons of his waistcoat, and let them in. The bitter eighteenth-century rain rushed down the kennel. Southampton Row, however, is chiefly remarkable nowadays for the fact that you will always find a man there trying to sell a tortoise to a tailor. "Showing off the tweed, sir; what the gentry wants is something singular to catch the eye, sir —and clean in their habits, sir!" So they display their tortoises.

At Mudie's corner in Oxford Street all the red and blue beads had run together on the string. The motor omnibuses were locked. Mr. Spalding going to the city looked at Mr. Charles Budgeon bound for Shepherd's Bush. The proximity of the omnibuses gave the outside passengers an opportunity to stare into each other's faces. Yet few took advantage of it. Each had his own business to think of. Each had his past shut in him like the leaves of a book known to him by heart; and his friends could only read the title, James Spalding, or Charles Budgeon, and the passengers going the opposite way could read nothing at all—save "a man with a red moustache," "a young man in grey smoking a pipe." The October sunlight rested upon all these men and women sitting immobile; and little Johnnie Sturgeon took the chance to swing down the staircase, carrying his large mysterious parcel, and so dodging a zigzag course between the wheels he reached the pavement, started to whistle a tune and was soon out of sight—for ever. The omnibuses jerked on, and every single person felt relief at being a little nearer to his journey's end, though some cajoled themselves past the immediate engagement by promise of indulgence beyond—steak and kidney pudding, drink, or a game of dominoes in the smoky corner of a city restaurant. Oh yes, human life is very tolerable on the top of an omnibus in Holborn, when the policeman holds up his arm and the sun beats on your back, and if there is such a thing as a shell secreted by man to fit man himself here we find it, on the banks of the Thames, where the great streets join and St. Paul's Cathedral, like the volute on the top of the snail shell, finishes it off. Jacob, getting off his omnibus, loitered up the steps, consulted his watch, and finally made up his mind to go in. . . . Does it need an effort? Yes. These changes of mood wear us out.

Dim it is, haunted by ghosts of white marble, to whom the organ for ever chaunts. If a boot creaks, it's awful; then the order; the discipline. The verger with his rod has life ironed out beneath him. Sweet and holy are the angelic choristers. And for ever round the marble shoulders, in and out of the folded fingers, go the thin high sounds of voice and organ. For ever requiem—repose. Tired with scrubbing the steps of the Prudential Society's office, which she did year in year out, Mrs. Lidgett took her seat beneath the great Duke's tomb, folded her hands, and half closed her eyes. A magnificent place for an old woman to rest in, by the very side of the great Duke's bones, whose victories mean nothing to her, whose name she knows not, though she never fails to greet the little angels opposite, as she passes out, wishing the like on her own tomb, for the leather curtain of the heart has flapped wide, and out steal on tiptoe thoughts of rest, sweet melodies. . . . Old Spicer, jute merchant, thought nothing of the kind though. Strangely enough he'd never been in St. Paul's these fifty years, though his office windows looked on the churchyard. "So that's all? Well, a gloomy old place. . . . Where's Nelson's tomb? No time now—come again—a coin to leave in the box. . . . Rain or fine is it? Well, if it would only make up its mind!" Idly the children stray in—the verger dissuades them—and another and another . . . man, woman, man, woman, boy . . . casting their eyes up, pursing their lips, the same shadow brushing the same faces; the leathern curtain of the heart flaps wide.

Nothing could appear more certain from the steps of St. Paul's than that each person is miraculously provided with coat, skirt, and boots; an income; an object. Only Jacob, carrying in his hand Finlay's *Byzantine Empire,* which he had bought in Ludgate Hill, looked a little different; for in his hand he carried a book, which book he would at nine-thirty precisely, by his own fireside, open and study, as no one else of all these multitudes would do. They have no houses. The streets belong to them; the shops; the churches; theirs the innumerable desks; the stretched office lights; the vans are theirs, and the railway slung high above the street. If you look closer you will see that three elderly men at a little distance from each other run spiders along the pavement as if the street were their parlour, and here, against the wall, a woman stares at nothing, boot-laces extended, which she does not ask you to buy. The posters are theirs too; and the news on them. A town destroyed; a race won. A homeless people, circling beneath the sky whose blue or white is held off by a ceiling cloth of steel filings and horse dung shredded to dust.

There, under the green shade, with his head bent over white paper, Mr. Sibley transferred figures to folios, and upon each desk you observe, like provender, a bunch of papers, the day's nutriment, slowly consumed by the industrious pen. Innumerable overcoats of the quality prescribed hung empty all day in the corridors, but as the clock struck six each was exactly filled, and the little figures, split apart into trousers or moulded into a single thickness, jerked rapidly with angular forward motion along the pavement; then dropped into darkness. Beneath the pavement, sunk in the earth, hollow drains lined with yellow light for ever conveyed them this way and that, and large letters upon enamel plates represented in the underworld the parks, squares, and circuses of the upper. "Marble Arch—Shepherd's Bush"— to the majority the Arch and the Bush are eternally white letters upon a blue ground. Only at one point—it may be Acton, Holloway, Kensal Rise, Caledonian Road—does the name mean shops where you buy things, and houses, in one of which, down to the right, where the pollard trees grow out of the paving stones, there is a square curtained window, and a bedroom.

Long past sunset an old blind woman sat on a camp-stool with her back to the stone wall of the Union of London and Smith's Bank, clasping a brown mongrel tight in her arms and singing out loud, not for coppers, no, from the depths of her gay wild heart—her sinful, tanned heart—for the child who fetches her is the fruit of sin, and should have been in bed, curtained, asleep, instead of hearing in the lamplight her mother's wild song, where she sits against the Bank, singing not for coppers, with her dog against her breast.

Home they went. The grey church spires received them; the hoary city, old, sinful, and majestic. One behind another, round or pointed, piercing the sky or massing themselves, like sailing ships, like granite cliffs, spires and offices, wharves and factories crowd the bank; eternally the pilgrims trudge; barges rest in mid stream heavy laden; as some believe, the city loves her prostitutes.

But few, it seems, are admitted to that degree. Of all the carriages that leave the arch of the Opera House, not one turns eastward, and when the little thief is caught in the empty market-place no one in black-and-white or rose-coloured evening dress blocks the way by pausing with a hand upon the carriage door to help or condemn—though Lady Charles, to do her justice, sighs sadly as she ascends her staircase, takes down Thomas à Kempis, and does not sleep till her mind has lost itself tunnelling into the complexity of things. "Why? Why? Why?" she sighs. On the whole it's best to walk back from the Opera House. Fatigue is the safest sleeping draught.

The autumn season was in full swing. Tristan was twitching his rug up under his armpits twice a week; Isolde waved her scarf in miraculous sympathy with the conductor's baton. In all parts of the house were to be found pink faces and glittering breasts. When a Royal hand attached to an invisible body slipped out and withdrew the red and white bouquet reposing on the scarlet ledge, the Queen of England seemed a name worth dying for. Beauty, in its hothouse variety (which is none of the worst), flowered in box after box; and though nothing was said of profound importance, and though it is generally agreed that wit deserted beautiful lips about the time that Walpole died—at any rate when Victoria in her nightgown descended to meet her ministers, the lips (through an opera glass) remained red, adorable. Bald distinguished men with gold-headed canes strolled down the crimson avenues between the stalls, and only broke from intercourse with the boxes when the lights went down, and the conductor, first bowing to the Queen, next to the bald-headed men, swept round on his feet and raised his wand.

Then two thousand hearts in the semi-darkness remembered, anticipated, travelled dark labyrinths; and Clara Durrant said farewell to Jacob Flanders, and tasted the sweetness of death in effigy; and Mrs. Durrant, sitting behind her in the dark of the box, sighed her sharp sigh; and Mr. Wortley, shifting his position behind the Italian Ambassador's wife, thought that Brangaena was a trifle hoarse; and suspended in the gallery many feet above their heads, Edward Whittaker surreptitiously held a torch to his miniature score; and . . . and . . .

In short, the observer is choked with observations. Only to pre-

vent us from being submerged by chaos, nature and society between them have arranged a system of classification which is simplicity itself; stalls, boxes, amphitheatre, gallery. The moulds are
filled nightly. There is no need to distinguish details. But the
difficulty remains—one has to choose. For though I have no wish
to be Queen of England—or only for a moment—I would willingly sit beside her; I would hear the Prime Minister's gossip; the
countess whisper, and share her memories of halls and gardens;
the massive fronts of the respectable conceal after all their secret
code; or why so impermeable? And then, doffing one's own
headpiece, how strange to assume for a moment some one's—any
one's—to be a man of valour who has ruled the Empire; to refer
while Brangaena sings to the fragments of Sophocles, or see in a
flash, as the shepherd pipes his tune, bridges and aqueducts. But
no—we must choose. Never was there a harsher necessity! or one
which entails greater pain, more certain disaster; for wherever
I seat myself, I die in exile: Whittaker in his lodging-house;
Lady Charles at the Manor.

A young man with a Wellington nose, who had occupied a
seven-and-sixpenny seat, made his way down the stone stairs
when the opera ended, as if he were still set a little apart from his
fellows by the influence of the music.

At midnight Jacob Flanders heard a rap on his door.

"By Jove!" he exclaimed. "You're the very man I want!" and
without more ado they discovered the lines which he had been
seeking all day; only they come not in Virgil, but in Lucretius.

"Yes; that should make him sit up," said Bonamy, as Jacob
stopped reading. Jacob was excited. It was the first time he had
read his essay aloud.

"Damned swine!" he said, rather too extravagantly; but the
praise had gone to his head. Professor Bulteel, of Leeds, had issued an edition of Wycherley without stating that he had left out,
disembowelled, or indicated only by asterisks, several indecent

words and some indecent phrases. An outrage, Jacob said; a breach of faith; sheer prudery; token of a lewd mind and a disgusting nature. Aristophanes and Shakespeare were cited. Modern life was repudiated. Great play was made with the professional title, and Leeds as a seat of learning was laughed to scorn. And the extraordinary thing was that these young men were perfectly right—extraordinary, because, even as Jacob copied his pages, he knew that no one would ever print them; and sure enough back they came from the *Fortnightly,* the *Contemporary,* the *Nineteenth Century*—when Jacob threw them into the black wooden box where he kept his mother's letters, his old flannel trousers, and a note or two with the Cornish postmark. The lid shut upon the truth.

This black wooden box, upon which his name was still legible in white paint, stood between the long windows of the sitting-room. The street ran beneath. No doubt the bedroom was behind. The furniture—three wicker chairs and a gate-legged table —came from Cambridge. These houses (Mrs. Garfit's daughter, Mrs. Whitehorn, was the landlady of this one) were built, say, a hundred and fifty years ago. The rooms are shapely, the ceilings high; over the doorway a rose, or a ram's skull, is carved in the wood. The eighteenth century has its distinction. Even the panels, painted in raspberry-coloured paint, have their distinction. . . .

"Distinction"—Mrs. Durrant said that Jacob Flanders was "distinguished-looking." "Extremely awkward," she said, "but so distinguished-looking." Seeing him for the first time that no doubt is the word for him. Lying back in his chair, taking his pipe from his lips, and saying to Bonamy: "About this opera now" (for they had done with indecency). "This fellow Wagner" . . . distinction was one of the words to use naturally, though, from looking at him, one would have found it difficult to say which seat in the opera house was his, stalls, gallery, or dress circle. A writer? He lacked self-consciousness. A painter? There was something in the shape of his hands (he was descended on his mother's side from a family of the greatest antiquity and deepest obscurity) which indicated taste. Then his mouth—but surely, of all futile occupations this of cataloguing features is the worst. One word is sufficient. But if one cannot find it?

"I like Jacob Flanders," wrote Clara Durrant in her diary. "He is so unworldly. He gives himself no airs and one can say what one likes to him, though he's frightening because . . ." But Mr. Letts allows little space in his shilling diaries. Clara was not the one to encroach upon Wednesday. Humblest, most candid of women! "No, no, no," she sighed, standing at the greenhouse door, "don't break—don't spoil"—what? Something infinitely wonderful.

But then, this is only a young woman's language, one, too, who loves, or refrains from loving. She wished the moment to continue for ever precisely as it was that July morning. And moments don't. Now, for instance, Jacob was telling a story about some walking tour he'd taken, and the inn was called "The Foaming Pot," which, considering the landlady's name . . . They shouted with laughter. The joke was indecent.

Then Julia Eliot said "the silent young man," and as she dined with Prime Ministers, no doubt she meant: "If he is going to get on in the world, he will have to find his tongue."

Timothy Durrant never made any comment at all.

The housemaid found herself very liberally rewarded.

Mr. Sopwith's opinion was as sentimental as Clara's, though far more skilfully expressed.

Betty Flanders was romantic about Archer and tender about John; she was unreasonably irritated by Jacob's clumsiness in the house.

Captain Barfoot liked him best of the boys; but as for saying why . . .

It seems then that men and women are equally at fault. It seems that a profound, impartial, and absolutely just opinion of our fellow-creatures is utterly unknown. Either we are men, or

we are women. Either we are cold, or we are sentimental. Either
we are young, or growing old. In any case life is but a procession
of shadows, and God knows why it is that we embrace them so
eagerly, and see them depart with such anguish, being shadows.
And why, if this and much more than this is true, why are we
yet surprised in the window corner by a sudden vision that
the young man in the chair is of all things in the world the most
real, the most solid, the best known to us—why indeed? For the
moment after we know nothing about him.

Such is the manner of our seeing. Such the conditions of our
love.

("I'm twenty-two. It's nearly the end of October. Life is thoroughly pleasant, although unfortunately there are a great number of fools about. One must apply oneself to something or other
—God knows what. Everything is really very jolly—except getting up in the morning and wearing a tail coat.")

"I say, Bonamy, what about Beethoven?"

("Bonamy is an amazing fellow. He knows practically everything—not more about English literature than I do—but then
he's read all those Frenchmen.")

"I rather suspect you're talking rot, Bonamy. In spite of what
you say, poor old Tennyson. . . ."

("The truth is one ought to have been taught French. Now, I
suppose, old Barfoot is talking to my mother. That's an odd
affair to be sure. But I can't see Bonamy down there. Damn London!") for the market carts were lumbering down the street.

"What about a walk on Saturday?"

("What's happening on Saturday?")

Then, taking out his pocket-book, he assured himself that
the night of the Durrants' party came next week.

But though all this may very well be true—so Jacob thought
and spoke—so he crossed his legs—filled his pipe—sipped his
whisky, and once looked at his pocket-book, rumpling his hair
as he did so, there remains over something which can never be

conveyed to a second person save by Jacob himself. Moreover, part of this is not Jacob but Richard Bonamy—the room; the market carts; the hour; the very moment of history. Then consider the effect of sex—how between man and woman it hangs wavy, tremulous, so that here's a valley, there's a peak, when in truth, perhaps, all's as flat as my hand. Even the exact words get the wrong accent on them. But something is always impelling one to hum vibrating, like the hawk moth, at the mouth of the cavern of mystery, endowing Jacob Flanders with all sorts of qualities he had not at all—for though, certainly, he sat talking to Bonamy, half of what he said was too dull to repeat; much unintelligible (about unknown people and Parliament); what remains is mostly a matter of guess work. Yet over him we hang vibrating.

"Yes," said Captain Barfoot, knocking out his pipe on Betty Flanders's hob, and buttoning his coat. "It doubles the work, but I don't mind that."

He was now town councillor. They looked at the night, which was the same as the London night, only a good deal more transparent. Church bells down in the town were striking eleven o'clock. The wind was off the sea. And all the bedroom windows were dark—the Pages were asleep; the Garfits were asleep; the Cranches were asleep—whereas in London at this hour they were burning Guy Fawkes on Parliament Hill.

he flames had fairly caught.

"There's St. Paul's!" some one cried.

As the wood caught the city of London was lit up for a second; on other sides of the fire there were trees. Of the faces which came out fresh and vivid as though painted in yellow and red, the most prominent was a girl's face. By a trick of the firelight she seemed to have no body. The oval of the face and hair hung beside the fire with a dark vacuum for background. As if dazed by the glare, her green-blue eyes stared at the flames. Every muscle of her face was taut. There was something tragic in her thus staring—her age between twenty and twenty-five.

A hand descending from the chequered darkness thrust on her head the conical white hat of a pierrot. Shaking her head, she still stared. A whiskered face appeared above her. They dropped two legs of a table upon the fire and a scattering of twigs and leaves. All this blazed up and showed faces far back, round, pale, smooth, bearded, some with billycock hats on; all intent; showed too St. Paul's floating on the uneven white mist, and two or three narrow, paper-white, extinguisher-shaped spires.

The flames were struggling through the wood and roaring up when, goodness knows where from, pails flung water in beautiful hollow shapes, as of polished tortoiseshell; flung again and again; until the hiss was like a swarm of bees; and all the faces went out.

"Oh Jacob," said the girl, as they pounded up the hill in the dark, "I'm so frightfully unhappy!"

Shouts of laughter came from the others—high, low; some before, others after.

The hotel dining-room was brightly lit. A stag's head in plaster was at one end of the table; at the other some Roman bust blackened and reddened to represent Guy Fawkes, whose night it was. The diners were linked together by lengths of paper roses, so that when it came to singing "Auld Lang Syne" with their hands crossed a pink and yellow line rose and fell the entire length of the table. There was an enormous tapping of green wine-glasses. A young man stood up, and Florinda, taking one of the purplish globes that lay on the table, flung it straight at his head. It crushed to powder.

"I'm so frightfully unhappy!" she said, turning to Jacob, who sat beside her.

The table ran, as if on invisible legs, to the side of the room, and a barrel organ decorated with a red cloth and two pots of paper flowers reeled out waltz music.

Jacob could not dance. He stood against the wall smoking a pipe.

"We think," said two of the dancers, breaking off from the rest, and bowing profoundly before him, "that you are the most beautiful man we have ever seen."

So they wreathed his head with paper flowers. Then somebody brought out a white and gilt chair and made him sit on it. As they passed, people hung glass grapes on his shoulders, until he looked like the figure-head of a wrecked ship. Then Florinda got upon his knee and hid her face in his waistcoat. With one hand he held her; with the other, his pipe.

"Now let us talk," said Jacob, as he walked down Haverstock Hill between four and five o'clock in the morning of November the sixth arm-in-arm with Timmy Durrant, "about something sensible."

The Greeks—yes, that was what they talked about—how when all's said and done, when one's rinsed one's mouth with every literature in the world, including Chinese and Russian (but these Slavs aren't civilized), it's the flavour of Greek that remains. Durrant quoted Aeschylus—Jacob Sophocles. It is true that no

Greek could have understood or professor refrained from pointing out— Never mind; what is Greek for if not to be shouted on
Haverstock Hill in the dawn? Moreover, Durrant never listened
to Sophocles, nor Jacob to Aeschylus. They were boastful, triumphant; it seemed to both that they had read every book in
the world; known every sin, passion, and joy. Civilizations stood
round them like flowers ready for picking. Ages lapped at their
feet like waves fit for sailing. And surveying all this, looming
through the fog, the lamplight, the shades of London, the two
young men decided in favour of Greece.

"Probably," said Jacob, "we are the only people in the world
who know what the Greeks meant."

They drank coffee at a stall where the urns were burnished
and little lamps burnt along the counter.

Taking Jacob for a military gentleman, the stall-keeper told
him about his boy at Gibraltar, and Jacob cursed the British army
and praised the Duke of Wellington. So on again they went down
the hill talking about the Greeks.

A strange thing—when you come to think of it—this love of
Greek, flourishing in such obscurity, distorted, discouraged, yet
leaping out, all of a sudden, especially on leaving crowded rooms,
or after a surfeit of print, or when the moon floats among the
waves of the hills, or in hollow, sallow, fruitless London days,
like a specific; a clean blade; always a miracle. Jacob knew no
more Greek than served him to stumble through a play. Of ancient history he knew nothing. However, as he tramped into
London it seemed to him that they were making the flagstones
ring on the road to the Acropolis, and that if Socrates saw them
coming he would bestir himself and say "my fine fellows," for the
whole sentiment of Athens was entirely after his heart; free, ven-
turesome, high-spirited. . . . She had called him Jacob without
asking his leave. She had sat upon his knee. Thus did all good
women in the days of the Greeks.

At this moment there shook out into the air a wavering, quav-

ering, doleful lamentation which seemed to lack strength to unfold itself, and yet flagged on; at the sound of which doors in
back streets burst sullenly open; workmen stumped forth.

Florinda was sick.

Mrs. Durrant, sleepless as usual, scored a mark by the side of
certain lines in the *Inferno*.

Clara slept buried in her pillows; on her dressing-table dishevelled roses and a pair of long white gloves.

Still wearing the conical white hat of a pierrot, Florinda was
sick.

The bedroom seemed fit for these catastrophes—cheap, mus-
tard-coloured, half attic, half studio, curiously ornamented with
silver paper stars, Welshwomen's hats, and rosaries pendent from
the gas brackets. As for Florinda's story, her name had been be-
stowed upon her by a painter who had wished it to signify that
the flower of her maidenhood was still unplucked. Be that as it
may, she was without a surname, and for parents had only the
photograph of a tombstone beneath which, she said, her father
lay buried. Sometimes she would dwell upon the size of it, and
rumour had it that Florinda's father had died from the growth
of his bones which nothing could stop; just as her mother enjoyed the confidence of a Royal master, and now and again Florinda herself was a Princess, but chiefly when drunk. Thus deserted, pretty into the bargain, with tragic eyes and the lips of a
child, she talked more about virginity than women mostly do;
and had lost it only the night before, or cherished it beyond the
heart in her breast, according to the man she talked to. But did
she always talk to men? No, she had her confidante: Mother
Stuart. Stuart, as the lady would point out, is the name of a Royal
house; but what that signified, and what her business was, no
one knew; only that Mrs. Stuart got postal orders every Monday
morning, kept a parrot, believed in the transmigration of souls,

and could read the future in tea leaves. Dirty lodging-house wall-paper she was behind the chastity of Florinda.

Now Florinda wept, and spent the day wandering the streets; stood at Chelsea watching the river swim past; trailed along the shopping streets; opened her bag and powdered her cheeks in omnibuses; read love letters, propping them against the milk pot in the A.B.C. shop; detected glass in the sugar bowl; accused the waitress of wishing to poison her; declared that young men stared at her; and found herself towards evening slowly saun-tering down Jacob's street, when it struck her that she liked that man Jacob better than dirty Jews, and sitting at his table (he was copying his essay upon the Ethics of Indecency), drew off her gloves and told him how Mother Stuart had banged her on the head with the tea-cosy.

Jacob took her word for it that she was chaste. She prattled, sitting by the fireside, of famous painters. The tomb of her father was mentioned. Wild and frail and beautiful she looked, and thus the women of the Greeks were, Jacob thought; and this was life; and himself a man and Florinda chaste.

She left with one of Shelley's poems beneath her arm. Mrs. Stuart, she said, often talked of him.

Marvellous are the innocent. To believe that the girl herself transcends all lies (for Jacob was not such a fool as to believe im-plicitly), to wonder enviously at the unanchored life—his own seeming petted and even cloistered in comparison—to have at hand as sovereign specifics for all disorders of the soul Adonais and the plays of Shakespeare; to figure out a comradeship all spirited on her side, protective on his, yet equal on both, for women, thought Jacob, are just the same as men—innocence such as this is marvellous enough, and perhaps not so foolish after all.

For when Florinda got home that night she first washed her head; then ate chocolate creams; then opened Shelley. True, she was horribly bored. What on earth was it *about?* She had to wager with herself that she would turn the page before she ate another. In fact she slept. But then her day had been a long one, Mother Stuart had thrown the tea-cosy;—there are formidable sights in the streets, and though Florinda was ignorant as an owl, and would never learn to read even her love letters correctly, still she had her feelings, liked some men better than others, and was entirely at the beck and call of life. Whether or not she was a virgin seems a matter of no importance whatever. Unless, indeed, it is the only thing of any importance at all.

Jacob was restless when she left him.

All night men and women seethed up and down the well-known beats. Late home-comers could see shadows against the blinds even in the most respectable suburbs. Not a square in snow or fog lacked its amorous couple. All plays turned on the same subject. Bullets went through heads in hotel bedrooms almost nightly on that account. When the body escaped mutilation, seldom did the heart go to the grave unscarred. Little else was talked of in theatres and popular novels. Yet we say it is a matter of no importance at all.

What with Shakespeare and Adonais, Mozart and Bishop Berkeley—choose whom you like—the fact is concealed and the evenings for most of us pass reputably, or with only the sort of tremor that a snake makes sliding through the grass. But then concealment by itself distracts the mind from the print and the sound. If Florinda had had a mind, she might have read with clearer eyes than we can. She and her sort have solved the question by turning it to a trifle of washing the hands nightly before going to bed, the only difficulty being whether you prefer your water hot or cold, which being settled, the mind can go about its business unassailed.

But it did occur to Jacob, half-way through dinner, to wonder whether she had a mind.

They sat at a little table in the restaurant.

Florinda leant the points of her elbows on the table and held her chin in the cup of her hands. Her cloak had slipped behind her. Gold and white with bright beads on her she emerged, her face flowering from her body, innocent, scarcely tinted, the eyes gazing frankly about her, or slowly settling on Jacob and resting there. She talked:

"You know that big black box the Australian left in my room ever so long ago? . . . I do think furs make a woman look old. . . . That's Bechstein come in now. . . . I was wondering what you looked like when you were a little boy, Jacob." She nibbled her roll and looked at him.

"Jacob. You're like one of those statues. . . . I think there are lovely things in the British Museum, don't you? Lots of lovely things . . ." she spoke dreamily. The room was filling; the heat increasing. Talk in a restaurant is dazed sleep-walkers' talk, so many things to look at—so much noise—other people talking. Can one overhear? Oh, but they mustn't overhear *us*.

"That's like Ellen Nagle—that girl . . ." and so on.

"I'm awfully happy since I've known you, Jacob. You're such a *good* man."

The room got fuller and fuller; talk louder; knives more clattering.

"Well, you see what makes her say things like that is . . ."

She stopped. So did every one.

"To-morrow . . . Sunday . . . a beastly . . . you tell me . . . go then!" Crash! And out she swept.

It was at the table next them that the voice spun higher and higher. Suddenly the woman dashed the plates to the floor. The man was left there. Everybody stared. Then—"Well, poor chap, we mustn't sit staring. What a go! Did you hear what she said? By God, he looks a fool! Didn't come up to the scratch, I suppose. All the mustard on the table-cloth. The waiters laughing."

Jacob observed Florinda. In her face there seemed to him something horribly brainless—as she sat staring.

Out she swept, the black woman with the dancing feather in her hat.

Yet she had to go somewhere. The night is not a tumultuous black ocean in which you sink or sail as a star. As a matter of fact it was a wet November night. The lamps of Soho made large greasy spots of light upon the pavement. The by-streets were dark enough to shelter man or woman leaning against the doorways. One detached herself as Jacob and Florinda approached.

"She's dropped her glove," said Florinda.

Jacob, pressing forward, gave it her.

Effusively she thanked him; retraced her steps; dropped her glove again. But why? For whom?

Meanwhile, where had the other woman got to? And the man?

The street lamps do not carry far enough to tell us. The voices, angry, lustful, despairing, passionate, were scarcely more than the voices of caged beasts at night. Only they are not caged, nor beasts. Stop a man; ask him the way; he'll tell it you; but one's afraid to ask him the way. What does one fear?—the human eye. At once the pavement narrows, the chasm deepens. There! They've melted into it—both man and woman. Further on, blatantly advertising its meritorious solidity, a boarding-house exhibits behind uncurtained windows its testimony to the soundness of London. There they sit, plainly illuminated, dressed like ladies and gentlemen, in bamboo chairs. The widows of business men prove laboriously that they are related to judges. The wives of coal merchants instantly retort that their fathers kept coachmen. A servant brings coffee, and the crochet basket has to be moved. And so on again into the dark, passing a girl here for sale, or there an old woman with only matches to offer, passing the crowd from the Tube station, the women with veiled hair, passing at length no one but shut doors, carved door-posts, and a solitary policeman, Jacob, with Florinda on his arm, reached his room and, lighting the lamp, said nothing at all.

"I don't like you when you look like that," said Florinda.

The problem is insoluble. The body is harnessed to a brain.

Beauty goes hand in hand with stupidity. There she sat staring at the fire as she had stared at the broken mustard-pot. In spite of defending indecency, Jacob doubted whether he liked it in the raw. He had a violent reversion towards male society, cloistered rooms, and the works of the classics; and was ready to turn with wrath upon whoever it was who had fashioned life thus.

Then Florinda laid her hand upon his knee.

After all, it was none of her fault. But the thought saddened him. It's not catastrophes, murders, deaths, diseases, that age and kill us; it's the way people look and laugh, and run up the steps of omnibuses.

Any excuse, though, serves a stupid woman. He told her his head ached.

But when she looked at him, dumbly, half-guessing, half-understanding, apologizing perhaps, anyhow saying as he had said, "It's none of my fault," straight and beautiful in body, her face like a shell within its cap, then he knew that cloisters and classics are no use whatever. The problem is insoluble.

SEVEN

About this time a firm of merchants having dealings with the East put on the market little paper flowers which opened on touching water. As it was the custom also to use finger-bowls at the end of dinner, the new discovery was found of excellent service. In these sheltered lakes the little coloured flowers swam and slid; surmounted smooth slippery waves, and sometimes foundered and lay like pebbles on the glass floor. Their fortunes were watched by eyes intent and lovely. It is surely a great discovery that leads to the union of hearts and foundation of homes. The paper flowers did no less.

It must not be thought, though, that they ousted the flowers of nature. Roses, lilies, carnations in particular, looked over the rims of vases and surveyed the bright lives and swift dooms of their artificial relations. Mr. Stuart Ormond made this very observation; and charming it was thought; and Kitty Craster married him on the strength of it six months later. But real flowers can never be dispensed with. If they could, human life would be a different affair altogether. For flowers fade; chrysanthemums are the worst; perfect over night; yellow and jaded next morning—not fit to be seen. On the whole, though the price is sinful, carnations pay best;—it's a question, however, whether it's wise to have them wired. Some shops advise it. Certainly it's the only way to keep them at a dance; but whether it is necessary at dinner parties, unless the rooms are very hot, remains in dispute. Old Mrs. Temple used to recommend an ivy leaf—just one— dropped into the bowl. She said it kept the water pure for days and days. But there is some reason to think that old Mrs. Temple was mistaken.

The little cards, however, with names engraved on them, are

a more serious problem than the flowers. More horses' legs have been worn out, more coachmen's lives consumed, more hours of sound afternoon time vainly lavished than served to win us the battle of Waterloo, and pay for it into the bargain. The little demons are the source of as many reprieves, calamities, and anxieties as the battle itself. Sometimes Mrs. Bonham has just gone out; at others she is at home. But, even if the cards should be superseded, which seems unlikely, there are unruly powers blowing life into storms, disordering sedulous mornings, and uprooting the stability of the afternoon—dressmakers, that is to say, and confectioners' shops. Six yards of silk will cover one body; but if you have to devise six hundred shapes for it, and twice as many colours?—in the middle of which there is the urgent question of the pudding with tufts of green cream and battlements of almond paste. It has not arrived.

The flamingo hours fluttered softly through the sky. But regularly they dipped their wings in pitch black; Notting Hill, for instance, or the purlieus of Clerkenwell. No wonder that Italian remained a hidden art, and the piano always played the same sonata. In order to buy one pair of elastic stockings for Mrs. Page, widow, aged sixty-three, in receipt of five shillings out-door relief, and help from her only son employed in Messrs. Mackie's dye-works, suffering in winter with his chest, letters must be written, columns filled up in the same round, simple hand that wrote in Mr. Letts's diary how the weather was fine, the children demons, and Jacob Flanders unworldly. Clara Durrant procured the stockings, played the sonata, filled the vases, fetched the pudding, left the cards, and when the great invention of paper flowers to swim in finger-bowls was discovered, was one of those who most marvelled at their brief lives.

Nor were there wanting poets to celebrate the theme. Edwin Mallett, for example, wrote his verses ending:

And read their doom in Chloe's eyes,

which caused Clara to blush at the first reading, and to laugh at the second, saying that it was just like him to call her Chloe when her name was Clara. Ridiculous young man! But when, between ten and eleven on a rainy morning, Edwin Mallett laid his life at her feet she ran out of the room and hid herself in her bedroom, and Timothy below could not get on with his work all that morning on account of her sobs.

"Which is the result of enjoying yourself," said Mrs. Durrant severely, surveying the dance programme all scored with the same initials, or rather they were different ones this time—R.B. instead of E.M.; Richard Bonamy it was now, the young man with the Wellington nose.

"But I could never marry a man with a nose like that," said Clara.

"Nonsense," said Mrs. Durrant.

"But I am too severe," she thought to herself. For Clara, losing all vivacity, tore up her dance programme and threw it in the fender.

Such were the very serious consequences of the invention of paper flowers to swim in bowls.

"Please," said Julia Eliot, taking up her position by the curtain almost opposite the door, "don't introduce me. I like to look on. The amusing thing," she went on, addressing Mr. Salvin, who, owing to his lameness, was accommodated with a chair, "the amusing thing about a party is to watch the people—coming and going, coming and going."

"Last time we met," said Mr. Salvin, "was at the Farquhars. Poor lady! She has much to put up with."

"Doesn't she look charming?" exclaimed Miss Eliot, as Clara Durrant passed them.

"And which of them . . . ?" asked Mr. Salvin, dropping his voice and speaking in quizzical tones.

"There are so many . . ." Miss Eliot replied. Three young men stood at the doorway looking about for their hostess.

"You don't remember Elizabeth as I do," said Mr. Salvin,

"dancing Highland reels at Banchorie. Clara lacks her mother's spirit. Clara is a little pale."

"What different people one sees here!" said Miss Eliot.

"Happily we are not governed by the evening papers," said Mr. Salvin.

"I never read them," said Miss Eliot. "I know nothing about politics," she added.

"The piano is in tune," said Clara, passing them, "but we may have to ask some one to move it for us."

"Are they going to dance?" asked Mr. Salvin.

"Nobody shall disturb you," said Mrs. Durrant peremptorily as she passed.

"Julia Eliot. It *is* Julia Eliot!" said old Lady Hibbert, holding out both her hands. "And Mr. Salvin. What is going to happen to us, Mr. Salvin? With all my experience of English politics—My dear, I was thinking of your father last night—one of my oldest friends, Mr. Salvin. Never tell me that girls of ten are incapable of love! I had all Shakespeare by heart before I was in my teens, Mr. Salvin!"

"You don't say so," said Mr. Salvin.

"But I do," said Lady Hibbert.

"Oh, Mr. Salvin, I'm so sorry. . . ."

"I will remove myself if you'll kindly lend me a hand," said Mr. Salvin.

"You shall sit by my mother," said Clara. "Everybody seems to come in here. . . . Mr. Calthorp, let me introduce you to Miss Edwards."

"Are you going away for Christmas?" said Mr. Calthorp.

"If my brother gets his leave," said Miss Edwards.

"What regiment is he in?" said Mr. Calthorp.

"The Twentieth Hussars," said Miss Edwards.

"Perhaps he knows my brother?" said Mr. Calthorp.

"I am afraid I did not catch your name," said Miss Edwards.

"Calthorp," said Mr. Calthorp.

"But what proof was there that the marriage service was actually performed?" said Mr. Crosby.

"There is no reason to doubt that Charles James Fox . . ." Mr. Burley began; but here Mrs. Stretton told him that she knew his sister well; had stayed with her not six weeks ago; and thought the house charming, but bleak in winter.

"Going about as girls do nowadays——" said Mrs. Forster.

Mr. Bowley looked round him, and catching sight of Rose Shaw moved towards her, threw out his hands, and exclaimed: "Well!"

"Nothing!" she replied. "Nothing at all—though I left them alone the entire afternoon on purpose."

"Dear me, dear me," said Mr. Bowley. "I will ask Jimmy to breakfast."

"But who could resist her?" cried Rose Shaw. "Dearest Clara—I know we mustn't try to stop you . . ."

"You and Mr. Bowley are talking dreadful gossip, I know," said Clara.

"Life is wicked—life is detestable!" cried Rose Shaw.

"There's not much to be said for this sort of thing, is there?" said Timothy Durrant to Jacob.

"Women like it."

"Like what?" said Charlotte Wilding, coming up to them.

"Where have you come from?" said Timothy. "Dining somewhere, I suppose."

"I don't see why not," said Charlotte.

"People must go downstairs," said Clara, passing. "Take Charlotte, Timothy. How d'you do, Mr. Flanders."

"How d'you do, Mr. Flanders," said Julia Eliot, holding out her hand. "What's been happening to you?"

> "Who is Silvia? what is she?
>   That all our swains commend her?"

sang Elsbeth Siddons.

Every one stood where they were, or sat down if a chair was empty.

"Ah," sighed Clara, who stood beside Jacob, half-way through.

> "Then to Silvia let us sing,
>   That Silvia is excelling;
> She excels each mortal thing
>   Upon the dull earth dwelling.
> To her let us garlands bring,"

sang Elsbeth Siddons.

"Ah!" Clara exclaimed out loud, and clapped her gloved hands; and Jacob clapped his bare ones; and then she moved forward and directed people to come in from the doorway.

"You are living in London?" asked Miss Julia Eliot.

"Yes," said Jacob.

"In rooms?"

"Yes."

"There is Mr. Clutterbuck. You always see Mr. Clutterbuck here. He is not very happy at home, I am afraid. They say that Mrs. Clutterbuck . . ." she dropped her voice. "That's why he stays with the Durrants. Were you there when they acted Mr. Wortley's play? Oh, no, of course not—at the last moment, did you hear—you had to go to join your mother, I remember, at Harrogate—At the last moment, as I was saying, just as everything was ready, the clothes finished and everything—Now Elsbeth is going to sing again. Clara is playing her accompaniment or turning over for Mr. Carter, I think. No, Mr. Carter is playing by himself—This is *Bach*," she whispered, as Mr. Carter played the first bars.

"Are you fond of music?" said Mrs. Durrant.

"Yes. I like hearing it," said Jacob. "I know nothing about it."

"Very few people do that," said Mrs. Durrant. "I daresay you were never taught. Why is that, Sir Jasper?—Sir Jasper Bigham —Mr. Flanders. Why is nobody taught anything that they ought to know, Sir Jasper?" She left them standing against the wall.

Neither of the gentlemen said anything for three minutes, though Jacob shifted perhaps five inches to the left, and then as many to the right. Then Jacob grunted, and suddenly crossed the room.

"Will you come and have something to eat?" he said to Clara Durrant.

"Yes, an ice. Quickly. Now," she said.

Downstairs they went.

But half-way down they met Mr. and Mrs. Gresham, Herbert Turner, Sylvia Rashleigh, and a friend, whom they had dared to bring, from America, "knowing that Mrs. Durant—wishing to show Mr. Pilcher.—Mr. Pilcher from New York—This is Miss Durrant."

"Whom I have heard so much of," said Mr. Pilcher, bowing low.

So Clara left him.

bout half-past nine Jacob left the house, his door slamming, other doors slamming, buying his paper, mounting his omnibus, or, weather permitting, walking his road as other people do. Head bent down, a desk, a telephone, books bound in green leather, electric light. . . . "Fresh coals, sir?" . . . "Your tea, sir." . . . Talk about football, the Hotspurs, the Harlequins; six-thirty *Star* brought in by the office boy; the rooks of Gray's Inn passing overhead; branches in the fog thin and brittle; and through the roar of traffic now and again a voice shouting: "Verdict—verdict—winner—winner," while letters accumulate in a basket, Jacob signs them, and each evening finds him, as he takes his coat down, with some muscle of the brain new stretched.

Then, sometimes a game of chess; or pictures in Bond Street, or a long way home to take the air with Bonamy on his arm, meditatively marching, head thrown back, the world a spectacle, the early moon above the steeples coming in for praise, the sea-gulls flying high, Nelson on his column surveying the horizon, and the world our ship.

Meanwhile, poor Betty Flanders's letter, having caught the second post, lay on the hall table—poor Betty Flanders writing her son's name, Jacob Alan Flanders, Esq., as mothers do, and the ink pale, profuse, suggesting how mothers down at Scarborough scribble over the fire with their feet on the fender, when tea's cleared away, and can never, never say, whatever it may be—probably this—Don't go with bad women, do be a good boy; wear your thick shirts; and come back, come back, come back to me.

But she said nothing of the kind. "Do you remember old Miss Wargrave, who used to be so kind when you had the whooping-cough?" she wrote; "she's dead at last, poor thing. They would like it if you wrote. Ellen came over and we spent a nice day shopping. Old Mouse gets very stiff, and we have to walk him up the smallest hill. Rebecca, at last, after I don't know how long, went into Mr. Adamson's. Three teeth, he says, must come out. Such mild weather for the time of year, the little buds actually on the pear trees. And Mrs. Jarvis tells me——" Mrs. Flanders liked Mrs. Jarvis, always said of her that she was too good for such a quiet place, and, though she never listened to her discontent and told her at the end of it (looking up, sucking her thread, or taking off her spectacles) that a little peat wrapped round the iris roots keeps them from the frost, and Parrot's great white sale is Tuesday next, "do remember,"—Mrs. Flanders knew precisely how Mrs. Jarvis felt; and how interesting her letters were, about Mrs. Jarvis, could one read them year in, year out—the unpublished works of women, written by the fireside in pale profusion, dried by the flame, for the blotting-paper's worn to holes and the nib cleft and clotted. Then Captain Barfoot. Him she called "the Captain," spoke of frankly, yet never without reserve. The Captain was enquiring for her about Garfit's acre; advised chickens; could promise profit; or had the sciatica; or Mrs. Barfoot had been indoors for weeks; or the Captain says things look bad, politics that is, for as Jacob knew, the Captain would sometimes talk, as the evening waned, about Ireland or India; and then Mrs. Flanders would fall musing about Morty, her brother, lost all these years—had the natives got him, was his ship sunk— would the Admiralty tell her?—the Captain knocking his pipe out, as Jacob knew, rising to go, stiffly stretching to pick up Mrs. Flanders's wool which had rolled beneath the chair. Talk of the chicken farm came back and back, the woman, even at fifty, impulsive at heart, sketching on the cloudy future flocks of Leghorns, Cochin Chinas, Orpingtons; like Jacob in the blur of her outline; but powerful as he was; fresh and vigorous, running about the house, scolding Rebecca.

The letter lay upon the hall table; Florinda coming in that

night took it up with her, put it on the table as she kissed Jacob, and Jacob seeing the hand, left it there under the lamp, between the biscuit-tin and the tobacco-box. They shut the bedroom door behind them.

The sitting-room neither knew nor cared. The door was shut; and to suppose that wood, when it creaks, transmits anything save that rats are busy and wood dry is childish. These old houses are only brick and wood, soaked in human sweat, grained with human dirt. But if the pale blue envelope lying by the biscuit-box had the feelings of a mother, the heart was torn by the little creak, the sudden stir. Behind the door was the obscene thing, the alarming presence, and terror would come over her as at death, or the birth of a child. Better, perhaps, burst in and face it than sit in the antechamber listening to the little creak, the sudden stir, for her heart was swollen, and pain threaded it. My son, my son—such would be her cry, uttered to hide her vision of him stretched with Florinda, inexcusable, irrational, in a woman with three children living at Scarborough. And the fault lay with Florinda. Indeed, when the door opened and the couple came out, Mrs. Flanders would have flounced upon her—only it was Jacob who came first, in his dressing-gown, amiable, authoritative, beautifully healthy, like a baby after an airing, with an eye clear as running water. Florinda followed, lazily stretching; yawning a little; arranging her hair at the looking-glass—while Jacob read his mother's letter.

Let us consider letters—how they come at breakfast, and at night, with their yellow stamps and their green stamps, immortalized by the postmark—for to see one's own envelope on another's table is to realize how soon deeds sever and become alien. Then at last the power of the mind to quit the body is manifest, and perhaps we fear or hate or wish annihilated this phantom of ourselves, lying on the table. Still, there are letters that merely say how dinner's at seven; others ordering coal; making appointments. The hand in them is scarcely perceptible, let alone the voice or the scowl. Ah, but when the post knocks and the letter comes always the miracle seems repeated—speech attempted. Venerable are letters, infinitely brave, forlorn, and lost.

Life would split asunder without them. "Come to tea, come to dinner, what's the truth of the story? have you heard the news? life in the capital is gay; the Russian dancers. . . ." These are our stays and props. These lace our days together and make of life a perfect globe. And yet, and yet . . . when we go to dinner, when pressing finger-tips we hope to meet somewhere soon, a doubt insinuates itself; is this the way to spend our days? the rare, the limited, so soon dealt out to us—drinking tea? dining out? And the notes accumulate. And the telephones ring. And everywhere we go wires and tubes surround us to carry the voices that try to penetrate before the last card is dealt and the days are over. "Try to penetrate," for as we lift the cup, shake the hand, express the hope, something whispers, Is this all? Can I never know, share, be certain? Am I doomed all my days to write letters, send voices, which fall upon the tea-table, fade upon the passage, making appointments, while life dwindles, to come and dine? Yet letters are venerable; and the telephone valiant, for the journey is a lonely one, and if bound together by notes and telephones we went in company, perhaps—who knows?—we might talk by the way.

Well, people have tried. Byron wrote letters. So did Cowper. For centuries the writing-desk has contained sheets fit precisely for the communications of friends. Masters of language, poets of long ages, have turned from the sheet that endures to the sheet that perishes, pushing aside the tea-tray, drawing close to the fire (for letters are written when the dark presses round a bright red cave), and addressed themselves to the task of reaching, touching, penetrating the individual heart. Were it possible! But words have been used too often; touched and turned, and left exposed to the dust of the street. The words we seek hang close to the tree. We come at dawn and find them sweet beneath the leaf.

Mrs. Flanders wrote letters; Mrs. Jarvis wrote them; Mrs. Durrant too; Mother Stuart actually scented her pages, thereby adding a flavour which the English language fails to provide; Jacob had written in his day long letters about art, morality, and politics to young men at college. Clara Durrant's letters were those of a child. Florinda—the impediment between Florinda and her pen was something impassable. Fancy a butterfly, gnat, or other winged insect, attached to a twig which, clogged with mud, it rolls across a page. Her spelling was abominable. Her sentiments infantile. And for some reason when she wrote she declared her belief in God. Then there were crosses—tear stains; and the hand itself rambling and redeemed only by the fact—which always did redeem Florinda—by the fact that she cared. Yes, whether it was for chocolate creams, hot baths, the shape of her face in the looking-glass, Florinda could no more pretend a feeling than swallow whisky. Incontinent was her rejection. Great men are truthful, and these little prostitutes, staring in the fire, taking out a powder-puff, decorating lips at an inch of looking-glass, have (so Jacob thought) an inviolable fidelity.

Then he saw her turning up Greek Street upon another man's arm.

The light from the arc lamp drenched him from head to toe. He stood for a minute motionless beneath it. Shadows chequered the street. Other figures, single and together, poured out, wavered across, and obliterated Florinda and the man.

The light drenched Jacob from head to toe. You could see the pattern on his trousers; the old thorns on his stick; his shoe laces; bare hands; and face.

It was as if a stone were ground to dust; as if white sparks flew from a livid whetstone, which was his spine; as if the switchback railway, having swooped to the depths, fell, fell, fell. This was in his face.

Whether we know what was in his mind is another question. Granted ten years' seniority and a difference of sex, fear of him comes first; this is swallowed up by a desire to help—overwhelming sense, reason, and the time of night; anger would follow close on that—with Florinda, with destiny; and then up would bubble an irresponsible optimism. "Surely there's enough light in the street at this moment to drown all our cares in gold!" Ah, what's the use of saying it? Even while you speak and look over your shoulder towards Shaftesbury Avenue, destiny is chipping a dent in him. He has turned to go. As for following him back to his rooms, no—that we won't do.

Yet that, of course, is precisely what one does. He let himself in and shut the door, though it was only striking ten on one of the city clocks. No one can go to bed at ten. Nobody was thinking of going to bed. It was January and dismal, but Mrs. Wagg stood on her doorstep, as if expecting something to happen. A barrel-organ played like an obscene nightingale beneath wet leaves. Children ran across the road. Here and there one could see brown panelling inside the hall door. . . . The march that the mind keeps beneath the windows of others is queer enough. Now distracted by brown panelling; now by a fern in a pot; here improvising a few phrases to dance with the barrel-organ; again snatching a detached gaiety from a drunken man; then altogether absorbed by words the poor shout across the street at each other (so outright, so lusty)—yet all the while having for centre, for magnet, a young man alone in his room.

"Life is wicked—life is detestable," cried Rose Shaw.

The strange thing about life is that though the nature of it must have been apparent to every one for hundreds of years, no one has left any adequate account of it. The streets of London have their map; but our passions are uncharted. What are you going to meet if you turn this corner?

"Holborn straight ahead of you," says the policeman. Ah, but where are you going if instead of brushing past the old man with the white beard, the silver medal, and the cheap violin, you let him go on with his story, which ends in an invitation to step somewhere, to his room, presumably, off Queen's Square, and there he shows you a collection of birds' eggs and a letter from the Prince of Wales's secretary, and this (skipping the intermediate stages) brings you one winter's day to the Essex coast, where the little boat makes off to the ship, and the ship sails and you behold on the skyline the Azores; and the flamingoes rise; and there you sit on the verge of the marsh drinking rum-punch, an outcast from civilization, for you have committed a crime, are infected with yellow fever as likely as not, and—fill in the sketch as you like.

As frequent as street corners in Holborn are these chasms in the continuity of our ways. Yet we keep straight on.

Rose Shaw, talking in rather an emotional manner to Mr. Bowley at Mrs. Durrant's evening party a few nights back, said that life was wicked because a man called Jimmy refused to marry a woman called (if memory serves) Helen Aitken.

Both were beautiful. Both were inanimate. The oval tea-table invariably separated them, and the plate of biscuits was all he ever gave her. He bowed; she inclined her head. They danced. He danced divinely. They sat in the alcove; never a word was said. Her pillow was wet with tears. Kind Mr. Bowley and dear Rose Shaw marvelled and deplored. Bowley had rooms in the Albany. Rose was re-born every evening precisely as the clock struck eight. All four were civilization's triumphs, and if you persist that a command of the English language is part of our inheritance, one can only reply that beauty is almost always dumb. Male beauty in association with female beauty breeds in the onlooker a sense of fear. Often have I seen them—Helen and Jimmy—and likened them to ships adrift, and feared for my own little craft. Or again, have you ever watched fine collie dogs couchant at twenty yards' distance? As she passed him his cup there was that quiver in her flanks. Bowley saw what was up— asked Jimmy to breakfast. Helen must have confided in Rose. For my own part, I find it exceedingly difficult to interpret songs

without words. And now Jimmy feeds crows in Flanders and
Helen visits hospitals. Oh, life is damnable, life is wicked, as
Rose Shaw said.

The lamps of London uphold the dark as upon the points of
burning bayonets. The yellow canopy sinks and swells over the
great four-poster. Passengers in the mail-coaches running into
London in the eighteenth century looked through leafless
branches and saw it flaring beneath them. The light burns behind yellow blinds and pink blinds, and above fanlights, and
down in basement windows. The street market in Soho is fierce
with light. Raw meat, china mugs, and silk stockings blaze in it.
Raw voices wrap themselves round the flaring gas-jets. Arms
akimbo, they stand on the pavement bawling—Messrs. Kettle
and Wilkinson; their wives sit in the shop, furs wrapped round
their necks, arms folded, eyes contemptuous. Such faces as one
sees. The little man fingering the meat must have squatted before the fire in innumerable lodging-houses, and heard and seen
and known so much that it seems to utter itself even volubly
from dark eyes, loose lips, as he fingers the meat silently, his face
sad as a poet's, and never a song sung. Shawled women carry
babies with purple eyelids; boys stand at street corners; girls look
across the road—rude illustrations, pictures in a book whose
pages we turn over and over as if we should at last find what we
look for. Every face, every shop, bedroom window, public-house,
and dark square is a picture feverishly turned—in search of what?
It is the same with books. What do we seek through millions of
pages? Still hopefully turning the pages—oh, here is Jacob's
room.

He sat at the table reading the *Globe*. The pinkish sheet was
spread flat before him. He propped his face in his hand, so that
the skin of his cheek was wrinkled in deep folds. Terribly severe
he looked, set, and defiant. (What people go through in half an
hour! But nothing could save him. These events are features of

our landscape. A foreigner coming to London could scarcely miss seeing St. Paul's.) He judged life. These pinkish and greenish newspapers are thin sheets of gelatine pressed nightly over the brain and heart of the world. They take the impression of the whole. Jacob cast his eye over it. A strike, a murder, football, bodies found; vociferation from all parts of England simultaneously. How miserable it is that the *Globe* newspaper offers nothing better to Jacob Flanders! When a child begins to read history one marvels, sorrowfully, to hear him spell out in his new voice the ancient words.

The Prime Minister's speech was reported in something over five columns. Feeling in his pocket, Jacob took out a pipe and proceeded to fill it. Five minutes, ten minutes, fifteen minutes passed. Jacob took the paper over to the fire. The Prime Minister proposed a measure for giving Home Rule to Ireland. Jacob knocked out his pipe. He was certainly thinking about Home Rule in Ireland—a very difficult matter. A very cold night.

The snow, which had been falling all night, lay at three o'clock in the afternoon over the fields and the hill. Clumps of withered grass stood out upon the hill-top; the furze bushes were black, and now and then a black shiver crossed the snow as the wind drove flurries of frozen particles before it. The sound was that of a broom sweeping—sweeping.

The stream crept along by the road unseen by any one. Sticks and leaves caught in the frozen grass. The sky was sullen grey and the trees of black iron. Uncompromising was the severity of the country. At four o'clock the snow was again falling. The day had gone out.

A window tinged yellow about two feet across alone combated the white fields and the black trees. . . . At six o'clock a man's figure carrying a lantern crossed the field. . . . A raft of twig stayed upon a stone, suddenly detached itself, and floated towards the culvert. . . . A load of snow slipped and fell from a fir branch. . . . Later there was a mournful cry. . . . A motor car came along the road shoving the dark before it. . . . The dark shut down behind it. . . .

Spaces of complete immobility separated each of these movements. The land seemed to lie dead. . . . Then the old shepherd returned stiffly across the field. Stiffly and painfully the frozen earth was trodden under and gave beneath pressure like a treadmill. The worn voices of clocks repeated the fact of the hour all night long.

Jacob, too, heard them, and raked out the fire. He rose. He stretched himself. He went to bed.

NINE

The Countess of Rocksbier sat at the head of the table alone with Jacob. Fed upon champagne and spices for at least two centuries (four, if you count the female line), the Countess Lucy looked well fed. A discriminating nose she had for scents, prolonged, as if in quest of them; her underlip protruded a narrow red shelf; her eyes were small, with sandy tufts for eyebrows, and her jowl was heavy. Behind her (the window looked on Grosvenor Square) stood Moll Pratt on the pavement, offering violets for sale; and Mrs. Hilda Thomas, lifting her skirts, preparing to cross the road. One was from Walworth; the other from Putney. Both wore black stockings, but Mrs. Thomas was coiled in furs. The comparison was much in Lady Rocksbier's favour. Moll had more humour, but was violent; stupid too. Hilda Thomas was mealy-mouthed, all her silver frames aslant; egg-cups in the drawing-room; and the windows shrouded. Lady Rocksbier, whatever the deficiencies of her profile, had been a great rider to hounds. She used her knife with authority, tore her chicken bones, asking Jacob's pardon, with her own hands.

"Who is that driving by?" she asked Boxall, the butler.

"Lady Fittlemere's carriage, my lady," which reminded her to send a card to ask after his lordship's health. A rude old lady, Jacob thought. The wine was excellent. She called herself "an old woman"—"so kind to lunch with an old woman"—which flattered him. She talked of Joseph Chamberlain, whom she had known. She said that Jacob must come and meet—one of our celebrities. And the Lady Alice came in with three dogs on a leash, and Jackie, who ran to kiss his grandmother, while Boxall brought in a telegram, and Jacob was given a good cigar.

* * *

A few moments before a horse jumps it slows, sidles, gathers itself together, goes up like a monster wave, and pitches down on the further side. Hedges and sky swoop in a semicircle. Then as if your own body ran into the horse's body and it was your own forelegs grown with his that sprang, rushing through the air you go, the ground resilient, bodies a mass of muscles, yet you have command too, upright stillness, eyes accurately judging. Then the curves cease, changing to downright hammer strokes, which jar; and you draw up with a jolt; sitting back a little, sparkling, tingling, glazed with ice over pounding arteries, gasping: "Ah! ho! Hah!" the steam going up from the horses as they jostle together at the cross-roads, where the signpost is, and the woman in the apron stands and stares at the doorway. The man raises himself from the cabbages to stare too.

So Jacob galloped over the fields of Essex, flopped in the mud, lost the hunt, and rode by himself eating sandwiches, looking over the hedges, noticing the colours as if new scraped, cursing his luck.

He had tea at the Inn; and there they all were, slapping, stamping, saying, "After you," clipped, curt, jocose, red as the wattles of turkeys, using free speech until Mrs. Horsefield and her friend Miss Dudding appeared at the doorway with their skirts hitched up, and hair looping down. Then Tom Dudding rapped at the window with his whip. A motor car throbbed in the courtyard. Gentlemen, feeling for matches, moved out, and Jacob went into the bar with Brandy Jones to smoke with the rustics. There was old Jevons with one eye gone, and his clothes the colour of mud, his bag over his back, and his brains laid feet down in earth among the violet roots and the nettle roots; Mary Sanders with her box of wood; and Tom sent for beer, the half-witted son of the sexton—all this within thirty miles of London.

Mrs. Papworth, of Endell Street, Covent Garden, did for Mr. Bonamy in New Square, Lincoln's Inn, and as she washed up the dinner things in the scullery she heard the young gentlemen talking in the room next door. Mr. Sanders was there again; Flanders she meant; and where an inquisitive old woman gets a name wrong, what chance is there that she will faithfully report an argument? As she held the plates under water and then dealt them on the pile beneath the hissing gas, she listened: heard Sanders speaking in a loud rather overbearing tone of voice: "good," he said, and "absolute" and "justice" and "punishment," and "the will of the majority." Then her gentleman piped up; she backed him for argument against Sanders. Yet Sanders was a fine young fellow (here all the scraps went swirling round the sink, scoured after by her purple, almost nailless hands). "Women"—she thought, and wondered what Sanders and her gentleman did in *that* line, one eyelid sinking perceptibly as she mused, for she was the mother of nine—three still-born and one deaf and dumb from birth. Putting the plates in the rack she heard once more Sanders at it again ("He don't give Bonamy a chance," she thought). "Objective something," said Bonamy; and "common ground" and something else—all very long words, she noted. "Book learning does it," she thought to herself, and, as she thrust her arms into her jacket, heard something—might be the little table by the fire—fall; and then stamp, stamp, stamp —as if they were having at each other—round the room, making the plates dance.

"To-morrow's breakfast, sir," she said, opening the door; and there were Sanders and Bonamy like two bulls of Bashan driving each other up and down, making such a racket, and all them chairs in the way. They never noticed her. She felt motherly towards them. "Your breakfast, sir," she said, as they came near. And Bonamy, all his hair touzled and his tie flying, broke off, and pushed Sanders into the arm-chair, and said Mr. Sanders had smashed the coffee-pot and he was teaching Mr. Sanders——

Sure enough, the coffee-pot lay broken on the hearthrug.

"Any day this week except Thursday," wrote Miss Perry, and

this was not the first invitation by any means. Were all Miss Perry's weeks blank with the exception of Thursday, and was her only desire to see her old friend's son? Time is issued to spinster ladies of wealth in long white ribbons. These they wind round and round, round and round, assisted by five female servants, a butler, a fine Mexican parrot, regular meals, Mudie's library, and friends dropping in. A little hurt she was already that Jacob had not called.

"Your mother," she said, "is one of my oldest friends."

Miss Rosseter, who was sitting by the fire, holding the *Spectator* between her cheek and the blaze, refused to have a fire screen, but finally accepted one. The weather was then discussed, for in deference to Parkes, who was opening little tables, graver matters were postponed. Miss Rosseter drew Jacob's attention to the beauty of the cabinet.

"So wonderfully clever in picking things up," she said. Miss Perry had found it in Yorkshire. The North of England was discussed. When Jacob spoke they both listened. Miss Perry was bethinking her of something suitable and manly to say when the door opened and Mr. Benson was announced. Now there were four people sitting in that room. Miss Perry aged 66; Miss Rosseter 42; Mr. Benson 38; and Jacob 25.

"My old friend looks as well as ever," said Mr. Benson, tapping the bars of the parrot's cage; Miss Rosseter simultaneously praised the tea; Jacob handed the wrong plates; and Miss Perry signified her desire to approach more closely. "Your brothers," she began vaguely.

"Archer and John," Jacob supplied her. Then to her pleasure she recovered Rebecca's name; and how one day "when you were all little boys, playing in the drawing-room——"

"But Miss Perry has the kettle-holder," said Miss Rosseter, and indeed Miss Perry was clasping it to her breast. (Had she, then, loved Jacob's father?)

"So clever"—"not so good as usual"—"I thought it most unfair," said Mr. Benson and Miss Rosseter, discussing the Saturday

Westminster. Did they not compete regularly for prizes? Had not Mr. Benson three times won a guinea, and Miss Rosseter once ten and sixpence? Of course Everard Benson had a weak heart, but still, to win prizes, remember parrots, toady Miss Perry, despise Miss Rosseter, give tea-parties in his rooms (which were in the style of Whistler, with pretty books on tables), all this, so Jacob felt without knowing him, made him a contemptible ass. As for Miss Rosseter, she had nursed cancer, and now painted water-colours.

"Running away so soon?" said Miss Perry vaguely. "At home every afternoon, if you've nothing better to do—except Thursdays."

"I've never known you desert your old ladies once," Miss Rosseter was saying, and Mr. Benson was stooping over the parrot's cage, and Miss Perry was moving towards the bell. . . .

The fire burnt clear between two pillars of greenish marble, and on the mantelpiece there was a green clock guarded by Britannia leaning on her spear. As for pictures—a maiden in a large hat offered roses over the garden gate to a gentleman in eighteenth-century costume. A mastiff lay extended against a battered door. The lower panes of the windows were of ground glass, and the curtains, accurately looped, were of plush and green too.

Laurette and Jacob sat with their toes in the fender side by side, in two large chairs covered in green plush. Laurette's skirts were short, her legs long, thin, and transparently covered. Her fingers stroked her ankles.

"It's not exactly that I don't understand them," she was saying thoughtfully. "I must go and try again."

"What time will you be there?" said Jacob.

She shrugged her shoulders.

"To-morrow?"

No, not to-morrow.

"This weather makes me long for the country," she said, look-

ing over her shoulder at the back view of tall houses through
the window.

"I wish you'd been with me on Saturday," said Jacob.

"I used to ride," she said. She got up gracefully, calmly. Jacob
got up. She smiled at him. As she shut the door he put so many
shillings on the mantelpiece.

Altogether a most reasonable conversation; a most respectable
room; an intelligent girl. Only Madame herself seeing Jacob out
had about her that leer, that lewdness, that quake of the surface
(visible in the eyes chiefly), which threatens to spill the whole
bag of ordure, with difficulty held together, over the pavement.
In short, something was wrong.

Not so very long ago the workmen had gilt the final "y" in
Lord Macaulay's name, and the names stretched in unbroken
file round the dome of the British Museum. At a considerable
depth beneath, many hundreds of the living sat at the spokes of
a cart-wheel copying from printed books into manuscript books;
now and then rising to consult the catalogue; regaining their
places stealthily, while from time to time a silent man replenished
their compartments.

There was a little catastrophe. Miss Marchmont's pile over-
balanced and fell into Jacob's compartment. Such things happened to Miss Marchmont. What was she seeking through
millions of pages, in her old plush dress, and her wig of claret-
coloured hair, with her gems and her chilblains? Sometimes one
thing, sometimes another, to confirm her philosophy that colour
is sound—or, perhaps, it has something to do with music. She
could never quite say, though it was not for lack of trying. And
she could not ask you back to her room, for it was "not very
clean, I'm afraid," so she must catch you in the passage, or take
a chair in Hyde Park to explain her philosophy. The rhythm of
the soul depends on it—("how rude the little boys are!" she
would say), and Mr. Asquith's Irish policy, and Shakespeare

comes in, "and Queen Alexandra most graciously once acknowledged a copy of my pamphlet," she would say, waving the little boys magnificently away. But she needs funds to publish her book, for "publishers are capitalists—publishers are cowards." And so, digging her elbow into her pile of books it fell over.

Jacob remained quite unmoved.

But Fraser, the atheist, on the other side, detesting plush, more than once accosted with leaflets, shifted irritably. He abhorred vagueness—the Christian religion, for example, and old Dean Parker's pronouncements. Dean Parker wrote books and Fraser utterly destroyed them by force of logic and left his children unbaptized—his wife did it secretly in the washing basin—but Fraser ignored her, and went on supporting blasphemers, distributing leaflets, getting up his facts in the British Museum, always in the same check suit and fiery tie, but pale, spotted, irritable. Indeed, what a work—to destroy religion!

Jacob transcribed a whole passage from Marlowe.

Miss Julia Hedge, the feminist, waited for her books. They did not come. She wetted her pen. She looked about her. Her eye was caught by the final letters in Lord Macaulay's name. And she read them all round the dome—the names of great men which remind us—— "Oh damn," said Julia Hedge, "why didn't they leave room for an Eliot or a Brontë?"

Unfortunate Julia! wetting her pen in bitterness, and leaving her shoe laces untied. When her books came she applied herself to her gigantic labours, but perceived through one of the nerves of her exasperated sensibility how composedly, unconcernedly, and with every consideration the male readers applied themselves to theirs. That young man for example. What had he got to do except copy out poetry? And she must study statistics. There are more women than men. Yes; but if you let women work as men work, they'll die off much quicker. They'll become extinct. That was her argument. Death and gall and bitter dust were on her pen-tip; and as the afternoon wore on, red had worked into her cheek-bones and a light was in her eyes.

But what brought Jacob Flanders to read Marlowe in the British Museum?

Youth, youth—something savage—something pedantic. For example, there is Mr. Masefield, there is Mr. Bennett. Stuff them into the flame of Marlowe and burn them to cinders. Let not a shred remain. Don't palter with the second rate. Detest your own age. Build a better one. And to set that on foot read incredibly dull essays upon Marlowe to your friends. For which purpose one must collate editions in the British Museum. One must do the thing oneself. Useless to trust to the Victorians, who disembowel, or to the living, who are mere publicists. The flesh and blood of the future depends entirely upon six young men. And as Jacob was one of them, no doubt he looked a little regal and pompous as he turned his page, and Julia Hedge disliked him naturally enough.

But then a pudding-faced man pushed a note towards Jacob, and Jacob, leaning back in his chair, began an uneasy murmured conversation, and they went off together (Julia Hedge watched them), and laughed aloud (she thought) directly they were in the hall.

Nobody laughed in the reading-room. There were shiftings, murmurings, apologetic sneezes, and sudden unashamed devastating coughs. The lesson hour was almost over. Ushers were collecting exercises. Lazy children wanted to stretch. Good ones scribbled assiduously—ah, another day over and so little done! And now and then was to be heard from the whole collection of human beings a heavy sigh, after which the humiliating old man would cough shamelessly, and Miss Marchmont hinnied like a horse.

Jacob came back only in time to return his books.

The books were now replaced. A few letters of the alphabet were sprinkled round the dome. Closely stood together in a ring round the dome were Plato, Aristotle, Sophocles, and Shakespeare; the literatures of Rome, Greece, China, India, Persia. One

leaf of poetry was pressed flat against another leaf, one burnished
letter laid smooth against another in a density of meaning, a conglomeration of loveliness.

"One does want one's tea," said Miss Marchmont, reclaiming
her shabby umbrella.

Miss Marchmont wanted her tea, but could never resist a last
look at the Elgin Marbles. She looked at them sideways, waving
her hand and muttering a word or two of salutation which made
Jacob and the other man turn round. She smiled at them amiably.
It all came into her philosophy—that colour is sound, or perhaps
it has something to do with music. And having done her service,
she hobbled off to tea. It was closing time. The public collected
in the hall to receive their umbrellas.

For the most part the students wait their turn very patiently.
To stand and wait while some one examines white discs is sooth-
ing. The umbrella will certainly be found. But the fact leads you
on all day through Macaulay, Hobbes, Gibbon; through octavos,
quartos, folios; sinks deeper and deeper through ivory pages and
morocco bindings into this density of thought, this conglomeration of knowledge.

Jacob's walking-stick was like all the others; they had mud-
dled the pigeon-holes perhaps.

There is in the British Museum an enormous mind. Consider
that Plato is there cheek by jowl with Aristotle; and Shakespeare
with Marlowe. This great mind is hoarded beyond the power of
any single mind to possess it. Nevertheless (as they take so long
finding one's walking-stick) one can't help thinking how one
might come with a notebook, sit at a desk, and read it all
through. A learned man is the most venerable of all—a man like
Huxtable of Trinity, who writes all his letters in Greek, they
say, and could have kept his end up with Bentley. And then
there is science, pictures, architecture,—an enormous mind.

They pushed the walking-stick across the counter. Jacob stood
beneath the porch of the British Museum. It was raining. Great
Russell Street was glazed and shining—here yellow, here, out-

side the chemist's, red and pale blue. People scuttled quickly close to the wall; carriages rattled rather helter-skelter down the streets. Well, but a little rain hurts nobody. Jacob walked off much as if he had been in the country; and late that night there he was sitting at his table with his pipe and his book.

The rain poured down. The British Museum stood in one solid immense mound, very pale, very sleek in the rain, not a quarter of a mile from him. The vast mind was sheeted with stone; and each compartment in the depths of it was safe and dry. The night-watchmen, flashing their lanterns over the backs of Plato and Shakespeare, saw that on the twenty-second of February neither flame, rat, nor burglar was going to violate these treasures—poor, highly respectable men, with wives and families at Kentish Town, do their best for twenty years to protect Plato and Shakespeare, and then are buried at Highgate.

Stone lies solid over the British Museum, as bone lies cool over the visions and heat of the brain. Only here the brain is Plato's brain and Shakespeare's; the brain has made pots and statues, great bulls and little jewels, and crossed the river of death this way and that incessantly, seeking some landing, now wrapping the body well for its long sleep; now laying a penny piece on the eyes; now turning the toes scrupulously to the East. Meanwhile, Plato continues his dialogue; in spite of the rain; in spite of the cab whistles; in spite of the woman in the mews behind Great Ormond Street who has come home drunk and cries all night long, "Let me in! Let me in!"

In the street below Jacob's room voices were raised.

But he read on. For after all Plato continues imperturbably. And Hamlet utters his soliloquy. And there the Elgin Marbles lie, all night long, old Jones's lantern sometimes recalling Ulysses, or a horse's head; or sometimes a flash of gold, or a mummy's sunk yellow cheek. Plato and Shakespeare continue; and Jacob, who was reading the *Phaedrus*, heard people vociferating round the lamp-post, and the woman battering at the door and crying, "Let me in!" as if a coal had dropped from the fire, or a fly, falling from the ceiling, had lain on its back, too weak to turn over.

The *Phaedrus* is very difficult. And so, when at length one reads straight ahead, falling into step, marching on, becoming (so it seems) momentarily part of this rolling, imperturbable energy, which has driven darkness before it since Plato walked the Acropolis, it is impossible to see to the fire.

The dialogue draws to its close. Plato's argument is done. Plato's argument is stowed away in Jacob's mind, and for five minutes Jacob's mind continues alone, onwards, into the darkness. Then, getting up, he parted the curtains, and saw, with astonishing clearness, how the Springetts opposite had gone to bed; how it rained; how the Jews and the foreign woman, at the end of the street, stood by the pillar-box, arguing.

Every time the door opened and fresh people came in, those already in the room shifted slightly; those who were standing looked over their shoulders; those who were sitting stopped in the middle of sentences. What with the light, the wine, the strumming of a guitar, something exciting happened each time the door opened. Who was coming in?

"That's Gibson."

"The painter?"

"But go on with what you were saying."

They were saying something that was far, far too intimate to be said outright. But the noise of the voices served like a clapper in little Mrs. Withers's mind, scaring into the air flocks of small birds, and then they'd settle, and then she'd feel afraid, put one hand to her hair, bind both round her knees, and look up at Oliver Skelton nervously, and say:

"Promise, *promise,* you'll tell no one." . . . so considerate he was, so tender. It was her husband's character that she discussed. He was cold, she said.

Down upon them came the splendid Magdalen, brown, warm, voluminous, scarcely brushing the grass with her sandalled feet.

Her hair flew; pins seemed scarcely to attach the flying silks. An actress of course, a line of light perpetually beneath her. It was only "My dear" that she said, but her voice went jodelling between Alpine passes. And down she tumbled on the floor, and sang, since there was nothing to be said, round ah's and oh's. Mangin, the poet, coming up to her, stood looking down at her, drawing at his pipe. The dancing began.

Grey-haired Mrs. Keymer asked Dick Graves to tell her who Mangin was, and said that she had seen too much of this sort of thing in Paris (Magdalen had got upon his knees; now his pipe was in her mouth) to be shocked. "Who is that?" she said, staying her glasses when they came to Jacob, for indeed he looked quiet, not indifferent, but like some one on a beach, watching.

"Oh, my dear, let me lean on you," gasped Helen Askew, hopping on one foot, for the silver cord round her ankle had worked loose. Mrs. Keymer turned and looked at the picture on the wall.

"Look at Jacob," said Helen (they were binding his eyes for some game).

And Dick Graves, being a little drunk, very faithful, and very simple-minded, told her that he thought Jacob the greatest man he had ever known. And down they sat cross-legged upon cushions and talked about Jacob, and Helen's voice trembled, for they both seemed heroes to her, and the friendship between them so much more beautiful than women's friendships. Anthony Pollett now asked her to dance, and as she danced she looked at them, over her shoulder, standing at the table, drinking together.

The magnificent world—the live, sane, vigorous world. . . . These words refer to the stretch of wood pavement between Hammersmith and Holborn in January between two and three in the morning. That was the ground beneath Jacob's feet. It was healthy and magnificent because one room, above a mews, somewhere near the river, contained fifty excited, talkative, friendly people. And then to stride over the pavement (there was scarcely a cab or policeman in sight) is of itself exhilarating. The long loop of Piccadilly, diamond-stitched, shows to best advantage when it is empty. A young man has nothing to fear. On the contrary, though he may not have said anything brilliant, he feels pretty confident he can hold his own. He was pleased to have met Mangin; he admired the young woman on the floor; he liked them all; he liked that sort of thing. In short, all the drums and trumpets were sounding. The street scavengers were the only people about at the moment. It is scarcely necessary to say how well-disposed Jacob felt towards them; how it pleased him to let himself in with his latch-key at his own door; how he seemed to bring back with him into the empty room ten or eleven people whom he had not known when he set out; how he looked about for something to read, and found it, and never read it, and fell asleep.

Indeed, drums and trumpets is no phrase. Indeed, Piccadilly and Holborn, and the empty sitting-room and the sitting-room with fifty people in it are liable at any moment to blow music into the air. Women perhaps are more excitable than men. It is seldom that any one says anything about it, and to see the hordes crossing Waterloo Bridge to catch the non-stop to Surbiton one might think that reason impelled them. No, no. It is the drums and trumpets. Only, should you turn aside into one of those little bays on Waterloo Bridge to think the matter over, it will probably seem to you all a muddle—all a mystery.

They cross the Bridge incessantly. Sometimes in the midst of carts and omnibuses a lorry will appear with great forest trees chained to it. Then, perhaps, a mason's van with newly lettered tombstones recording how some one loved some one who is buried at Putney. Then the motor car in front jerks forward, and the tombstones pass too quick for you to read more. All the time the stream of people never ceases passing from the Surrey side to the Strand; from the Strand to the Surrey side. It seems as if the poor had gone raiding the town, and now trapesed back to their own quarters, like beetles scurrying to their holes, for that old woman fairly hobbles towards Waterloo, grasping a shiny bag, as if she had been out into the light and now made off with some scraped chicken bones to her hovel underground. On the other hand, though the wind is rough and blowing in their faces, those girls there, striding hand in hand, shouting out a song, seem to feel neither cold nor shame. They are hatless. They triumph.

The wind has blown up the waves. The river races beneath us, and the men standing on the barges have to lean all their weight on the tiller. A black tarpaulin is tied down over a swelling load of gold. Avalanches of coal glitter blackly. As usual, painters are slung on planks across the great riverside hotels, and the hotel windows have already points of light in them. On the other side the city is white as if with age; St. Paul's swells white above the fretted, pointed, or oblong buildings beside it. The cross alone shines rosy-gilt. But what century have we reached? Has this procession from the Surrey side to the Strand gone on for ever? That old man has been crossing the Bridge these six hundred years, with the rabble of little boys at his heels, for he is drunk, or blind with misery, and tied round with old clouts of clothing such as pilgrims might have worn. He shuffles on. No one stands still. It seems as if we marched to the sound of music; perhaps the wind and the river; perhaps these same drums and trumpets —the ecstasy and hubbub of the soul. Why, even the unhappy laugh, and the policeman, far from judging the drunk man, surveys him humorously, and the little boys scamper back again, and the clerk from Somerset House has nothing but tolerance for him, and the man who is reading half a page of *Lothair* at the bookstall muses charitably, with his eyes off the print, and the girl hesitates at the crossing and turns on him the bright yet vague glance of the young.

Bright yet vague. She is perhaps twenty-two. She is shabby. She crosses the road and looks at the daffodils and the red tulips in the florist's window. She hesitates, and makes off in the direction of Temple Bar. She walks fast, and yet anything distracts her. Now she seems to see, and now to notice nothing.

hrough the disused graveyard in the parish of St. Pancras, Fanny Elmer strayed between the white tombs which lean against the wall, crossing the grass to read a name, hurrying on when the grave-keeper approached, hurrying into the street, pausing now by a window with blue china, now quickly making up for lost time, abruptly entering a baker's shop, buying rolls, adding cakes, going on again so that any one wishing to follow must fairly trot. She was not drably shabby, though. She wore silk stockings, and silver-buckled shoes, only the red feather in her hat drooped, and the clasp of her bag was weak, for out fell a copy of Madame Tussaud's programme as she walked. She had the ankles of a stag. Her face was hidden. Of course, in this dusk, rapid movements, quick glances, and soaring hopes come naturally enough. She passed right beneath Jacob's window.

The house was flat, dark, and silent. Jacob was at home engaged upon a chess problem, the board being on a stool between his knees. One hand was fingering the hair at the back of his head. He slowly brought it forward and raised the white queen from her square; then put her down again on the same spot. He filled his pipe; ruminated; moved two pawns; advanced the white knight; then ruminated with one finger upon the bishop. Now Fanny Elmer passed beneath the window.

She was on her way to sit to Nick Bramham the painter.

She sat in a flowered Spanish shawl, holding in her hand a yellow novel.

"A little lower, a little looser, so—better, that's right," Bramham mumbled, who was drawing her, and smoking at the same

time, and was naturally speechless. His head might have been
the work of a sculptor, who had squared the forehead, stretched
the mouth, and left marks of his thumbs and streaks from his
fingers in the clay. But the eyes had never been shut. They were
rather prominent, and rather bloodshot, as if from staring and
staring, and when he spoke they looked for a second disturbed,
but went on staring. An unshaded electric light hung above her
head.

As for the beauty of women, it is like the light on the sea, never
constant to a single wave. They all have it; they all lose it. Now
she is dull and thick as bacon; now transparent as a hanging
glass. The fixed faces are the dull ones. Here comes Lady Venice
displayed like a monument for admiration, but carved in ala-
baster, to be set on the mantelpiece and never dusted. A dapper
brunette complete from head to foot serves only as an illustration to lie upon the drawing-room table. The women in the
streets have the faces of playing cards; the outlines accurately
filled in with pink or yellow, and the line drawn tightly round
them. Then, at a top-floor window, leaning out, looking down,
you see beauty itself; or in the corner of an omnibus; or squatted
in a ditch—beauty glowing, suddenly expressive, withdrawn the
moment after. No one can count on it or seize it or have it
wrapped in paper. Nothing is to be won from the shops, and
Heaven knows it would be better to sit at home than haunt the
plate-glass windows in the hope of lifting the shining green, the
glowing ruby, out of them alive. Sea glass in a saucer loses its
lustre no sooner than silks do. Thus if you talk of a beautiful
woman you mean only something flying fast which for a second
uses the eyes, lips, or cheeks of Fanny Elmer, for example, to
glow through.

She was not beautiful, as she sat stiffly; her underlip too prominent; her nose too large; her eyes too near together. She was a
thin girl, with brilliant cheeks and dark hair, sulky just now, or
stiff with sitting. When Bramham snapped his stick of charcoal
she started. Bramham was out of temper. He squatted before the

gas fire warming his hands. Meanwhile she looked at his drawing. He grunted. Fanny threw on a dressing-gown and boiled a
kettle.

"By God, it's bad," said Bramham.

Fanny dropped on to the floor, clasped her hands round her
knees, and looked at him, her beautiful eyes—yes, beauty, flying
through the room, shone there for a second. Fanny's eyes seemed
to question, to commiserate, to be, for a second, love itself. But
she exaggerated. Bramham noticed nothing. And when the kettle
boiled, up she scrambled, more like a colt or a puppy than a loving woman.

Now Jacob walked over to the window and stood with his
hands in his pockets. Mr. Springett opposite came out, looked
at his shop window, and went in again. The children drifted
past, eyeing the pink sticks of sweetstuff. Pickford's van swung
down the street. A small boy twirled from a rope. Jacob turned
away. Two minutes later he opened the front door, and walked
off in the direction of Holborn.

Fanny Elmer took down her cloak from the hook. Nick Bramham unpinned his drawing and rolled it under his arm. They
turned out the lights and set off down the street, holding on
their way through all the people, motor cars, omnibuses, carts,
until they reached Leicester Square, five minutes before Jacob
reached it, for his way was slightly longer, and he had been
stopped by a block in Holborn waiting to see the King drive by,
so that Nick and Fanny were already leaning over the barrier in
the promenade at the Empire when Jacob pushed through the
swing doors and took his place beside them.

"Hullo, never noticed you," said Nick, five minutes later.

"Bloody rot," said Jacob.

"Miss Elmer," said Nick.

Jacob took his pipe out of his mouth very awkwardly.

Very awkward he was. And when they sat upon a plush sofa and let the smoke go up between them and the stage, and heard far off the high-pitched voices and the jolly orchestra breaking in opportunely he was still awkward, only Fanny thought: "What a beautiful voice!" She thought how little he said yet how firm it was. She thought how young men are dignified and aloof, and how unconscious they are, and how quietly one might sit beside Jacob and look at him. And how childlike he would be, come in tired of an evening, she thought, and how majestic; a little overbearing perhaps; "But I wouldn't give way," she thought. He got up and leant over the barrier. The smoke hung about him.

And for ever the beauty of young men seems to be set in smoke, however lustily they chase footballs, or drive cricket balls, dance, run, or stride along roads. Possibly they are soon to lose it. Possibly they look into the eyes of faraway heroes, and take their station among us half contemptuously, she thought (vibrating like a fiddle-string, to be played on and snapped). Anyhow, they love silence, and speak beautifully, each word falling like a disc new cut, not a hubble-bubble of small smooth coins such as girls use; and they move decidedly, as if they knew how long to stay and when to go—oh, but Mr. Flanders was only gone to get a programme.

"The dancers come right at the end," he said, coming back to them.

And isn't it pleasant, Fanny went on thinking, how young men bring out lots of silver coins from their trouser pockets, and look at them, instead of having just so many in a purse?

Then there she was herself, whirling across the stage in white flounces, and the music was the dance and fling of her own soul, and the whole machinery, rock and gear of the world was spun smoothly into those swift eddies and falls, she felt, as she stood rigid leaning over the barrier two feet from Jacob Flanders.

Her screwed-up black glove dropped to the floor. When Jacob

gave it her, she started angrily. For never was there a more irrational passion. And Jacob was afraid of her for a moment—so violent, so dangerous is it when young women stand rigid; grasp the barrier; fall in love.

It was the middle of February. The roofs of Hampstead Garden Suburb lay in a tremulous haze. It was too hot to walk. A dog barked, barked, barked down in the hollow. The liquid shadows went over the plain.

The body after long illness is languid, passive, receptive of sweetness, but too weak to contain it. The tears well and fall as the dog barks in the hollow, the children skim after hoops, the country darkens and brightens. Beyond a veil it seems. Ah, but draw the veil thicker lest I faint with sweetness, Fanny Elmer sighed, as she sat on a bench in Judges Walk looking at Hampstead Garden Suburb. But the dog went on barking. The motor cars hooted on the road. She heard a far-away rush and humming. Agitation was at her heart. Up she got and walked. The grass was freshly green; the sun hot. All round the pond children were stooping to launch little boats; or were drawn back screaming by their nurses.

At mid-day young women walk out into the air. All the men are busy in the town. They stand by the edge of the blue pond. The fresh wind scatters the children's voices all about. *My* children, thought Fanny Elmer. The women stand round the pond, beating off great prancing shaggy dogs. Gently the baby is rocked in the perambulator. The eyes of all the nurses, mothers, and wandering women are a little glazed, absorbed. They gently nod instead of answering when the little boys tug at their skirts, begging them to move on.

And Fanny moved, hearing some cry—a workman's whistle perhaps—high in mid-air. Now, among the trees, it was the thrush trilling out into the warm air a flutter of jubilation, but fear seemed to spur him, Fanny thought; as if he too were anxious with such joy at his heart—as if he were watched as he sang, and pressed by tumult to sing. There! Restless, he flew to the next tree. She heard his song more faintly. Beyond it was the humming of the wheels and the wind rushing.

She spent tenpence on lunch.

"Dear, miss, she's left her umberella," grumbled the mottled woman in the glass box near the door at the Express Dairy Company's shop.

"Perhaps I'll catch her," answered Milly Edwards, the waitress with the pale plaits of hair; and she dashed through the door.

"No good," she said, coming back a moment later with Fanny's cheap umbrella. She put her hand to her plaits.

"Oh, that door!" grumbled the cashier.

Her hands were cased in black mittens, and the finger-tips that drew in the paper slips were swollen as sausages.

"Pie and greens for one. Large coffee and crumpets. Eggs on toast. Two fruit cakes."

Thus the sharp voices of the waitresses snapped. The lunchers heard their orders repeated with approval; saw the next table served with anticipation. Their own eggs on toast were at last delivered. Their eyes strayed no more.

Damp cubes of pastry fell into mouths opened like triangular bags.

Nelly Jenkinson, the typist, crumbled her cake indifferently enough. Every time the door opened she looked up. What did she expect to see?

The coal merchant read the *Telegraph* without stopping, missed the saucer, and, feeling abstractedly, put the cup down on the table-cloth.

"Did you ever hear the like of that for impertinence?" Mrs. Parsons wound up, brushing the crumbs from her furs.

"Hot milk and scone for one. Pot of tea. Roll and butter," cried the waitresses.

The door opened and shut.

Such is the life of the elderly.

It is curious, lying in a boat, to watch the waves. Here are three coming regularly one after another, all much of a size. Then, hurrying after them comes a fourth, very large and menacing; it lifts the boat; on it goes; somehow merges without accomplishing anything; flattens itself out with the rest.

What can be more violent than the fling of boughs in a gale, the tree yielding itself all up the trunk, to the very tip of the branch, streaming and shuddering the way the wind blows, yet never flying in dishevelment away?

The corn squirms and abases itself as if preparing to tug itself free from the roots, and yet is tied down.

Why, from the very windows, even in the dusk, you see a swelling run through the street, an aspiration, as with arms outstretched, eyes desiring, mouths agape. And then we peaceably subside. For if the exaltation lasted we should be blown like foam into the air. The stars would shine through us. We should go down the gale in salt drops—as sometimes happens. For the impetuous spirits will have none of this cradling. Never any swaying or aimlessly lolling for them. Never any making believe, or lying cosily, or genially supposing that one is much like another, fire warm, wine pleasant, extravagance a sin.

"People are so nice, once you know them."

"I couldn't think ill of her. One must remember——" But Nick perhaps, or Fanny Elmer, believing implicitly in the truth of the moment, fling off, sting the cheek, are gone like sharp hail.

"Oh," said Fanny, bursting into the studio three-quarters of an hour late because she had been hanging about the neighbourhood of the Foundling Hospital merely for the chance of seeing Jacob walk down the street, take out his latch-key, and open the door,

"I'm afraid I'm late"; upon which Nick said nothing and Fanny grew defiant.

"I'll never come again!" she cried at length.

"Don't, then," Nick replied, and off she ran without so much as good-night.

How exquisite it was—that dress in Evelina's shop off Shaftesbury Avenue! It was four o'clock on a fine day early in April, and was Fanny the one to spend four o'clock on a fine day indoors? Other girls in that very street sat over ledgers, or drew long threads wearily between silk and gauze; or, festooned with ribbons in Swan and Edgars, rapidly added up pence and farthings on the back of the bill and twisted the yard and three-quarters in tissue paper and asked "Your pleasure?" of the next comer.

In Evelina's shop off Shaftesbury Avenue the parts of a woman were shown separate. In the left hand was her skirt. Twining round a pole in the middle was a feather boa. Ranged like the heads of malefactors on Temple Bar were hats—emerald and white, lightly wreathed or drooping beneath deep-dyed feathers. And on the carpet were her feet—pointed gold, or patent leather slashed with scarlet.

Feasted upon by the eyes of women, the clothes by four o'clock were flyblown like sugar cakes in a baker's window. Fanny eyed them too.

But coming along Gerrard Street was a tall man in a shabby coat. A shadow fell across Evelina's window—Jacob's shadow, though it was not Jacob. And Fanny turned and walked along Gerrard Street and wished that she had read books. Nick never read books, never talked of Ireland, or the House of Lords; and as for his finger-nails! She would learn Latin and read Virgil. She had been a great reader. She had read Scott; she had read Dumas. At the Slade no one read. But no one knew Fanny at the Slade, or guessed how empty it seemed to her; the passion for ear-rings,

for dances, for Tonks and Steer—when it was only the French
who could paint, Jacob said. For the moderns were futile; painting the least respectable of the arts; and why read anything but
Marlowe and Shakespeare, Jacob said, and Fielding if you must
read novels?

"Fielding," said Fanny, when the man in Charing Cross Road
asked her what book she wanted.

She bought *Tom Jones.*

At ten o'clock in the morning, in a room which she shared
with a school teacher, Fanny Elmer read *Tom Jones*—that mystic book. For this dull stuff (Fanny thought) about people with
odd names is what Jacob likes. Good people like it. Dowdy
women who don't mind how they cross their legs read *Tom
Jones*—a mystic book; for there is something, Fanny thought,
about books which if I had been educated I could have liked—
much better than ear-rings and flowers, she sighed, thinking of
the corridors at the Slade and the fancy-dress dance next week.
She had nothing to wear.

They are real, thought Fanny Elmer, setting her feet on the
mantelpiece. Some people are. Nick perhaps, only he was so stupid. And women never—except Miss Sargent, but she went off
at lunch-time and gave herself airs. There they sat quietly of a
night reading, she thought. Not going to music-halls; not looking in at shop windows; not wearing each other's clothes, like
Robertson who had worn her shawl, and she had worn his waistcoat, which Jacob could only do very awkwardly; for he liked
Tom Jones.

There it lay on her lap, in double columns, price three and sixpence; the mystic book in which Henry Fielding ever so many
years ago rebuked Fanny Elmer for feasting on scarlet, in perfect prose, Jacob said. For he never read modern novels. He
liked *Tom Jones.*

"I do like *Tom Jones,*" said Fanny, at five-thirty that same day
early in April when Jacob took out his pipe in the arm-chair
opposite.

Alas, women lie! But not Clara Durrant. A flawless mind; a candid nature; a virgin chained to a rock (somewhere off Lowndes Square) eternally pouring out tea for old men in white waistcoats, blue-eyed, looking you straight in the face, playing Bach. Of all women, Jacob honoured her most. But to sit at a table with bread and butter, with dowagers in velvet, and never say more to Clara Durrant than Benson said to the parrot when old Miss Perry poured out tea, was an insufferable outrage upon the liberties and decencies of human nature—or words to that effect. For Jacob said nothing. Only he glared at the fire. Fanny laid down *Tom Jones*.

She stitched or knitted.

"What's that?" asked Jacob.

"For the dance at the Slade."

And she fetched her head-dress; her trousers; her shoes with red tassels. What should she wear?

"I shall be in Paris," said Jacob.

And what is the point of fancy-dress dances? thought Fanny. You meet the same people; you wear the same clothes; Mangin gets drunk; Florinda sits on his knee. She flirts outrageously— with Nick Bramham just now.

"In Paris?" said Fanny.

"On my way to Greece," he replied.

For, he said, there is nothing so detestable as London in May. He would forget her.

A sparrow flew past the window trailing a straw—a straw from a stack stood by a barn in a farmyard. The old brown spaniel snuffs at the base for a rat. Already the upper branches of the elm trees are blotted with nests. The chestnuts have flirted their fans. And the butterflies are flaunting across the rides in the Forest. Perhaps the Purple Emperor is feasting, as Morris says, upon a mass of putrid carrion at the base of an oak tree.

Fanny thought it all came from *Tom Jones*. He could go alone with a book in his pocket and watch the badgers. He would take a train at eight-thirty and walk all night. He saw fire-flies, and brought back glow-worms in pill-boxes. He would hunt with the New Forest Staghounds. It all came from *Tom Jones*; and he would go to Greece with a book in his pocket and forget her.

She fetched her hand-glass. There was her face. And suppose one wreathed Jacob in a turban? There was his face. She lit the lamp. But as the daylight came through the window only half was lit up by the lamp. And though he looked terrible and magnificent and would chuck the Forest, he said, and come to the Slade, and be a Turkish knight or a Roman emperor (and he let her blacken his lips and clenched his teeth and scowled in the glass), still—there lay *Tom Jones*.

rcher," said Mrs. Flanders with that tenderness which mothers so often display towards their eldest sons, "will be at Gibraltar to-morrow."

The post for which she was waiting (strolling up Dods Hill while the random church bells swung a hymn tune about her head, the clock striking four straight through the circling notes; the grass purpling under a storm-cloud; and the two dozen houses of the village cowering, infinitely humble, in company under a leaf of shadow), the post, with all its variety of messages, envelopes addressed in bold hands, in slanting hands, stamped now with English stamps, again with Colonial stamps, or sometimes hastily dabbed with a yellow bar, the post was about to scatter a myriad messages over the world. Whether we gain or not by this habit of profuse communication it is not for us to say. But that letter-writing is practised mendaciously nowadays, particularly by young men travelling in foreign parts, seems likely enough.

For example, take this scene.

Here was Jacob Flanders gone abroad and staying to break his journey in Paris. (Old Miss Birkbeck, his mother's cousin, had died last June and left him a hundred pounds.)

"You needn't repeat the whole damned thing over again, Cruttendon," said Mallinson, the little bald painter who was sitting at a marble table, splashed with coffee and ringed with wine, talking very fast, and undoubtedly more than a little drunk.

"Well, Flanders, finished writing to your lady?" said Cruttendon, as Jacob came and took his seat beside them, holding in his hand an envelope addressed to Mrs. Flanders, near Scarborough, England.

"Do you uphold Velasquez?" said Cruttendon.

"By God, he does," said Mallinson.

"He always gets like this," said Cruttendon irritably.

Jacob looked at Mallinson with excessive composure.

"I'll tell you the three greatest things that were ever written in the whole of literature," Cruttendon burst out. " 'Hang there like fruit my soul,' " he began. . . .

"Don't listen to a man who don't like Velasquez," said Mallinson.

"Adolphe, don't give Mr. Mallinson any more wine," said Cruttendon.

"Fair play, fair play," said Jacob judicially. "Let a man get drunk if he likes. That's Shakespeare, Cruttendon. I'm with you there. Shakespeare had more guts than all these damned frogs put together. 'Hang there like fruit my soul,' " he began quoting, in a musical rhetorical voice, flourishing his wine-glass. "The devil damn you black, you cream-faced loon!" he exclaimed as the wine washed over the rim.

" 'Hang there like fruit my soul,' " Cruttendon and Jacob both began again at the same moment, and both burst out laughing.

"Curse these flies," said Mallinson, flicking at his bald head. "What do they take me for?"

"Something sweet-smelling," said Cruttendon.

"Shut up, Cruttendon," said Jacob. "The fellow has no manners," he explained to Mallinson very politely. "Wants to cut people off their drink. Look here. I want grilled bone. What's the French for grilled bone? Grilled bone, Adolphe. Now you juggins, don't you understand?"

"And I'll tell you, Flanders, the second most beautiful thing in the whole of literature," said Cruttendon, bringing his feet down on to the floor, and leaning right across the table, so that his face almost touched Jacob's face.

" 'Hey diddle diddle, the cat and the fiddle,' " Mallinson interrupted, strumming his fingers on the table. "The most exqui-sitely beautiful thing in the whole of literature. . . . Cruttendon is a very good fellow," he remarked confidentially. "But he's a bit of a fool." And he jerked his head forward.

Well, not a word of this was ever told to Mrs. Flanders; nor what happened when they paid the bill and left the restaurant, and walked along the Boulevard Raspaille.

Then here is another scrap of conversation; the time about eleven in the morning; the scene a studio; and the day Sunday.

"I tell you, Flanders," said Cruttendon, "I'd as soon have one of Mallinson's little pictures as a Chardin. And when I say that . . ." he squeezed the tail of an emaciated tube . . . "Chardin was a great swell. . . . He sells 'em to pay his dinner now. But wait till the dealers get hold of him. A great swell—oh, a very great swell."

"It's an awfully pleasant life," said Jacob, "messing away up here. Still, it's a stupid art, Cruttendon." He wandered off across the room. "There's this man, Pierre Louÿs now." He took up a book.

"Now my good sir, are you going to settle down?" said Cruttendon.

"That's a solid piece of work," said Jacob, standing a canvas on a chair.

"Oh, that I did ages ago," said Cruttendon, looking over his shoulder.

"You're a pretty competent painter in my opinion," said Jacob after a time.

"Now if you'd like to see what I'm after at the present moment," said Cruttendon, putting a canvas before Jacob. "There. That's it. That's more like it. That's . . ." he squirmed his thumb in a circle round a lamp globe painted white.

"A pretty solid piece of work," said Jacob, straddling his legs in front of it. "But what I wish you'd explain . . ."

Miss Jinny Carslake, pale, freckled, morbid, came into the room.

"Oh Jinny, here's a friend. Flanders. An Englishman. Wealthy. Highly connected. Go on, Flanders. . . ."

Jacob said nothing.

"It's *that*—that's not right," said Jinny Carslake.

"No," said Cruttendon decidedly. "Can't be done."

He took the canvas off the chair and stood it on the floor with its back to them.

"Sit down, ladies and gentlemen. Miss Carslake comes from your part of the world, Flanders. From Devonshire. Oh, I thought you said Devonshire. Very well. She's a daughter of the church too. The black sheep of the family. Her mother writes her such letters. I say—have you one about you? It's generally Sundays they come. Sort of church-bell effect, you know."

"Have you met all the painter men?" said Jinny. "Was Mallinson drunk? If you go to his studio he'll give you one of his pictures. I say, Teddy . . ."

"Half a jiff," said Cruttendon. "What's the season of the year?" He looked out of the window.

"We take a day off on Sundays, Flanders."

"Will he . . ." said Jinny, looking at Jacob. "You . . ."

"Yes, he'll come with us," said Cruttendon.

And then, here is Versailles.

Jinny stood on the stone rim and leant over the pond, clasped by Cruttendon's arms or she would have fallen in. "There! There!" she cried. "Right up to the top!" Some sluggish, sloping-shouldered fish had floated up from the depths to nip her crumbs. "You look," she said, jumping down. And then the dazzling white water, rough and throttled, shot up into the air. The fountain spread itself. Through it came the sound of military music far away. All the water was puckered with drops. A blue air-ball gently bumped the surface. How all the nurses and children and old men and young crowded to the edge, leant over and waved their sticks! The little girl ran stretching her arms towards her air-ball, but it sank beneath the fountain.

Edward Cruttendon, Jinny Carslake, and Jacob Flanders walked in a row along the yellow gravel path; got on to the grass; so passed under the trees; and came out at the summer-house where Marie Antoinette used to drink chocolate. In went Edward and Jinny, but Jacob waited outside, sitting on the handle of his walking-stick. Out they came again.

"Well?" said Cruttendon, smiling at Jacob.

Jinny waited; Edward waited; and both looked at Jacob.

"Well?" said Jacob, smiling and pressing both hands on his stick.

"Come along," he decided; and started off. The others followed him, smiling.

And then they went to the little café in the by-street where people sit drinking coffee, watching the soldiers, meditatively knocking ashes into trays.

"But he's quite different," said Jinny, folding her hands over the top of her glass. "I don't suppose you know what Ted means when he says a thing like that," she said, looking at Jacob. "But I do. Sometimes I could kill myself. Sometimes he lies in bed all day long—just lies there. . . . I don't want you right on the table"; she waved her hands. Swollen iridescent pigeons were waddling round their feet.

"Look at that woman's hat," said Cruttendon. "How do they come to think of it? . . . No, Flanders, I don't think I could live like you. When one walks down that street opposite the British Museum—what's it called?—that's what I mean. It's all like that. Those fat women—and the man standing in the middle of the road as if he were going to have a fit . . ."

"Everybody feeds them," said Jinny, waving the pigeons away. "They're stupid old things."

"Well, I don't know," said Jacob, smoking his cigarette. "There's St. Paul's."

"I mean going to an office," said Cruttendon.

"Hang it all," Jacob expostulated.

"But you don't count," said Jinny, looking at Cruttendon. "You're mad. I mean, you just think of painting."

"Yes, I know. I can't help it. I say, will King George give way about the peers?"

"He'll jolly well have to," said Jacob.

"There!" said Jinny. "He really knows."

"You see, I would if I could," said Cruttendon, "but I simply can't."

"I *think* I could," said Jinny. "Only, it's all the people one dislikes who do it. At home, I mean. They talk of nothing else. Even people like my mother."

"Now if I came and lived here——" said Jacob. "What's my share, Cruttendon? Oh, very well. Have it your own way. Those silly birds, directly one wants them—they've flown away."

And finally under the arc lamps in the Gare des Invalides, with one of those queer movements which are so slight yet so definite, which may wound or pass unnoticed but generally inflict a good deal of discomfort, Jinny and Cruttendon drew together; Jacob stood apart. They had to separate. Something must be said. Nothing was said. A man wheeled a trolley past Jacob's legs so near that he almost grazed them. When Jacob recovered his balance the other two were turning away, though Jinny looked over her shoulder, and Cruttendon, waving his hand, disappeared like the very great genius that he was.

No—Mrs. Flanders was told none of this, though Jacob felt, it is safe to say, that nothing in the world was of greater importance; and as for Cruttendon and Jinny, he thought them the most remarkable people he had ever met—being of course unable to foresee how it fell out in the course of time that Cruttendon took to painting orchards; had therefore to live in Kent; and must, one would think, see through apple blossom by this time, since his wife, for whose sake he did it, eloped with a novelist; but no; Cruttendon still paints orchards, savagely, in solitude.

Then Jinny Carslake, after her affair with Lefanu the American painter, frequented Indian philosophers, and now you find her in pensions in Italy cherishing a little jeweller's box containing ordinary pebbles picked off the road. But if you look at them steadily, she says, multiplicity becomes unity, which is somehow the secret of life, though it does not prevent her from following the macaroni as it goes round the table, and sometimes, on spring nights, she makes the strangest confidences to shy young Englishmen.

Jacob had nothing to hide from his mother. It was only that he could make no sense himself of his extraordinary excitement, and as for writing it down——

"Jacob's letters are so like him," said Mrs. Jarvis, folding the sheet.

"Indeed he seems to be having . . ." said Mrs. Flanders, and paused, for she was cutting out a dress and had to straighten the pattern, ". . . a very gay time."

Mrs. Jarvis thought of Paris. At her back the window was open, for it was a mild night; a calm night; when the moon seemed muffled and the apple trees stood perfectly still.

"I never pity the dead," said Mrs. Jarvis, shifting the cushion at her back, and clasping her hands behind her head. Betty Flanders did not hear, for her scissors made so much noise on the table.

"They are at rest," said Mrs. Jarvis. "And we spend our days doing foolish unnecessary things without knowing why."

Mrs. Jarvis was not liked in the village.

"You never walk at this time of night?" she asked Mrs. Flanders.

"It is certainly wonderfully mild," said Mrs. Flanders.

Yet it was years since she had opened the orchard gate and gone out on Dods Hill after dinner.

"It is perfectly dry," said Mrs. Jarvis, as they shut the orchard door and stepped on to the turf.

"I shan't go far," said Betty Flanders. "Yes, Jacob will leave Paris on Wednesday."

"Jacob was always my friend of the three," said Mrs. Jarvis.

"Now, my dear, I am going no further," said Mrs. Flanders. They had climbed the dark hill and reached the Roman camp.

The rampart rose at their feet—the smooth circle surrounding the camp or the grave. How many needles Betty Flanders had lost there! and her garnet brooch.

"It is much clearer than this sometimes," said Mrs. Jarvis, standing upon the ridge. There were no clouds, and yet there was a haze over the sea, and over the moors. The lights of Scarborough flashed, as if a woman wearing a diamond necklace turned her head this way and that.

"How quiet it is!" said Mrs. Jarvis.

Mrs. Flanders rubbed the turf with her toe, thinking of her garnet brooch.

Mrs. Jarvis found it difficult to think of herself to-night. It was so calm. There was no wind; nothing racing, flying, escaping. Black shadows stood still over the silver moors. The furze bushes stood perfectly still. Neither did Mrs. Jarvis think of God. There was a church behind them, of course. The church clock struck ten. Did the strokes reach the furze bush, or did the thorn tree hear them?

Mrs. Flanders was stooping down to pick up a pebble. Sometimes people do find things, Mrs. Jarvis thought, and yet in this hazy moonlight it was impossible to see anything, except bones, and little pieces of chalk.

"Jacob bought it with his own money, and then I brought Mr. Parker up to see the view, and it must have dropped——" Mrs. Flanders murmured.

Did the bones stir, or the rusty swords? Was Mrs. Flanders's twopenny-halfpenny brooch for ever part of the rich accumulation? and if all the ghosts flocked thick and rubbed shoulders with Mrs. Flanders in the circle, would she not have seemed perfectly in her place, a live English matron, growing stout?

The clock struck the quarter.

The frail waves of sound broke among the stiff gorse and the hawthorn twigs as the church clock divided time into quarters.

Motionless and broad-backed the moors received the statement "It is fifteen minutes past the hour," but made no answer, unless a bramble stirred.

Yet even in this light the legends on the tombstones could be read, brief voices saying, "I am Bertha Ruck," "I am Tom Gage." And they say which day of the year they died, and the New Testament says something for them, very proud, very emphatic, or consoling.

The moors accept all that too.

The moonlight falls like a pale page upon the church wall, and illumines the kneeling family in the niche, and the tablet set up in 1780 to the Squire of the parish who relieved the poor, and believed in God—so the measured voice goes on down the marble scroll, as though it could impose itself upon time and the open air.

Now a fox steals out from behind the gorse bushes.

Often, even at night, the church seems full of people. The pews are worn and greasy, and the cassocks in place, and the hymn-books on the ledges. It is a ship with all its crew aboard. The timbers strain to hold the dead and the living, the ploughmen, the carpenters, the fox-hunting gentlemen and the farmers smelling of mud and brandy. Their tongues join together in syllabling the sharp-cut words, which for ever slice asunder time and the broad-backed moors. Plaint and belief and elegy, despair and triumph, but for the most part good sense and jolly indifference, go trampling out of the windows any time these five hundred years.

Still, as Mrs. Jarvis said, stepping out on to the moors, "How quiet it is!" Quiet at midday, except when the hunt scatters across it; quiet in the afternoon, save for the drifting sheep; at night the moor is perfectly quiet.

A garnet brooch has dropped into its grass. A fox pads stealthily. A leaf turns on its edge. Mrs. Jarvis, who is fifty years of age, reposes in the camp in the hazy moonlight.

". . . and," said Mrs. Flanders, straightening her back, "I never cared for Mr. Parker."

"Neither did I," said Mrs. Jarvis. They began to walk home.

But their voices floated for a little above the camp. The moonlight destroyed nothing. The moor accepted everything. Tom Gage cries aloud so long as his tombstone endures. The Roman skeletons are in safe keeping. Betty Flanders's darning needles are safe too and her garnet brooch. And sometimes at midday, in the sunshine, the moor seems to hoard these little treasures, like a nurse. But at midnight when no one speaks or gallops, and the thorn tree is perfectly still, it would be foolish to vex the moor with questions—what? and why?

The church clock, however, strikes twelve.

he water fell off a ledge like lead—like a chain with thick white links. The train ran out into a steep green meadow, and Jacob saw striped tulips growing and heard a bird singing, in Italy.

A motor car full of Italian officers ran along the flat road and kept up with the train, raising dust behind it. There were trees laced together with vines—as Virgil said. Here was a station; and a tremendous leave-taking going on, with women in high yellow boots and odd pale boys in ringed socks. Virgil's bees had gone about the plains of Lombardy. It was the custom of the ancients to train vines between elms. Then at Milan there were sharp-winged hawks, of a bright brown, cutting figures over the roofs.

These Italian carriages get damnably hot with the afternoon sun on them, and the chances are that before the engine has pulled to the top of the gorge the clanking chain will have broken. Up, up, up, it goes, like a train on a scenic railway. Every peak is covered with sharp trees, and amazing white villages are crowded on ledges. There is always a white tower on the very summit, flat red-frilled roofs, and a sheer drop beneath. It is not a country in which one walks after tea. For one thing there is no grass. A whole hillside will be ruled with olive trees. Already in April the earth is clotted into dry dust between them. And there are neither stiles nor footpaths, nor lanes chequered with the shadows of leaves nor eighteenth-century inns with bow-windows, where one eats ham and eggs. Oh no, Italy is all fierceness, bareness, exposure, and black priests shuffling along the roads. It is strange, too, how you never get away from villas.

Still, to be travelling on one's own with a hundred pounds to spend is a fine affair. And if his money gave out, as it probably would, he would go on foot. He could live on bread and wine—the wine in straw bottles—for after doing Greece he was going to knock off Rome. The Roman civilization was a very inferior affair, no doubt. But Bonamy talked a lot of rot, all the same. "You ought to have been in Athens," he would say to Bonamy when he got back. "Standing on the Parthenon," he would say, or "The ruins of the Coliseum suggest some fairly sublime reflections," which he would write out at length in letters. It might turn to an essay upon civilization. A comparison between the ancients and moderns, with some pretty sharp hits at Mr. Asquith—something in the style of Gibbon.

A stout gentleman laboriously hauled himself in, dusty, baggy, slung with gold chains, and Jacob, regretting that he did not come of the Latin race, looked out of the window.

It is a strange reflection that by travelling two days and nights you are in the heart of Italy. Accidental villas among olive trees appear; and men-servants watering the cactuses. Black victorias drive in between pompous pillars with plaster shields stuck to them. It is at once momentary and astonishingly intimate—to be displayed before the eyes of a foreigner. And there is a lonely hill-top where no one ever comes, and yet it is seen by me who was lately driving down Piccadilly on an omnibus. And what I should like would be to get out among the fields, sit down and hear the grasshoppers, and take up a handful of earth—Italian earth, as this is Italian dust upon my shoes.

Jacob heard them crying strange names at railway stations through the night. The train stopped and he heard frogs croaking close by, and he wrinkled back the blind cautiously and saw a vast strange marsh all white in the moonlight. The carriage was thick with cigar smoke, which floated round the globe with the green shade on it. The Italian gentleman lay snoring with his boots off and his waistcoat unbuttoned. . . . And all this business of going to Greece seemed to Jacob an intolerable weariness—sitting in hotels by oneself and looking at monuments—he'd have done better to go to Cornwall with Timmy Durrant. . . .

"O—h," Jacob protested, as the darkness began breaking in front of him and the light showed through, but the man was reaching across him to get something—the fat Italian man in his dicky, unshaven, crumpled, obese, was opening the door and going off to have a wash.

So Jacob sat up, and saw a lean Italian sportsman with a gun walking down the road in the early morning light, and the whole idea of the Parthenon came upon him in a clap.

"By Jove!" he thought, "we must be nearly there!" and he stuck his head out of the window and got the air full in his face.

It is highly exasperating that twenty-five people of your acquaintance should be able to say straight off something very much to the point about being in Greece, while for yourself there is a stopper upon all emotions whatsoever. For after washing at the hotel at Patras, Jacob had followed the tram lines a mile or so out; and followed them a mile or so back; he had met several droves of turkeys; several strings of donkeys; had got lost in back streets; had read advertisements of corsets and of Maggi's consommé; children had trodden on his toes; the place smelt of bad cheese; and he was glad to find himself suddenly come out opposite his hotel. There was an old copy of the *Daily Mail* lying among coffee-cups; which he read. But what could he do after dinner?

No doubt we should be, on the whole, much worse off than we are without our astonishing gift for illusion. At the age of twelve or so, having given up dolls and broken our steam engines, France, but much more probably Italy, and India almost for a certainty, draws the superfluous imagination. One's aunts have been to Rome; and every one has an uncle who was last heard of—poor man—in Rangoon. He will never come back any more. But it is the governesses who start the Greek myth. Look at that for a head (they say)—nose, you see, straight as a dart, curls, eyebrows—everything appropriate to manly beauty; while his legs and arms have lines on them which indicate a perfect degree of development—the Greeks caring for the body as much as for the face. And the Greeks could paint fruit so that birds pecked at it. First you read Xenophon; then Euripides. One day—that was an occasion, by God—what people have said appears to have sense in it; "the Greek spirit"; the Greek this, that, and the other; though it is absurd, by the way, to say that any Greek comes near Shakespeare. The point is, however, that we have been brought up in an illusion.

Jacob, no doubt, thought something in this fashion, the *Daily Mail* crumpled in his hand; his legs extended; the very picture of boredom.

"But it's the way we're brought up," he went on.

And it all seemed to him very distasteful. Something ought to be done about it. And from being moderately depressed he became like a man about to be executed. Clara Durrant had left him at a party to talk to an American called Pilchard. And he had come all the way to Greece and left her. They wore evening-dresses, and talked nonsense—what damned nonsense—and he put out his hand for the *Globe Trotter,* an international magazine which is supplied free of charge to the proprietors of hotels.

In spite of its ramshackle condition modern Greece is highly advanced in the electric tramway system, so that while Jacob sat in the hotel sitting-room the trams clanked, chimed, rang, rang, rang imperiously to get the donkeys out of the way, and one old woman who refused to budge, beneath the windows. The whole of civilization was being condemned.

The waiter was quite indifferent to that too. Aristotle, a dirty man, carnivorously interested in the body of the only guest now occupying the only arm-chair, came into the room ostentatiously, put something down, put something straight, and saw that Jacob was still there.

"I shall want to be called early to-morrow," said Jacob, over his shoulder. "I am going to Olympia."

This gloom, this surrender to the dark waters which lap us about, is a modern invention. Perhaps, as Cruttendon said, we do not believe enough. Our fathers at any rate had something to demolish. So have we for the matter of that, thought Jacob, crumpling the *Daily Mail* in his hand. He would go into Parliament and make fine speeches—but what use are fine speeches and Parliament, once you surrender an inch to the black waters? Indeed there has never been any explanation of the ebb and flow in our veins—of happiness and unhappiness. That respectability and evening parties where one has to dress, and wretched slums at the back of Gray's Inn—something solid, immovable, and grotesque—is at the back of it, Jacob thought probable. But then there was the British Empire which was beginning to puzzle him; nor was he altogether in favour of giving Home Rule to Ireland. What did the *Daily Mail* say about that?

For he had grown to be a man, and was about to be immersed in things—as indeed the chambermaid, emptying his basin upstairs, fingering keys, studs, pencils, and bottles of tabloids strewn on the dressing-table, was aware.

That he had grown to be a man was a fact that Florinda knew, as she knew everything, by instinct.

And Betty Flanders even now suspected it, as she read his letter, posted at Milan, "Telling me," she complained to Mrs. Jarvis, "really nothing that I want to know"; but she brooded over it.

Fanny Elmer felt it to desperation. For he would take his stick and his hat and would walk to the window, and look perfectly absent-minded and very stern too, she thought.

"I am going," he would say, "to cadge a meal of Bonamy."

"Anyhow, I can drown myself in the Thames," Fanny cried, as she hurried past the Foundling Hospital.

"But the *Daily Mail* isn't to be trusted," Jacob said to himself, looking about for something else to read. And he sighed again, being indeed so profoundly gloomy that gloom must have been lodged in him to cloud him at any moment, which was odd in a man who enjoyed things so, was not much given to analysis, but was horribly romantic, of course, Bonamy thought, in his rooms in Lincoln's Inn.

"He will fall in love," thought Bonamy. "Some Greek woman with a straight nose."

It was to Bonamy that Jacob wrote from Patras—to Bonamy who couldn't love a woman and never read a foolish book.

There are very few good books after all, for we can't count profuse histories, travels in mule carts to discover the sources of the Nile, or the volubility of fiction.

I like books whose virtue is all drawn together in a page or two. I like sentences that don't budge though armies cross them. I like words to be hard—such were Bonamy's views, and they won him the hostility of those whose taste is all for the fresh growths of the morning, who throw up the window, and find the poppies spread in the sun, and can't forbear a shout of jubilation at the astonishing fertility of English literature. That was not Bonamy's way at all. That his taste in literature affected his friendships, and made him silent, secretive, fastidious, and only quite at his ease with one or two young men of his own way of thinking, was the charge against him.

But then Jacob Flanders was not at all of his own way of thinking—far from it, Bonamy sighed, laying the thin sheets of notepaper on the table and falling into thought about Jacob's character, not for the first time.

The trouble was this romantic vein in him. "But mixed with the stupidity which leads him into these absurd predicaments," thought Bonamy, "there is something—something"—he sighed, for he was fonder of Jacob than of any one in the world.

Jacob went to the window and stood with his hands in his pockets. There he saw three Greeks in kilts; the masts of ships; idle or busy people of the lower classes strolling or stepping out briskly, or falling into groups and gesticulating with their hands. Their lack of concern for him was not the cause of his gloom;

but some more profound conviction—it was not that he himself happened to be lonely, but that all people are.

Yet next day, as the train slowly rounded a hill on the way to Olympia, the Greek peasant women were out among the vines; the old Greek men were sitting at the stations, sipping sweet wine. And though Jacob remained gloomy he had never suspected how tremendously pleasant it is to be alone; out of England; on one's own; cut off from the whole thing. There are very sharp bare hills on the way to Olympia; and between them blue sea in triangular spaces. A little like the Cornish coast. Well now, to go walking by oneself all day—to get on to that track and follow it up between the bushes—or are they small trees?— to the top of that mountain from which one can see half the nations of antiquity——

"Yes," said Jacob, for his carriage was empty, "let's look at the map."

Blame it or praise it, there is no denying the wild horse in us. To gallop intemperately; fall on the sand tired out; to feel the earth spin; to have—positively—a rush of friendship for stones and grasses, as if humanity were over, and as for men and women, let them go hang—there is no getting over the fact that this desire seizes us pretty often.

The evening air slightly moved the dirty curtains in the hotel window at Olympia.

"I am full of love for every one," thought Mrs. Wentworth Williams, "—for the poor most of all—for the peasants coming back in the evening with their burdens. And everything is soft and vague and very sad. It is sad, it is sad. But everything has meaning," thought Sandra Wentworth Williams, raising her head a little and looking very beautiful, tragic, and exalted. "One must love everything."

She held in her hand a little book convenient for travelling— stories by Tchekov—as she stood, veiled, in white, in the window of the hotel at Olympia. How beautiful the evening was! and her beauty was its beauty. The tragedy of Greece was the tragedy of all high souls. The inevitable compromise. She seemed to have grasped something. She would write it down. And moving to the table where her husband sat reading she leant her chin in her hands and thought of the peasants, of suffering, of her own beauty, of the inevitable compromise, and of how she would write it down. Nor did Evan Williams say anything brutal, banal, or foolish when he shut his book and put it away to make room for the plates of soup which were now being placed before them. Only his drooping bloodhound eyes and his heavy sallow cheeks expressed his melancholy tolerance, his conviction that though forced to live with circumspection and deliberation he could never possibly achieve any of those objects which, as he knew, are the only ones worth pursuing. His consideration was flawless; his silence unbroken.

"Everything seems to mean so much," said Sandra. But with the sound of her own voice the spell was broken. She forgot the peasants. Only there remained with her a sense of her own beauty, and in front, luckily, there was a looking-glass.

"I am very beautiful," she thought.

She shifted her hat slightly. Her husband saw her looking in the glass; and agreed that beauty is important; it is an inheritance; one cannot ignore it. But it is a barrier; it is in fact rather a bore. So he drank his soup; and kept his eyes fixed upon the window.

"Quails," said Mrs. Wentworth Williams languidly. "And then goat, I suppose; and then . . ."

"Caramel custard presumably," said her husband in the same cadence, with his toothpick out already.

She laid her spoon upon her plate, and her soup was taken away half finished. Never did she do anything without dignity; for hers was the English type which is so Greek, save that villagers have touched their hats to it, the vicarage reveres it; and upper-gardeners and under-gardeners respectfully straighten

their backs as she comes down the broad terrace on Sunday
morning, dallying at the stone urns with the Prime Minister to
pick a rose—which, perhaps, she was trying to forget, as her eye
wandered round the dining-room of the inn at Olympia, seeking
the window where her book lay, where a few minutes ago she
had discovered something—something very profound it had
been, about love and sadness and the peasants.

But it was Evan who sighed; not in despair nor indeed in re-
bellion. But, being the most ambitious of men and tempera-
mentally the most sluggish, he had accomplished nothing; had
the political history of England at his finger-ends, and living
much in company with Chatham, Pitt, Burke, and Charles James
Fox could not help contrasting himself and his age with them
and theirs. "Yet there never was a time when great men are more
needed," he was in the habit of saying to himself, with a sigh.
Here he was picking his teeth in an inn at Olympia. He had
done. But Sandra's eyes wandered.

"Those pink melons are sure to be dangerous," he said gloom-
ily. And as he spoke the door opened and in came a young man
in a grey check suit.

"Beautiful but dangerous," said Sandra, immediately talking
to her husband in the presence of a third person. ("Ah, an English boy on tour," she thought to herself.)

And Evan knew all that too.

Yes, he knew all that; and he admired her. Very pleasant, he
thought, to have affairs. But for himself, what with his height
(Napoleon was five feet four, he remembered), his bulk, his inability to impose his own personality (and yet great men are
needed more than ever now, he sighed), it was useless. He threw
away his cigar, went up to Jacob and asked him, with a simple
sort of sincerity which Jacob liked, whether he had come straight
out from England.

"How very English!" Sandra laughed when the waiter told
them next morning that the young gentleman had left at five to
climb the mountain. "I am sure he asked you for a bath?" at

which the waiter shook his head, and said that he would ask the manager.

"You do not understand," laughed Sandra. "Never mind."

Stretched on the top of the mountain, quite alone, Jacob enjoyed himself immensely. Probably he had never been so happy in the whole of his life.

But at dinner that night Mr. Williams asked him whether he would like to see the paper; then Mrs. Williams asked him (as they strolled on the terrace smoking—and how could he refuse that man's cigar?) whether he'd seen the theatre by moonlight; whether he knew Everard Sherborn; whether he read Greek and whether (Evan rose silently and went in) if he had to sacrifice one it would be the French literature or the Russian?

"And now," wrote Jacob in his letter to Bonamy, "I shall have to read her cursed book"—her Tchekov, he meant, for she had lent it him.

Though the opinion is unpopular it seems likely enough that bare places, fields too thick with stones to be ploughed, tossing sea-meadows half-way between England and America, suit us better than cities.

There is something absolute in us which despises qualification. It is this which is teased and twisted in society. People come together in a room. "So delighted," says somebody, "to meet you," and that is a lie. And then: "I enjoy the spring more than the autumn now. One does, I think, as one gets older." For women are always, always, always talking about what one feels, and if they say "as one gets older," they mean you to reply with something quite off the point.

Jacob sat himself down in the quarry where the Greeks had cut marble for the theatre. It is hot work walking up Greek hills at midday. The wild red cyclamen was out; he had seen the little tortoises hobbling from clump to clump; the air smelt strong and suddenly sweet, and the sun, striking on jagged splinters of marble, was very dazzling to the eyes. Composed, commanding, contemptuous, a little melancholy, and bored with an august kind of boredom, there he sat smoking his pipe.

Bonamy would have said that this was the sort of thing that made him uneasy—when Jacob got into the doldrums, looked like a Margate fisherman out of a job, or a British Admiral. You couldn't make him understand a thing when he was in a mood like that. One had better leave him alone. He was dull. He was apt to be grumpy.

He was up very early, looking at the statues with his Baedeker.

Sandra Wentworth Williams, ranging the world before breakfast in quest of adventure or a point of view, all in white, not so very tall perhaps, but uncommonly upright—Sandra Williams got Jacob's head exactly on a level with the head of the Hermes of Praxiteles. The comparison was all in his favour. But before she could say a single word he had gone out of the Museum and left her.

Still, a lady of fashion travels with more than one dress, and if white suits the morning hour, perhaps sandy yellow with purple spots on it, a black hat, and a volume of Balzac, suit the evening. Thus she was arranged on the terrace when Jacob came in. Very beautiful she looked. With her hands folded she mused, seemed to listen to her husband, seemed to watch the peasants coming down with brushwood on their backs, seemed to notice how the hill changed from blue to black, seemed to discriminate between truth and falsehood, Jacob thought, and crossed his legs suddenly, observing the extreme shabbiness of his trousers.

"But he is very distinguished looking," Sandra decided.

And Evan Williams, lying back in his chair with the paper on his knees, envied them. The best thing he could do would be to publish, with Macmillans, his monograph upon the foreign policy of Chatham. But confound this tumid, queasy feeling—this restlessness, swelling, and heat—it was jealousy! jealousy! jealousy! which he had sworn never to feel again.

"Come with us to Corinth, Flanders," he said with more than

his usual energy, stopping by Jacob's chair. He was relieved by Jacob's reply, or rather by the solid, direct, if shy manner in which he said that he would like very much to come with them to Corinth.

"Here is a fellow," thought Evan Williams, "who might do very well in politics."

"I intend to come to Greece every year so long as I live," Jacob wrote to Bonamy. "It is the only chance I can see of protecting oneself from civilization."

"Goodness knows what he means by that," Bonamy sighed. For as he never said a clumsy thing himself, these dark sayings of Jacob's made him feel apprehensive, yet somehow impressed, his own turn being all for the definite, the concrete, and the rational.

Nothing could be much simpler than what Sandra said as she descended the Acro-Corinth, keeping to the little path, while Jacob strode over rougher ground by her side. She had been left motherless at the age of four; and the Park was vast.

"One never seemed able to get out of it," she laughed. Of course there was the library, and dear Mr. Jones, and notions about things. "I used to stray into the kitchen and sit upon the butler's knees," she laughed, sadly though.

Jacob thought that if he had been there he would have saved her; for she had been exposed to great dangers, he felt, and, he thought to himself, "People wouldn't understand a woman talking as she talks."

She made little of the roughness of the hill; and wore breeches, he saw, under her short skirts.

"Women like Fanny Elmer don't," he thought. "What's-her-name Carslake didn't; yet they pretend . . ."

Mrs. Williams said things straight out. He was surprised by his own knowledge of the rules of behaviour; how much more can be said than one thought; how open one can be with a woman; and how little he had known himself before.

Evan joined them on the road; and as they drove along up hill and down hill (for Greece is in a state of effervescence, yet astonishingly clean-cut, a treeless land, where you see the ground between the blades, each hill cut and shaped and outlined as often as not against sparkling deep blue waters, islands white as sand floating on the horizon, occasional groves of palm trees standing in the valleys, which are scattered with black goats, spotted with little olive trees and sometimes have white hollows, rayed and criss-crossed, in their flanks), as they drove up hill and down he scowled in the corner of the carriage, with his paw so tightly closed that the skin was stretched between the knuckles and the little hairs stood upright. Sandra rode opposite, dominant, like a Victory prepared to fling into the air.

"Heartless!" thought Evan (which was untrue).

"Brainless!" he suspected (and that was not true either). "Still . . . !" He envied her.

When bedtime came the difficulty was to write to Bonamy, Jacob found. Yet he had seen Salamis, and Marathon in the distance. Poor old Bonamy! No; there was something queer about it. He could not write to Bonamy.

"I shall go to Athens all the same," he resolved, looking very set, with this hook dragging in his side.

The Williamses had already been to Athens.

Athens is still quite capable of striking a young man as the oddest combination, the most incongruous assortment. Now it is suburban; now immortal. Now cheap continental jewellery is laid upon plush trays. Now the stately woman stands naked, save for a wave of drapery above the knee. No form can he set on his sensations as he strolls, one blazing afternoon, along the Parisian boulevard and skips out of the way of the royal landau which, looking indescribably ramshackle, rattles along the pitted roadway, saluted by citizens of both sexes cheaply dressed in bowler hats and continental costumes; though a shepherd in kilt, cap, and gaiters very nearly drives his herd of goats between the royal wheels; and all the time the Acropolis surges into the air, raises itself above the town, like a large immobile wave with the yellow columns of the Parthenon firmly planted upon it.

The yellow columns of the Parthenon are to be seen at all hours of the day firmly planted upon the Acropolis; though at sunset, when the ships in the Piraeus fire their guns, a bell rings, a man in uniform (the waistcoat unbuttoned) appears; and the women roll up the black stockings which they are knitting in the shadow of the columns, call to the children, and troop off down the hill back to their houses.

There they are again, the pillars, the pediment, the Temple of Victory and the Erechtheum, set on a tawny rock cleft with shadows, directly you unlatch your shutters in the morning and, leaning out, hear the clatter, the clamour, the whip cracking in the street below. There they are.

The extreme definiteness with which they stand, now a brilliant white, again yellow, and in some lights red, imposes ideas of durability, of the emergence through the earth of some spiritual energy elsewhere dissipated in elegant trifles. But this durability exists quite independently of our admiration. Although the beauty is sufficiently humane to weaken us, to stir the deep deposit of mud—memories, abandonments, regrets, sentimental devotions—the Parthenon is separate from all that; and if you consider how it has stood out all night, for centuries, you begin to connect the blaze (at midday the glare is dazzling and the frieze almost invisible) with the idea that perhaps it is beauty alone that is immortal.

Added to this, compared with the blistered stucco, the new love songs rasped out to the strum of guitar and gramophone, and the mobile yet insignificant faces of the street, the Parthenon is really astonishing in its silent composure; which is so vigorous that, far from being decayed, the Parthenon appears, on the contrary, likely to outlast the entire world.

* * *

"And the Greeks, like sensible men, never bothered to finish the backs of their statues," said Jacob, shading his eyes and observing that the side of the figure which is turned away from view is left in the rough.

He noted the slight irregularity in the line of the steps which "the artistic sense of the Greeks preferred to mathematical accuracy," he read in his guide-book.

He stood on the exact spot where the great statue of Athena used to stand, and identified the more famous landmarks of the scene beneath.

In short he was accurate and diligent; but profoundly morose. Moreover he was pestered by guides. This was on Monday.

But on Wednesday he wrote a telegram to Bonamy, telling him to come at once. And then he crumpled it in his hand and threw it in the gutter.

"For one thing he wouldn't come," he thought. "And then I daresay this sort of thing wears off." "This sort of thing" being that uneasy, painful feeling, something like selfishness—one wishes almost that the thing would stop—it is getting more and more beyond what is possible—"If it goes on much longer I shan't be able to cope with it—but if some one else were seeing it at the same time—Bonamy is stuffed in his room in Lincoln's Inn —oh, I say, damn it all, I say,"—the sight of Hymettus, Pentelicus, Lycabettus on one side, and the sea on the other, as one stands in the Parthenon at sunset, the sky pink feathered, the plain all colours, the marble tawny in one's eyes, is thus oppressive. Luckily Jacob had little sense of personal association; he seldom thought of Plato or Socrates in the flesh; on the other hand his feeling for architecture was very strong; he preferred statues to pictures; and he was beginning to think a great deal about the problems of civilization, which were solved, of course, so very remarkably by the ancient Greeks, though their solution is no help to us. Then the hook gave a great tug in his side as he lay in bed on Wednesday night; and he turned over with a des-

perate sort of tumble, remembering Sandra Wentworth Williams
with whom he was in love.

Next day he climbed Pentelicus.

The day after he went up to the Acropolis. The hour was
early; the place almost deserted; and possibly there was thunder
in the air. But the sun struck full upon the Acropolis.

Jacob's intention was to sit down and read, and, finding a drum
of marble conveniently placed, from which Marathon could be
seen, and yet it was in the shade, while the Erechtheum blazed
white in front of him, there he sat. And after reading a page he
put his thumb in his book. Why not rule countries in the way
they should be ruled? And he read again.

No doubt his position there overlooking Marathon somehow
raised his spirits. Or it may have been that a slow capacious brain
has these moments of flowering. Or he had, insensibly, while he
was abroad, got into the way of thinking about politics.

And then looking up and seeing the sharp outline, his medita-
tions were given an extraordinary edge; Greece was over; the
Parthenon in ruins; yet there he was.

(Ladies with green and white umbrellas passed through the
courtyard—French ladies on their way to join their husbands
in Constantinople.)

Jacob read on again. And laying the book on the ground he began, as if inspired by what he had read, to write a note upon the
importance of history—upon democracy—one of those scribbles
upon which the work of a lifetime may be based; or again, it
falls out of a book twenty years later, and one can't remember a
word of it. It is a little painful. It had better be burnt.

Jacob wrote; began to draw a straight nose; when all the
French ladies opening and shutting their umbrellas just beneath
him exclaimed, looking at the sky, that one did not know what
to expect—rain or fine weather?

Jacob got up and strolled across to the Erechtheum. There are
still several women standing there holding the roof on their

heads. Jacob straightened himself slightly; for stability and balance affect the body first. These statues annulled things so! He stared at them, then turned, and there was Madame Lucien Gravé perched on a block of marble with her kodak pointed at his head. Of course she jumped down, in spite of her age, her figure, and her tight boots—having, now that her daughter was married, lapsed with a luxurious abandonment, grand enough in its way, into the fleshy grotesque; she jumped down, but not before Jacob had seen her.

"Damn these women—damn these women!" he thought. And he went to fetch his book which he had left lying on the ground in the Parthenon.

"How they spoil things," he murmured, leaning against one of the pillars, pressing his book tight between his arm and his side. (As for the weather, no doubt the storm would break soon; Athens was under cloud.)

"It is those damned women," said Jacob, without any trace of bitterness, but rather with sadness and disappointment that what might have been should never be.

(This violent disillusionment is generally to be expected in young men in the prime of life, sound of wind and limb, who will soon become fathers of families and directors of banks.)

Then, making sure that the Frenchwomen had gone, and looking cautiously round him, Jacob strolled over to the Erechtheum and looked rather furtively at the goddess on the left-hand side holding the roof on her head. She reminded him of Sandra Wentworth Williams. He looked at her, then looked away. He looked at her, then looked away. He was extraordinarily moved, and with the battered Greek nose in his head, with Sandra in his head, with all sorts of things in his head, off he started to walk right up to the top of Mount Hymettus, alone, in the heat.

That very afternoon Bonamy went expressly to talk about Jacob to tea with Clara Durrant in the square behind Sloane

Street where, on hot spring days, there are striped blinds over the front windows, single horses pawing the macadam outside the doors, and elderly gentlemen in yellow waistcoats ringing bells and stepping in very politely when the maid demurely replies that Mrs. Durrant is at home.

Bonamy sat with Clara in the sunny front room with the barrel organ piping sweetly outside; the water-cart going slowly along spraying the pavement; the carriages jingling, and all the silver and chintz, brown and blue rugs and vases filled with green boughs, striped with trembling yellow bars.

The insipidity of what was said needs no illustration— Bonamy kept on gently returning quiet answers and accumulating amazement at an existence squeezed and emasculated within a white satin shoe (Mrs. Durrant meanwhile enunciating strident politics with Sir Somebody in the back room) until the virginity of Clara's soul appeared to him candid; the depths unknown; and he would have brought out Jacob's name had he not begun to feel positively certain that Clara loved him—and could do nothing whatever.

"Nothing whatever!" he exclaimed, as the door shut, and, for a man of his temperament, got a very queer feeling, as he walked through the park, of carriages irresistibly driven; of flower beds uncompromisingly geometrical; of force rushing round geometrical patterns in the most senseless way in the world. "Was Clara," he thought, pausing to watch the boys bathing in the Serpentine, "the silent woman?—would Jacob marry her?"

But in Athens in the sunshine, in Athens, where it is almost impossible to get afternoon tea, and elderly gentlemen who talk politics talk them all the other way round, in Athens sat Sandra Wentworth Williams, veiled, in white, her legs stretched in front of her, one elbow on the arm of the bamboo chair, blue clouds wavering and drifting from her cigarette.

The orange trees which flourish in the Square of the Constitution, the band, the dragging of feet, the sky, the houses, lemon and rose coloured—all this became so significant to Mrs. Wentworth Williams after her second cup of coffee that she began dramatizing the story of the noble and impulsive Englishwoman who had offered a seat in her carriage to the old American lady at Mycenae (Mrs. Duggan)—not altogether a false story, though it said nothing of Evan, standing first on one foot, then on the other, waiting for the women to stop chattering.

"I am putting the life of Father Damien into verse," Mrs. Duggan had said, for she had lost everything—everything in the world, husband and child and everything, but faith remained.

Sandra, floating from the particular to the universal, lay back in a trance.

The flight of time which hurries us so tragically along; the eternal drudge and drone, now bursting into fiery flame like those brief balls of yellow among green leaves (she was looking at orange trees); kisses on lips that are to die; the world turning, turning in mazes of heat and sound—though to be sure there is the quiet evening with its lovely pallor, "For I am sensitive to every side of it," Sandra thought, "and Mrs. Duggan will write to me for ever, and I shall answer her letters." Now the royal band marching by with the national flag stirred wider rings of emotion, and life became something that the courageous mount and ride out to sea on—the hair blown back (so she envisaged it, and the breeze stirred slightly among the orange trees) and she herself was emerging from silver spray—when she saw Jacob. He was standing in the Square with a book under his arm looking vacantly about him. That he was heavily built and might become stout in time was a fact.

But she suspected him of being a mere bumpkin.

"There is that young man," she said, peevishly, throwing away her cigarette, "that Mr. Flanders."

"Where?" said Evan. "I don't see him."

"Oh, walking away—behind the trees now. No, you can't see

him. But we are sure to run into him," which, of course, they did.

But how far was he a mere bumpkin? How far was Jacob Flanders at the age of twenty-six a stupid fellow? It is no use trying to sum people up. One must follow hints, not exactly what is said, nor yet entirely what is done. Some, it is true, take ineffaceable impressions of character at once. Others dally, loiter, and get blown this way and that. Kind old ladies assure us that cats are often the best judges of character. A cat will always go to a good man, they say; but then, Mrs. Whitehorn, Jacob's landlady, loathed cats.

There is also the highly respectable opinion that character-mongering is much overdone nowadays. After all, what does it matter—that Fanny Elmer was all sentiment and sensation, and Mrs. Durrant hard as iron? that Clara, owing (so the character-mongers said) largely to her mother's influence, never yet had the chance to do anything off her own bat, and only to very observant eyes displayed deeps of feeling which were positively alarming; and would certainly throw herself away upon some one unworthy of her one of these days unless, so the character-mongers said, she had a spark of her mother's spirit in her—was somehow heroic. But what a term to apply to Clara Durrant! Simple to a degree, others thought her. And that is the very reason, so they said, why she attracts Dick Bonamy—the young man with the Wellington nose. Now *he's* a dark horse if you like. And there these gossips would suddenly pause. Obviously they meant to hint at his peculiar disposition—long rumoured among them.

"But sometimes it is precisely a woman like Clara that men of that temperament need . . ." Miss Julia Eliot would hint.

"Well," Mr. Bowley would reply, "it may be so."

For however long these gossips sit, and however they stuff out their victims' characters till they are swollen and tender as the livers of geese exposed to a hot fire, they never come to a decision.

"That young man, Jacob Flanders," they would say, "so distinguished looking—and yet so awkward." Then they would apply themselves to Jacob and vacillate eternally between the two extremes. He rode to hounds—after a fashion, for he hadn't a penny.

"Did you ever hear who his father was?" asked Julia Eliot.

"His mother, they say, is somehow connected with the Rocksbiers," replied Mr. Bowley.

"He doesn't overwork himself anyhow."

"His friends are very fond of him."

"Dick Bonamy, you mean?"

"No, I didn't mean that. It's evidently the other way with Jacob. He is precisely the young man to fall headlong in love and repent it for the rest of his life."

"Oh, Mr. Bowley," said Mrs. Durrant, sweeping down upon them in her imperious manner, "you remember Mrs. Adams? Well, that is her niece." And Mr. Bowley, getting up, bowed politely and fetched strawberries.

So we are driven back to see what the other side means—the men in clubs and Cabinets—when they say that character-drawing is a frivolous fireside art, a matter of pins and needles, exquisite outlines enclosing vacancy, flourishes, and mere scrawls.

The battleships ray out over the North Sea, keeping their stations accurately apart. At a given signal all the guns are trained on a target which (the master gunner counts the seconds, watch in hand—at the sixth he looks up) flames into splinters. With equal nonchalance a dozen young men in the prime of life descend with composed faces into the depths of the sea; and there impassively (though with perfect mastery of machinery) suffocate uncomplainingly together. Like blocks of tin soldiers the army covers the cornfield, moves up the hillside, stops, reels slightly this way and that, and falls flat, save that, through field-glasses, it can be seen that one or two pieces still agitate up and down like fragments of broken match-stick.

These actions, together with the incessant commerce of banks, laboratories, chancellories, and houses of business, are the strokes which oar the world forward, they say. And they are dealt by men as smoothly sculptured as the impassive policeman at Ludgate Circus. But you will observe that far from being padded to rotundity his face is stiff from force of will, and lean from the efforts of keeping it so. When his right arm rises, all the force in his veins flows straight from shoulder to finger-tips; not an ounce is diverted into sudden impulses, sentimental regrets, wire-drawn distinctions. The buses punctually stop.

It is thus that we live, they say, driven by an unseizable force. They say that the novelists never catch it; that it goes hurtling through their nets and leaves them torn to ribbons. This, they say, is what we live by—this unseizable force.

"Where are the men?" said old General Gibbons, looking round the drawing-room, full as usual on Sunday afternoons of well-dressed people. "Where are the guns?"

Mrs. Durrant looked too.

Clara, thinking that her mother wanted her, came in; then went out again.

They were talking about Germany at the Durrants, and Jacob (driven by this unseizable force) walked rapidly down Hermes Street and ran straight into the Williamses.

"Oh!" cried Sandra, with a cordiality which she suddenly felt. And Evan added, "What luck!"

The dinner which they gave him in the hotel which looks on to the Square of the Constitution was excellent. Plated baskets contained fresh rolls. There was real butter. And the meat scarcely needed the disguise of innumerable little red and green vegetables glazed in sauce.

It was strange, though. There were the little tables set out at intervals on the scarlet floor with the Greek King's monogram wrought in yellow. Sandra dined in her hat, veiled as usual. Evan looked this way and that over his shoulder; imperturbable yet supple; and sometimes sighed. It was strange. For they were English people come together in Athens on a May evening. Jacob, helping himself to this and that, answered intelligently, yet with a ring in his voice.

The Williamses were going to Constantinople early next morning, they said.

"Before you are up," said Sandra.

They would leave Jacob alone, then. Turning very slightly, Evan ordered something—a bottle of wine—from which he helped Jacob, with a kind of solicitude, with a kind of paternal solicitude, if that were possible. To be left alone—that was good for a young fellow. Never was there a time when the country had more need of men. He sighed.

"And you have been to the Acropolis?" asked Sandra.

"Yes," said Jacob. And they moved off to the window together, while Evan spoke to the head waiter about calling them early.

"It is astonishing," said Jacob, in a gruff voice.

Sandra opened her eyes very slightly. Possibly her nostrils expanded a little too.

"At half-past six then," said Evan, coming towards them, looking as if he faced something in facing his wife and Jacob standing with their backs to the window.

Sandra smiled at him.

And, as he went to the window and had nothing to say she added, in broken half-sentences:

"Well, but how lovely—wouldn't it be? The Acropolis, Evan —or are you too tired?"

At that Evan looked at them, or, since Jacob was staring ahead of him, at his wife, surlily, sullenly, yet with a kind of distress— not that she would pity him. Nor would the implacable spirit of love, for anything he could do, cease its tortures.

They left him and he sat in the smoking-room, which looks out on to the Square of the Constitution.

"Evan is happier alone," said Sandra. "We have been separated from the newspapers. Well, it is better that people should have what they want. . . . You have seen all these wonderful things since we met. . . . What impression . . . I think that you are changed."

"You want to go to the Acropolis," said Jacob. "Up here then."

"One will remember it all one's life," said Sandra.

"Yes," said Jacob. "I wish you could have come in the day-time."

"This is more wonderful," said Sandra, waving her hand.

Jacob looked vaguely.

"But you should see the Parthenon in the day-time," he said. "You couldn't come to-morrow—it would be too early?"

"You have sat there for hours and hours by yourself?"

"There were some awful women this morning," said Jacob.

"Awful women?" Sandra echoed.

"Frenchwomen."

"But something very wonderful has happened," said Sandra. Ten minutes, fifteen minutes, half an hour—that was all the time before her.

"Yes," he said.

"When one is your age—when one is young. What will you do? You will fall in love—oh yes! But don't be in too great a hurry. I am so much older."

She was brushed off the pavement by parading men.

"Shall we go on?" Jacob asked.

"Let us go on," she insisted.

For she could not stop until she had told him—or heard him say—or was it some action on his part that she required? Far away on the horizon she discerned it and could not rest.

"You'd never get English people to sit out like this," he said.

"Never—no. When you get back to England you won't forget this—or come with us to Constantinople!" she cried suddenly.

"But then . . ."

Sandra sighed.

"You must go to Delphi, of course," she said. "But," she asked herself, "what do I want from him? Perhaps it is something that I have missed. . . ."

"You will get there about six in the evening," she said. "You will see the eagles."

Jacob looked set and even desperate by the light at the street corner; and yet composed. He was suffering, perhaps. He was credulous. Yet there was something caustic about him. He had in him the seeds of extreme disillusionment, which would come to him from women in middle life. Perhaps if one strove hard enough to reach the top of the hill it need not come to him—this disillusionment from women in middle life.

"The hotel is awful," she said. "The last visitors had left their basins full of dirty water. There is always that," she laughed.

"The people one meets *are* beastly," Jacob said.

His excitement was clear enough.

"Write and tell me about it," she said. "And tell me what you feel and what you think. Tell me everything."

The night was dark. The Acropolis was a jagged mound.

"I should like to, awfully," he said.

"When we get back to London, we shall meet . . ."

"Yes."

"I suppose they leave the gates open?" he asked.

"We could climb them!" she answered wildly.

Obscuring the moon and altogether darkening the Acropolis the clouds passed from east to west. The clouds solidified; the vapours thickened; the trailing veils stayed and accumulated.

It was dark now over Athens, except for gauzy red streaks where the streets ran; and the front of the Palace was cadaverous from electric light. At sea the piers stood out, marked by separate dots; the waves being invisible, and promontories and islands were dark humps with a few lights.

"I'd love to bring my brother, if I may," Jacob murmured.

"And then when your mother comes to London——," said Sandra.

The mainland of Greece was dark; and somewhere off Euboea a cloud must have touched the waves and spattered them—the dolphins circling deeper and deeper into the sea. Violent was the wind now rushing down the Sea of Marmara between Greece and the plains of Troy.

In Greece and the uplands of Albania and Turkey, the wind scours the sand and the dust, and sows itself thick with dry particles. And then it pelts the smooth domes of the mosques, and makes the cypresses, standing stiff by the turbaned tombstones of Mohammedans, creak and bristle.

Sandra's veils were swirled about her.

"I will give you my copy," said Jacob. "Here. Will you keep it?"

(The book was the poems of Donne.)

Now the agitation of the air uncovered a racing star. Now it was dark. Now one after another lights were extinguished. Now great towns—Paris—Constantinople—London—were black as strewn rocks. Waterways might be distinguished. In England the trees were heavy in leaf. Here perhaps in some southern wood an old man lit dry ferns and the birds were startled. The sheep coughed; one flower bent slightly towards another. The English sky is softer, milkier than the Eastern. Something gentle has passed into it from the grass-rounded hills, something damp. The salt gale blew in at Betty Flanders's bedroom window, and the widow lady, raising herself slightly on her elbow, sighed like one who realizes, but would fain ward off a little longer—oh, a little longer!—the oppression of eternity.

But to return to Jacob and Sandra.

They had vanished. There was the Acropolis; but had they reached it? The columns and the Temple remain; the emotion of the living breaks fresh on them year after year; and of that what remains?

As for reaching the Acropolis who shall say that we ever do it, or that when Jacob woke next morning he found anything hard and durable to keep for ever? Still, he went with them to Constantinople.

Sandra Wentworth Williams certainly woke to find a copy of Donne's poems upon her dressing-table. And the book would be stood on the shelf in the English country house where Sally Duggan's *Life of Father Damien* in verse would join it one of these days. There were ten or twelve little volumes already. Strolling in at dusk, Sandra would open the books and her eyes would brighten (but not at the print), and subsiding into the arm-chair she would suck back again the soul of the moment; or, for sometimes she was restless, would pull out book after book and swing across the whole space of her life like an acrobat from bar to bar. She had had her moments. Meanwhile, the great clock on the landing ticked and Sandra would hear time accumulating, and ask herself, "What for? What for?"

"What for? What for?" Sandra would say, putting the book back, and strolling to the looking-glass and pressing her hair. And Miss Edwards would be startled at dinner, as she opened her mouth to admit roast mutton, by Sandra's sudden solicitude: "Are you happy, Miss Edwards?"—a thing Cissy Edwards hadn't thought of for years.

"What for? What for?" Jacob never asked himself any such questions, to judge by the way he laced his boots; shaved himself; to judge by the depth of his sleep that night, with the wind fidgeting at the shutters, and half-a-dozen mosquitoes singing in his ears. He was young—a man. And then Sandra was right when she judged him to be credulous as yet. At forty it might be a different matter. Already he had marked the things he liked in Donne, and they were savage enough. However, you might place beside them passages of the purest poetry in Shakespeare.

But the wind was rolling the darkness through the streets

of Athens, rolling it, one might suppose, with a sort of trampling
energy of mood which forbids too close an analysis of the feelings
of any single person, or inspection of features. All faces—Greek,
Levantine, Turkish, English—would have looked much the
same in that darkness. At length the columns and the Temples
whiten, yellow, turn rose; and the Pyramids and St. Peter's arise,
and at last sluggish St. Paul's looms up.

The Christians have the right to rouse most cities with their
interpretation of the day's meaning. Then, less melodiously, dis-
senters of different sects issue a cantankerous emendation. The
steamers, resounding like gigantic tuning-forks, state the old
old fact—how there is a sea coldly, greenly, swaying outside. But
nowadays it is the thin voice of duty, piping in a white thread
from the top of a funnel, that collects the largest multitudes, and
night is nothing but a long-drawn sigh between hammer-strokes,
a deep breath—you can hear it from an open window even in the
heart of London.

But who, save the nerve-worn and sleepless, or thinkers standing with hands to the eyes on some crag above the multitude, see
things thus in skeleton outline, bare of flesh? In Surbiton the
skeleton is wrapped in flesh.

"The kettle never boils so well on a sunny morning," says Mrs.
Grandage, glancing at the clock on the mantelpiece. Then the
grey Persian cat stretches itself on the window-seat, and buffets
a moth with soft round paws. And before breakfast is half over
(they were late to-day), a baby is deposited in her lap, and she
must guard the sugar basin while Tom Grandage reads the
golfing article in the *Times,* sips his coffee, wipes his moustaches,
and is off to the office, where he is the greatest authority upon
the foreign exchanges and marked for promotion.

The skeleton is well wrapped in flesh. Even this dark night
when the wind rolls the darkness through Lombard Street and
Fetter Lane and Bedford Square it stirs (since it is summer-time
and the height of the season), plane trees spangled with electric
light, and curtains still preserving the room from the dawn. Peo-

ple still murmur over the last word said on the staircase, or strain, all through their dreams, for the voice of the alarum clock. So when the wind roams through a forest innumerable twigs stir; hives are brushed; insects sway on grass blades; the spider runs rapidly up a crease in the bark; and the whole air is tremulous with breathing; elastic with filaments.

Only here—in Lombard Street and Fetter Lane and Bedford Square—each insect carries a globe of the world in his head, and the webs of the forest are schemes evolved for the smooth conduct of business; and honey is treasure of one sort and another; and the stir in the air is the indescribable agitation of life.

But colour returns; runs up the stalks of the grass; blows out into tulips and crocuses; solidly stripes the tree trunks; and fills the gauze of the air and the grasses and pools.

The Bank of England emerges; and the Monument with its bristling head of golden hair; the dray horses crossing London Bridge show grey and strawberry and iron-coloured. There is a whir of wings as the suburban trains rush into the terminus. And the light mounts over the faces of all the tall blind houses, slides through a chink and paints the lustrous bellying crimson curtains; the green wine-glasses; the coffee-cups; and the chairs standing askew.

Sunlight strikes in upon shaving-glasses; and gleaming brass cans; upon all the jolly trappings of the day; the bright, inquisitive, armoured, resplendent, summer's day, which has long since vanquished chaos; which has dried the melancholy mediaeval mists; drained the swamp and stood glass and stone upon it; and equipped our brains and bodies with such an armoury of weapons that merely to see the flash and thrust of limbs engaged in the conduct of daily life is better than the old pageant of armies drawn out in battle array upon the plain.

he height of the season," said Bonamy.

The sun had already blistered the paint on the backs of the green chairs in Hyde Park; peeled the bark off the plane trees; and turned the earth to powder and to smooth yellow pebbles. Hyde Park was circled, incessantly, by turning wheels.

"The height of the season," said Bonamy sarcastically.

He was sarcastic because of Clara Durrant; because Jacob had come back from Greece very brown and lean, with his pockets full of Greek notes, which he pulled out when the chair man came for pence; because Jacob was silent.

"He has not said a word to show that he is glad to see me," thought Bonamy bitterly.

The motor cars passed incessantly over the bridge of the Serpentine; the upper classes walked upright, or bent themselves gracefully over the palings; the lower classes lay with their knees cocked up, flat on their backs; the sheep grazed on pointed wooden legs; small children ran down the sloping grass, stretched their arms, and fell.

"Very urbane," Jacob brought out.

"Urbane" on the lips of Jacob had mysteriously all the shapeliness of a character which Bonamy thought daily more sublime, devastating, terrific than ever, though he was still, and perhaps would be for ever, barbaric, obscure.

What superlatives! What adjectives! How acquit Bonamy of sentimentality of the grossest sort; of being tossed like a cork on the waves; of having no steady insight into character; of being unsupported by reason, and of drawing no comfort whatever from the works of the classics?

"The height of civilization," said Jacob.

He was fond of using Latin words.

Magnanimity, virtue—such words when Jacob used them in talk with Bonamy meant that he took control of the situation; that Bonamy would play round him like an affectionate spaniel; and that (as likely as not) they would end by rolling on the floor.

"And Greece?" said Bonamy. "The Parthenon and all that?"

"There's none of this European mysticism," said Jacob.

"It's the atmosphere, I suppose," said Bonamy. "And you went to Constantinople?"

"Yes," said Jacob.

Bonamy paused, moved a pebble; then darted in with the rapidity and certainty of a lizard's tongue.

"You are in love!" he exclaimed.

Jacob blushed.

The sharpest of knives never cut so deep.

As for responding, or taking the least account of it, Jacob stared straight ahead of him, fixed, monolithic—oh, very beautiful!—like a British Admiral, exclaimed Bonamy in a rage, rising from his seat and walking off; waiting for some sound; none came; too proud to look back; walking quicker and quicker until he found himself gazing into motor cars and cursing women. Where was the pretty woman's face? Clara's—Fanny's—Florinda's? Who was the pretty little creature?

Not Clara Durrant.

The Aberdeen terrier must be exercised, and as Mr. Bowley was going that very moment—would like nothing better than a walk—they went together, Clara and kind little Bowley—Bowley who had rooms in the Albany, Bowley who wrote letters to the *Times* in a jocular vein about foreign hotels and the Aurora Borealis—Bowley who liked young people and walked down Piccadilly with his right arm resting on the boss of his back.

"Little demon!" cried Clara, and attached Troy to his chain.

Bowley anticipated—hoped for—a confidence. Devoted to her mother, Clara sometimes felt her a little, well, her mother was so sure of herself that she could not understand other people be-ing—being—"as ludicrous as I am," Clara jerked out (the dog tugging her forwards). And Bowley thought she looked like a huntress and turned over in his mind which it should be—some pale virgin with a slip of the moon in her hair, which was a flight for Bowley.

The colour was in her cheeks. To have spoken outright about her mother—still, it was only to Mr. Bowley, who loved her, as everybody must; but to speak was unnatural to her, yet it was awful to feel, as she had done all day, that she *must* tell some one.

"Wait till we cross the road," she said to the dog, bending down.

Happily she had recovered by that time.

"She thinks so much about England," she said. "She is so anx-ious——"

Bowley was defrauded as usual. Clara never confided in any one.

"Why don't the young people settle it, eh?" he wanted to ask. "What's all this about England?"—a question poor Clara could not have answered, since, as Mrs. Durrant discussed with Sir Edgar the policy of Sir Edward Grey, Clara only wondered why the cabinet looked dusty, and Jacob had never come. Oh, here was Mrs. Cowley Johnson . . .

And Clara would hand the pretty china teacups, and smile at the compliment—that no one in London made tea so well as she did.

"We get it at Brocklebank's," she said, "in Cursitor Street."

Ought she not to be grateful? Ought she not to be happy? Especially since her mother looked so well and enjoyed so much talking to Sir Edgar about Morocco, Venezuela, or some such place.

"Jacob! Jacob!" thought Clara; and kind Mr. Bowley, who was ever so good with old ladies, looked; stopped; wondered whether Elizabeth wasn't too harsh with her daughter; wondered about

Bonamy, Jacob—which young fellow was it?—and jumped up directly Clara said she must exercise Troy.

They had reached the site of the old Exhibition. They looked at the tulips. Stiff and curled, the little rods of waxy smoothness rose from the earth, nourished yet contained, suffused with scarlet and coral pink. Each had its shadow; each grew trimly in the diamond-shaped wedge as the gardener had planned it.

"Barnes never gets them to grow like that," Clara mused; she sighed.

"You are neglecting your friends," said Bowley, as some one, going the other way, lifted his hat. She started; acknowledged Mr. Lionel Parry's bow; wasted on him what had sprung for Jacob.

("Jacob! Jacob!" she thought.)

"But you'll get run over if I let you go," she said to the dog.

"England seems all right," said Mr. Bowley.

The loop of the railing beneath the statue of Achilles was full of parasols and waistcoats; chains and bangles; of ladies and gentlemen, lounging elegantly, lightly observant.

"'This statue was erected by the women of England . . .'" Clara read out with a foolish little laugh. "Oh, Mr. Bowley! Oh!" Gallop—gallop—gallop—a horse galloped past without a rider. The stirrups swung; the pebbles spurted.

"Oh, stop! Stop it, Mr. Bowley!" she cried, white, trembling, gripping his arm, utterly unconscious, the tears coming.

"Tut-tut!" said Mr. Bowley in his dressing-room an hour later. "Tut-tut!"—a comment that was profound enough, though inarticulately expressed, since his valet was handing his shirt studs.

Julia Eliot, too, had seen the horse run away, and had risen from her seat to watch the end of the incident, which, since she came of a sporting family, seemed to her slightly ridiculous. Sure enough the little man came pounding behind with his breeches dusty; looked thoroughly annoyed; and was being helped to mount by a policeman when Julia Eliot, with a sardonic smile, turned towards the Marble Arch on her errand of mercy. It was only to visit a sick old lady who had known her mother and perhaps the Duke of Wellington; for Julia shared the love of her sex for the distressed; liked to visit death-beds; threw slippers at weddings; received confidences by the dozen; knew more pedigrees than a scholar knows dates, and was one of the kindliest, most generous, least continent of women.

Yet five minutes after she had passed the statue of Achilles she had the rapt look of one brushing through crowds on a summer's afternoon, when the trees are rustling, the wheels churning yellow, and the tumult of the present seems like an elegy for past youth and past summers, and there rose in her mind a curious sadness, as if time and eternity showed through skirts and waistcoats, and she saw people passing tragically to destruction. Yet, Heaven knows, Julia was no fool. A sharper woman at a bargain did not exist. She was always punctual. The watch on her wrist gave her twelve minutes and a half in which to reach Bruton Street. Lady Congreve expected her at five.

The gilt clock at Verrey's was striking five.

Florinda looked at it with a dull expression, like an animal. She looked at the clock; looked at the door; looked at the long glass opposite; disposed her cloak; drew closer to the table, for she was pregnant—no doubt about it, Mother Stuart said, recommending remedies, consulting friends; sunk, caught by the heel, as she tripped so lightly over the surface.

Her tumbler of pinkish sweet stuff was set down by the waiter; and she sucked, through a straw, her eyes on the looking-glass, on the door, now soothed by the sweet taste. When Nick Bramham came in it was plain, even to the young Swiss waiter, that there was a bargain between them. Nick hitched his clothes together clumsily; ran his fingers through his hair; sat down, to an ordeal, nervously. She looked at him; and set off laughing;

laughed—laughed—laughed. The young Swiss waiter, standing with crossed legs by the pillar, laughed too.

The door opened; in came the roar of Regent Street, the roar of traffic, impersonal, unpitying; and sunshine grained with dirt. The Swiss waiter must see to the newcomers. Bramham lifted his glass.

"He's like Jacob," said Florinda, looking at the newcomer.

"The way he stares." She stopped laughing.

Jacob, leaning forward, drew a plan of the Parthenon in the dust in Hyde Park, a network of strokes at least, which may have been the Parthenon, or again a mathematical diagram. And why was the pebble so emphatically ground in at the corner? It was not to count his notes that he took out a wad of papers and read a long flowing letter which Sandra had written two days ago at Milton Dower House with his book before her and in her mind the memory of something said or attempted, some moment in the dark on the road to the Acropolis which (such was her creed) mattered for ever.

"He is," she mused, "like that man in Molière."

She meant Alceste. She meant that he was severe. She meant that she could deceive him.

"Or could I not?" she thought, putting the poems of Donne back in the bookcase. "Jacob," she went on, going to the window and looking over the spotted flower-beds across the grass where the piebald cows grazed under beech trees, "Jacob would be shocked."

The perambulator was going through the little gate in the railing. She kissed her hand; directed by the nurse, Jimmy waved his.

"*He's* a small boy," she said, thinking of Jacob.

And yet—Alceste?

"What a nuisance you are!" Jacob grumbled, stretching out first one leg and then the other and feeling in each trouser-pocket for his chair ticket.

"I expect the sheep have eaten it," he said. "Why do you keep sheep?"

"Sorry to disturb you, sir," said the ticket-collector, his hand deep in the enormous pouch of pence.

"Well, I hope they pay you for it," said Jacob. "There you are. No. You can stick to it. Go and get drunk."

He had parted with half-a-crown, tolerantly, compassionately, with considerable contempt for his species.

Even now poor Fanny Elmer was dealing, as she walked along the Strand, in her incompetent way with this very careless, indifferent, sublime manner he had of talking to railway guards or porters; or Mrs. Whitehorn, when she consulted him about her little boy who was beaten by the schoolmaster.

Sustained entirely upon picture post cards for the past two months, Fanny's idea of Jacob was more statuesque, noble, and eyeless than ever. To reinforce her vision she had taken to visiting the British Museum, where, keeping her eyes downcast until she was alongside of the battered Ulysses, she opened them and got a fresh shock of Jacob's presence, enough to last her half a day. But this was wearing thin. And she wrote now—poems, letters that were never posted, saw his face in advertisements on hoardings, and would cross the road to let the barrel-organ turn her musings to rhapsody. But at breakfast (she shared rooms with a teacher), when the butter was smeared about the plate, and the prongs of the forks were clotted with old egg yolk, she revised these visions violently; was, in truth, very cross; was losing her complexion, as Margery Jackson told her, bringing the whole thing down (as she laced her stout boots) to a level of mother-wit, vulgarity, and sentiment, for she had loved too; and been a fool.

"One's godmothers ought to have told one," said Fanny, looking in at the window of Bacon, the mapseller, in the Strand— told one that it is no use making a fuss; this is life, they should have said, as Fanny said it now, looking at the large yellow globe marked with steamship lines.

"This is life. This is life," said Fanny.

"A very hard face," thought Miss Barrett, on the other side of the glass, buying maps of the Syrian desert and waiting impatiently to be served. "Girls look old so soon nowadays."

The equator swam behind tears.

"Piccadilly?" Fanny asked the conductor of the omnibus, and climbed to the top. After all, he would, he must, come back to her.

But Jacob might have been thinking of Rome; of architecture; of jurisprudence; as he sat under the plane tree in Hyde Park.

The omnibus stopped outside Charing Cross; and behind it were clogged omnibuses, vans, motor-cars, for a procession with banners was passing down Whitehall, and elderly people were stiffly descending from between the paws of the slippery lions, where they had been testifying to their faith, singing lustily, raising their eyes from their music to look into the sky, and still their eyes were on the sky as they marched behind the gold letters of their creed.

The traffic stopped, and the sun, no longer sprayed out by the breeze, became almost too hot. But the procession passed; the banners glittered far away down Whitehall; the traffic was released; lurched on; spun to a smooth continuous uproar; swerving round the curve of Cockspur Street; and sweeping past Government offices and equestrian statues down Whitehall to the prickly spires, the tethered grey fleet of masonry, and the large white clock of Westminster.

Five strokes Big Ben intoned; Nelson received the salute. The wires of the Admiralty shivered with some far-away communication. A voice kept remarking that Prime Ministers and Viceroys spoke in the Reichstag; entered Lahore; said that the Emperor travelled; in Milan they rioted; said there were rumours in Vienna; said that the Ambassador at Constantinople had audience with the Sultan; the fleet was at Gibraltar. The voice continued, imprinting on the faces of the clerks in Whitehall

(Timothy Durrant was one of them) something of its own in-
exorable gravity, as they listened, deciphered, wrote down. Papers accumulated, inscribed with the utterances of Kaisers, the
statistics of ricefields, the growling of hundreds of work-people,
plotting sedition in back streets, or gathering in the Calcutta
bazaars, or mustering their forces in the uplands of Albania,
where the hills are sand-coloured, and bones lie unburied.

The voice spoke plainly in the square quiet room with heavy
tables, where one elderly man made notes on the margin of type-
written sheets, his silver-topped umbrella leaning against the
bookcase.

His head—bald, red-veined, hollow-looking—represented all
the heads in the building. His head, with the amiable pale eyes,
carried the burden of knowledge across the street; laid it before
his colleagues, who came equally burdened; and then the sixteen
gentlemen, lifting their pens or turning perhaps rather wearily in
their chairs, decreed that the course of history should shape itself
this way or that way, being manfully determined, as their faces
showed, to impose some coherency upon Rajahs and Kaisers and
the muttering in bazaars, the secret gatherings, plainly visible
in Whitehall, of kilted peasants in Albanian uplands; to control
the course of events.

Pitt and Chatham, Burke and Gladstone looked from side to
side with fixed marble eyes and an air of immortal quiescence
which perhaps the living may have envied, the air being full of
whistling and concussions, as the procession with its banners
passed down Whitehall. Moreover, some were troubled with dys-
pepsia; one had at that very moment cracked the glass of his
spectacles; another spoke in Glasgow to-morrow; altogether
they looked too red, fat, pale or lean, to be dealing, as the marble
heads had dealt, with the course of history.

Timmy Durrant in his little room in the Admiralty, going to
consult a Blue book, stopped for a moment by the window and
observed the placard tied round the lamp-post.

Miss Thomas, one of the typists, said to her friend that if the

Cabinet was going to sit much longer she should miss her boy outside the Gaiety.

Timmy Durrant, returning with his Blue book under his arm, noticed a little knot of people at the street corner; conglomerated as though one of them knew something; and the others, pressing round him, looked up, looked down, looked along the street. What was it that he knew?

Timothy, placing the Blue book before him, studied a paper sent round by the Treasury for information. Mr. Crawley, his fellow-clerk, impaled a letter on a skewer.

Jacob rose from his chair in Hyde Park, tore his ticket to pieces, and walked away.

"Such a sunset," wrote Mrs. Flanders in her letter to Archer at Singapore. "One couldn't make up one's mind to come indoors," she wrote. "It seemed wicked to waste even a moment."

The long windows of Kensington Palace flushed fiery rose as Jacob walked away; a flock of wild duck flew over the Serpentine; and the trees were stood against the sky, blackly, magnificently.

"Jacob," wrote Mrs. Flanders, with the red light on her page, "is hard at work after his delightful journey . . ."

"The Kaiser," the far-away voice remarked in Whitehall, "received me in audience."

"Now I know that face—" said the Reverend Andrew Floyd, coming out of Carter's shop in Piccadilly, "but who the dickens—?" and he watched Jacob, turned round to look at him, but could not be sure——

"Oh, Jacob Flanders!" he remembered in a flash.

But he was so tall; so unconscious; such a fine young fellow.

"I gave him Byron's works," Andrew Floyd mused, and started forward, as Jacob crossed the road; but hesitated, and let the moment pass, and lost the opportunity.

Another procession, without banners, was blocking Long Acre. Carriages, with dowagers in amethyst and gentlemen spot-

ted with carnations, intercepted cabs and motor-cars turned in
the opposite direction, in which jaded men in white waistcoats
lolled, on their way home to shrubberies and billiard-rooms in
Putney and Wimbledon.

Two barrel-organs played by the kerb, and horses coming out
of Aldridge's with white labels on their buttocks straddled across
the road and were smartly jerked back.

Mrs. Durrant, sitting with Mr. Wortley in a motor-car, was
impatient lest they should miss the overture.

But Mr. Wortley, always urbane, always in time for the overture, buttoned his gloves, and admired Miss Clara.

"A shame to spend such a night in the theatre!" said Mrs.
Durrant, seeing all the windows of the coachmakers in Long
Acre ablaze.

"Think of your moors!" said Mr. Wortley to Clara.

"Ah! but Clara likes this better," Mrs. Durrant laughed.

"I don't know—really," said Clara, looking at the blazing windows. She started.

She saw Jacob.

"Who?" asked Mrs. Durrant sharply, leaning forward.

But she saw no one.

Under the arch of the Opera House large faces and lean ones,
the powdered and the hairy, all alike were red in the sunset; and,
quickened by the great hanging lamps with their repressed prim-
rose lights, by the tramp, and the scarlet, and the pompous ceremony, some ladies looked for a moment into steaming bedrooms
near by, where women with loose hair leaned out of windows,
where girls—where children—(the long mirrors held the ladies
suspended) but one must follow; one must not block the way.

Clara's moors were fine enough. The Phoenicians slept under
their piled grey rocks; the chimneys of the old mines pointed
starkly; early moths blurred the heather-bells; cartwheels could
be heard grinding on the road far beneath; and the suck and
sighing of the waves sounded gently, persistently, for ever.

Shading her eyes with her hand Mrs. Pascoe stood in her cabbage-garden looking out to sea. Two steamers and a sailing-ship crossed each other; passed each other; and in the bay the gulls kept alighting on a log, rising high, returning again to the log, while some rode in upon the waves and stood on the rim of the water until the moon blanched all to whiteness.

Mrs. Pascoe had gone indoors long ago.

But the red light was on the columns of the Parthenon, and the Greek women who were knitting their stockings and sometimes crying to a child to come and have the insects picked from its head were as jolly as sand-martins in the heat, quarrelling, scolding, suckling their babies, until the ships in the Piraeus fired their guns.

The sound spread itself flat, and then went tunnelling its way with fitful explosions among the channels of the islands.

Darkness drops like a knife over Greece.

"The guns?" said Betty Flanders, half asleep, getting out of bed and going to the window, which was decorated with a fringe of dark leaves.

"Not at this distance," she thought. "It is the sea."

Again, far away, she heard the dull sound, as if nocturnal women were beating great carpets. There was Morty lost, and Seabrook dead; her sons fighting for their country. But were the chickens safe? Was that some one moving downstairs? Rebecca with the toothache? No. The nocturnal women were beating great carpets. Her hens shifted slightly on their perches.

FOURTEEN

"He left everything just as it was," Bonamy marvelled. "Nothing arranged. All his letters strewn about for any one to read. What did he expect? Did he think he would come back?" he mused, standing in the middle of Jacob's room.

The eighteenth century has its distinction. These houses were built, say, a hundred and fifty years ago. The rooms are shapely, the ceilings high; over the doorways a rose or a ram's skull is carved in the wood. Even the panels, painted in raspberry-coloured paint, have their distinction.

Bonamy took up a bill for a hunting-crop.

"That seems to be paid," he said.

There were Sandra's letters.

Mrs. Durrant was taking a party to Greenwich.

Lady Rocksbier hoped for the pleasure. . . .

Listless is the air in an empty room, just swelling the curtain; the flowers in the jar shift. One fibre in the wicker arm-chair creaks, though no one sits there.

Bonamy crossed to the window. Pickford's van swung down the street. The omnibuses were locked together at Mudie's corner. Engines throbbed, and carters, jamming the brakes down, pulled their horses sharp up. A harsh and unhappy voice cried something unintelligible. And then suddenly all the leaves seemed to raise themselves.

"Jacob! Jacob!" cried Bonamy, standing by the window. The leaves sank down again.

"Such confusion everywhere!" exclaimed Betty Flanders, bursting open the bedroom door.

Bonamy turned away from the window.

"What am I to do with these, Mr. Bonamy?"

She held out a pair of Jacob's old shoes.

THE WAVES

he sun had not yet risen. The sea was indistinguishable from the sky, except that the sea was slightly creased as if a cloth had wrinkles in it. Gradually as the sky whitened a dark line lay on the horizon dividing the sea from the sky and the grey cloth became barred with thick strokes moving, one after another, beneath the surface, following each other, pursuing each other, perpetually.

As they neared the shore each bar rose, heaped itself, broke and swept a thin veil of white water across the sand. The wave paused, and then drew out again, sighing like a sleeper whose breath comes and goes unconsciously. Gradually the dark bar on the horizon became clear as if the sediment in an old wine-bottle had sunk and left the glass green. Behind it, too, the sky cleared as if the white sediment there had sunk, or as if the arm of a woman couched beneath the horizon had raised a lamp and flat bars of white, green and yellow, spread across the sky like the blades of a fan. Then she raised her lamp higher and the air seemed to become fibrous and to tear away from the green surface flickering and flaming in red and yellow fibres like the smoky fire that roars from a bonfire. Gradually the fibres of the burning bonfire were fused into one haze, one incandescence which lifted the weight of the woollen grey sky on top of it and turned it to a million atoms of soft blue. The surface of the sea slowly became transparent and lay rippling and sparkling until the dark stripes were almost rubbed out. Slowly the arm that held the lamp raised it higher and then higher until a broad flame became visible; an arc of fire burnt on the rim of the horizon, and all round it the sea blazed gold.

The light struck upon the trees in the garden, making one leaf transparent and then another. One bird chirped high up; there was a pause; another chirped lower down. The sun sharp-

ened the walls of the house, and rested like the tip of a fan upon
a white blind and made a blue fingerprint of shadow under the
leaf by the bedroom window. The blind stirred slightly, but all
within was dim and unsubstantial. The birds sang their blank
melody outside.

"I see a ring," said Bernard, "hanging above me. It quivers and
hangs in a loop of light."

"I see a slab of pale yellow," said Susan, "spreading away until
it meets a purple stripe."

"I hear a sound," said Rhoda, "cheep, chirp; cheep, chirp; going up and down."

"I see a globe," said Neville, "hanging down in a drop against
the enormous flanks of some hill."

"I see a crimson tassel," said Jinny, "twisted with gold
threads."

"I hear something stamping," said Louis. "A great beast's foot
is chained. It stamps, and stamps, and stamps."

"Look at the spider's web on the corner of the balcony," said
Bernard. "It has beads of water on it, drops of white light."

"The leaves are gathered round the window like pointed ears,"
said Susan.

"A shadow falls on the path," said Louis, "like an elbow bent."

"Islands of light are swimming on the grass," said Rhoda.
"They have fallen through the trees."

"The birds' eyes are bright in the tunnels between the leaves,"
said Neville.

"The stalks are covered with harsh, short hairs," said Jinny,
"and drops of water have stuck to them."

"A caterpillar is curled in a green ring," said Susan, "notched
with blunt feet."

"The grey-shelled snail draws across the path and flattens the
blades behind him," said Rhoda.

"And burning lights from the window-panes flash in and out on the grasses," said Louis.

"Stones are cold to my feet," said Neville. "I feel each one, round or pointed, separately."

"The back of my hand burns," said Jinny, "but the palm is clammy and damp with dew."

"Now the cock crows like a spurt of hard, red water in the white tide," said Bernard.

"Birds are singing up and down and in and out all round us," said Susan.

"The beast stamps; the elephant with its foot chained; the great brute on the beach stamps," said Louis.

"Look at the house," said Jinny, "with all its windows white with blinds."

"Cold water begins to run from the scullery tap," said Rhoda, "over the mackerel in the bowl."

"The walls are cracked with gold cracks," said Bernard, "and there are blue, finger-shaped shadows of leaves beneath the windows."

"Now Mrs. Constable pulls up her thick, black stockings," said Susan.

"When the smoke rises, sleep curls off the roof like a mist," said Louis.

"The birds sang in chorus first," said Rhoda. "Now the scullery door is unbarred. Off they fly. Off they fly like a fling of seed. But one sings by the bedroom window alone."

"Bubbles form on the floor of the saucepan," said Jinny. "Then they rise, quicker and quicker in a silver chain to the top."

"Now Biddy scrapes the fish-scales with a jagged knife on to a wooden board," said Neville.

"The dining-room window is dark blue now," said Bernard, "and the air ripples above the chimneys."

"A swallow is perched on the lightning-conductor," said Susan. "And Biddy has smacked down the bucket on the kitchen flags."

"That is the first stroke of the church bell," said Louis. "Then the others follow; one, two; one, two; one, two."

"Look at the table-cloth, flying white along the table," said Rhoda. "Now there are rounds of white china, and silver streaks beside each plate."

"Suddenly a bee booms in my ear," said Neville. "It is here; it is past."

"I burn, I shiver," said Jinny, "out of this sun, into this shadow."

"Now they have all gone," said Louis. "I am alone. They have gone into the house for breakfast, and I am left standing by the wall among the flowers. It is very early, before lessons. Flower after flower is specked on the depths of green. The petals are harlequins. Stalks rise from the black hollows beneath. The flowers swim like fish made of light upon the dark, green waters. I hold a stalk in my hand. I am the stalk. My roots go down to the depths of the world, through earth dry with brick, and damp earth, through veins of lead and silver. I am all fibre. All tremors shake me, and the weight of the earth is pressed to my ribs. Up here my eyes are green leaves, unseeing. I am a boy in grey flannels with a belt fastened by a brass snake up here. Down there my eyes are the lidless eyes of a stone figure in a desert by the Nile. I see women passing with red pitchers to the river; I see camels swaying and men in turbans. I hear tramplings, tremblings, stirrings round me.

"Up here Bernard, Neville, Jinny and Susan (but not Rhoda) skim the flower-beds with their nets. They skim the butterflies from the nodding tops of the flowers. They brush the surface of the world. Their nets are full of fluttering wings. 'Louis! Louis! Louis!' they shout. But they cannot see me. I am on the other side of the hedge. There are only little eyeholes among the leaves. Oh, Lord, let them pass. Lord, let them lay their butterflies on a pocket-handkerchief on the gravel. Let them count out their tortoise-shells, their red admirals and cabbage whites. But let me be unseen. I am green as a yew tree in the shade of the hedge.

My hair is made of leaves. I am rooted to the middle of the earth. My body is a stalk. I press the stalk. A drop oozes from the hole at the mouth and slowly, thickly, grows larger and larger. Now something pink passes the eyehole. Now an eyebeam is slid through the chink. Its beam strikes me. I am a boy in a grey flannel suit. She has found me. I am struck on the nape of the neck. She has kissed me. All is shattered."

"I was running," said Jinny, "after breakfast. I saw leaves moving in a hole in the hedge. I thought, 'That is a bird on its nest.' I parted them and looked; but there was no bird on a nest. The leaves went on moving. I was frightened. I ran past Susan, past Rhoda, and Neville and Bernard in the tool-house talking. I cried as I ran, faster and faster. What moved the leaves? What moves my heart, my legs? And I dashed in here, seeing you green as a bush, like a branch, very still, Louis, with your eyes fixed. 'Is he dead?' I thought, and kissed you, with my heart jumping under my pink frock like the leaves, which go on moving, though there is nothing to move them. Now I smell geraniums; I smell earth mould. I dance. I ripple. I am thrown over you like a net of light. I lie quivering flung over you."

"Through the chink in the hedge," said Susan, "I saw her kiss him. I raised my head from my flower-pot and looked through a chink in the hedge. I saw her kiss him. I saw them, Jinny and Louis, kissing. Now I will wrap my agony inside my pocket-handkerchief. It shall be screwed tight into a ball. I will go to the beech wood alone, before lessons. I will not sit at a table, doing sums. I will not sit next Jinny and next Louis. I will take my anguish and lay it upon the roots under the beech trees. I will examine it and take it between my fingers. They will not find me. I shall eat nuts and peer for eggs through the brambles and my hair will be matted and I shall sleep under hedges and drink water from ditches and die there."

"Susan has passed us," said Bernard. "She has passed the tool-house door with her handkerchief screwed into a ball. She was not crying, but her eyes, which are so beautiful, were narrow as cats' eyes before they spring. I shall follow her, Neville. I shall go gently behind her, to be at hand, with my curiosity, to comfort her when she bursts out in a rage and thinks, 'I am alone.'

"Now she walks across the field with a swing, nonchalantly, to deceive us. Then she comes to the dip; she thinks she is unseen; she begins to run with her fists clenched in front of her. Her nails meet in the ball of her pocket-handkerchief. She is making for the beech woods out of the light. She spreads her arms as she comes to them and takes to the shade like a swimmer. But she is blind after the light and trips and flings herself down on the roots under the trees, where the light seems to pant in and out, in and out. The branches heave up and down. There is agitation and trouble here. There is gloom. The light is fitful. There is anguish here. The roots make a skeleton on the ground, with dead leaves heaped in the angles. Susan has spread her anguish out. Her pocket-handkerchief is laid on the roots of the beech trees and she sobs, sitting crumpled where she has fallen."

"I saw her kiss him," said Susan. "I looked between the leaves and saw her. She danced in flecked with diamonds light as dust. And I am squat, Bernard, I am short. I have eyes that look close to the ground and see insects in the grass. The yellow warmth in my side turned to stone when I saw Jinny kiss Louis. I shall eat grass and die in a ditch in the brown water where dead leaves have rotted."

"I saw you go," said Bernard. "As you passed the door of the tool-house I heard you cry, 'I am unhappy.' I put down my knife. I was making boats out of firewood with Neville. And my hair is untidy, because when Mrs. Constable told me to brush it there was a fly in a web, and I asked, 'Shall I free the fly? Shall I let the fly be eaten?' So I am late always. My hair is unbrushed and these chips of wood stick in it. When I heard you cry I followed you, and saw you put down your handkerchief, screwed up, with its rage, with its hate, knotted in it. But soon that will cease. Our bodies are close now. You hear me breathe. You see the beetle too carrying off a leaf on its back. It runs this way, then that way, so that even your desire while you watch the beetle, to possess one single thing (it is Louis now) must waver, like the light in and out of the beech leaves; and then words, moving darkly, in the depths of your mind will break up this knot of hardness, screwed in your pocket-handkerchief."

"I love," said Susan, "and I hate. I desire one thing only. My eyes are hard. Jinny's eyes break into a thousand lights. Rhoda's are like those pale flowers to which moths come in the evening. Yours grow full and brim and never break. But I am already set on my pursuit. I see insects in the grass. Though my mother still knits white socks for me and hems pinafores and I am a child, I love and I hate."

"But when we sit together, close," said Bernard, "we melt into each other with phrases. We are edged with mist. We make an unsubstantial territory."

"I see the beetle," said Susan. "It is black, I see; it is green, I see; I am tied down with single words. But you wander off; you slip away; you rise up higher, with words and words in phrases."

"Now," said Bernard, "let us explore. There is the white house lying among the trees. It lies down there ever so far beneath us. We shall sink like swimmers just touching the ground with the tips of their toes. We shall sink through the green air of the leaves, Susan. We sink as we run. The waves close over us, the beech leaves meet above our heads. There is the stable clock with its gilt hands shining. Those are the flats and heights of the roofs of the great house. There is the stable-boy clattering in the yard in rubber-boots. That is Elvedon.

"Now we have fallen through the tree-tops to the earth. The air no longer rolls its long, unhappy, purple waves over us. We touch earth; we tread ground. That is the close-clipped hedge of the ladies' garden. There they walk at noon, with scissors, clipping roses. Now we are in the ringed wood with the wall round it. This is Elvedon. I have seen signposts at the crossroads with one arm pointing 'To Elvedon.' No one has been there. The ferns smell very strong, and there are red funguses growing beneath them. Now we wake the sleeping daws who have never seen a human form; now we tread on rotten oak apples, red with age and slippery. There is a ring of wall round this wood; nobody comes here. Listen! That is the flop of a giant toad in the undergrowth; that is the patter of some primeval fir-cone falling to rot among the ferns.

"Put your foot on this brick. Look over the wall. That is Elvedon. The lady sits between the two long windows, writing. The gardeners sweep the lawn with giant brooms. We are the first to come here. We are the discoverers of an unknown land. Do not stir; if the gardeners saw us they would shoot us. We should be nailed like stoats to the stable door. Look! Do not move. Grasp the ferns tight on the top of the wall."

"I see the lady writing. I see the gardeners sweeping," said Susan. "If we died here, nobody would bury us."

"Run!" said Bernard. "Run! The gardener with the black beard has seen us! We shall be shot! We shall be shot like jays and pinned to the wall! We are in a hostile country. We must escape to the beech wood. We must hide under the trees. I turned a twig as we came. There is a secret path. Bend as low as you can. Follow without looking back. They will think we are foxes. Run!

"Now we are safe. Now we can stand upright again. Now we can stretch our arms in this high canopy, in this vast wood. I hear nothing. That is only the murmur of the waves in the air. That is a wood-pigeon breaking cover in the tops of the beech trees. The pigeon beats the air; the pigeon beats the air with wooden wings."

"Now you trail away," said Susan, "making phrases. Now you mount like an air-ball's string, higher and higher through the layers of the leaves, out of reach. Now you lag. Now you tug at my skirts, looking back, making phrases. You have escaped me. Here is the garden. Here is the hedge. Here is Rhoda on the path rocking petals to and fro in her brown basin."

"All my ships are white," said Rhoda. "I do not want red petals of hollyhocks or geranium. I want white petals that float when I tip the basin up. I have a fleet now swimming from shore to shore. I will drop a twig in as a raft for a drowning sailor. I will drop a stone in and see bubbles rise from the depths of the sea. Neville has gone and Susan has gone; Jinny is in the kitchen garden picking currants with Louis perhaps. I have a short time alone, while Miss Hudson spreads our copy-books on the school-room table. I have a short space of freedom. I have picked all the fallen petals and made them swim. I have put raindrops in some. I will plant a lighthouse here, a head of Sweet Alice. And I will now rock the brown basin from side to side so that my ships may ride the waves. Some will founder. Some will dash themselves against the cliffs. One sails alone. That is my ship. It sails into icy caverns where the sea-bear barks and stalactites swing green chains. The waves rise; their crests curl; look at the lights on the mastheads. They have scattered, they have foundered, all except my ship which mounts the wave and sweeps before the gale and reaches the islands where the parrots chatter and the creepers . . ."

"Where is Bernard?" said Neville. "He has my knife. We were in the tool-shed making boats, and Susan came past the door. And Bernard dropped his boat and went after her taking my knife, the sharp one that cuts the keel. He is like a dangling wire, a broken bell-pull, always twangling. He is like the sea-weed hung outside the window, damp now, now dry. He leaves me in the lurch; he follows Susan; and if Susan cries he will take my knife and tell her stories. The big blade is an emperor; the broken blade a Negro. I hate dangling things; I hate dampish things. I hate wandering and mixing things together. Now the bell rings and we shall be late. Now we must drop our toys. Now we must go in together. The copy-books are laid out side by side on the green baize table."

"I will not conjugate the verb," said Louis, "until Bernard has said it. My father is a banker in Brisbane and I speak with an Australian accent. I will wait and copy Bernard. He is English. They are all English. Susan's father is a clergyman. Rhoda has no father. Bernard and Neville are the sons of gentlemen. Jinny lives with her grandmother in London. Now they suck their pens. Now they twist their copy-books, and, looking sideways at Miss Hudson, count the purple buttons on her bodice. Bernard has a chip in his hair. Susan has a red look in her eyes. Both are flushed. But I am pale; I am neat, and my knickerbockers are drawn together by a belt with a brass snake. I know the lesson by heart. I know more than they will ever know. I know my cases and my genders; I could know everything in the world if I wished. But I do not wish to come to the top and say my lesson. My roots are threaded, like fibres in a flower-pot, round and round about the world. I do not wish to come to the top and live in the light of this great clock, yellow-faced, which ticks and ticks. Jinny and Susan, Bernard and Neville bind themselves into a thong with which to lash me. They laugh at my neatness, at my Australian accent. I will now try to imitate Bernard softly lisping Latin."

"Those are white words," said Susan, "like stones one picks up by the seashore."

"They flick their tails right and left as I speak them," said Bernard. "They wag their tails; they flick their tails; they move through the air in flocks, now this way, now that way, moving all together, now dividing, now coming together."

"Those are yellow words, those are fiery words," said Jinny. "I should like a fiery dress, a yellow dress, a fulvous dress to wear in the evening."

"Each tense," said Neville, "means differently. There is an order in this world; there are distinctions, there are differences in this world, upon whose verge I step. For this is only a beginning."

"Now Miss Hudson," said Rhoda, "has shut the book. Now the terror is beginning. Now taking her lump of chalk she draws figures, six, seven, eight, and then a cross and then a line on the blackboard. What is the answer? The others look; they look with understanding. Louis writes; Susan writes; Neville writes; Jinny writes; even Bernard has now begun to write. But I cannot write. I see only figures. The others are handing in their answers, one by one. Now it is my turn. But I have no answer. The others are allowed to go. They slam the door. Miss Hudson goes. I am left alone to find an answer. The figures mean nothing now. Meaning has gone. The clock ticks. The two hands are convoys marching through a desert. The black bars on the clock face are green oases. The long hand has marched ahead to find water. The other painfully stumbles among hot stones in the desert. It will die in the desert. The kitchen door slams. Wild dogs bark far away. Look, the loop of the figure is beginning to fill with time; it holds the world in it. I begin to draw a figure and the world is looped in it, and I myself am outside the loop; which I now join—so—and seal up, and make entire. The world is entire, and I am outside of it, crying, 'Oh, save me, from being blown for ever outside the loop of time!' "

"There Rhoda sits staring at the blackboard," said Louis, "in the schoolroom, while we ramble off, picking here a bit of thyme, pinching here a leaf of southernwood while Bernard tells a story. Her shoulderblades meet across her back like the wings of a small butterfly. And as she stares at the chalk figures, her mind lodges in those white circles; it steps through those white loops into emptiness, alone. They have no meaning for her. She has no answer for them. She has no body as the others have. And I, who speak with an Australian accent, whose father is a banker in Brisbane, do not fear her as I fear the others."

"Let us now crawl," said Bernard, "under the canopy of the currant leaves, and tell stories. Let us inhabit the underworld. Let us take possession of our secret territory, which is lit by pendant currants like candelabra, shining red on one side, black on the other. Here, Jinny, if we curl up close, we can sit under the canopy of the currant leaves and watch the censers swing. This is our universe. The others pass down the carriage-drive. The skirts of Miss Hudson and Miss Curry sweep by like candle extinguishers. Those are Susan's white socks. Those are Louis' neat sandshoes firmly printing the gravel. Here come warm gusts of decomposing leaves, of rotting vegetation. We are in a swamp now; in a malarial jungle. There is an elephant white with maggots, killed by an arrow shot dead in its eye. The bright eyes of hopping-birds—eagles, vultures—are apparent. They take us for fallen trees. They pick at a worm—that is a hooded cobra—and leave it with a festering brown scar to be mauled by lions. This is our world, lit with crescents and stars of light; and great petals half transparent block the openings like purple windows. Everything is strange. Things are huge and very small. The stalks of flowers are thick as oak trees. Leaves are high as the domes of vast cathedrals. We are giants, lying here, who can make forests quiver."

"This is here," said Jinny, "this is now. But soon we shall go. Soon Miss Curry will blow her whistle. We shall walk. We shall part. You will go to school. You will have masters wearing crosses with white ties. I shall have a mistress in a school on the East Coast who sits under a portrait of Queen Alexandra. That is where I am going, and Susan and Rhoda. This is only here; this is only now. Now we lie under the currant bushes and every time the breeze stirs we are mottled all over. My hand is like a snake's skin. My knees are pink floating islands. Your face is like an apple tree netted under."

"The heat is going," said Bernard, "from the Jungle. The leaves flap black wings over us. Miss Curry has blown her whistle on the terrace. We must creep out from the awning of the currant leaves and stand upright. There are twigs in your hair, Jinny. There is a green caterpillar on your neck. We must form, two by two. Miss Curry is taking us for a brisk walk, while Miss Hudson sits at her desk settling her accounts."

"It is dull," said Jinny, "walking along the high road with no windows to look at, with no bleared eyes of blue glass let into the pavement."

"We must form into pairs," said Susan, "and walk in order,

not shuffling our feet, not lagging, with Louis going first to lead us, because Louis is alert and not a wool-gatherer."

"Since I am supposed," said Neville, "to be too delicate to go with them, since I get so easily tired and then am sick, I will use this hour of solitude, this reprieve from conversation, to coast round the purlieus of the house and recover, if I can, by standing on the same stair half-way up the landing, what I felt when I heard about the dead man through the swing-door last night when cook was shoving in and out the dampers. He was found with his throat cut. The apple-tree leaves became fixed in the sky; the moon glared; I was unable to lift my foot up the stair. He was found in the gutter. His blood gurgled down the gutter. His jowl was white as a dead codfish. I shall call this stricture, this rigidity, 'death among the apple trees' for ever. There were the floating, pale-grey clouds; and the immitigable tree; the implacable tree with its greaved silver bark. The ripple of my life was unavailing. I was unable to pass by. There was an obstacle. 'I cannot surmount this unintelligible obstacle,' I said. And the others passed on. But we are doomed, all of us by the apple trees, by the immitigable tree which we cannot pass.

"Now the stricture and rigidity are over; and I will continue to make my survey of the purlieus of the house in the late afternoon, in the sunset, when the sun makes oleaginous spots on the linoleum, and a crack of light kneels on the wall, making the chair legs look broken."

"I saw Florrie in the kitchen garden," said Susan, "as we came back from our walk, with the washing blown out round her, the pyjamas, the drawers, the night-gowns blown tight. And Ernest kissed her. He was in his green baize apron, cleaning silver; and his mouth was sucked like a purse in wrinkles and he seized her with the pyjamas blown out hard between them. He was blind as a bull, and she swooned in anguish, only little veins streaking her white cheeks red. Now though they pass plates of bread and butter and cups of milk at tea-time I see a crack in the earth and

hot steam hisses up; and the urn roars as Ernest roared, and I
am blown out hard like the pyjamas, even while my teeth meet
in the soft bread and butter, and I lap the sweet milk. I am not
afraid of heat, nor of the frozen winter. Rhoda dreams, sucking
a crust soaked in milk; Louis regards the wall opposite with
snail-green eyes; Bernard moulds his bread into pellets and calls
them 'people.' Neville with his clean and decisive ways has finished. He has rolled his napkin and slipped it through the silver
ring. Jinny spins her fingers on the table-cloth, as if they were
dancing in the sunshine, pirouetting. But I am not afraid of the
heat or of the frozen winter."

"Now," said Louis, "we all rise; we all stand up. Miss Curry
spreads wide the black book on the harmonium. It is difficult not
to weep as we sing, as we pray that God may keep us safe while
we sleep, calling ourselves little children. When we are sad and
trembling with apprehension it is sweet to sing together, leaning slightly, I towards Susan, Susan towards Bernard, clasping
hands, afraid of much, I of my accent, Rhoda of figures; yet resolute to conquer."

"We troop upstairs like ponies," said Bernard, "stamping, clattering one behind another to take our turns in the bathroom.
We buffet, we tussle, we spring up and down on the hard, white
beds. My turn has come. I come now.

"Mrs. Constable, girt in a bath-towel, takes her lemon-coloured
sponge and soaks it in water; it turns chocolate-brown; it drips,
and, holding it high above me, shivering beneath her, she
squeezes it. Water pours down the runnel of my spine. Bright
arrows of sensation shoot on either side. I am covered with warm
flesh. My dry crannies are wetted; my cold body is warmed; it is
sluiced and gleaming. Water descends and sheets me like an eel.
Now hot towels envelop me, and their roughness, as I rub my
back, makes my blood purr. Rich and heavy sensations form on
the roof of my mind; down showers the day—the woods; and
Elvedon; Susan and the pigeon. Pouring down the walls of my
mind, running together, the day falls copious, resplendent. Now

I tie my pyjamas loosely round me, and lie under this thin sheet afloat in the shallow light which is like a film of water drawn over my eyes by a wave. I hear through it far off, far away, faint and far, the chorus beginning; wheels; dogs; men shouting; church bells; the chorus beginning."

"As I fold up my frock and my chemise," said Rhoda, "so I put off my hopeless desire to be Susan, to be Jinny. But I will stretch my toes so that they touch the rail at the end of the bed; I will assure myself, touching the rail, of something hard. Now I cannot sink; cannot altogether fall through the thin sheet now. Now I spread my body on this frail mattress and hang suspended. I am above the earth now. I am no longer upright, to be knocked against and damaged. All is soft, and bending. Walls and cupboards whiten and bend their yellow squares on top of which a pale glass gleams. Out of me now my mind can pour. I can think of my Armadas sailing on the high waves. I am relieved of hard contacts and collisions. I sail on alone under white cliffs. Oh, but I sink, I fall! That is the corner of the cupboard; that is the nursery looking-glass. But they stretch, they elongate. I sink down on the black plumes of sleep; its thick wings are pressed to my eyes. Travelling through darkness I see the stretched flower-beds, and Mrs. Constable runs from behind the corner of the pampas-grass to say my aunt has come to fetch me in a carriage. I mount; I escape; I rise on springheeled boots over the tree-tops. But I am now fallen into the carriage at the hall door, where she sits nodding yellow plumes with eyes hard like glazed marbles. Oh, to awake from dreaming! Look, there is the chest of drawers. Let me pull myself out of these waters. But they heap themselves on me; they sweep me between their great shoulders; I am turned; I am tumbled; I am stretched, among these long lights, these long waves, these endless paths, with people pursuing, pursuing."

he sun rose higher. Blue waves, green waves swept a quick fan over the beach, circling the spike of sea-holly and leaving shallow pools of light here and there on the sand. A faint black rim was left behind them. The rocks which had been misty and soft hardened and were marked with red clefts.

Sharp stripes of shadow lay on the grass, and the dew dancing on the tips of the flowers and leaves made the garden like a mosaic of single sparks not yet formed into one whole. The birds, whose breasts were specked canary and rose, now sang a strain or two together, wildly, like skaters rollicking arm-in-arm, and were suddenly silent, breaking asunder.

The sun laid broader blades upon the house. The light touched something green in the window corner and made it a lump of emerald, a cave of pure green like stoneless fruit. It sharpened the edges of chairs and tables and stitched white table-cloths with fine gold wires. As the light increased a bud here and there split asunder and shook out flowers, green veined and quivering, as if the effort of opening had set them rocking, and pealing a faint carillon as they beat their frail clappers against their white walls. Everything became softly amorphous, as if the china of the plate flowed and the steel of the knife were liquid. Meanwhile the concussion of the waves breaking fell with muffled thuds, like logs falling, on the shore.

"Now," said Bernard, "the time has come. The day has come. The cab is at the door. My huge box bends George's bandy-legs even wider. The horrible ceremony is over, the tips, and the good-byes in the hall. Now there is this gulping ceremony with my mother, this hand-shaking ceremony with my father; now I must go on waving, I must go on waving, till we turn the corner. Now that ceremony is over. Heaven be praised, all ceremonies are over. I am alone; I am going to school for the first time.

"Everybody seems to be doing things for this moment only; and never again. Never again. The urgency of it all is fearful. Everybody knows I am going to school, going to school for the first time. 'That boy is going to school for the first time,' says the housemaid, cleaning the steps. I must not cry. I must behold them indifferently. Now the awful portals of the station gape; 'the moon-faced clock regards me.' I must make phrases and phrases and so interpose something hard between myself and the stare of housemaids, the stare of clocks, staring faces, indifferent faces, or I shall cry. There is Louis; there is Neville in long coats, carrying handbags, by the booking-office. They are composed. But they look different."

"Here is Bernard," said Louis. "He is composed; he is easy. He swings his bag as he walks. I will follow Bernard, because he is not afraid. We are drawn through the booking-office on to the platform as a stream draws twigs and straws round the piers of a bridge. There is the very powerful, bottle-green engine without a neck, all back and thighs, breathing steam. The guard blows his whistle; the flag is dipped; without an effort, of its own momentum, like an avalanche started by a gentle push, we start forward. Bernard spreads a rug and plays knucklebones. Neville reads. London crumbles. London heaves and surges. There is a bristling of chimneys and towers. There a white church; there a mast among the spires. There a canal. Now there are open spaces with asphalt paths upon which it is strange that people should now be walking. There is a hill striped with red houses. A man crosses a bridge with a dog at his heels. Now the red boy begins firing at a pheasant. The blue boy shoves him aside. 'My uncle is the best shot in England. My cousin is Master of Foxhounds.' Boasting begins. And I cannot boast, for my father is a banker in Brisbane, and I speak with an Australian accent."

"After all this hubbub," said Neville, "all this scuffling and hubbub, we have arrived. This is indeed a moment—this is indeed a solemn moment. I come, like a lord to his hall appointed. That is our founder; our illustrious founder, standing in the courtyard with one foot raised. I salute our founder. A noble Roman air hangs over these austere quadrangles. Already the lights are lit in the form rooms. Those are laboratories perhaps; and that a library, where I shall explore the exactitude of the Latin language, and step firmly upon the well-laid sentences, and pronounce the explicit, the sonorous hexameters of Virgil; of Lucretius; and chant with a passion that is never obscure or formless the loves of Catullus, reading from a big book, a quarto with margins. I shall lie, too, in the fields among the tickling grasses. I shall lie with my friends under the towering elm trees.

"Behold, the Headmaster. Alas, that he should excite my ridicule. He is too sleek, he is altogether too shiny and black, like some statue in a public garden. And on the left side of his waistcoat, his taut, his drum-like waistcoat, hangs a crucifix."

"Old Crane," said Bernard, "now rises to address us. Old Crane, the Headmaster, has a nose like a mountain at sunset, and a blue cleft in his chin, like a wooded ravine, which some tripper has fired; like a wooded ravine seen from the train window. He sways slightly, mouthing out his tremendous and sonorous words. I love tremendous and sonorous words. But his words are too hearty to be true. Yet he is by this time convinced of their truth. And when he leaves the room, lurching rather heavily from side to side, and hurls his way through the swing-doors, all the masters, lurching rather heavily from side to side, hurl themselves also through the swing-doors. This is our first night at school, apart from our sisters."

"This is my first night at school," said Susan, "away from my father, away from my home. My eyes swell; my eyes prick with tears. I hate the smell of pine and linoleum. I hate the wind-bitten shrubs and the sanitary tiles. I hate the cheerful jokes and the glazed look of every one. I left my squirrel and my doves for the boy to look after. The kitchen door slams, and shot patters among the leaves when Percy fires at the rocks. All here is false; all is meretricious. Rhoda and Jinny sit far off in brown serge, and look at Miss Lambert who sits under a picture of Queen Alexandra reading from a book before her. There is also a blue scroll of needlework embroidered by some old girl. If I do not purse my lips, if I do not screw my handkerchief, I shall cry."

"The purple light," said Rhoda, "in Miss Lambert's ring passes to and fro across the black stain on the white page of the Prayer Book. It is a vinous, it is an amorous light. Now that our boxes are unpacked in the dormitories, we sit herded together under maps of the entire world. There are desks with wells for the ink. We shall write our exercises in ink here. But here I am nobody. I have no face. This great company, all dressed in brown serge, has robbed me of my identity. We are all callous, unfriended. I will seek out a face, a composed, a monumental face, and will endow it with omniscience, and wear it under my dress like a talisman and then (I promise this) I will find some dingle in a wood where I can display my assortment of curious treasures. I promise myself this. So I will not cry."

"That dark woman," said Jinny, "with high cheekbones, has a shiny dress, like a shell, veined, for wearing in the evening. That is nice for summer, but for winter I should like a thin dress shot with red threads that would gleam in the firelight. Then when the lamps were lit, I should put on my red dress and it would be thin as a veil, and would wind about my body, and billow out as I came into the room, pirouetting. It would make a flower shape as I sank down, in the middle of the room, on a gilt chair. But Miss Lambert wears an opaque dress, that falls in a cascade from her snow-white ruffle as she sits under a picture of Queen Alexandra pressing one white finger firmly on the page. And we pray."

"Now we march, two by two," said Louis, "orderly, processional, into chapel. I like the dimness that falls as we enter the sacred building. I like the orderly progress. We file in; we seat ourselves. We put off our distinctions as we enter. I like it now, when, lurching slightly, but only from his momentum, Dr. Crane mounts the pulpit and reads the lesson from a Bible spread on the back of the brass eagle. I rejoice; my heart expands in his bulk, in his authority. He lays the whirling dust clouds in my tremulous, my ignominiously agitated mind—how we danced round the Christmas tree and handing parcels they forgot me, and the fat woman said, 'This little boy has no present,' and gave me a shiny Union Jack from the top of the tree, and I cried with fury—to be remembered with pity. Now all is laid by his authority, his crucifix, and I feel come over me the sense of the earth under me, and my roots going down and down till they wrap themselves round some hardness at the centre. I recover my continuity, as he reads. I become a figure in the procession, a spoke in the huge wheel that turning, at last erects me, here and now. I have been in the dark; I have been hidden; but when the wheel turns (as he reads) I rise into this dim light where I just perceive, but scarcely, kneeling boys, pillars and memorial brasses. There is no crudity here, no sudden kisses."

"The brute menaces my liberty," said Neville, "when he prays. Unwarmed by imagination, his words fall cold on my head like paving-stones, while the gilt cross heaves on his waistcoat. The words of authority are corrupted by those who speak them. I gibe and mock at this sad religion, at these tremulous, grief-stricken figures advancing, cadaverous and wounded, down a white road shadowed by fig trees where boys sprawl in the dust —naked boys; and goat-skins distended with wine hang at the tavern door. I was in Rome travelling with my father at Easter; and the trembling figure of Christ's mother was borne niddle-noddling along the streets; there went by also the stricken figure of Christ in a glass case.

"Now I will lean sideways as if to scratch my thigh. So I shall see Percival. There he sits, upright among the smaller fry. He breathes through his straight nose rather heavily. His blue, and oddly inexpressive eyes, are fixed with pagan indifference upon the pillar opposite. He would make an admirable churchwarden. He should have a birch and beat little boys for misdemeanours. He is allied with the Latin phrases on the memorial brasses. He sees nothing; he hears nothing. He is remote from us all in a pagan universe. But look—he flicks his hand to the back of his neck. For such gestures one falls hopelessly in love for a lifetime. Dalton, Jones, Edgar and Bateman flick their hands to the backs of their necks likewise. But they do not succeed."

"At last," said Bernard, "the growl ceases. The sermon ends. He has minced the dance of the white butterflies at the door to powder. His rough and hairy voice is like an unshaven chin. Now he lurches back to his seat like a drunken sailor. It is an action that all the other masters will try to imitate; but, being flimsy, being floppy, wearing grey trousers, they will only succeed in making themselves ridiculous. I do not despise them. Their antics seem pitiable in my eyes. I note the fact for future reference with many others in my notebook. When I am grown up I shall carry a notebook—a fat book with many pages, methodically lettered. I shall enter my phrases. Under B shall come 'Butterfly powder.' If, in my novel, I describe the sun on the window-sill, I shall look under B and find butterfly powder. That will be useful. The tree 'shades the window with green fingers.' That will be useful. But alas! I am so soon distracted—by a hair like twisted candy, by Celia's Prayer Book, ivory covered. Louis can contemplate nature, unwinking, by the hour. Soon I fail, unless talked to. 'The lake of my mind, unbroken by oars, heaves placidly and soon sinks into an oily somnolence.' That will be useful."

"Now we move out of this cool temple, into the yellow playing-fields," said Louis. "And, as it is a half-holiday (the Duke's birthday) we will settle among the long grasses, while they play cricket. Could I be 'they' I would choose it; I would buckle on my pads and stride across the playing-field at the head of the batsmen. Look now, how everybody follows Percival. He is heavy. He walks clumsily down the field, through the long grass, to where the great elm trees stand. His magnificence is that of some mediaeval commander. A wake of light seems to lie on the grass behind him. Look at us trooping after him, his faithful servants, to be shot like sheep, for he will certainly attempt some forlorn enterprise and die in battle. My heart turns rough; it abrades my side like a file with two edges; one, that I adore his magnificence; the other I despise his slovenly accents—I who am so much his superior—and am jealous."

"And now," said Neville, "let Bernard begin. Let him burble on, telling us stories, while we lie recumbent. Let him describe what we have all seen so that it becomes a sequence. Bernard says there is always a story. I am a story. Louis is a story. There is the story of the boot-boy, the story of the man with one eye, the story of the woman who sells winkles. Let him burble on with his story while I lie back and regard the stiff-legged figures of the padded batsmen through the trembling grasses. It seems as if the whole world were flowing and curving—on the earth the trees, in the sky the clouds. I look up, through the trees, into the sky. The match seems to be played up there. Faintly among the soft, white clouds I hear the cry 'Run,' I hear the cry 'How's that?' The clouds lose tufts of whiteness as the breeze dishevels them. If that blue could stay for ever; if that hole could remain for ever; if this moment could stay for ever—

"But Bernard goes on talking. Up they bubble—images. 'Like a camel,' . . . 'a vulture.' The camel is a vulture; the vulture a camel; for Bernard is a dangling wire, loose, but seductive. Yes, for when he talks, when he makes his foolish comparisons, a lightness comes over one. One floats, too, as if one were that bubble; one is freed; I have escaped, one feels. Even the chubby little boys (Dalton, Larpent and Baker) feel the same abandonment. They like this better than the cricket. They catch the phrases as they bubble. They let the feathery grasses tickle their noses. And then we all feel Percival lying heavy among us. His curious guffaw seems to sanction our laughter. But now he has rolled himself over in the long grass. He is, I think, chewing a stalk between his teeth. He feels bored; I too feel bored. Bernard at once perceives that we are bored. I detect a certain effort, an extravagance in his phrase, as if he said 'Look!' but Percival says 'No.' For he is always the first to detect insincerity; and is brutal in the extreme. The sentence tails off feebly. Yes, the appalling moment has come when Bernard's power fails him and there is no longer any sequence and he sags and twiddles a bit of string and falls silent, gaping as if about to burst into tears. Among the tortures and devastations of life is this then—our friends are not able to finish their stories."

"Now let me try," said Louis, "before we rise, before we go to tea, to fix the moment in one effort of supreme endeavour. This shall endure. We are parting; some to tea; some to the nets; I to show my essay to Mr. Barker. This will endure. From discord, from hatred (I despise dabblers in imagery—I resent the power of Percival intensely) my shattered mind is pieced together by some sudden perception. I take the trees, the clouds, to be witnesses of my complete integration. I, Louis, I, who shall walk the earth these seventy years, am born entire, out of hatred, out of discord. Here on this ring of grass we have sat together, bound by the tremendous power of some inner compulsion. The trees wave, the clouds pass. The time approaches when these soliloquies shall be shared. We shall not always give out a sound like a beaten gong as one sensation strikes and then another. Children, our lives have been gongs striking; clamour and boasting; cries of despair; blows on the nape of the neck in gardens.

"Now grass and trees, the travelling air blowing empty spaces in the blue which they then recover, shaking the leaves which then replace themselves, and our ring here, sitting, with our arms binding our knees, hint at some other order, and better, which makes a reason everlastingly. This I see for a second, and shall try tonight to fix in words, to forge in a ring of steel, though

Percival destroys it, as he blunders off, crushing the grasses, with the small fry trotting subservient after him. Yet it is Percival I need; for it is Percival who inspires poetry."

"For how many months," said Susan, "for how many years, have I run up these stairs, in the dismal days of winter, in the chilly days of spring? Now it is midsummer. We go upstairs to change into white frocks to play tennis—Jinny and I with Rhoda following after. I count each step as I mount, counting each step something done with. So each night I tear off the old day from the calendar, and screw it tight into a ball. I do this vindictively, while Betty and Clara are on their knees. I do not pray. I revenge myself upon the day. I wreak my spite upon its image. You are dead now, I say, school day, hated day. They have made all the days of June—this is the twenty-fifth—shiny and orderly, with gongs, with lessons, with orders to wash, to change, to work, to eat. We listen to missionaries from China. We drive off in brakes along the asphalt pavement, to attend concerts in halls. We are shown galleries and pictures.

"At home the hay waves over the meadows. My father leans upon the stile, smoking. In the house one door bangs and then another, as the summer air puffs along the empty passages. Some old picture perhaps swings on the wall. A petal drops from the rose in the jar. The farm wagons strew the hedges with tufts of hay. All this I see, I always see, as I pass the looking-glass on the landing, with Jinny in front and Rhoda lagging behind. Jinny dances. Jinny always dances in the hall on the ugly, the encaustic tiles; she turns cartwheels in the playground; she picks some flower forbiddenly, and sticks it behind her ear so that Miss Perry's dark eyes smoulder with admiration, for Jinny, not me. Miss Perry loves Jinny; and I could have loved her, but now love no one, except my father, my doves and the squirrel whom I left in the cage at home for the boy to look after."

"I hate the small looking-glass on the stairs," said Jinny. "It shows our heads only; it cuts off our heads. And my lips are too wide, and my eyes are too close together; I show my gums too much when I laugh. Susan's head, with its fell look, with its grass-green eyes which poets will love, Bernard said, because they fall upon close white stitching, put mine out; even Rhoda's face mooning, vacant, is completed, like those white petals she used to swim in her bowl. So I skip up the stairs past them, to the next landing, where the long glass hangs, and I see myself entire. I see my body and head in one now; for even in this serge frock they are one, my body and my head. Look, when I move my head I ripple all down my narrow body; even my thin legs ripple like a stalk in the wind. I flicker between the set face of Susan and Rhoda's vagueness; I leap like one of those flames that run between the cracks of the earth; I move, I dance; I never cease to move and to dance. I move like the leaf that moved in the hedge as a child and frightened me. I dance over these streaked, these impersonal, distempered walls with their yellow skirting as firelight dances over teapots. I catch fire even from women's cold eyes. When I read, a purple rim runs round the black edge of the textbook. Yet I cannot follow any word through its changes. I cannot follow any thought from present to past. I do not stand lost, like Susan, with tears in my eyes remembering home; or lie, like Rhoda, crumpled among the ferns, staining my pink cotton green, while I dream of plants that flower under the sea, and rocks through which the fish swim slowly. I do not dream.

"Now let us be quick. Now let me be the first to pull off these coarse clothes. Here are my clean white stockings. Here are my new shoes. I bind my hair with a white ribbon, so that when I leap across the court the ribbon will stream out in a flash, yet curl round my neck, perfectly in its place. Not a hair shall be untidy."

"That is my face," said Rhoda, "in the looking-glass behind Susan's shoulder—that face is my face. But I will duck behind her to hide it, for I am not here. I have no face. Other people have faces; Susan and Jinny have faces; they are here. Their world is the real world. The things they lift are heavy. They say Yes, they say No; whereas I shift and change and am seen through in a second. If they meet a housemaid she looks at them without laughing. But she laughs at me. They know what to say if spoken to. They laugh really; they get angry really; while I have to look first and do what other people do when they have done it.

"See now with what extraordinary certainty Jinny pulls on her stockings, simply to play tennis. That I admire. But I like Susan's way better, for she is more resolute, and less ambitious of distinction than Jinny. Both despise me for copying what they do; but Susan sometimes teaches me, for instance, how to tie a bow, while Jinny has her own knowledge but keeps it to herself. They have friends to sit by. They have things to say privately in corners. But I attach myself only to names and faces; and hoard them like amulets against disaster. I choose out across the hall some unknown face and can hardly drink my tea when she whose name I do not know sits opposite. I choke. I am rocked from side to side by the violence of my emotion. I imagine these nameless, these immaculate people, watching me from behind bushes. I leap high to excite their admiration. At night, in bed, I excite their complete wonder. I often die pierced with arrows to win their tears. If they should say, or I should see from a label on their boxes that they were in Scarborough last holidays, the whole town runs gold, the whole pavement is illuminated. Therefore I hate looking-glasses which show me my real face. Alone, I often fall down into nothingness. I must push my foot stealthily lest I should fall off the edge of the world into nothingness. I have to bang my hand against some hard door to call myself back to the body."

"We are late," said Susan. "We must wait our turn to play. We will pitch here in the long grass and pretend to watch Jinny and Clara, Betty and Mavis. But we will not watch them. I hate watching other people play games. I will make images of all the things I hate most and bury them in the ground. This shiny pebble is Madame Carlo, and I will bury her deep because of her fawning and ingratiating manners, because of the sixpence she gave me for keeping my knuckles flat when I played my scales. I buried her sixpence. I would bury the whole school; the gymnasium; the classroom, the dining-room that always smells of meat, and the chapel. I would bury the red-brown tiles and the oily portraits of old men—benefactors, founders of schools. There are some trees I like; the cherry tree with lumps of clear gum on the bark; and one view from the attic towards some far hills. Save for these, I would bury it all as I bury these ugly stones that are always scattered about this briny coast, with its piers and its trippers. At home, the waves are mile long. On winter nights we hear them booming. Last Christmas a man was drowned sitting alone in his cart."

"When Miss Lambert passes," said Rhoda, "talking to the clergyman, the others laugh and imitate her hunch behind her back; yet everything changes and becomes luminous. Jinny leaps higher too when Miss Lambert passes. Suppose she saw that daisy, it would change. Wherever she goes, things are changed under her eyes; and yet when she has passed is not the thing the same again? Miss Lambert is taking the clergyman through the wicket-gate to her private garden; and when she comes to the pond, she sees a frog on a leaf, and that will change. All is solemn, all is pale where she stands, like a statue in a grove. She lets her tasselled silken cloak slip down, and only her purple ring still glows, her vinous, her amethystine ring. There is this mystery about people when they leave us. When they leave us I can companion them to the pond and make them stately. When Miss Lambert passes, she makes the daisy change; and everything runs like streaks of fire when she carves the beef. Month by month things are losing their hardness; even my body now lets the light through; my spine is soft like wax near the flame of the candle. I dream; I dream."

"I have won the game," said Jinny. "Now it is your turn. I must throw myself on the ground and pant. I am out of breath with running, with triumph. Everything in my body seems thinned out with running and triumph. My blood must be bright red, whipped up, slapping against my ribs. My soles tingle, as if wire rings opened and shut in my feet. I see every blade of grass very clear. But the pulse drums so in my forehead, behind my eyes, that everything dances—the net, the grass; your faces leap like butterflies; the trees seem to jump up and down. There is nothing staid, nothing settled in this universe. All is rippling, all is dancing; all is quickness and triumph. Only, when I have lain alone on the hard ground, watching you play your game, I begin to feel the wish to be singled out; to be summoned, to be called away by one person who comes to find me, who is attracted towards me, who cannot keep himself from me, but comes to where I sit on my gilt chair, with my frock billowing round me like a flower. And withdrawing into an alcove, sitting alone on a balcony we talk together.

"Now the tide sinks. Now the trees come to earth; the brisk waves that slap my ribs rock more gently, and my heart rides at anchor, like a sailing-boat whose sails slide slowly down on to the white deck. The game is over. We must go to tea now."

"The boasting boys," said Louis, "have gone now in a vast team to play cricket. They have driven off in their great brake, singing in chorus. All their heads turn simultaneously at the corner by the laurel bushes. Now they are boasting. Larpent's brother played football for Oxford; Smith's father made a century at Lords. Archie and Hugh; Parker and Dalton; Larpent and Smith; then again Archie and Hugh; Parker and Dalton; Larpent and Smith—the names repeat themselves; the names are the same always. They are the volunteers; they are the cricketers; they are the officers of the Natural History Society. They are always forming into fours and marching in troops with badges on their caps; they salute simultaneously passing the figure of their general. How majestic is their order, how beautiful is their obedience! If I could follow, if I could be with them I would sacrifice all I know. But they also leave butterflies trembling with their wings pinched off; they throw dirty pocket-handkerchiefs clotted with blood screwed up into corners. They make little boys sob in dark passages. They have big red ears that stand out under their caps. Yet that is what we wish to be, Neville and I. I watch them go with envy. Peeping from behind a curtain, I note the simultaneity of their movements with delight. If my legs were reinforced by theirs, how they would run! If I had been with them and won matches and rowed in great races, and galloped all day, how I should thunder out songs at midnight! In what a torrent the words would rush from my throat!"

"Percival has gone now," said Neville. "He is thinking of nothing but the match. He never waved his hand as the brake turned the corner by the laurel bush. He despises me for being too weak to play (yet he is always kind to my weakness). He despises me for not caring if they win or lose except that he cares. He takes my devotion; he accepts my tremulous, no doubt abject offering, mixed with contempt as it is for his mind. For he cannot read. Yet when I read Shakespeare or Catullus, lying in the long grass, he understands more than Louis. Not the words—but what are words? Do I not know already how to rhyme, how to imitate Pope, Dryden, even Shakespeare? But I cannot stand all day in the sun with my eyes on the ball; I cannot feel the flight of the ball through my body and think only of the ball. I shall be a clinger to the outsides of words all my life. Yet I could not live with him and suffer his stupidity. He will coarsen and snore. He will marry and there will be scenes of tenderness at breakfast. But now he is young. Not a thread, not a sheet of paper lies between him and the sun, between him and the rain, between him and the moon as she lies naked, tumbled, hot, on his bed. Now as they drive along the high road in their brake his face is mottled red and yellow. He will throw off his coat and stand with his legs apart, with his hands ready, watching the wicket. And he will pray, 'Lord, let us win'; he will think of one thing only, that they should win.

"How could I go with them in a brake to play cricket? Only

Bernard could go with them, but Bernard is too late to go with them. He is always too late. He is prevented by his incorrigible moodiness from going with them. He stops, when he washes his hands, to say, 'There is a fly in that web. Shall I rescue that fly; shall I let the spider eat it?' He is shaded with innumerable perplexities, or he would go with them to play cricket, and would lie in the grass, watching the sky, and would start when the ball was hit. But they would forgive him; for he would tell them a story."

"They have bowled off," said Bernard, "and I am too late to go with them. The horrid little boys, who are also so beautiful, whom you and Louis, Neville, envy so deeply, have bowled off with their heads all turned the same way. But I am unaware of these profound distinctions. My fingers slip over the keyboard without knowing which is black and which white. Archie makes easily a hundred; I by a fluke make sometimes fifteen. But what is the difference between us? Wait though, Neville; let me talk. The bubbles are rising like the silver bubbles from the floor of a saucepan; image on top of image. I cannot sit down to my book, like Louis, with ferocious tenacity. I must open the little trap-door and let out these linked phrases in which I run together whatever happens so that instead of incoherence there is perceived a wandering thread, lightly joining one thing to another. I will tell you the story of the doctor.

"When Dr. Crane lurches through the swing-doors after prayers he is convinced, it seems, of his immense superiority; and indeed, Neville, we cannot deny that his departure leaves us not only with a sense of relief, but also with a sense of something removed, like a tooth. Now let us follow him as he heaves through the swing-door to his own apartments. Let us imagine him in his private room over the stables undressing. He unfastens his sock suspenders (let us be trivial, let us be intimate). Then with a characteristic gesture (it is difficult to avoid these ready-made phrases, and they are, in his case, somehow appropriate) he takes the silver, he takes the coppers from his trouser pockets and places them there, and there, on his dressing-table. With both arms stretched on the arms of his chair he reflects (this is his private moment; it is here we must try to catch him) shall he cross the pink bridge into his bedroom or shall he not cross it? The two rooms are united by a bridge of rosy light from the lamp at the bedside where Mrs. Crane lies with her hair on the pillow reading a French memoir. As she reads, she sweeps her hand with an abandoned and despairing gesture over her forehead and sighs, 'Is this all?' comparing herself with some French duchess. Now, says the doctor, in two years I shall retire. I shall clip yew hedges in a west country garden. An admiral I might have been; or a judge; not a schoolmaster. What forces, he asks, staring at the gas-fire with his shoulders hunched up more hugely than we know them (he is in his shirtsleeves remember) have brought me to this? What vast forces? he thinks, getting into the stride of his majestic phrases as he looks over his shoulder at the window. It is a stormy night; the branches of the chestnut trees are ploughing up and down. Stars flash between them. What vast forces of good and evil have brought me here? he asks, and sees with sorrow that his chair has worn a little hole in the pile of the purple carpet. So there he sits, swinging his braces. But stories that follow people into their private rooms are difficult. I cannot go on with this story. I twiddle a piece of string; I turn over four or five coins in my trouser pocket."

"Bernard's stories amuse me," said Neville, "at the start. But when they tail off absurdly and he gapes, twiddling a bit of string, I feel my own solitude. He sees every one with blurred edges. Hence I cannot talk to him of Percival. I cannot expose my absurd and violent passion to his sympathetic understanding. It, too, would make a 'story.' I need some one whose mind falls like a chopper on a block; to whom the pitch of absurdity is sublime; and a shoe-string adorable. To whom can I expose the urgency of my own passion? Louis is too cold, too universal. There is nobody—here among these grey arches, and moaning pigeons, and cheerful games and tradition and emulation, all so

skillfully organised to prevent feeling alone. Yet I am struck
still as I walk by sudden premonitions of what is to come. Yesterday, passing the open door leading into the private garden,
I saw Fenwick with his mallet raised. The steam from the tea-
urn rose in the middle of the lawn. There were banks of blue
flowers. Then suddenly descended upon me the obscure, the
mystic sense of adoration, of completeness that triumphed over
chaos. Nobody saw my poised and intent figure as I stood at the
open door. Nobody guessed the need I had to offer my being
to one god; and perish, and disappear. His mallet descended; the
vision broke.

"Should I seek out some tree? Should I desert these form
rooms and libraries, and the broad yellow page in which I read
Catullus, for woods and fields? Should I walk under beech trees,
or saunter along the river bank, where the trees meet united like
lovers in the water? But nature is too vegetable, too vapid. She
has only sublimities and vastitudes and water and leaves. I begin
to wish for firelight, privacy, and the limbs of one person."

"I begin to wish," said Louis, "for night to come. As I stand
here with my hand on the grained oak panel of Mr. Wickham's
door I think myself the friend of Richelieu, or the Duke of St.
Simon holding out a snuff-box to the King himself. It is my privilege. My witticisms 'run like wildfire through the court.' Duch-
esses tear emeralds from their ear-rings out of admiration—but
these rockets rise best in darkness, in my cubicle at night. I am
now a boy only with a colonial accent holding my knuckles
against Mr. Wickham's grained oak door. The day has been full
of ignominies and triumphs concealed from fear of laughter. I
am the best scholar in the school. But when darkness comes I
put off this unenviable body—my large nose, my thin lips, my
colonial accent—and inhabit space. I am then Virgil's companion, and Plato's. I am then the last scion of one of the great
houses of France. But I am also one who will force himself to
desert these windy and moonlit territories, these midnight wan-
derings, and confront grained oak doors. I will achieve in my life

—Heaven grant that it be not long—some gigantic amalgama-
tion between the two discrepancies so hideously apparent to me.
Out of my suffering I will do it. I will knock. I will enter."

"I have torn off the whole of May and June," said Susan, "and
twenty days of July. I have torn them off and screwed them up
so that they no longer exist, save as a weight in my side. They
have been crippled days, like moths with shrivelled wings unable
to fly. There are only eight days left. In eight days' time I shall
get out of the train and stand on the platform at six-twenty-five.
Then my freedom will unfurl, and all these restrictions that
wrinkle and shrivel—hours and order and discipline, and being
here and there exactly at the right moment—will crack asunder.
Out the day will spring, as I open the carriage-door and see my
father in his old hat and gaiters. I shall tremble. I shall burst into
tears. Then next morning I shall get up at dawn. I shall let myself out by the kitchen door. I shall walk on the moor. The great
horses of the phantom riders will thunder behind me and stop
suddenly. I shall see the swallow skim the grass. I shall throw
myself on a bank by the river and watch the fish slip in and out
among the reeds. The palms of my hands will be printed with
pine-needles. I shall there unfold and take out whatever it is I
have made here; something hard. For something has grown in
me here, through the winters and summers, on staircases, in
bedrooms. I do not want, as Jinny wants, to be admired. I do not
want people, when I come in, to look up with admiration. I want
to give, to be given, and solitude in which to unfold my possessions.

"Then I shall come back through the trembling lanes under
the arches of the nut leaves. I shall pass an old woman wheeling
a perambulator full of sticks; and the shepherd. But we shall not
speak. I shall come back through the kitchen garden, and see
the curved leaves of the cabbages pebbled with dew, and the
house in the garden, blind with curtained windows. I shall go upstairs to my room, and turn over my own things, locked care-

fully in the wardrobe; my shells; my eggs; my curious grasses. I shall feed my doves and my squirrel. I shall go to the kennel and comb my spaniel. So gradually I shall turn over the hard thing that has grown here in my side. But here bells ring; feet shuffle perpetually."

"I hate darkness and sleep and night," said Jinny, "and lie longing for the day to come. I long that the week should be all one day without divisions. When I wake early—and the birds wake me—I lie and watch the brass handles on the cupboard grow clear; then the basin; then the towel-horse. As each thing in the bedroom grows clear, my heart beats quicker. I feel my body harden, and become pink, yellow, brown. My hands pass over my legs and body. I feel its slopes, its thinness. I love to hear the gong roar through the house and the stir begin—here a thud, there a patter. Doors slam; water rushes. Here is another day, here is another day, I cry, as my feet touch the floor. It may be a bruised day, an imperfect day. I am often scolded. I am often in disgrace for idleness, for laughing; but even as Miss Matthews grumbles at my feather-headed carelessness, I catch sight of something moving—a speck of sun perhaps on a picture, or the donkey drawing the mowing-machine across the lawn; or a sail that passes between the laurel leaves, so that I am never cast down. I cannot be prevented from pirouetting behind Miss Matthews into prayers.

"Now, too, the time is coming when we shall leave school and wear long skirts. I shall wear necklaces and a white dress without sleeves at night. There will be parties in brilliant rooms; and one man will single me out and will tell me what he has told no other person. He will like me better than Susan or Rhoda. He will find in me some quality, some peculiar thing. But I shall not let myself be attached to one person only. I do not want to be fixed, to be pinioned. I tremble, I quiver, like the leaf in the hedge, as I sit dangling my feet, on the edge of the bed, with a new day to break open. I have fifty years, I have sixty years to spend. I have not yet broken into my hoard. This is the beginning."

"There are hours and hours," said Rhoda, "before I can put out the light and lie suspended on my bed above the world, before I can let the day drop down, before I can let my tree grow, quivering in green pavilions above my head. Here I cannot let it grow. Somebody knocks through it. They ask questions, they interrupt, they throw it down.

"Now I will go to the bathroom and take off my shoes and wash; but as I wash, as I bend my head down over the basin, I will let the Russian Empress's veil flow about my shoulders. The diamonds of the Imperial crown blaze on my forehead. I hear the roar of the hostile mob as I step out on to the balcony. Now I dry my hands, vigorously, so that Miss, whose name I forget, cannot suspect that I am waving my fist at an infuriated mob. 'I am your Empress, people.' My attitude is one of defiance. I am fearless. I conquer.

"But this is a thin dream. This is a papery tree. Miss Lambert blows it down. Even the sight of her vanishing down the corridor blows it to atoms. It is not solid; it gives me no satisfaction —this Empress dream. It leaves me, now that it has fallen, here in the passage rather shivering. Things seem paler. I will go now into the library and take out some book, and read and look; and read again and look. Here is a poem about a hedge. I will wander down it and pick flowers, green cowbind and the moonlight coloured may, wild roses and ivy serpentine. I will clasp them in my hands and lay them on the desk's shiny surface. I will sit by the river's trembling edge and look at the water-lilies, broad and bright, which lit the oak that overhung the hedge with moonlight beams of their own watery light. I will pick flowers; I will bind flowers in one garland and clasp them and present them— Oh! to whom? There is some check in the flow of my being; a deep stream presses on some obstacle; it jerks; it tugs; some knot in the centre resists. Oh, this is pain, this is anguish!

I faint, I fail. Now my body thaws; I am unsealed, I am incandescent. Now the stream pours in a deep tide fertilising, opening the shut, forcing the tight-folded, flooding free. To whom shall I give all that now flows through me, from my warm, my porous body? I will gather my flowers and present them— Oh! to whom?

"Sailors loiter on the parade, and amorous couples; the omnibuses rattle along the sea front to the town. I will give; I will enrich; I will return to the world this beauty. I will bind my flowers in one garland and advancing with my hand outstretched will present them— Oh! to whom?"

"Now we have received," said Louis, "for this is the last day of the last term—Neville's and Bernard's and my last day—whatever our masters have had to give us. The introduction has been made; the world presented. They stay, we depart. The great Doctor, whom of all men I most revere, swaying a little from side to side among the tables, the bound volumes, has dealt out Horace, Tennyson, the complete works of Keats and Matthew Arnold suitably inscribed. I respect the hand which gave them. He speaks with complete conviction. To him his words are true, though not to us. Speaking in the gruff voice of deep emotion, fiercely, tenderly, he has told us that we are about to go. He has bid us 'quit ourselves like men.' (On his lips quotations from the Bible, from the *Times,* seem equally magnificent.) Some will do this; others that. Some will not meet again. Neville, Bernard and I shall not meet here again. Life will divide us. But we have formed certain ties. Our boyish, our irresponsible years are over. But we have forged certain links. Above all, we have inherited traditions. These stone flags have been worn for six hundred years. On these walls are inscribed the names of men of war, of statesmen, of some unhappy poets (mine shall be among them). Blessings be on all traditions, on all safeguards and circumscriptions! I am most grateful to you men in black gowns, and you, dead, for your leading, for your guardianship; yet after all, the problem remains. The differences are not yet solved. Flowers toss their heads outside the window. I see wild birds, and impulses wilder than the wildest birds strike from my wild heart. My eyes are wild; my lips tight pressed. The bird flies; the flower dances; but I hear always the sullen thud of the waves; and the chained beast stamps on the beach. It stamps and stamps."

"This is the final ceremony," said Bernard. "This is the last of all our ceremonies. We are overcome by strange feelings. The guard holding his flag is about to blow his whistle; the train breathing steam in another moment is about to start. One wants to say something, to feel something, absolutely appropriate to the occasion. One's mind is primed; one's lips are pursed. And then a bee drifts in and hums round the flowers in the bouquet which Lady Hampton, the wife of the General, keeps smelling to show her appreciation of the compliment. If the bee were to sting her nose? We are all deeply moved; yet irreverent; yet penitent; yet anxious to get it over; yet reluctant to part. The bee distracts us; its casual flight seems to deride our intensity. Humming vaguely, skimming widely, it is settled now on the carnation. Many of us will not meet again. We shall not enjoy certain pleasures again, when we are free to go to bed, or to sit up, when I need no longer smuggle in bits of candle ends and immoral literature. The bee now hums round the head of the great Doctor. Larpent, John, Archie, Percival, Baker and Smith —I have liked them enormously. I have known one mad boy only. I have hated one mean boy only. I enjoy in retrospect my terribly awkward breakfasts at the Headmaster's table with toast and marmalade. He alone does not notice the bee. If it were to settle on his nose he would flick it off with one magnificent gesture. Now he has made his joke; now his voice has almost broken but not quite. Now we are dismissed—Louis, Neville and I for ever. We take our highly-polished books scholastically inscribed in a little crabbed hand. We rise, we disperse; the pressure is removed. The bee has become an insignificant, a disregarded insect, flown through the open window into obscurity. Tomorrow we go."

"We are about to part," said Neville. "Here are the boxes; here are the cabs. There is Percival in his billy-cock hat. He will forget me. He will leave my letters lying about among guns and dogs unanswered. I shall send him poems and he will perhaps reply with a picture post card. But it is for that that I love him. I shall propose meeting—under a clock, by some Cross; and shall wait, and he will not come. It is for that that I love him. Oblivious, almost entirely ignorant, he will pass from my life. And I shall pass, incredible as it seems, into other lives; this is only an escapade perhaps, a prelude only. I feel already, though I cannot endure the Doctor's pompous mummery, and faked emotions, that things we have only dimly perceived draw near. I shall be free to enter the garden where Fenwick raises his mallet. Those who have despised me shall acknowledge my sovereignty. But by some inscrutable law of my being sovereignty and the possession of power will not be enough; I shall always push through curtains to privacy, and want some whispered words alone. Therefore I go, dubious, but elate; apprehensive of intolerable pain; yet I think bound in my adventuring to conquer after huge suffering, bound, surely, to discover my desire in the end. There, for the last time, I see the statue of our pious founder with the doves about his head. They will wheel for ever about his head, whitening it, while the organ moans in the chapel. So I take my seat; and, when I have found my place in the corner of our reserved compartment, I will shade my eyes with a book to hide one tear; I will shade my eyes to observe; to peep at one face. It is the first day of the summer holidays."

"It is the first day of the summer holidays," said Susan. "But the day is still rolled up. I will not examine it until I step out on to the platform in the evening. I will not let myself even smell it until I smell the cold green air off the fields. But already these are not school fields; these are not school hedges; the men in these fields are doing real things; they fill carts with real hay; and those are real cows, not school cows. But the carbolic smell of corridors and the chalky smell of schoolrooms is still in my nostrils. The glazed, shiny look of matchboard is still in my eyes. I must wait for fields and hedges, and woods and fields, and steep railway cuttings, sprinkled with gorse bushes, and trucks in sidings, and tunnels and suburban gardens with women hanging out washing, and then fields again and children swinging on gates to cover it over, to bury it deep, this school that I have hated.

"I will not send my children to school nor spend a night all my life in London. Here in this vast station everything echoes and booms hollowly. The light is like the yellow light under an awning. Jinny lives here. Jinny takes her dog for walks on these pavements. People here shoot through the streets silently. They look at nothing but shop-windows. Their heads bob up and down all at about the same height. The streets are laced together with telegraph wires. The houses are all glass, all festoons and glitter; now all front doors and lace curtains, all pillars and white steps. But now I pass on, out of London again; the fields begin again; and the houses, and women hanging washing, and trees and fields. London is now veiled, now vanished, now crumbled, now fallen. The carbolic and the pitch-pine begin to lose their savour. I smell corn and turnips. I undo a paper packet tied with a piece of white cotton. The egg shells slide in to the cleft between my knees. Now we stop at station after station, rolling out milk cans. Now women kiss each other and help with baskets. Now I will let myself lean out of the window. The air rushes down my nose and throat—the cold air, the salt air with the smell of turnip fields in it. And there is my father, with his back turned, talking to a farmer. I tremble. I cry. There is my father in gaiters. There is my father."

"I sit snug in my own corner going North," said Jinny, "in this roaring express which is yet so smooth that it flattens hedges, lengthens hills. We flash past signal-boxes; we make the earth rock slightly from side to side. The distance closes for ever in a point; and we for ever open the distance wide again. The telegraph poles bob up incessantly; one is felled, another rises. Now we roar and swing into a tunnel. The gentleman pulls up the window. I see reflections on the shining glass which lines the tunnel. I see him lower his paper. He smiles at my reflection in the tunnel. My body instantly of its own accord puts forth a frill under his gaze. My body lives a life of its own. Now the black window glass is green again. We are out of the tunnel. He reads his paper. But we have exchanged the approval of our bodies. There is then a great society of bodies, and mine is introduced; mine has come into the room where the gilt chairs are. Look—all the windows of the villas and their white-tented curtains dance; and the men sitting in the hedges in the cornfields with knotted blue handkerchiefs are aware too, as I am aware, of heat and rapture. One waves as we pass him. There are bowers and arbours in these villa gardens and young men in shirt-sleeves on ladders trimming roses. A man on a horse canters over the field. His horse plunges as we pass. And the rider turns to look at us. We roar again through blackness. And I lie back; I give myself up to rapture; I think that at the end of the tunnel I enter a lamp-lit room with chairs into one of which I sink, much admired, my dress billowing round me. But behold, looking up, I meet the eyes of a sour woman, who suspects me of rapture. My body shuts in her face, impertinently, like a parasol. I open my body, I shut my body at my will. Life is beginning. I now break into my hoard of life."

"It is the first day of the summer holidays," said Rhoda. "And now, as the train passes by these red rocks, by this blue sea, the term, done with, forms itself into one shape behind me. I see its colour. June was white. I see the fields white with daisies, and white with dresses; and tennis courts marked with white. Then there was wind and violent thunder. There was a star riding through clouds one night, and I said to the star, 'Consume me.' That was at midsummer, after the garden party, and my humiliation at the garden party. Wind and storm coloured July. Also, in the middle, cadaverous, awful, lay the grey puddle in the courtyard, when, holding an envelope in my hand, I carried a message. I came to the puddle. I could not cross it. Identity failed me. We are nothing, I said, and fell. I was blown like a feather. I was wafted down tunnels. Then very gingerly, I pushed my foot across. I laid my hands against a brick wall. I returned very painfully, drawing myself back into my body over the grey, cadaverous space of the puddle. This is life then to which I am committed.

"So I detach the summer term. With intermittent shocks, sudden as the springs of a tiger, life emerges heaving its dark crest from the sea. It is to this we are attached; it is to this we are bound, as bodies to wild horses. And yet we have invented devices for filling up the crevices and disguising these fissures. Here is the ticket collector. Here are two men; three women; there is a cat in a basket; myself with my elbow on the window-sill—this is here and now. We draw on, we make off, through whispering fields of golden corn. Women in the fields are surprised to be left behind there, hoeing. The train now stamps heavily, breathes stertorously, as it climbs up and up. At last we are on the top of the moor. Only a few wild sheep live here; a few shaggy ponies; yet we are provided with every comfort; with tables to hold our newspapers, with rings to hold our tumblers. We come carrying these appliances with us over the top of the moor. Now we are on the summit. Silence will close behind us. If I look back over that bald head, I can see silence already closing and the shadows of clouds chasing each other over the empty moor; silence closes over our transient passage. This I say is the present moment; this is the first day of the summer holidays. This is part of the emerging monster to whom we are attached."

"Now we are off," said Louis. "Now I hang suspended without attachments. We are nowhere. We are passing through England in a train. England slips by the window, always changing from hill to wood, from rivers and willows to towns again. And I have no firm ground to which I go. Bernard and Neville, Percival, Archie, Larpent and Baker go to Oxford or Cambridge, to Edinburgh, Rome, Paris, Berlin, or to some American University. I go vaguely, to make money vaguely. Therefore a poignant shadow, a keen accent, falls on these golden bristles, on these poppy-red fields, this flowing corn that never overflows its boundaries; but runs rippling to the edge. This is the first day of a new life, another spoke of the rising wheel. But my body passes vagrant as a bird's shadow. I should be transient as the shadow on the meadow, soon fading, soon darkening and dying there where it meets the wood, were it not that I coerce my brain to form in my forehead; I force myself to state, if only in one line of unwritten poetry, this moment; to mark this inch in the long, long history that began in Egypt, in the time of the Pharaohs, when women carried red pitchers to the Nile. I seem already to have lived many thousand years. But if I now shut my eyes, if I fail to realise the meeting-place of past and present, that I sit in a third-class railway carriage full of boys going home for the holidays, human history is defrauded of a moment's vision. Its eye, that would see through me, shuts—if I sleep now, through slovenliness, or cowardice, burying myself in the past, in the dark; or acquiesce, as Bernard acquiesces, telling stories; or boast, as Percival, Archie, John, Walter, Lathom, Larpent, Roper, Smith boast—the names are the same always, the names of the boasting boys. They are all boasting, all talking, except Neville, who slips a look occasionally over the edge of a French novel, and so will always slip into cushioned firelit rooms, with many books and one friend, while I tilt on an office chair behind a counter. Then I shall grow bitter and mock at them. I shall envy them their continuance down the safe traditional ways under the shade of old yew trees while I consort with cockneys and clerks, and tap the pavements of the city.

"But now disembodied, passing over fields without lodgment —(there is a river; a man fishes; there is a spire, there is the village street with its bow-windowed inn)—all is dreamlike and dim to me. These hard thoughts, this envy, this bitterness, make no lodgment in me. I am the ghost of Louis, an ephemeral passer-by, in whose mind dreams have power, and garden sounds when in the early morning petals float on fathomless depths, and the birds sing. I dash and sprinkle myself with the bright waters of childhood. Its thin veil quivers. But the chained beast stamps and stamps on the shore."

"Louis and Neville," said Bernard, "both sit silent. Both are absorbed. Both feel the presence of other people as a separating wall. But if I find myself in company with other people, words at once make smoke rings—see how phrases at once begin to wreathe off my lips. It seems that a match is set to a fire; something burns. An elderly and apparently prosperous man, a traveller, now gets in. And I at once wish to approach him; I instinctively dislike the sense of his presence, cold, unassimilated, among us. I do not believe in separation. We are not single. Also I wish to add to my collection of valuable observations upon the true nature of human life. My book will certainly run to many volumes embracing every known variety of man and woman. I fill my mind with whatever happens to be the contents of a room or a railway carriage as one fills a fountain-pen in an inkpot. I have a steady unquenchable thirst. Now I feel by imperceptible signs, which I cannot yet interpret but will later, that his defiance is about to thaw. His solitude shows signs of cracking. He has passed a remark about a country house. A smoke ring issues from my lips (about crops) and circles him, bringing him into contact. The human voice has a disarming quality—(we are not single, we are one). As we exchange these few but amiable remarks, about country houses, I furbish him up and make him concrete. He is indulgent as a husband but not faithful; a small builder who employs a few men. In local society he is important; is already a councillor, and perhaps in time will be mayor. He wears a large ornament, like a double tooth torn up by the roots, made of coral, hanging at his watch-chain. Walter J. Trumble is the sort of name that would fit him. He has been in America, on a business trip with his wife, and a double room in a smallish hotel cost him a whole month's wages. His front tooth is stopped with gold.

"The fact is that I have little aptitude for reflection. I require the concrete in everything. It is so only that I lay hands upon the world. A good phrase, however, seems to me to have an independent existence. Yet I think it is likely that the best are made in solitude. They require some final refrigeration which I cannot give them dabbling always in warm soluble words. My method, nevertheless, has certain advantages over theirs. Neville is repelled by the grossness of Trumble. Louis, glancing, tripping with the high step of a disdainful crane, picks up words as if in sugar-tongs. It is true that his eyes—wild, laughing, yet desperate—express something that we have not gauged. There is about both Neville and Louis a precision, an exactitude that I admire and shall never possess. Now I begin to be aware that action is demanded. We approach a junction; at a junction I have to change. I have to board a train for Edinburgh. I cannot precisely lay fingers on this fact—it lodges loosely among my thoughts like a button, like a small coin. Here is the jolly old boy who collects tickets. I had one—I had one certainly. But it does not matter. Either I shall find it, or I shall not find it. I examine my note-case. I look in all my pockets. These are the things that for ever interrupt the process upon which I am eternally engaged of finding some perfect phrase that fits this very moment exactly."

"Bernard has gone," said Neville, "without a ticket. He has escaped us, making a phrase, waving his hand. He talked as easily to the horse-breeder or to the plumber as to us. The plumber accepted him with devotion. 'If he had a son like that,' he was thinking, 'he would manage to send him to Oxford.' But what did Bernard feel for the plumber? Did he not only wish to continue the sequence of the story which he never stops telling himself? He began it when he rolled his bread into pellets as a child. One pellet was a man, one was a woman. We are all pellets. We are all phrases in Bernard's story, things he writes down in his notebook under A or under B. He tells our story with extraordinary understanding, except of what we most feel. For he does not need us. He is never at our mercy. There he is, waving his arms on the platform. The train has gone without him. He has missed his connection. He has lost his ticket. But that does not matter. He will talk to the barmaid about the nature of human destiny. We are off; he has forgotten us already; we pass out of his view; we go on, filled with lingering sensations, half bitter, half sweet, for he is somehow to be pitied breasting the world with half-finished phrases, having lost his ticket; he is also to be loved.

"Now I pretend again to read. I raise my book, till it almost covers my eyes. But I cannot read in the presence of horse-dealers and plumbers. I have no power of ingratiating myself. I do not admire that man; he does not admire me. Let me at least be honest. Let me denounce this piffling, trifling, self-satisfied world; these horse-hair seats; these coloured photographs of piers and parades. I could shriek aloud at the smug self-satisfaction, at the mediocrity of this world, which breeds horse-dealers with coral ornaments hanging from their watch-chains. There is that in me which will consume them entirely. My laughter shall make them twist in their seats; shall drive them howling before me. No; they are immortal. They triumph. They will make it impossible for me always to read Catullus in a third-class railway carriage. They will drive me in October to take refuge in one of the universities, where I shall become a don; and go with schoolmasters to Greece; and lecture on the ruins of the Parthenon. It would be better to breed horses and live in one of those red villas than to run in and out of the skulls of Sophocles and Euripides like a maggot, with a high-minded wife, one of those University women. That, however, will be my fate. I shall suffer. I am already at eighteen capable of such contempt that horse-breeders hate me. That is my triumph; I do not compromise. I am not timid; I have no accent. I do not finick about fearing what people think of 'my father a banker at Brisbane' like Louis.

"Now we draw near the centre of the civilised world. There are the familiar gasometers. There are the public gardens intersected by asphalt paths. There are the lovers lying shamelessly mouth to mouth on the burnt grass. Percival is now almost in Scotland; his train draws through the red moors; he sees the long line of the border hills and the Roman wall. He reads a detective novel, yet understands everything.

"The train slows and lengthens, as we approach London, the centre, and my heart draws out too, in fear, in exultation. I am about to meet—what? What extraordinary adventure waits me, among these mail vans, these porters, these swarms of people calling taxis? I feel insignificant, lost, but exultant. With a soft shock we stop. I will let the others get out before me. I will sit still one moment before I emerge into that chaos, that tumult. I will not anticipate what is to come. The huge uproar is in my ears. It sounds and resounds under this glass roof like the surge of a sea. We are cast down on the platform with our handbags. We are whirled asunder. My sense of self almost perishes; my contempt. I become drawn in, tossed down, thrown sky-high. I step out on to the platform, grasping tightly all that I possess— one bag."

he sun rose. Bars of yellow and green fell on the shore gilding the ribs of the eaten-out boat and making the sea-holly and its mailed leaves gleam blue as steel. Light almost pierced the thin swift waves as they raced fan-shaped over the beach. The girl who had shaken her head and made all the jewels, the topaz, the aquamarine, the water-coloured jewels with sparks of fire in them dance, now bared her brows and with wide-opened eyes drove a straight pathway over the waves. Their quivering mackerel sparkling was darkened; they massed themselves; their green hollows deepened and darkened and might be traversed by shoals of wandering fish. As they splashed and drew back they left a black rim of twigs and cork on the shore and straws and sticks of wood as if some light shallop had foundered and burst its sides and the sailor had swum to land and bounded up the cliff and left his frail cargo to be washed ashore.

In the garden the birds that had sung erratically and spasmodically in the dawn on that tree, on that bush, now sang together in chorus, shrill and sharp; now together, as if conscious of companionship, now alone as if to the pale blue sky. They swerved, all in one flight, when the black cat moved among the bushes, when the cook threw cinders on the ash heap and startled them. Fear was in their song, and apprehension of pain, and joy to be snatched quickly now at this instant. Also they sang emulously in the clear morning air, swerving high over the elm tree, singing together as they chased each other, escaping, pursuing, pecking each other as they turned high in the air. And then tiring of pursuit and flight, lovelily they came descending, delicately declining, dropped down and sat silent on the tree, on the wall, with their bright eyes glancing, and their heads turned this way, that way; aware, awake; intensely conscious of one thing, one object in particular.

Perhaps it was a snail shell, rising in the grass like a grey cathedral, a swelling building burnt with dark rings and shadowed green by the grass. Or perhaps they saw the splendour of the flowers making a light of flowing purple over the beds, through which dark tunnels of purple shade were driven between the stalks. Or they fixed their gaze on the small bright apple leaves, dancing yet withheld, stiffly sparkling among the pink-tipped blossoms. Or they saw the rain drop on the hedge, pendent but not falling, with a whole house bent in it, and towering elms; or, gazing straight at the sun, their eyes became gold beads.

Now glancing this side, that side, they looked deeper, beneath the flowers, down the dark avenues into the unlit world where the leaf rots and the flower has fallen. Then one of them, beautifully darting, accurately alighting, spiked the soft, monstrous body of the defenceless worm, pecked again and yet again, and left it to fester. Down there among the roots where the flowers decayed, gusts of dead smells were wafted; drops formed on the bloated sides of swollen things. The skin of rotten fruit broke, and matter oozed too thick to run. Yellow excretions were exuded by slugs and now and again an amorphous body with a head at either end swayed slowly from side to side. The gold-eyed birds darting in between the leaves observed that purulence, that wetness, quizzically. Now and then they plunged the tips of their beaks savagely into the sticky mixture.

Now, too, the rising sun came in at the window, touching the red-edged curtain and began to bring out circles and lines. Now in the growing light its whiteness settled in the plate; the blade condensed its gleam. Chairs and cupboards loomed behind so that though each was separate they seemed inextricably involved. The looking-glass whitened its pool upon the wall. The real flower on the window-sill was attended by a phantom flower. Yet the phantom was part of the flower for when a bud broke free, the paler flower in the glass opened a bud too.

The wind rose. The waves drummed on the shore, like tur-
baned warriors, like turbaned men with poisoned assegais who,
whirling their arms on high, advance upon the feeding flocks,
the white sheep.

"The complexity of things becomes more close," said Bernard,
"here at college, where the stir and pressure of life are so
extreme, where the excitement of mere living becomes daily
more urgent. Every hour something new is unburied in the
great bran pie. What am I? I ask. This? No, I am that. Especially
now, when I have left a room, and people talking, and the stone
flags ring out with my solitary footsteps, and I behold the moon
rising, sublimely, indifferently, over the ancient chapel—then it
becomes clear that I am not one and simple, but complex and
many. Bernard in public, bubbles; in private, is secretive. That
is what they do not understand, for they are now undoubtedly
discussing me, saying I escape them, am evasive. They do not
understand that I have to effect different transitions; have to
cover the entrances and exits of several different men who alternately act their parts as Bernard. I am abnormally aware of circumstances. I can never read a book in a railway carriage without asking, Is he a builder? Is she unhappy? I was aware today
acutely that poor Simes, with his pimple was feeling, how bitterly, that his chance of making a good impression upon Billy
Jackson was remote. Feeling this painfully I invited him to dinner with ardour. This he will attribute to an admiration which
is not mine. That is true. But 'joined to the sensibility of a
woman' (I am here quoting my own biographer) 'Bernard pos-
sessed the logical sobriety of a man.' Now people who make a
single impression, and that, in the main, a good one (for there
seems to be a virtue in simplicity) are those who keep their equi-
librium in mid-stream. (I instantly see fish with their noses one
way, the stream rushing past another.) Canon, Lycett, Peters,
Hawkins, Larpent, Neville—all fish in mid-stream. But *you* un-

derstand, *you,* my self, who always comes at a call (that would
be a harrowing experience to call and for no one to come; that
would make the midnight hollow, and explains the expression
of old men in clubs—they have given up calling for a self who
does not come) you understand that I am only superficially
represented by what I was saying tonight. Underneath, and, at
the moment when I am most disparate, I am also integrated. I
sympathise effusively; I also sit like a toad in a hole, receiving
with perfect coldness whatever comes. Very few of you who are
now discussing me have the double capacity to feel, to reason.
Lycett, you see, believes in running after hares; Hawkins has
spent a most industrious afternoon in the library. Peters has his
young lady at the circulating library. You are all engaged, involved, drawn in, and absolutely energised to the top of your
bent—all save Neville, whose mind is far too complex to
be roused by any single activity. I also am too complex. In my
case something remains floating, unattached.

"Now, as a proof of my susceptibility to atmosphere, here, as
I come into my room, and turn on the light, and see the sheet of
paper, the table, my gown lying negligently over the back of the
chair, I feel that I am that dashing yet reflective man, that bold
and deleterious figure, who, lightly throwing off his cloak, seizes
his pen and at once flings off the following letter to the girl with
whom he is passionately in love.

"Yes, all is propitious. I am now in the mood. I can write the
letter straight off which I have begun ever so many times. I have
just come in; I have flung down my hat and my stick; I am writing the first thing that comes into my head without troubling to
put the paper straight. It is going to be a brilliant sketch which,
she must think, was written without a pause, without an
erasure. Look how unformed the letters are—there is a careless
blot. All must be sacrificed to speed and carelessness. I will write
a quick, running, small hand, exaggerating the down stroke of
the 'y' and crossing the 't' thus—with a dash. The date shall be
only Tuesday, the 17th, and then a question mark. But also I

must give her the impression that though he—for this is not my-self—is writing in such an off-hand, such a slap-dash way, there is some subtle suggestion of intimacy and respect. I must allude to talks we have had together—bring back some remembered scene. But I must seem to her (this is very important) to be pass-ing from thing to thing with the greatest ease in the world. I shall pass from the service for the man who was drowned (I have a phrase for that) to Mrs. Moffat and her sayings (I have a note of them) and so to some reflections apparently casual but full of profundity (profound criticism is often written casually) about some book I have been reading, some out-of-the-way book. I want her to say as she brushes her hair or puts out the candle, 'Where did I read that? Oh, in Bernard's letter.' It is the speed, the hot, molten effect, the lava flow of sentence into sentence that I need. Who am I thinking of? Byron of course. I am, in some ways, like Byron. Perhaps a sip of Byron will help to put me in the vein. Let me read a page. No; this is dull; this is scrappy. This is rather too formal. Now I am getting the hang of it. Now I am getting his beat into my brain (the rhythm is the main thing in writing). Now, without pausing I will begin, on the very lilt of the stroke—

"Yet it falls flat. It peters out. I cannot get up steam enough to carry me over the transition. My true self breaks off from my assumed. And if I begin to rewrite it, she will feel, 'Bernard is posing as a literary man; Bernard is thinking of his biographer' (which is true). No, I will write the letter tomorrow directly after breakfast.

"Now let me fill my mind with imaginary pictures. Let me suppose that I am asked to stay at Restover, King's Laughton, Station Langley three miles. I arrive in the dusk. In the courtyard of this shabby but distinguished house there are two or three dogs, slinking, long legged. There are faded rugs in the hall; a military gentleman smokes a pipe as he paces the terrace. The note is of distinguished poverty and military connections. A hunter's hoof on the writing-table—a favourite horse. 'Do you ride?' 'Yes, sir, I love riding.' 'My daughter expects us in the drawing-room.' My heart pounds against my ribs. She is standing at a low table; she has been hunting; she munches sandwiches like a tomboy. I make a fairly good impression on the Colonel. I am not too clever, he thinks; I am not too raw. Also I play billiards. Then the nice maid who has been with the family thirty years comes in. The pattern on the plates is of Oriental long-tailed birds. Her mother's portrait in muslin hangs over the fireplace. I can sketch the surroundings up to a point with extraordinary ease. But can I make it work? Can I hear her voice —the precise tone with which, when we are alone, she says 'Bernard'? And then what next?

"The truth is that I need the stimulus of other people. Alone, over my dead fire, I tend to see the thin places in my own stories. The real novelist, the perfectly simple human being, could go on, indefinitely, imagining. He would not integrate, as I do. He would not have this devastating sense of grey ashes in a burnt-out grate. Some blind flaps in my eyes. Everything becomes impervious. I cease to invent.

"Let me recollect. It has been on the whole a good day. The drop that forms on the roof of the soul in the evening is round, many-coloured. There was the morning, fine; there was the afternoon, walking. I like views of spires across grey fields. I like glimpses between people's shoulders. Things kept popping into my head. I was imaginative, subtle. After dinner, I was dramatic. I put into concrete form many things that we had dimly observed about our common friends. I made my transitions easily. But now let me ask myself the final question, as I sit over this grey fire, with its naked promontories of black coal, which of these people am I? It depends so much upon the room. When I say to myself, 'Bernard,' who comes? A faithful, sardonic man, disillusioned, but not embittered. A man of no particular age or calling. Myself, merely. It is he who now takes the poker and rattles the cinders so that they fall in showers through the grate. 'Lord,' he says to himself, watching them fall, 'what a pother!' and then he adds, lugubriously, but with some sense of consolation, 'Mrs. Moffat will come and sweep it all up—' I fancy I shall often repeat to myself that phrase, as I rattle and bang through life, hitting first this side of the carriage then the other, 'Oh, yes, Mrs. Moffat will come and sweep it all up.' And so to bed."

"In a world which contains the present moment," said Neville, "why discriminate? Nothing should be named lest by so doing we change it. Let it exist, this bank, this beauty, and I, for one instant, steeped in pleasure. The sun is hot. I see the river. I see trees specked and burnt in the autumn sunlight. Boats float past, through the red, through the green. Far away a bell tolls, but not for death. There are bells that ring for life. A leaf falls, from joy. Oh, I am in love with life! Look how the willow shoots its fine sprays into the air! Look how through them a boat passes, filled with indolent, with unconscious, with powerful young men. They are listening to the gramophone; they are eating fruit out of paper bags. They are tossing the skins of bananas, which then sink eel-like, into the river. All they do is beautiful. There are cruets behind them and ornaments; their rooms are full of oars and oleographs but they have turned all to beauty. That boat passes under the bridge. Another comes. Then another. That is Percival, lounging on the cushions, monolithic, in giant repose. No, it is only one of his satellites, imitating his monolithic, his giant repose. He alone is unconscious of their tricks, and when he catches them at it he buffets them good-humouredly with a blow of his paw. They, too, have passed under the bridge through 'the fountains of the pendent trees,' through its fine strokes of yellow and plum colour. The breeze stirs; the curtain quivers; I see behind the leaves the grave, yet eternally joyous buildings, which seem porous, not gravid; light, though set so immemorially in the ancient turf. Now begins to rise in me the familiar rhythm; words that have lain dormant now lift, now toss their crests, and fall and rise, and fall and rise again. I am a poet, yes. Surely I am a great poet. Boats and youth passing and distant trees, 'the falling fountains of the pendent trees.' I see it all. I feel it all. I am inspired. My eyes fill with tears. Yet even as I feel this, I lash my frenzy higher and higher. It foams. It becomes artificial, insincere. Words and words and words, how they gallop—how they lash their long manes and tails, but for some fault in me I cannot give myself to their backs; I cannot fly with them, scattering women and string bags. There is some flaw in me—some fatal hesitancy, which, if I pass it over, turns to foam and falsity. Yet it is incredible that I should not be a great poet. What did I write last night if it was not poetry? Am I too fast, too facile? I do not know. I do not know myself sometimes, or how to measure and name and count out the grains that make me what I am.

"Something now leaves me; something goes from me to meet that figure who is coming, and assures me that I know him before I see who it is. How curiously one is changed by the addition, even at a distance, of a friend. How useful an office one's friends perform when they recall us. Yet how painful to be recalled, to be mitigated, to have one's self adulterated, mixed up, become part of another. As he approaches I become not myself but Neville mixed with somebody—with whom?—with Bernard? Yes, it is Bernard, and it is to Bernard that I shall put the question, Who am I?"

"How strange," said Bernard, "the willow looks seen together. I was Byron, and the tree was Byron's tree, lachrymose, down-showering, lamenting. Now that we look at the tree together, it has a combed look, each branch distinct, and I will tell you what I feel, under the compulsion of your clarity.

"I feel your disapproval, I feel your force. I become, with you, an untidy, an impulsive human being whose bandanna handkerchief is for ever stained with the grease of crumpets. Yes, I hold Gray's *Elegy* in one hand; with the other I scoop out the bottom crumpet, that has absorbed all the butter and sticks to the bottom of the plate. This offends you; I feel your distress acutely. Inspired by it and anxious to regain your good opinion,

I proceed to tell you how I have just pulled Percival out of bed; I describe his slippers, his table, his guttered candle; his surly and complaining accents as I pull the blanket off his feet; he burrowing, like some vast cocoon meanwhile. I describe all this in such a way that, centred as you are upon some private sorrow (for a hooded shape presides over our encounter) you give way, you laugh and delight in me. My charm and flow of language, unexpected and spontaneous as it is delights me too. I am astonished, as I draw the veil off things with words, how much, how infinitely more than I can say I have observed. More and more bubbles into my mind as I talk, images and images. This, I say to myself, is what I need; why, I ask, can I not finish the letter that I am writing? For my room is always scattered with unfinished letters. I begin to suspect, when I am with you, that I am among the most gifted of men. I am filled with the delight of youth, with potency, with the sense of what is to come. Blundering, but fervid, I see myself buzzing round flowers, humming down scarlet cups, making blue funnels resound with my prodigious booming. How richly I shall enjoy my youth (you make me feel). And London. And freedom. But stop. You are not listening. You are making some protest, as you slide with an inexpressibly familiar gesture, your hand along your knee. By such signs we diagnose our friends' diseases. 'Do not, in your affluence and plenty,' you seem to say, 'pass me by.' 'Stop,' you say. 'Ask me what I suffer.'

"Let me then create you. (You have done as much for me.) You lie on this hot bank, in this lovely, this fading, this still bright October day, watching boat after boat float through the combed-out twigs of the willow tree. And you wish to be a poet; and you wish to be a lover. But the splendid clarity of your intelligence, and the remorseless honesty of your intellect (these Latin words I owe you; these qualities of yours make me shift a little uneasily and see the faded patches, the thin strands in my own equipment) bring you to a halt. You indulge in no mystifications. You do not fog yourself with rosy clouds, or yellow.

"Am I right? Have I read the little gesture of your left hand correctly? If so, give me your poems; hand over the sheets you wrote last night in such a fervour of inspiration that you now feel a little sheepish. For you distrust inspiration, yours or mine. Let us go back together, over the bridge, under the elm trees, to my room, where, with walls round us and red serge curtains drawn, we can shut out these distracting voices, scents and savours of lime trees, and other lives; these pert shop-girls, disdainfully tripping, these shuffling, heavy-laden old women; these furtive glimpses of some vague and vanishing figure—it might be Jinny, it might be Susan, or was that Rhoda disappearing down the avenue? Again, from some slight twitch I guess your feeling; I have escaped you; I have gone buzzing like a swarm of bees, endlessly vagrant, with none of your power of fixing remorselessly upon a single object. But I will return."

"When there are buildings like these," said Neville, "I cannot endure that there should be shop-girls. Their titter, their gossip, offends me; breaks into my stillness, and nudges me, in moments of purest exultation, to remember our degradation.

"But now we have regained our territory after that brief brush with the bicycles and the lime scent and the vanishing figures in the distracted street. Here we are masters of tranquillity and order; inheritors of proud tradition. The lights are beginning to make yellow slits across the square. Mists from the river are filling these ancient spaces. They cling, gently, to the hoary stone. The leaves now are thick in country lanes, sheep cough in the damp fields; but here in your room we are dry. We talk privately. The fire leaps and sinks, making some knob bright.

"You have been reading Byron. You have been marking the passages that seem to approve of your own character. I find marks against all those sentences which seem to express a sardonic yet passionate nature; a moth-like impetuosity dashing itself against hard glass. You thought, as you drew your pencil there, 'I too throw off my cloak like that. I too snap my fingers in the face of destiny.' Yet Byron never made tea as you do, who fill the pot so that when you put the lid on the tea spills over. There is a brown pool on the table—it is running among your books and papers. Now you mop it up, clumsily, with your pocket-handkerchief. You then stuff your handkerchief back into your pocket—that is not Byron; that is you; that is so essentially you that if I think of you in twenty years' time, when we are both famous, gouty and intolerable, it will be by that scene: and if you are dead, I shall weep. Once you were Tolstoi's young man; now you are Byron's young man; perhaps you will be Meredith's young man; then you will visit Paris in the Easter vacation and come back wearing a black tie, some detestable Frenchman whom nobody has ever heard of. Then I shall drop you.

"I am one person—myself. I do not impersonate Catullus, whom I adore. I am the most slavish of students, with here a dictionary; there a notebook in which I enter curious uses of the past participle. But one cannot go on for ever cutting these ancient inscriptions clearer with a knife. Shall I always draw the red serge curtain close and see my book, laid like a block of marble, pale under the lamp? That would be a glorious life, to addict oneself to perfection; to follow the curve of the sentence wherever it might lead, into deserts, under drifts of sand, regardless of lures, of seductions; to be poor always and unkempt; to be ridiculous in Piccadilly.

"But I am too nervous to end my sentence properly. I speak quickly, as I pace up and down, to conceal my agitation. I hate your greasy handkerchiefs—you will stain your copy of *Don Juan*. You are not listening to me. You are making phrases about Byron. And while you gesticulate, with your cloak, your cane, I am trying to expose a secret told to nobody yet; I am asking you (as I stand with my back to you) to take my life in your hands and tell me whether I am doomed always to cause repulsion in those I love?

"I stand with my back to you fidgeting. No, my hands are now perfectly still. Precisely, opening a space in the bookcase, I insert *Don Juan*; there. I would rather be loved, I would rather be famous than follow perfection through the sand. But am I doomed to cause disgust? Am I a poet? Take it. The desire which is loaded behind my lips, cold as lead, fell as a bullet, the thing I aim at shop-girls, women, the pretence, the vulgarity of life (because I love it) shoots at you as I throw—catch it—my poem."

"He has shot like an arrow from the room," said Bernard. "He has left me his poem. O friendship, I too will press flowers between the pages of Shakespeare's sonnets! O friendship, how piercing are your darts—there, there, again there. He looked at me, turning to face me; he gave me his poem. All mists curl off the roof of my being. That confidence I shall keep to my dying day. Like a long wave, like a roll of heavy waters, he went over me, his devastating presence—dragging me open, laying bare the pebbles on the shore of my soul. It was humiliating; I was turned to small stones. All semblances were rolled up. 'You are not Byron; you are your self.' To be contracted by another person into a single being—how strange.

"How strange to feel the line that is spun from us lengthening its fine filament across the misty spaces of the intervening world. He is gone; I stand here, holding his poem. Between us is this line. But now, how comfortable, how reassuring to feel that alien presence removed, that scrutiny darkened and hooded over! How grateful to draw the blinds, and admit no other presence; to feel returning from the dark corners in which they took refuge, those shabby inmates, those familiars, whom, with his superior force, he drove into hiding. The mocking, the observant spirits who, even in the crisis and stab of the moment watched on my behalf, now come flocking home again. With their addition, I am Bernard; I am Byron; I am this, that and the other. They darken the air and enrich me, as of old with their antics, their comments, and cloud the fine simplicity of my moment of emotion. For I am more selves than Neville thinks. We are not simple as our friends would have us to meet their needs. Yet love is simple.

"Now they have returned, my inmates, my familiars. Now the stab, the rent in my defences that Neville made with his astonishing fine rapier is repaired. I am almost whole now; and see how jubilant I am, bringing into play all that Neville ignores in me. I feel, as I look from the window, parting the curtains, 'That would give him no pleasure; but it rejoices me.' (We use our friends to measure our own stature.) My scope embraces what Neville never reaches. They are shouting hunting-songs over the way. They are celebrating some run with the beagles. The little boys in caps who always turned at the same moment when the brake went round the corner are clapping each other on the shoulder and boasting. But Neville, delicately avoiding interference, stealthily, like a conspirator, hastens back to his room. I see him sunk in his low chair gazing at the fire which has assumed for the moment an architectural solidity. If life, he thinks, could wear that permanence, if life could have that order —for above all he desires order, and detests my Byronic untidiness; and so draws his curtain; and bolts his door. His eyes (for he is in love; the sinister figure of love presided at our encounter) fill with longing; fill with tears. He snatches the poker and with one blow destroys that momentary appearance of solidity in the burning coals. All changes. And youth and love. The boat has floated through the arch of the willows and is now under the bridge. Percival, Tony, Archie, or another, will go to India. We shall not meet again. Then he stretches his hand for his copybook—a neat volume bound in mottled paper—and writes feverishly long lines of poetry, in the manner of whomever he admires most at the moment.

"But I want to linger; to lean from the window; to listen. There again comes that rollicking chorus. They are now smashing china—that also is the convention. The chorus, like a torrent jumping rocks, brutally assaulting old trees, pours with splendid abandonment headlong over precipices. On they roll; on they gallop; after hounds, after footballs; they pump up and down attached to oars like sacks of flour. All divisions are merged—they act like one man. The gusty October wind blows the uproar in bursts of sound and silence across the court. Now again they are smashing the china—that is the convention. An old, unsteady woman carrying a bag trots home under the fire-red windows. She is half afraid that they will fall on her and tumble her into the gutter. Yet she pauses as if to warm her knobbed, her rheumaticky hands at the bonfire which flares away with streams of sparks and bits of blown paper. The old woman pauses against the lit window. A contrast. That I see and Neville does not see; that I feel and Neville does not feel. Hence he will reach perfection, and I shall fail and shall leave nothing behind me but imperfect phrases littered with sand.

"I think of Louis now. What malevolent yet searching light would Louis throw upon this dwindling autumn evening, upon this china smashing and trolling of hunting-songs, upon Neville, Byron and our life here? His thin lips are somewhat pursed; his cheeks are pale; he pores in an office over some obscure commercial document. 'My father, a banker at Brisbane'—being ashamed of him he always talks of him—failed. So he sits in an office, Louis the best scholar in the school. But I seeking contrasts often feel his eye on us, his laughing eye, his wild eye, adding us up like insignificant items in some grand total which he is for ever pursuing, in his office. And one day taking a fine pen and dipping it in red ink, the addition will be complete; our total will be known; but it will not be enough.

"Bang! They have thrown a chair now against the wall. We are damned then. My case is dubious too. Am I not indulging in unwarranted emotions? Yes, as I lean out of the window and drop my cigarette so that it twirls lightly to the ground I feel Louis watching even my cigarette. And Louis says, 'That means something. But what?' "

"People go on passing," said Louis. "They pass the window of this eating-shop incessantly. Motor-cars, vans, motor-omnibuses;

and again motor-omnibuses, vans, motor-cars—they pass the window. In the background I perceive shops and houses; also the grey spires of a city church. In the foreground are glass shelves set with plates of buns and ham sandwiches. All is somewhat obscured by steam from a tea-urn. A meaty, vapourish smell of beef and mutton, sausages and mash, hangs down like a damp net in the middle of the eating-house. I prop my book against a bottle of Worcester sauce and try to look like the rest.

"Yet I cannot. (They go on passing, they go on passing in disorderly procession.) I cannot read my book, or order my beef, with conviction. I repeat, 'I am an average Englishman; I am an average clerk,' yet I look at the little men at the next table to be sure that I do what they do. Supple-faced, with rippling skins, that are always twitching with the multiplicity of their sensations, prehensile like monkeys, greased to this particular moment, they are discussing with all the right gestures the sale of a piano. It blocks up the hall; so he would take a tenner. People go on passing; they go on passing against the spires of the church and the plates of ham sandwiches. The streamers of my consciousness waver out and are perpetually torn and distressed by their disorder. I cannot therefore concentrate on my dinner. 'I would take a tenner. The case is handsome; but it blocks up the hall.' They dive and plunge like guillemots whose feathers are slippery with oil. All excesses beyond that norm are vanity. That is the mean; that is the average. Meanwhile the hats bob up and down; the door perpetually shuts and opens. I am conscious of flux, of disorder; of annihilation and despair. If this is all, this is worthless. Yet I feel, too, the rhythm of the eating-house. It is like a waltz tune, eddying in and out, round and round. The waitresses, balancing trays, swing in and out, round and round, dealing plates of greens, of apricot and custard, dealing them at the right time, to the right customers. The average men, including her rhythm in their rhythm ('I would take a tenner; for it blocks up the hall') take their greens, take their apricots and custard. Where then is the break in this continuity? What the fissure through which one sees disaster? The circle is unbroken; the harmony complete. Here is the central rhythm; here the common mainspring. I watch it expand, contract; and then expand again. Yet I am not included. If I speak, imitating their accent, they prick their ears, waiting for me to speak again, in order that they may place me—if I come from Canada or Australia, I, who desire above all things to be taken to the arms with love, an alien, external. I, who would wish to feel close over me the protective waves of the ordinary, catch with the tail of my eye some far horizon; am aware of hats bobbing up and down in perpetual disorder. To me is addressed the plaint of the wandering and distracted spirit—(a woman with bad teeth falters at the counter). Bring us back to the fold, we who pass so disjectedly, bobbing up and down, past windows with plates of ham sandwiches in the foreground. Yes; I will reduce you to order.

"I will read in the book that is propped against the bottle of Worcester sauce. It contains some forged rings, some perfect statements, a few words, but poetry. You, all of you, ignore it. What the dead poet said, you have forgotten. And I cannot translate it to you so that its binding power ropes you in, and makes it clear to you that you are aimless; and the rhythm is cheap and worthless; and so remove that degradation which, if you are unaware of your aimlessness, pervades you, making you senile, even while you are young. To translate that poem so that it is easily read is to be my endeavour. I, the companion of Plato, of Virgil, will knock at the grained oak door. I oppose to what is passing this ramrod of beaten steel. I will not submit to this aimless passing of billycock hats and Homburg hats and all the plumed and variegated head-dresses of women. (Susan, whom I respect, would wear a plain straw hat on a summer's day.) And the grinding and the steam that runs in unequal drops down the window pane; and the stopping and the starting with a jerk of motor-omnibuses; and the hesitations at counters; and the words that trail drearily without human meaning; I will reduce you to order.

"My roots go down through veins ot lead and silver, through damp, marshy places that exhale odours to a knot made of oak roots bound together in the centre. Sealed and blind, with each stopping my ears, I have yet heard rumours of wars; and the nightingale; have felt the hurrying of many troops of men flocking hither and thither in quest of civilisation like flocks of birds migrating seeking the summer; I have seen women carrying red pitchers to the banks of the Nile. I woke in a garden, with a blow on the nape of my neck, a hot kiss, Jinny's; remembering all this as one remembers confused cries and toppling pillars and shafts of red and black in some nocturnal conflagration. I am for ever sleeping and waking. Now I sleep; now I wake. I see the gleaming tea-urn; the glass cases full of pale-yellow sandwiches; the men in round coats perched on stools at the counter; and also behind them, eternity. It is a stigma burnt on my quivering flesh by a cowled man with a red-hot iron. I see this eating-shop against the packed and fluttering birds' wings, many feathered, folded, of the past. Hence my pursed lips, my sickly pallor; my distasteful and uninviting aspect as I turn my face with hatred and bitterness upon Bernard and Neville, who saunter under yew trees; who inherit arm-chairs; and draw their curtains close, so that lamplight falls on their books.

"Susan, I respect; because she sits stitching. She sews under a quiet lamp in a house where the corn sighs close to the window and gives me safety. For I am the weakest, the youngest of them all. I am a child looking at his feet and the little runnels that the stream has made in the gravel. That is a snail, I say, that is a leaf. I delight in the snails; I delight in the leaf. I am always the youngest, the most innocent, the most trustful. You are all protected. I am naked. When the waitress with the plaited wreaths of hair swings past, she deals you your apricots and custard unhesitatingly, like a sister. You are her brothers. But when I get up, brushing the crumbs from my waistcoat, I slip too large a tip, a shilling, under the edge of my plate, so that she may not find it till I am gone, and her scorn, as she picks it up with laughter, may not strike on me till I am past the swing-doors."

"Now the wind lifts the blind," said Susan. "Jars, bowls, matting and the shabby arm-chair with the hole in it are now become distinct. The usual faded ribbons sprinkle the wall-paper. The bird chorus is over, only one bird now sings close to the bedroom window. I will pull on my stockings and go quietly past the bedroom doors, and down through the kitchen, out through the garden past the greenhouse into the field. It is still early morning. The mist is on the marshes. The day is stark and stiff as a linen shroud. But it will soften; it will warm. At this hour, this still early hour, I think I am the field, I am the barn, I am the trees; mine are the flocks of birds, and this young hare who leaps, at the last moment when I step almost on him. Mine is the heron that stretches its vast wings lazily; and the cow that creaks as it pushes one foot before another, munching; and the wild, swooping swallow; and the faint red in the sky, and the green when the red fades; the silence and the bell; the call of the man fetching cart-horses from the fields—all are mine.

"I cannot be divided, or kept apart. I was sent to school; I was sent to Switzerland to finish my education. I hate linoleum; I hate fir trees and mountains. Let me now fling myself on this flat ground under a pale sky where the clouds pace slowly. The cart grows gradually larger as it comes along the road. The sheep gather in the middle of the field. The birds gather in the middle of the road—they need not fly yet. The wood smoke rises. The starkness of the dawn is going out of it. Now the day stirs. Colour returns. The day waves yellow with all its crops. The earth hangs heavy beneath me.

"But who am I, who lean on this gate and watch my setter nose in a circle? I think sometimes (I am not twenty yet) I am not a woman, but the light that falls on this gate, on this ground. I am the seasons, I think sometimes, January, May, November; the mud, the mist, the dawn. I cannot be tossed about, or float gently, or mix with other people. Yet now leaning here, till the gate prints my arm, I feel the weight that has formed itself in my side. Something has formed, at school, in Switzerland, some hard thing. Not sighs and laughter; not circling and ingenious phrases; not Rhoda's strange communications when she looks past us, over our shoulders; not Jinny's pirouetting, all of a piece, limbs and body. What I give is fell. I cannot float gently, mixing with other people. I like best the stare of shepherds met in the road; the stare of gipsy women beside a cart in a ditch suckling their children as I shall suckle my children. For soon in the hot midday when the bees hum round the hollyhocks my lover will come. He will stand under the cedar tree. To his one word I shall answer my one word. What has formed in me I shall give him. I shall have children; I shall have maids in aprons; men with pitchforks; a kitchen where they bring the ailing lambs to warm in baskets, where the hams hang and the onions glisten. I shall be like my mother, silent in a blue apron locking up the cupboards.

"Now I am hungry. I will call my setter. I think of crusts and bread and butter and white plates in a sunny room. I will go back across the fields. I will walk along this grass path with strong, even strides, now swerving to avoid the puddle, now leaping lightly to a clump. Beads of wet form on my rough skirt; my shoes become supple and dark. The stiffness has gone from the day; it is shaded with grey, green and umber. The birds no longer settle on the high road.

"I return, like a cat or fox returning, whose fur is grey with rime, whose pads are hardened by the coarse earth. I push through the cabbages, making their leaves squeak and their drops spill. I sit waiting for my father's footsteps as he shuffles down the passage pinching some herb between his fingers. I pour out cup after cup while the unopened flowers hold themselves erect on the table among the pots of jam, the loaves and the butter. We are silent.

"I go then to the cupboard, and take the damp bags of rich sultanas; I lift the heavy flour on to the clean scrubbed kitchen table. I knead; I stretch; I pull, plunging my hands in the warm inwards of the dough. I let the cold water stream fanwise through my fingers. The fire roars; the flies buzz in a circle. All my currants and rices, the silver bags and the blue bags, are locked again in the cupboard. The meat is stood in the oven; the bread rises in a soft dome under the clean towel. I walk in the afternoon down to the river. All the world is breeding. The flies are going from grass to grass. The flowers are thick with pollen. The swans ride the stream in order. The clouds warm now, sun-spotted, sweep over the hills, leaving gold in the water, and gold on the necks of the swans. Pushing one foot before the other, the cows munch their way across the field. I feel through the grass for the white-domed mushroom; and break its stalk and pick the purple orchid that grows beside it and lay the orchid by the mushroom with the earth at its root, and so home to make the kettle boil for my father among the just reddened roses on the tea-table.

"But evening comes and the lamps are lit. And when evening comes and the lamps are lit they make a yellow fire in the ivy. I sit with my sewing by the table. I think of Jinny; of Rhoda; and hear the rattle of wheels on the pavement as the farm horses plod home; I hear traffic roaring in the evening wind. I look at the quivering leaves in the dark garden and think, 'They dance in London. Jinny kisses Louis.' "

"How strange," said Jinny, "that people should sleep, that people should put out the lights and go upstairs. They have taken off their dresses, they have put on white night-gowns. There are no lights in any of these houses. There is a line of chimney-pots against the sky; and a street lamp or two burning, as lamps burn when nobody needs them. The only people in the streets are poor people hurrying. There is no one coming or going in this street; the day is over. A few policemen stand at the corners. Yet night is beginning. I feel myself shining in the dark. Silk is on my knee. My silk legs rub smoothly together. The stones of a necklace lie cold on my throat. My feet feel the pinch of shoes. I sit bolt upright so that my hair may not touch the back of the seat. I am arrayed, I am prepared. This is the momentary pause; the dark moment. The fiddlers have lifted their bows.

"Now the car slides to a stop. A strip of pavement is lighted. The door is opening and shutting. People are arriving; they do not speak; they hasten in. There is the swishing sound of cloaks falling in the hall. This is the prelude, this is the beginning. I glance, I peep, I powder. All is exact, prepared. My hair is swept in one curve. My lips are precisely red. I am ready now to join men and women on the stairs, my peers. I pass them, exposed to their gaze, as they are to mine. Like lightning we look but do not soften or show signs of recognition. Our bodies communicate. This is my calling. This is my world. All is decided and ready; the servants, standing here, and again here, take my name, my fresh, my unknown name, and toss it before me. I enter.

"Here are gilt chairs in the empty, the expectant rooms, and flowers, stiller, statelier, than flowers that grow, spread green, spread white, against the walls. And on one small table is one bound book. This is what I have dreamt; this is what I have foretold. I am native here. I tread naturally on thick carpets. I slide easily on smooth-polished floors. I now begin to unfurl, in this scent, in this radiance, as a fern when its curled leaves unfurl. I stop. I take stock of this world. I look among the groups of unknown people. Among the lustrous green, pink, pearl-grey women stand upright the bodies of men. They are black and white; they are grooved beneath their clothes with deep rills. I feel again the reflection in the window of the tunnel; it moves. The black-and-white figures of unknown men look at me as I lean forward; as I turn aside to look at a picture, they turn too. Their hands go fluttering to their ties. They touch their waistcoats, their pocket-handkerchiefs. They are very young. They are anxious to make a good impression. I feel a thousand capacities spring up in me. I am arch, gay, languid, melancholy by turns. I am rooted, but I flow. All gold, flowing that way, I say to this one, 'Come.' Rippling black, I say to that one, 'No.' One breaks off from his station under the glass cabinet. He approaches. He makes towards me. This is the most exciting moment I have ever known. I flutter. I ripple. I stream like a plant in the river, flowing this way, flowing that way, but rooted, so that he may come to me. 'Come,' I say, 'come.' Pale, with dark hair the one who is coming is melancholy, romantic. And I am arch and fluent and capricious; for he is melancholy, he is romantic. He is here; he stands at my side.

"Now with a little jerk, like a limpet broken from a rock, I am broken off: I fall with him; I am carried off. We yield to this slow flood. We go in and out of this hesitating music. Rocks break the current of the dance; it jars, it shivers. In and out, we are swept now into this large figure; it holds us together; we cannot step outside its sinuous, its hesitating, its abrupt, its perfectly encircling walls. Our bodies, his hard, mine flowing, are pressed together within its body; it holds us together; and then lengthening out, in smooth, in sinuous folds, rolls us between it, on and on. Suddenly the music breaks. My blood runs on but my body stands still. The room reels past my eyes. It stops.

"Come then, let us wander whirling to the gilt chairs. The body is stronger than I thought. I am dizzier than I supposed. I do not care for anything in this world. I do not care for anybody save this man whose name I do not know. Are we not acceptable, moon? Are we not lovely sitting together here, I in my satin; he in black and white? My peers may look at me now. I look straight back at you, men and women. I am one of you. This is my world. Now I take this thin-stemmed glass and sip. Wine has a drastic, an astringent taste. I cannot help wincing as I drink. Scent and flowers, radiance and heat, are distilled here to a fiery, to a yellow liquid. Just behind my shoulder-blades some dry thing, wide-eyed, gently closes, gradually lulls itself to sleep. This is rapture; this is relief. The bar at the back of my throat lowers itself. Words crowd and cluster and push forth one on top of another. It does not matter which. They jostle and mount on each other's shoulders. The single and the solitary mate, tumble and become many. It does not matter what I say. Crowding, like a fluttering bird, one sentence crosses the empty space between us. It settles on his lips. I fill my glass again. I drink. The veils drop between us. I am admitted to the warmth and privacy of another soul. We are together, high up, on some Alpine pass. He stands melancholy on the crest of the road. I stoop. I pick a blue flower and fix it, standing on tiptoe to reach him, in his coat. There! That is my moment of ecstasy. Now it is over.

"Now slackness and indifference invade us. Other people brush past. We have lost consciousness of our bodies uniting under the table. I also like fair-haired men with blue eyes. The door opens. The door goes on opening. Now I think, next time it opens the whole of my life will be changed. Who comes? But it is only a servant, bringing glasses. That is an old man—I should be a child with him. That is a great lady—with her I should dissemble. There are girls of my own age, for whom I feel the drawn swords of an honourable antagonism. For these are my peers. I am a native of this world. Here is my risk, here is my adventure. The door opens. Oh, come, I say to this one, rippling gold from head to heels. 'Come,' and he comes towards me."

"I shall edge behind them," said Rhoda, "as if I saw some one I know. But I know no one. I shall twitch the curtain and look at the moon. Draughts of oblivion shall quench my agitation. The door opens; the tiger leaps. The door opens; terror rushes in; terror upon terror, pursuing me. Let me visit furtively the treasures I have laid apart. Pools lie on the other side of the world reflecting marble columns. The swallow dips her wing in dark pools. But here the door opens and people come; they come towards me. Throwing faint smiles to mask their cruelty, their indifference, they seize me. The swallow dips her wings; the moon rides through blue seas alone. I must take his hand; I must answer. But what answer shall I give? I am thrust back to stand burning in this clumsy, this ill-fitting body, to receive the shafts of his indifference, and his scorn, I who long for marble columns and pools on the other side of the world where the swallow dips her wings.

"Night has wheeled a little further over the chimney-pots. I see out of the window over his shoulder some unembarrassed cat, not drowned in light, not trapped in silk, free to pause, to stretch, and to move again. I hate all details of the individual life. But I am fixed here to listen. An immense pressure is on me. I cannot move without dislodging the weight of centuries. A million arrows pierce me. Scorn and ridicule pierce me. I, who could beat my breast against the storm and let the hail choke me joyfully, am pinned down here; am exposed. The tiger leaps. Tongues with their whips are upon me. Mobile, incessant, they flicker over me. I must prevaricate and fence them off with lies. What amulet is there against this disaster? What face can I summon to lay cool upon this heat? I think of names on boxes; of mothers from whose wide knees skirts descend; of glades where the many-backed steep hills come down. Hide me, I cry, protect me, for I am the youngest, the most naked of you all. Jinny rides like a gull on the wave, dealing her looks adroitly here and there, saying this, saying that, with truth. But I lie; I prevaricate.

"Alone, I rock my basins; I am mistress of my fleet of ships. But here, twisting the tassels of this brocaded curtain in my hostess's window, I am broken into separate pieces; I am no longer one. What then is the knowledge that Jinny has as she dances; the assurance that Susan has as, stooping quietly beneath the lamplight, she draws the white cotton through the eye of her needle? They say, Yes; they say, No; they bring their fists down with a bang on the table. But I doubt; I tremble; I see the wild thorn tree shake its shadow in the desert.

"Now I will walk, as if I had an end in view, across the room, to the balcony under the awning. I see the sky, softly feathered with its sudden effulgence of moon. I also see the railings of the square, and two people without faces, leaning like statues against the sky. There is then a world immune from change. When I have passed through this drawing-room flickering with tongues that cut me like knives, making me stammer, making me lie, I find faces rid of features, robed in beauty. The lovers crouch under the plane tree. The policeman stands sentinel at the corner. A man passes. There is then a world immune from change. But I am not composed enough, standing on tiptoe on the verge of fire, still scorched by the hot breath, afraid of the door opening and the leap of the tiger, to make even one sentence. What I say is perpetually contradicted. Each time the door opens I am interrupted. I am not yet twenty-one. I am to be broken. I am to be derided all my life. I am to be cast up and down among these men and women, with their twitching faces, with their lying tongues, like a cork on a rough sea. Like a ribbon of weed I am flung far every time the door opens. The wave breaks. I am the foam that sweeps and fills the uttermost rims of the rocks with whiteness; I am also a girl, here in this room."

The sun, risen, no longer couched on a green mattress darting a fitful glance through watery jewels, bared its face and looked straight over the waves. They fell with a regular thud. They fell with the concussion of horses' hooves on the turf. Their spray rose like the tossing of lances and assegais over the riders' heads. They swept the beach with steel blue and diamond-tipped water. They drew in and out with the energy, the muscularity of an engine which sweeps its force out and in again. The sun fell on cornfields and woods. Rivers became blue, and many-plaited, lawns that sloped down to the water's edge became green as birds' feathers softly ruffling their plumes. The hills curved and controlled, seemed bound back by thongs, as a limb is laced by muscles; and the woods which bristled proudly on their flanks were like the curt, clipped mane on the neck of a horse.

In the garden where the trees stood thick over flower-beds, ponds, and greenhouses the birds sang in the hot sunshine, each alone. One sang under the bedroom window; another on the topmost twig of the lilac bush; another on the edge of the wall. Each sang stridently, with passion, with vehemence, as if to let the song burst out of it, no matter if it shattered the song of another bird with harsh discord. Their round eyes bulged with brightness; their claws gripped the twig or rail. They sang exposed without shelter, to the air and the sun, beautiful in their new plumage, shell-veined or brightly mailed, here barred with soft blues, here splashed with gold, or striped with one bright feather. They sang as if the song were urged out of them by the pressure of the morning. They sang as if the edge of being were sharpened and must cut, must split the softness of the blue-green light, the dampness of the wet earth; the fumes and steams of the greasy kitchen vapour; the hot breath of mutton and beef; the richness of pastry and fruit; the damp shreds and peelings thrown from the kitchen bucket, from which a slow steam oozed on the rubbish heap. On all the sodden, the damp-spotted, the curled with wetness, they descended, dry-beaked, ruthless, abrupt. They swooped suddenly from the lilac bough or the fence. They spied a snail and tapped the shell against a stone. They tapped furiously, methodically, until the shell broke and something slimy oozed from the crack. They swept and soared sharply in flights high into the air, twittering short, sharp notes, and perched in the upper branches of some tree, and looked down upon leaves and spires beneath, and the country white with blossom, flowing with grass, and the sea which beat like a drum that raises a regiment of plumed and turbaned soldiers. Now and again their songs ran together in swift scales like the interlacings of a mountain stream whose waters, meeting, foam and then mix, and hasten quicker and quicker down the same channel brushing the same broad leaves. But there is a rock; they sever.

The sun fell in sharp wedges inside the room. Whatever the light touched became dowered with a fanatical existence. A plate was like a white lake. A knife looked like a dagger of ice. Suddenly tumblers revealed themselves upheld by streaks of light. Tables and chairs rose to the surface as if they had been sunk under water and rose, filmed with red, orange, purple like the bloom on the skin of ripe fruit. The veins on the glaze of the china, the grain of the wood, the fibres of the matting became more and more finely engraved. Everything was without shadow. A jar was so green that the eye seemed sucked up through a funnel by its intensity and stuck to it like a limpet. Then shapes took on mass and edge. Here was the boss of a chair; here the bulk of a cupboard. And as the light increased, flocks of shadow were driven before it and conglomerated and hung in many-pleated folds in the background.

"How fair, how strange," said Bernard, "glittering, many-pointed and many-domed London lies before me under mist. Guarded by gasometers, by factory chimneys, she lies sleeping as we approach. She folds the ant-heap to her breast. All cries, all clamour are softly enveloped in silence. Not Rome herself looks more majestic. But we are aimed at her. Already her maternal somnolence is uneasy. Ridges fledged with houses rise from the mist. Factories, cathedrals, glass domes, institutions and theatres erect themselves. The early train from the north is hurled at her like a missile. We draw a curtain as we pass. Blank expectant faces stare at us as we rattle and flash through stations. Men clutch their newspapers a little tighter, as our wind sweeps them, envisaging death. But we roar on. We are about to explode in the flanks of the city like a shell in the side of some ponderous, maternal, majestic animal. She hums and murmurs; she awaits us.

"Meanwhile as I stand looking from the train window, I feel strangely, persuasively, that because of my great happiness (being engaged to be married), I am become part of this speed, this missile, hurled at the city. I am numbed to tolerance and acquiescence. My dear sir, I could say, why do you fidget, taking down your suitcase and pressing into it the cap that you have worn all night? Nothing we can do will avail. Over us all broods a splendid unanimity. We are enlarged and solemnised and brushed into uniformity as with the grey wing of some enormous goose (it is a fine, but colourless morning) because we have only one desire —to arrive at the station. I do not want the train to stop with a thud. I do not want the connection which has bound us together sitting opposite each other all night long to be broken. I do not want to feel that hate and rivalry have resumed their sway; and different desires. Our community in the rushing train sitting together with only one wish to arrive at Euston was very welcome. But behold! It is over. We have attained our desire. We have drawn up at the platform. Hurry and confusion and the wish to be first through the gate into the lift assert themselves.

But I do not wish to be first through the gate, to assume the burden of individual life. I, who have been since Monday, when she accepted me, charged in every nerve with a sense of identity, who could not see a tooth-brush in a glass without saying, '*My* tooth-brush,' now wish to unclasp my hands and let fall my possessions, and merely stand here in the street, taking no part, watching the omnibuses, without desire; without envy; with what would be boundless curiosity about human destiny if there were any longer an edge to my mind. But it has none. I have arrived; am accepted. I ask nothing.

"Having dropped off satisfied like a child from the breast, I am at liberty now to sink down, deep, into what passes, this omnipresent, general life. (How much, let me note, depends upon trousers; the intelligent head is entirely handicapped by shabby trousers.) One observes curious hesitations at the door of the lift. This way, that way, the other? Then individuality asserts itself. They are off. They are all impelled by some necessity. Some miserable affair of keeping an appointment, of buying a hat, severs these beautiful human beings once so united. For myself, I have no aim. I have no ambition. I will let myself be carried on by the general impulse. The surface of my mind slips along like a pale-grey stream reflecting what passes. I cannot remember my past, my nose, or the colour of my eyes, or what my general opinion of myself is. Only in moments of emergency, at a crossing, at a kerb, the wish to preserve my body springs out and seizes me and stops me, here, before this omnibus. We insist, it seems, on living. Then again, indifference descends. The roar of the traffic, the passage of undifferentiated faces, this way and that way, drugs me into dreams; rubs the features from faces. People might walk through me. And, what is this moment of time, this particular day in which I have found myself caught? The growl of traffic might be any uproar—forest trees or the roar of wild beasts. Time has whizzed back an inch or two on its reel; our short progress has been cancelled. I think also that our bodies are in truth naked. We are only lightly covered with buttoned cloth; and beneath these pavements are shells, bones and silence.

"It is, however, true that my dreaming, my tentative advance like one carried beneath the surface of a stream, is interrupted, torn, pricked and plucked at by sensations, spontaneous and irrelevant, of curiosity, greed, desire, irresponsible as in sleep. (I covet that bag—etc.) No, but I wish to go under; to visit the profound depths; once in a while to exercise my prerogative not always to act, but to explore; to hear vague, ancestral sounds of boughs creaking, of mammoths, to indulge impossible desires to embrace the whole world with the arms of understanding, impossible to those who act. Am I not, as I walk, trembling with strange oscillations and vibrations of sympathy, which, unmoored as I am from a private being, bid me embrace these engrossed flocks; these starers and trippers; these errand-boys and furtive and fugitive girls who, ignoring their doom, look in at shop-windows? But I am aware of our ephemeral passage.

"It is, however, true that I cannot deny a sense that life for me is now mysteriously prolonged. Is it that I may have children, may cast a fling of seed wider, beyond this generation, this doom-encircled population, shuffling each other in endless competition along the street? My daughters shall come here, in other summers; my sons shall turn new fields. Hence we are not raindrops, soon dried by the wind; we make gardens blow and forests roar; we come up differently, for ever and ever. This then serves to explain my confidence, my central stability, otherwise so monstrously absurd as I breast the stream of this crowded thoroughfare, making always a passage for myself between people's bodies, taking advantage of safe moments to cross. It is not vanity; for I am emptied of ambition; I do not remember my special gifts, or idiosyncrasy, or the marks I bear on my person, eyes, nose or mouth. I am not, at this moment, myself.

"Yet behold, it returns. One cannot extinguish that persistent smell. It steals in through some crack in the structure—one's identity. I am not part of the street—no, I observe the street. One splits off, therefore. For instance, up that back street a girl stands

waiting; for whom? A romantic story. On the wall of that shop
is fixed a small crane, and for what reason, I ask, was that crane
fixed there? and invent a purple lady swelling, circumambient,
hauled from a barouche landau by a perspiring husband sometime in the sixties. A grotesque story. That is, I am a natural
coiner of words, a blower of bubbles through one thing and another. And striking off these observations spontaneously I elabo-
rate myself; differentiate myself and listening to the voice that
says as I stroll past, 'Look! Take note of that!' I conceive myself
called upon to provide, some winter's night, a meaning for all
my observations—a line that runs from one to another, a summing up that completes. But soliloquies in back streets soon pall.
I need an audience. That is my downfall. That always ruffles the
edge of the final statement and prevents it from forming. I cannot seat myself in some sordid eating-house and order the same
glass day after day and imbue myself entirely in one fluid—this
life. I make my phrase and run off with it to some furnished
room where it will be lit by dozens of candles. I need eyes on me
to draw out these frills and furbelows. To be myself (I note) I
need the illumination of other people's eyes, and therefore cannot
be entirely sure what is my self. The authentics, like Louis, like
Rhoda, exist most completely in solitude. They resent illumination, reduplication. They toss their pictures, once painted, face
downward on the field. On Louis's words the ice is packed thick.
His words issue pressed, condensed, enduring.

"I wish then after this somnolence to sparkle, many-faceted
under the light of my friends' faces. I have been traversing the
sunless territory of non-identity. A strange land. I have heard in
my moment of appeasement, in my moment of obliterating satisfaction, the sigh, as it goes in, comes out, of the tide that draws
beyond this circle of bright light, this drumming of insensate
fury. I have had one moment of enormous peace. This is perhaps
happiness. Now I am drawn back by pricking sensations; by curiosity, greed (I am hungry) and the irresistible desire to be myself. I think of people to whom I could say things; Louis;

Neville; Susan; Jinny and Rhoda. With them I am many-sided. They retrieve me from darkness. We shall meet tonight, thank Heaven. Thank Heaven, I need not be alone. We shall dine together. We shall say good-bye to Percival, who goes to India. The hour is still distant but I feel already those harbingers, those outriders, figures of one's friends in absence. I see Louis, stone-carved, sculpturesque; Neville, scissor-cutting, exact; Susan with eyes like lumps of crystal; Jinny dancing like a flame, febrile, hot, over dry earth; and Rhoda the nymph of the fountain always wet. These are fantastic pictures—these are figments, these visions of friends in absence, grotesque, dropsical, vanishing at the first touch of the toe of a real boot. Yet they drum me alive. They brush off these vapours. I begin to be impatient of solitude —to feel its draperies hang sweltering, unwholesome about me. Oh, to toss them off and be active! Anybody will do. I am not fastidious. The crossing-sweeper will do; the postman; the waiter in this French restaurant; better still the genial proprietor, whose geniality seems reserved for oneself. He mixes the salad with his own hands for some privileged guest. Which is the privileged guest, I ask, and why? And what is he saying to the lady in ear-rings, is she a friend or a customer? I feel at once, as I sit down at a table, the delicious jostle of confusion, of uncertainty, of possibility, of speculation. Images breed instantly. I am embarrassed by my own fertility. I could describe every chair, table, luncher here copiously, freely. My mind hums hither and thither with its veil of words for everything. To speak, about wine even to the waiter, is to bring about an explosion. Up goes the rocket. Its golden grain falls, fertilising, upon the rich soil of my imagination. The entirely unexpected nature of this explosion—that is the joy of intercourse. I, mixed with an unknown Italian waiter—what am I? There is no stability in this world. Who is to say what meaning there is in anything? Who is to foretell the flight of a word? It is a balloon that sails over tree-tops. To speak of knowledge is futile. All is experiment and adventure. We are for ever mixing ourselves with unknown quantities. What is to come? I know not. But, as I put down my glass I remember; I am engaged to be married. I am to dine with my friends tonight. I am Bernard."

"It is now five minutes to eight," said Neville. "I have come early. I have taken my place at the table ten minutes before the time in order to taste every moment of anticipation; to see the door open and to say, 'Is it Percival? No; it is not Percival.' There is a morbid pleasure in saying, 'No, it is not Percival.' I have seen the door open and shut twenty times already; each time the suspense sharpens. This is the place to which he is coming. This is the table at which he will sit. Here, incredible as it seems, will be his actual body. This table, these chairs, this metal vase with its three red flowers are about to undergo an extraordinary transformation. Already the room, with its swing-doors, its tables heaped with fruit, with cold joints, wears the wavering, unreal appearance of a place where one waits expecting something to happen. Things quiver as if not yet in being. The blankness of the white table-cloth glares. The hostility, the indifference of other people dining here is oppressive. We look at each other; see that we do not know each other, stare, and go off. Such looks are lashes. I feel the whole cruelty and indifference of the world in them. If he should not come I could not bear it. I should go. Yet somebody must be seeing him now. He must be in some cab; he must be passing some shop. And every moment he seems to pump into this room this prickly light, this intensity of being so that things have lost their normal uses—this knife-blade is only a flash of light, not a thing to cut with. The normal is abolished.

"The door opens, but he does not come. That is Louis hesitating there. That is his strange mixture of assurance and timidity. He looks at himself in the looking-glass as he comes in; he touches his hair; he is dissatisfied with his appearance. He says, 'I am a Duke—the last of an ancient race.' He is acrid, suspicious, domineering, difficult (I am comparing him with Percival). At the same time he is formidable, for there is laughter in his eyes. He has seen me. Here he is."

"There is Susan," said Louis. "She does not see us. She has not dressed, because she despises the futility of London. She stands for a moment at the swing-door, looking about her like a creature dazed by the light of a lamp. Now she moves. She has the stealthy yet assured movements (even among tables and chairs) of a wild beast. She seems to find her way by instinct in and out among these little tables, touching no one, disregarding waiters, yet comes straight to our table in the corner. When she sees us (Neville, and myself) her face assumes a certainty which is alarming, as if she had what she wanted. To be loved by Susan would be to be impaled by a bird's sharp beak, to be nailed to a barnyard door. Yet there are moments when I could wish to be speared by a beak, to be nailed to a barnyard door, positively, once and for all.

"Rhoda comes now, from nowhere, having slipped in while we were not looking. She must have made a tortuous course, taking cover now behind a waiter, now behind some ornamental pillar, so as to put off as long as possible the shock of recognition, so as to be secure for one more moment to rock her petals in her basin. We wake her. We torture her. She dreads us, she despises us, yet comes cringing to our sides because for all our cruelty there is always some name, some face which sheds a radiance, which lights up her pavements and makes it possible for her to replenish her dreams."

"The door opens, the door goes on opening," said Neville, "yet he does not come."

"There is Jinny," said Susan. "She stands in the door. Everything seems stayed. The waiter stops. The diners at the table by the door look. She seems to centre everything; round her tables, lines of doors, windows, ceilings, ray themselves, like rays round the star in the middle of a smashed window-pane. She brings things to a point, to order. Now she sees us, and moves, and all the rays ripple and flow and waver over us, bringing in new tides of sensation. We change. Louis puts his hand to his tie. Neville, who sits waiting with agonised intensity, nervously straightens the forks in front of him. Rhoda sees her with surprise, as if on some far horizon a fire blazed. And I, though I pile my mind with damp grass, with wet fields, with the sound of rain on the roof and the gusts of wind that batter at the house in winter and so protect my soul against her, feel her derision steal round me, feel her laughter curl its tongues of fire round me and light up unsparingly my shabby dress, my square-tipped finger-nails, which I at once hide under the table-cloth."

"He has not come," said Neville. "The door opens and he does not come. That is Bernard. As he pulls off his coat he shows, of course, the blue shirt under his arm-pits. And then, unlike the rest of us, he comes in without pushing open a door, without knowing that he comes into a room full of strangers. He does not look in the glass. His hair is untidy, but he does not know it. He has no perception that we differ, or that this table is his goal. He hesitates on his way here. Who is that? he asks himself, for he half knows a woman in an opera cloak. He half knows everybody; he knows nobody (I compare him with Percival). But now, perceiving us, he waves a benevolent salute; he bears down with such benignity, with such love of mankind (crossed with humour at the futility of 'loving mankind'), that, if it were not for Percival, who turns all this to vapour, one would feel, as the others already feel: Now is our festival; now we are together. But without Percival there is no solidity. We are silhouettes, hollow phantoms moving mistily without a background."

"The swing-door goes on opening," said Rhoda. "Strangers keep on coming, people we shall never see again, people who brush us disagreeably with their familiarity, their indifference, and the sense of a world continuing without us. We cannot sink down, we cannot forget our faces. Even I who have no face, who make no difference when I come in (Susan and Jinny change bodies and faces), flutter unattached, without anchorage anywhere, unconsolidated, incapable of composing any blankness or continuity or wall against which their bodies move. It is because of Neville and his misery. The sharp breath of his misery scatters my being. Nothing can settle; nothing can subside. Every time the door opens he looks fixedly at the table—he dare not raise his eyes—then looks for one second and says, 'He has not come.' But here he is."

"Now," said Neville, "my tree flowers. My heart rises. All oppression is relieved. All impediment is removed. The reign of chaos is over. He has imposed order. Knives cut again."

"Here is Percival," said Jinny. "He has not dressed."

"Here is Percival," said Bernard, "smoothing his hair, not from vanity (he does not look in the glass), but to propitiate the god of decency. He is conventional; he is a hero. The little boys trooped after him across the playing-fields. They blew their noses as he blew his nose, but unsuccessfully, for he is Percival. Now, when he is about to leave us, to go to India, all these trifles come together. He is a hero. Oh, yes, that is not to be denied, and when he takes his seat by Susan, whom he loves, the occasion is crowned. We who yelped like jackals biting at each other's heels now assume the sober and confident air of soldiers in the presence of their captain. We who have been separated by our youth (the oldest is not yet twenty-five), who have sung like eager birds each his own song and tapped with the remorseless and savage egotism of the young our own snail-shell till it cracked (I am engaged), or perched solitary outside some bedroom window and sang of love, of fame and other single experiences so dear to the callow bird with a yellow tuft on its beak, now come nearer; and shuffling closer on our perch in this restaurant where everybody's interests are at variance, and the incessant passage of traffic chafes us with distractions, and the door opening perpetually its glass cage solicits us with myriad temptations and offers insults and wounds to our confidence—sitting together now we love each other and believe in our own endurance."

"Now let us issue from the darkness of solitude," said Louis.

"Now let us say, brutally and directly, what is in our minds," said Neville. "Our isolation, our preparation, is over. The furtive days of secrecy and hiding, the revelations on staircases, moments of terror and ecstasy."

"Old Mrs. Constable lifted her sponge and warmth poured over us," said Bernard. "We became clothed in this changing, this feeling garment of flesh."

"The boot boy made love to the scullery-maid in the kitchen garden," said Susan, "among the blown-out washing."

"The breath of the wind was like a tiger panting," said Rhoda.

"The man lay livid with his throat cut in the gutter," said Neville. "And going upstairs I could not raise my foot against the immitigable apple-tree with its silver leaves held stiff!"

"The leaf danced in the hedge without any one to blow it," said Jinny.

"In the sun-baked corner," said Louis, "the petals swam on depths of green."

"At Elvedon the gardeners swept and swept with their great brooms, and the woman sat at a table writing," said Bernard.

"From these close-furled balls of string we draw now every filament," said Louis, "remembering, when we meet."

"And then," said Bernard, "the cab came to the door, and, pressing our new bowler hats tightly over our eyes to hide our unmanly tears, we drove through streets in which even the house-maids looked at us, and our names painted in white letters on our boxes proclaimed to all the world that we were going to school with the regulation number of socks and drawers, on which our mothers for some nights previously had stitched our initials, in our boxes. A second severance from the body of our mother."

"And Miss Lambert, Miss Cutting, and Miss Bard," said Jinny, "monumental ladies, white-ruffed, stone-coloured, enigmatic, with amethyst rings moving like virginal tapers, dim glowworms over the pages of French, geography and arithmetic, presided; and there were maps, green-baize boards, and rows of shoes on a shelf."

"Bells rang punctually," said Susan, "maids scuffled and giggled. There was a drawing in of chairs and a drawing out of chairs on the linoleum. But from one attic there was a blue view, a distant view of a field unstained by the corruption of this regimented, unreal existence."

"Down from our heads veils fell," said Rhoda. "We clasped the flowers with their green leaves rustling in garlands."

"We changed, we became unrecognisable," said Louis. "Exposed to all these different lights, what we had in us (for we are all so different) came intermittently, in violent patches, spaced by blank voids, to the surface as if some acid had dropped unequally on the plate. I was this, Neville that, Rhoda different again, and Bernard too."

"Then canoes slipped through palely tinted willow branches," said Neville, "and Bernard, advancing in his casual way against breadths of green, against houses of very ancient foundation, tumbled in a heap on the ground beside me. In an access of emotion—winds are not more raving, nor lightning more sudden—I took my poem, I flung my poem, I slammed the door behind me."

"I, however," said Louis, "losing sight of you, sat in my office and tore the date from the calendar, and announced to the world of ship-brokers, corn-chandlers and actuaries that Friday the tenth, or Tuesday the eighteenth, had dawned on the city of London."

"Then," said Jinny, "Rhoda and I, exposed in bright dresses, with a few precious stones nestling on a cold ring round our throats, bowed, shook hands and took a sandwich from a plate with a smile."

"The tiger leapt, and the swallow dipped her wings in dark pools on the other side of the world," said Rhoda.

"But here and now we are together," said Bernard. "We have come together, at a particular time, to this particular spot. We are drawn into this communion by some deep, some common emotion. Shall we call it, conveniently, 'love'? Shall we say 'love of Percival' because Percival is going to India?

"No, that is too small, too particular a name. We cannot attach the width and spread of our feelings to so small a mark. We have come together (from the North, from the South, from Susan's farm, from Louis's house of business) to make one thing, not enduring—for what endures?—but seen by many eyes simul-taneously. There is a red carnation in that vase. A single flower as we sat here waiting, but now a seven-sided flower, many-petalled, red, puce, purple-shaded, stiff with silver-tinted leaves —a whole flower to which every eye brings its own contribu-tion."

"After the capricious fires, the abysmal dulness of youth," said Neville, "the light falls upon real objects now. Here are knives and forks. The world is displayed, and we too, so that we can talk."

"We differ, it may be too profoundly," said Louis, "for ex-planation. But let us attempt it. I smoothed my hair when I came in, hoping to look like the rest of you. But I cannot, for I am not single and entire as you are. I have lived a thousand lives already. Every day I unbury—I dig up. I find relics of myself in the sand that women made thousands of years ago, when I heard songs by the Nile and the chained beast stamping. What you see beside you, this man, this Louis, is only the cinders and refuse of something once splendid. I was an Arab prince; behold my free gestures. I was a great poet in the time of Elizabeth. I was a Duke at the court of Louis the Fourteenth. I am very vain, very confident; I have an immeasurable desire that women should sigh in sympathy. I have eaten no lunch today in order that Susan may think me cadaverous and that Jinny may extend to me the exquisite balm of her sympathy. But while I admire Susan and Percival, I hate the others, because it is for them that I do these antics, smoothing my hair, concealing my accent. I am the little ape who chatters over a nut, and you are the dowdy women with shiny bags of stale buns; I am also the caged tiger, and you are the keepers with red-hot bars. That is, I am fiercer and stronger than you are, yet the apparition that appears above ground after ages of non-entity will be spent in terror lest you should laugh at me, in veerings with the wind against the soot storms, in efforts to make a steel ring of clear poetry that shall connect the gulls and the women with bad teeth, the church spire and the bobbing billycock hats as I see them when I take my luncheon and prop my poet—is it Lucretius?—against a cruet and the gravy-splashed bill of fare."

"But you will never hate me," said Jinny. "You will never see me, even across a room full of gilt chairs and ambassadors, without coming to me across the room to seek my sympathy. When I came in just now everything stood still in a pattern. Waiters stopped, diners raised their forks and held them. I had the air of being prepared for what would happen. When I sat down you put your hands to your ties, you hid them under the table. But I hide nothing. I am prepared. Every time the door opens I cry 'More!' But my imagination is the bodies. I can imagine nothing beyond the circle cast by my body. My body goes before me, like a lantern down a dark lane, bringing one thing after another out of darkness into a ring of light. I dazzle you; I make you believe that this is all."

"But when you stand in the door," said Neville, "you inflict stillness, demanding admiration, and that is a great impediment to the freedom of intercourse. You stand in the door making us notice you. But none of you saw me approach. I came early; I came quickly and directly, *here,* to sit for the person whom I love. My life has a rapidity that yours lack. I am like a hound on the scent. I hunt from dawn to dusk. Nothing, not the pursuit of perfection through the sand, nor fame, nor money has meaning for me. I shall have riches; I shall have fame. But I shall never have what I want, for I lack bodily grace and the courage that comes with it. The swiftness of my mind is too strong for my body. I fail before I reach the end and fall in a heap, damp, perhaps disgusting. I excite pity in the crises of life, not love. Therefore I suffer horribly. But I do not suffer, as Louis does, to make myself a spectacle. I have too fine a sense of fact to allow myself these juggleries, these pretences. I see everything —except one thing—with complete clarity. That is my saving. That is what gives my suffering an unceasing excitement. That is what makes me dictate, even when I am silent. And since I am, in one respect, deluded, since the person is always changing, though not the desire, and I do not know in the morning by whom I shall sit at night, I am never stagnant; I rise from my worst disasters, I turn, I change. Pebbles bounce off the mail of my muscular, my extended body. In this pursuit I shall grow old."

"If I could believe," said Rhoda, "that I should grow old in pursuit and change, I should be rid of my fear: nothing persists. One moment does not lead to another. The door opens and the tiger leaps. You did not see me come. I circled round the chairs to avoid the horror of the spring. I am afraid of you all. I am afraid of the shock of sensation that leaps upon me, because I cannot deal with it as you do—I cannot make one moment merge in the next. To me they are all violent, all separate; and if I fall under the shock of the leap of the moment you will be on me, tearing me to pieces. I have no end in view. I do not know how to run minute to minute and hour to hour, solving them by some natural force until they make the whole and indivisible mass that you call life. Because you have an end in view—one person, is it, to sit beside, an idea is it, your beauty is it? I do not know— your days and hours pass like the boughs of forest trees and the smooth green of forest rides to a hound running on the scent. But there is no single scent, no single body for me to follow. And I have no face. I am like the foam that races over the beach or the moonlight that falls arrowlike here on a tin can, here on a spike of the mailed sea holly, or a bone or a half-eaten boat. I am whirled down caverns, and flap like paper against endless corridors, and must press my hand against the wall to draw myself back.

"But since I wish above all things to have lodgment, I pretend, as I go upstairs lagging behind Jinny and Susan, to have an end in view. I pull on my stockings as I see them pull on theirs. I wait for you to speak and then speak like you. I am drawn here across London to a particular spot, to a particular place, not to see you or you or you, but to light my fire at the general blaze of you who live wholly, indivisibly and without caring in the moment."

"When I came into the room tonight," said Susan, "I stopped, I peered about like an animal with its eyes near to the ground. The smell of carpets and furniture and scent disgusts me. I like to walk through wet fields alone, or to stop at a gate and watch my setter nose in a circle, and to ask, Where is the hare? I like to be with people who twist herbs, and spit into the fire and shuffle down long passages in slippers like my father. The only sayings I understand are cries of love, hate, rage and pain. This talking is undressing an old woman whose dress had seemed to be part of her, but now, as we talk, she turns pinkish underneath, and has wrinkled thighs and sagging breasts. When you are silent you are again beautiful. I shall never have anything but natural happiness. It will almost content me. I shall go to bed tired. I shall lie like a field bearing crops in rotation; in the summer heat will dance over me; in the winter I shall be cracked with the cold. But heat and cold will follow each other naturally without my willing or unwilling. My children will carry me on; their teething, their crying, their going to school and coming back will be like the waves of the sea under me. No day will be without its movement. I shall be lifted higher than any of you on the backs of the seasons. I shall possess more than Jinny, more than Rhoda, by the time I die. But on the other hand, where you are various and dimple a million times to the ideas and laughter of others, I shall be sullen, storm-tinted and all one purple. I shall be debased and hide-bound by the bestial and beautiful passion of maternity. I shall push the fortunes of my children unscrupulously. I shall hate those who see their faults. I shall lie basely to help them. I shall let them wall me away from you, from you and from you. Also, I am torn with jealousy. I hate Jinny because she shows me that my hands are red, my nails bitten. I love with such ferocity that it kills me when the object of my love shows by a phrase that he can escape. He escapes, and I am left clutching at a string that slips in and out among the leaves on the tree-tops. I do not understand phrases."

"Had I been born," said Bernard, "not knowing that one word follows another I might have been, who knows, perhaps anything. As it is, finding sequences everywhere, I cannot bear the pressure of solitude. When I cannot see words curling like rings of smoke round me I am in darkness—I am nothing. When I am alone I fall into lethargy, and say to myself dismally as I poke the cinders through the bars of the grate, Mrs. Moffat will come. She will come and sweep it all up. When Louis is alone he sees with astonishing intensity, and will write some words that may outlast us all. Rhoda loves to be alone. She fears us because we shatter the sense of being which is so extreme in solitude—see how she grasps her fork—her weapon against us. But I only come into existence when the plumber, or the horse-dealers, or whoever it may be, says something which sets me alight. Then how lovely the smoke of my phrase is, rising and falling, flaunting and falling, upon red lobsters and yellow fruit, wreathing them into one beauty. But observe how meretricious the phrase is—made up of what evasions and old lies. Thus my character is in part made of the stimulus which other people provide, and is not mine, as yours are. There is some fatal streak, some wandering and irregular vein of silver, weakening it. Hence the fact that used to enrage Neville at school, that I left him. I went with the boasting boys with little caps and badges, driving off in big brakes—there are some here tonight, dining together, correctly dressed before they go off in perfect concord to the music hall;

I loved them. For they bring me into existence as certainly as you do. Hence, too, when I am leaving you and the train is going, you feel that it is not the train that is going, but I, Bernard, who does not care, who does not feel, who has no ticket, and has lost perhaps his purse. Susan, staring at the string that slips in and out among the leaves of the beech trees, cries: 'He is gone! He has escaped me!' For there is nothing to lay hold of. I am made and remade continually. Different people draw different words from me.

"Thus there is not one person but fifty people whom I want to sit beside tonight. But I am the only one of you who is at home here without taking liberties. I am not gross; I am not a snob. If I lie open to the pressure of society I often succeed with the dexterity of my tongue in putting something difficult into the currency. See my little toys, twisted out of nothing in a second, how they entertain. I am no hoarder—I shall leave only a cupboard of old clothes when I die—and am almost indifferent to the minor vanities of life which cause Louis so much torture. But I have sacrificed much. Veined as I am with iron, with silver and streaks of common mud, I cannot contract into the firm fist which those clench who do not depend upon stimulus. I am incapable of the denials, the heroisms of Louis and Rhoda. I shall never succeed, even in talk, in making a perfect phrase. But I shall have contributed more to the passing moment than any of you; I shall go into more rooms, more different rooms, than any of you. But because there is something that comes from outside and not from within I shall be forgotten; when my voice is silent you will not remember me, save as the echo of a voice that once wreathed the fruit into phrases."

"Look," said Rhoda; "listen. Look how the light becomes richer, second by second, and bloom and ripeness lie everywhere; and our eyes, as they range round this room with all its tables, seem to push through curtains of colour, red, orange, umber and queer ambiguous tints, which yield like veils and close behind them, and one thing melts into another."

"Yes," said Jinny, "our senses have widened. Membranes, webs of nerve that lay white and limp, have filled and spread themselves and float round us like filaments, making the air tangible and catching in them far-away sounds unheard before."

"The roar of London," said Louis, "is round us. Motor-cars, vans, omnibuses pass and repass continuously. All are merged in one turning wheel of single sound. All separate sounds— wheels, bells, the cries of drunkards, of merrymakers—all churned into one sound, steel blue, circular. Then a siren hoots. At that shores slip away, chimneys flatten themselves, the ship makes for the open sea."

"Percival is going," said Neville. "We sit here, surrounded, lit up, many coloured; all things—hands, curtains, knives and forks, other people dining—run into each other. We are walled in here. But India lies outside."

"I see India," said Bernard. "I see the low, long shore; I see the tortuous lanes of stamped mud that lead in and out among ramshackle pagodas; I see the gilt and crenellated buildings which have an air of fragility and decay as if they were temporarily run up buildings in some Oriental exhibition. I see a pair of bullocks who drag a low cart along the sun-baked road. The cart sways incompetently from side to side. Now one wheel sticks in the rut, and at once innumerable natives in loin-cloths swarm round it, chattering excitedly. But they do nothing. Time seems endless, ambition vain. Over all broods a sense of the uselessness of human exertion. There are strange sour smells. An old man in a ditch continues to chew betel and to contemplate his navel. But now, behold, Percival advances; Percival rides a flea-bitten mare, and wears a sun-helmet. By applying the standards of the West, by using the violent language that is natural to him, the bullock-cart is righted in less than five minutes. The Oriental problem is solved. He rides on; the multitude cluster round him, regarding him as if he were—what indeed he is—a God."

"Unknown, with or without a secret, it does not matter," said Rhoda, "he is like a stone fallen into a pond round which minnows swarm. Like minnows, we who had been shooting this way, that way, all shot round him when he came. Like minnows, conscious of the presence of a great stone, we undulate and eddy contentedly. Comfort steals over us. Gold runs in our blood. One, two; one, two; the heart beats in serenity, in confidence, in some trance of well-being, in some rapture of benignity; and look—the outermost parts of the earth—pale shadows on the utmost horizon, India for instance, rise into our purview. The world that had been shrivelled, rounds itself; remote provinces are fetched up out of darkness; we see muddy roads, twisted jungle, swarms of men, and the vulture that feeds on some bloated carcass as within our scope, part of our proud and splendid province, since Percival, riding alone on a flea-bitten mare, advances down a solitary path, has his camp pitched among desolate trees, and sits alone, looking at the enormous mountains."

"It is Percival," said Louis, "sitting silent as he sat among the tickling grasses when the breeze parted the clouds and they formed again, who makes us aware that these attempts to say, 'I am this, I am that,' which we make, coming together, like separated parts of one body and soul, are false. Something has been left out from fear. Something has been altered, from vanity. We have tried to accentuate differences. From the desire to be separate we have laid stress upon our faults, and what is particular to us. But there is a chain whirling round, round, in a steel-blue circle beneath."

"It is hate, it is love," said Susan. "That is the furious coal-black stream that makes us dizzy if we look down into it. We stand on a ledge here, but if we look down we turn giddy."

"It is love," said Jinny, "it is hate, such as Susan feels for me because I kissed Louis once in the garden; because equipped as I am, I make her think when I come in, 'My hands are red,' and hide them. But our hatred is almost indistinguishable from our love."

"Yet these roaring waters," said Neville, "upon which we build our crazy platforms are more stable than the wild, the weak and inconsequent cries that we utter when, trying to speak, we rise; when we reason and jerk out these false sayings, 'I am this; I am that!' Speech is false.

"But I eat. I gradually lose all knowledge of particulars as I eat. I am becoming weighed down with food. These delicious mouthfuls of roast duck, fitly piled with vegetables, following each other in exquisite rotation of warmth, weight, sweet and bitter, past my palate, down my gullet, into my stomach, have stabilised my body. I feel quiet, gravity, control. All is solid now. Instinctively my palate now requires and anticipates sweetness and lightness, something sugared and evanescent; and cool wine, fitting glove-like over those finer nerves that seem to tremble from the roof of my mouth and make it spread (as I drink) into a domed cavern, green with vine leaves, musk-scented, purple with grapes. Now I can look steadily into the mill-race that foams beneath. By what particular name are we to call it? Let Rhoda speak, whose face I see reflected mistily in the looking-glass opposite; Rhoda whom I interrupted when she rocked her petals in a brown basin, asking for the pocket-knife that Bernard had stolen. Love is not a whirlpool to her. She is not giddy when she looks down. She looks far away over our heads, beyond India."

"Yes, between your shoulders, over your heads, to a landscape," said Rhoda, "to a hollow where the many-backed steep hills come down like birds' wings folded. There, on the short, firm turf, are bushes, dark leaved, and against their darkness I see a shape, white, but not of stone, moving, perhaps alive. But it is not you, it is not you, it is not you; not Percival, Susan, Jinny, Neville or Louis. When the white arm rests upon the knee it is a triangle; now it is upright—a column; now a fountain, falling. It makes no sign, it does not beckon, it does not see us. Behind it roars the sea. It is beyond our reach. Yet there I venture. There I go to replenish my emptiness, to stretch my nights and fill them fuller and fuller with dreams. And for a second even now, even here, I reach my object and say, 'Wander no more. All else is trial and make-believe. Here is the end.' But these pilgrimages, these moments of departure, start always in your presence, from this table, these lights, from Percival and Susan, here and now. Always I see the grove over your heads, between your shoulders, or from a window when I have crossed the room at a party and stand looking down into the street."

"But his slippers?" said Neville. "And his voice downstairs in the hall? And catching sight of him when he does not see one? One waits and he does not come. It gets later and later. He has forgotten. He is with some one else. He is faithless, his love meant nothing. Oh, then the agony—then the intolerable despair! And then the door opens. He is here."

"Rippling gold, I say to him, 'Come,'" said Jinny. "And he comes; he crosses the room to where I sit, with my dress like a veil billowing round me on the gilt chair. Our hands touch, our bodies burst into fire. The chair, the cup, the table—nothing remains unlit. All quivers, all kindles, all burns clear."

("Look, Rhoda," said Louis, "they have become nocturnal, rapt. Their eyes are like moths' wings moving so quickly that they do not seem to move at all."

"Horns and trumpets," said Rhoda, "ring out. Leaves unfold; the stag blares in the thicket. There is a dancing and a drumming, like the dancing and the drumming of naked men with assegais."

"Like the dance of savages," said Louis, "round the camp fire. They are savage; they are ruthless. They dance in a circle, flapping bladders. The flames leap over their painted faces, over the leopard skins and the bleeding limbs which they have torn from the living body."

"The flames of the festival rise high," said Rhoda. "The great procession passes, flinging green boughs and flowering branches. Their horns spill blue smoke; their skins are dappled red and yellow in the torchlight. They throw violets. They deck the beloved with garlands and with laurel leaves, there on the ring of turf where the steep-backed hills come down. The procession passes. And while it passes, Louis, we are aware of downfalling, we forebode decay. The shadow slants. We who are conspirators, withdrawn together to lean over some cold urn, note how the purple flame flows downwards."

"Death is woven in with the violets," said Louis. "Death and again death.")

"How proudly we sit here," said Jinny, "we who are not yet twenty-five! Outside the trees flower; outside the women linger; outside the cabs swerve and sweep. Emerged from the tentative ways, the obscurities and dazzle of youth, we look straight in front of us, ready for what may come (the door opens, the door keeps on opening). All is real; all is firm without shadow or illusion. Beauty rides our brows. There is mine, there is Susan's. Our flesh is firm and cool. Our differences are clear-cut as the shadows of rocks in full sunlight. Beside us lie crisp rolls, yellow-glazed and hard; the table-cloth is white, our hands lie half curled, ready to contract. Days and days are to come; winter days, summer days; we have scarcely broken into our hoard. Now the fruit is swollen beneath the leaf. The room is golden, and I say to him, 'Come.' "

"He has red ears," said Louis, "and the smell of meat hangs down in a damp net while the city clerks take snacks at the lunch bar."

"With infinite time before us," said Neville, "we ask what shall we do? Shall we loiter down Bond Street, looking here and there, and buying perhaps a fountain-pen because it is green, or asking how much is the ring with the blue stone? Or shall we sit indoors and watch the coals turn crimson? Shall we stretch our hands for books and read here a passage and there a passage? Shall we shout with laughter for no reason? Shall we push through flowering meadows and make daisy chains? Shall we find out when the next train starts for the Hebrides and engage a reserved compartment? All is to come."

"For you," said Bernard, "but yesterday I walked bang into a pillar-box. Yesterday I became engaged."

"How strange," said Susan, "the little heaps of sugar look by the side of our plates. Also the mottled peelings of pears, and the plush rims to the looking-glasses. I had not seen them before. Everything is now set; everything is fixed. Bernard is engaged. Something irrevocable has happened. A circle has been cast on the waters; a chain is imposed. We shall never flow freely again."

"For one moment only," said Louis. "Before the chain breaks, before disorder returns, see us fixed, see us displayed, see us held in a vice.

"But now the circle breaks. Now the current flows. Now we rush faster than before. Now passions that lay in wait down there in the dark weeds which grow at the bottom rise and pound us with their waves. Pain and jealousy, envy and desire, and something deeper than they are, stronger than love and more subterranean. The voice of action speaks. Listen, Rhoda (for we are conspirators, with our hands on the cold urn), to the casual, quick, exciting voice of action, of hounds running on the scent. They speak now without troubling to finish their sentences. They talk a little language such as lovers use. An imperious brute possesses them. The nerves thrill in their thighs. Their hearts pound and churn in their sides. Susan screws her pocket-handkerchief. Jinny's eyes dance with fire."

"They are immune," said Rhoda, "from picking fingers and searching eyes. How easily they turn and glance; what poses they take of energy and pride! What life shines in Jinny's eyes; how fell, how entire Susan's glance is, searching for insects at the roots! Their hair shines lustrous. Their eyes burn like the eyes of animals brushing through leaves on the scent of the prey. The circle is destroyed. We are thrown asunder."

"But soon, too soon," said Bernard, "this egotistic exultation fails. Too soon the moment of ravenous identity is over, and the appetite for happiness, and happiness, and still more happiness is glutted. The stone is sunk; the moment is over. Round me there spreads a wide margin of indifference. Now open in my eyes a thousand eyes of curiosity. Any one now is at liberty to murder Bernard, who is engaged to be married, so long as they leave untouched this margin of unknown territory, this forest of the unknown world. Why, I ask (whispering discreetly), do women dine alone together there? Who are they? And what has brought them on this particular evening to this particular spot? The youth in the corner, judging from the nervous way in which he puts his hand from time to time to the back of his head, is from the country. He is suppliant, and so anxious to respond suitably to the kindness of his father's friend, his host, that he can scarcely enjoy now what he will enjoy very much at about half-past eleven tomorrow morning. I have also seen that lady powder her nose three times in the midst of an absorbing conversation—about love perhaps, about the unhappiness of their dearest friend perhaps. 'Ah, but the state of my nose!' she thinks, and out comes her powder-puff, obliterating in its passage all the most fervent feelings of the human heart. There remains, however, the insoluble problem of the solitary man with the eyeglass; of the elderly lady drinking champagne alone. Who and what are these unknown people? I ask. I could make a dozen stories of what he said, of what she said—I can see a dozen pictures. But what are stories? Toys I twist, bubbles I blow, one ring passing through another. And sometimes I begin to doubt if there are stories. What is my story? What is Rhoda's? What is Neville's? There are facts, as, for example: 'The handsome young man in the grey suit, whose reserve contrasted so strangely with the loquacity of the others, now brushed the crumbs from his waistcoat and, with a characteristic gesture at once commanding and benign, made a sign to the waiter, who came instantly and returned a moment later with the bill discreetly folded upon a plate.' That is the truth; that is the fact, but beyond it all is darkness and conjecture."

"Now once more," said Louis, "as we are about to part, having paid our bill, the circle in our blood, broken so often, so sharply, for we are so different, closes in a ring. Something is made. Yes, as we rise and fidget, a little nervously, we pray, holding in our hands this common feeling, 'Do not move, do not let the swing-door cut to pieces the thing that we have made, that globes itself here, among these lights, these peelings, this litter of bread crumbs and people passing. Do not move, do not go. Hold it for ever.' "

"Let us hold it for one moment," said Jinny; "love, hatred, by whatever name we call it, this globe whose walls are made of Percival, of youth and beauty, and something so deep sunk within us that we shall perhaps never make this moment out of one man again."

"Forests and far countries on the other side of the world," said Rhoda, "are in it; seas and jungles; the howlings of jackals and moonlight falling upon some high peak where the eagle soars."

"Happiness is in it," said Neville, "and the quiet of ordinary things. A table, a chair, a book with a paper-knife stuck between the pages. And the petal falling from the rose, and the light flickering as we sit silent, or, perhaps, bethinking us of some trifle, suddenly speak."

"Week-days are in it," said Susan, "Monday, Tuesday, Wednesday; the horses going up to the fields, and the horses returning; the rooks rising and falling, and catching the elm-trees in their net, whether it is April, whether it is November."

"What is to come is in it," said Bernard. "That is the last drop and the brightest that we let fall like some supernal quicksilver into the swelling and splendid moment created by us from Percival. What is to come? I ask, brushing the crumbs from my waistcoat, what is outside? We have proved, sitting eating, sitting talking, that we can add to the treasury of moments. We are not slaves bound to suffer incessantly unrecorded petty blows on our bent backs. We are not sheep either, following a master. We are creators. We too have made something that will join the innumerable congregations of past time. We too, as we put on our hats and push open the door, stride not into chaos, but into a

world that our own force can subjugate and make part of the
illumined and everlasting road.

"Look, Percival, while they fetch the taxi, at the prospect
which you are so soon to lose. The street is hard and burnished
with the churning of innumerable wheels. The yellow canopy
of our tremendous energy hangs like a burning cloth above our
heads. Theatres, music halls and lamps in private houses make
that light."

"Peaked clouds," said Rhoda, "voyage over a sky dark like
polished whalebone."

"Now the agony begins; now the horror has seized me with
its fangs," said Neville. "Now the cab comes; now Percival goes.
What can we do to keep him? How bridge the distance between
us? How fan the fire so that it blazes for ever? How signal to
all time to come that we, who stand in the street, in the lamplight, loved Percival? Now Percival is gone."

he sun had risen to its full height. It was no longer half seen and guessed at, from hints and gleams, as if a girl couched on her green-sea mattress tired her brows with water-globed jewels that sent lances of opal-tinted light falling and flashing in the uncertain air like the flanks of a dolphin leaping, or the flash of a falling blade. Now the sun burnt uncompromising, undeniable. It struck upon the hard sand, and the rocks became furnaces of red heat; it searched each pool and caught the minnow hiding in the cranny, and showed the rusty cartwheel, the white bone, or the boot without laces stuck, black as iron, in the sand. It gave to everything its exact measure of colour; to the sandhills their innumerable glitter, to the wild grasses their glancing green; or it fell upon the arid waste of the desert, here wind-scourged into furrows, here swept into desolate cairns, here sprinkled with stunted dark-green jungle-trees. It lit up the smooth gilt mosque, the frail pink-and-white card houses of the southern village, and the long-breasted, white-haired women who knelt in the river bed beating wrinkled cloths upon stones. Steamers thudding slowly over the sea were caught in the level stare of the sun, and it beat through the yellow awnings upon passengers who dozed or paced the deck, shading their eyes to look for the land, while day after day, compressed in its oily throbbing sides, the ship bore them on monotonously over the waters.

The sun beat on the crowded pinnacles of southern hills and glared into deep, stony river beds where the water was shrunk beneath the high slung bridge so that washerwomen kneeling on hot stones could scarcely wet their linen; and lean mules went picking their way among the chattering grey stones with panniers slung across their narrow shoulders. At midday the heat of the sun made the hills grey as if shaved and singed in an explo-

278

*sion, while, further north, in cloudier and rainier countries, hills
smoothed into slabs as with the back of a spade had a light in
them as if a murder, deep within, went from chamber to chamber carrying a green lamp. Through atoms of grey-blue air the
sun struck at English fields and lit up marshes and pools, a white
gull on a stake, the slow sail of shadows over blunt-headed woods
and young corn and flowing hayfields. It beat on the orchard
wall, and every pit and grain of the brick was silver pointed, purple, fiery as if soft to touch, as if touched it must melt into hot-
baked grains of dust. The currants hung against the wall in
ripples and cascades of polished red; plums swelled out their
leaves, and all the blades of the grass were run together in one
fluent green blaze. The trees' shadow was sunk to a dark pool at
the root. Light descending in floods dissolved the separate folia-
tion into one green mound.*

*The birds sang passionate songs addressed to one ear only
and then stopped. Bubbling and chuckling they carried little bits
of straw and twig to the dark knots in the higher branches of
the trees. Gilt and purpled they perched in the garden, where
cones of laburnum and purple shook down gold and lilac, for
now at midday the garden was all blossom and profusion and
even the tunnels under the plants were green and purple and
tawny as the sun beat through the red petal, or the broad yellow
petal, or was barred by some thickly furred green stalk.*

*The sun struck straight upon the house, making the white
walls glare between the dark windows. Their panes, woven
thickly with green branches, held circles of impenetrable darkness. Sharp-edged wedges of light lay upon the window-sill and
showed inside the room plates with blue rings, cups with curved
handles, the bulge of a great bowl, the criss-cross pattern in the
rug, and the formidable corners and lines of cabinets and book-
cases. Behind their conglomeration hung a zone of shadow in
which might be a further shape to be disencumbered of shadow
or still denser depths of darkness.*

The waves broke and spread their waters swiftly over the shore.

One after another they massed themselves and fell; the spray tossed itself back with the energy of their fall. The waves were steeped deep-blue save for a pattern of diamond-pointed light on their backs which rippled as the backs of great horses ripple with muscles as they move. The waves fell; withdrew and fell again, like the thud of a great beast stamping.

"He is dead," said Neville. "He fell. His horse tripped. He was thrown. The sails of the world have swung round and caught me on the head. All is over. The lights of the world have gone out. There stands the tree which I cannot pass.

"Oh, to crumple this telegram in my fingers—to let the light of the world flood back—to say this has not happened! But why turn one's head hither and thither? This is the truth. This is the fact. His horse stumbled; he was thrown. The flashing trees and white rails went up in a shower. There was a surge; a drumming in his ears. Then the blow; the world crashed; he breathed heavily. He died where he fell.

"Barns and summer days in the country, rooms where we sat —all now lies in the unreal world which is gone. My past is cut from me. They came running. They carried him to some pavilion, men in riding-boots, men in sun helmets; among unknown men he died. Loneliness and silence often surrounded him. He often left me. And then, returning, 'See where he comes!' I said.

"Women shuffle past the window as if there were no gulf cut in the street; no tree with stiff leaves which we cannot pass. We deserve then to be tripped by mole-hills. We are infinitely abject, shuffling past with our eyes shut. But why should I submit? Why try to lift my foot and mount the stair? This is where I stand; here, holding the telegram. The past summer days and rooms where we sat stream away like burnt paper with red eyes in it. Why meet and resume? Why talk and eat and make up other combinations with other people? From this moment I am solitary. No one will know me now. I have three letters, 'I am about to play quoits with a colonel, so no more,' thus he ends our friendship, shouldering his way through the crowd with a wave of his hand. This farce is worth no more formal celebration. Yet if some one had but said: 'Wait'; had pulled the strap three holes tighter—he would have done justice for fifty years, and sat in Court and ridden alone at the head of troops and denounced some monstrous tyranny, and come back to us.

"Now I say there is a grinning, there is a subterfuge. There is something sneering behind our backs. That boy almost lost his footing as he leapt on the bus. Percival fell; was killed; is buried, and I watch people passing; holding tight to the rails of omnibuses; determined to save their lives.

"I will not lift my foot to climb the stair. I will stand for one moment beneath the immitigable tree, alone with the man whose throat is cut, while downstairs the cook shoves in and out the dampers. I will not climb the stair. We are doomed, all of us. Women shuffle past with shopping-bags. People keep on passing. Yet you shall not destroy me. For this moment, this one moment, we are together. I press you to me. Come, pain, feed on me. Bury your fangs in my flesh. Tear me asunder. I sob, I sob."

"Such is the incomprehensible combination," said Bernard, "such is the complexity of things, that as I descend the staircase I do not know which is sorrow, which joy. My son is born; Percival is dead. I am upheld by pillars, shored up on either side by stark emotions; but which is sorrow, which is joy? I ask, and do not know, only that I need silence, and to be alone and to go out, and to save one hour to consider what has happened to my world, what death has done to my world.

"This then is the world that Percival sees no longer. Let me look. The butcher delivers meat next door; two old men stumble along the pavement; sparrows alight. The machine then works; I note the rhythm, the throb, but as a thing in which I have no part, since he sees it no longer. (He lies pale and bandaged in some room.) Now then is my chance to find out what is of great importance, and I must be careful, and tell no lies. About him my feeling was: he sat there in the centre. Now I go to that spot no longer. The place is empty.

"Oh, yes, I can assure you, men in felt-hats and women carrying baskets—you have lost something that would have been very valuable to you. You have lost a leader, whom you would have followed; and one of you has lost happiness and children. He is dead who would have given you that. He lies on a camp-bed, bandaged, in some hot Indian hospital while coolies squatted on the floor agitate those fans—I forget how they call them. But this is important; 'You are well out of it,' I said, while the doves descended over the roofs and my son was born, as if it were a fact. I remember, as a boy, his curious air of detachment. And I go on to say (my eyes fill with tears and then are dry), 'But this is better than one had dared to hope.' I say, addressing what is abstract, facing me eyeless at the end of the avenue, in the sky, 'Is this the utmost you can do?' 'Then we have triumphed. You have done your utmost,' I say, addressing that blank and brutal face (for he was twenty-five and should have lived to be eighty) without avail. I am not going to lie down and weep away a life of care. (An entry to be made in my pocket-book; contempt for those who inflict meaningless death.) Further, this is important; that I should be able to place him in trifling and ridiculous situations, so that he may not feel himself absurd, perched on a great horse. I must be able to say, 'Percival, a ridiculous name.' At the same time let me tell you, men and women, hurrying to the tube station, you would have had to respect him. You would have had to form up and follow behind him. How strange to oar one's way through crowds seeing life through hollow eyes, burning eyes.

"Yet already signals begin, beckonings, attempts to lure me back. Curiosity is knocked out only for a short time. One cannot live outside the machine for more perhaps than half an hour. Bodies, I note, already begin to look ordinary; but what is behind them differs—the perspective. Behind that newspaper placard is the hospital; the long room with black men pulling ropes; and then they bury him. Yet since it says a famous actress has been divorced, I ask instantly Which? Yet I cannot take out my penny; I cannot buy a paper; I cannot suffer interruption yet.

"I ask, if I shall never see you again and fix my eyes on that solidity, what form will our communication take? You have gone across the court, further and further, drawing finer and finer the thread between us. But you exist somewhere. Something of you remains. A judge. That is, if I discover a new vein in myself I shall submit it to you privately. I shall ask, 'What is your verdict?' You shall remain the arbiter. But for how long? Things will become too difficult to explain: there will be new things; already my son. I am now at the zenith of an experience. It will decline. Already I no longer cry with conviction, 'What luck!' Exaltation, the flight of doves descending, is over. Chaos, detail, return. I am no longer amazed by names written over shop-windows. I do not feel Why hurry? Why catch trains? The sequence returns; one thing leads to another—the usual order.

"Yes, but I still resent the usual order. I will not let myself be made yet to accept the sequence of things. I will walk; I will not change the rhythm of my mind by stopping, by looking; I will walk. I will go up these steps into the gallery and submit myself to the influence of minds like mine outside the sequence. There is little time left to answer the question; my powers flag; I become torpid. Here are pictures. Here are cold madonnas among their pillars. Let them lay to rest the incessant activity of the mind's eye, the bandaged head, the men with ropes, so that I may find something unvisual beneath. Here are gardens; and Venus among her flowers; here are saints and blue madonnas. Mercifully these pictures make no reference; they do not nudge; they do not point. Thus they expand my consciousness of him and bring him back to me differently. I remember his beauty. 'Look, where he comes,' I said.

"Lines and colours almost persuade me that I too can be heroic, I, who make phrases so easily, am so soon seduced, love what comes next, and cannot clench my fist, but vacillate weakly making phrases according to my circumstances. Now, through my own infirmity I recover what he was to me: my opposite. Being naturally truthful, he did not see the point of these exaggerations, and was borne on by a natural sense of the fitting, was indeed a great master of the art of living so that he seems to have lived long, and to have spread calm round him, indifference one might almost say, certainly to his own advancement, save that he had also great compassion. A child playing—a summer evening—door will open and shut, will keep opening and shutting, through which I see sights that make me weep. For they cannot be imparted. Hence our loneliness; hence our desolation. I turn to that spot in my mind and find it empty. My own infirmities oppress me. There is no longer him to oppose them.

"Behold then, the blue madonna streaked with tears. This is my funeral service. We have no ceremonies, only private dirges and no conclusions, only violent sensations, each separate. Nothing that has been said meets our case. We sit in the Italian room at the National Gallery picking up fragments. I doubt that Titian ever felt this rat gnaw. Painters live lives of methodical absorption, adding stroke to stroke. They are not like poets—scapegoats; they are not chained to the rock. Hence the silence, the sublimity. Yet that crimson must have burnt in Titian's gizzard. No doubt he rose with the great arms holding the cornucopia, and fell, in that descent. But the silence weighs on me—the perpetual solicitation of the eye. The pressure is intermittent and muffled. I distinguish too little and too vaguely. The bell is pressed and I do not ring or give out irrelevant clamours all jangled. I am titillated inordinately by some splendour; the ruffled crimson against the green lining; the march of pillars; the orange light behind the black, pricked ears of the olive trees. Arrows of sensation strike from my spine, but without order.

"Yet something is added to my interpretation. Something lies deeply buried. For one moment I thought to grasp it. But bury it, bury it; let it breed, hidden in the depths of my mind some day to fructify. After a long lifetime, loosely, in a moment of revelation, I may lay hands on it, but now the idea breaks in my hand. Ideas break a thousand times for once that they globe themselves entire. They break; they fall over me. 'Line and colours they survive, therefore . . .'

"I am yawning. I am glutted with sensations. I am exhausted with the strain and the long, long time—twenty-five minutes, half an hour—that I have held myself alone outside the machine. I grow numb; I grow stiff. How shall I break up this numbness which discredits my sympathetic heart? There are others suffering—multitudes of people suffering. Neville suffers. He loved Percival. But I can no longer endure extremities; I want some one with whom to laugh, with whom to yawn, with whom to remember how he scratched his head; some one he was at ease with and liked (not Susan, whom he loved but Jinny rather). In her room also I could do penance. I could ask, Did he tell you how I refused him when he asked me to go to Hampton Court that day? Those are the thoughts that will wake me leaping in anguish in the middle of the night—the crimes for which one would do penance in all the markets of the world bareheaded; that one did not go to Hampton Court that day.

"But now I want life round me, and books and little ornaments, and the usual sounds of tradesmen calling on which to pillow my head after this exhaustion, and shut my eyes after this revelation. I will go straight then down the stairs, and hail the first taxi and drive to Jinny."

"There is the puddle," said Rhoda, "and I cannot cross it. I hear the rush of the great grindstone within an inch of my head. Its wind roars in my face. All palpable forms of life have failed me. Unless I can stretch and touch something hard, I shall be blown down the eternal corridors for ever. What then can I touch? What brick, what stone? and so draw myself across the enormous gulf into my body safely?

"Now the shadow has fallen and the purple light slants downwards. The figure that was robed in beauty is now clothed in ruin. The figure that stood in the grove where the steep backed hills come down falls in ruin, as I told them when they said they loved his voice on the stair, and his old shoes and moments of being together.

"Now I will walk down Oxford Street envisaging a world rent by lightning; I will look at oaks cracked asunder and red where the flowering branch has fallen. I will go to Oxford Street and buy stockings for a party. I will do the usual things under the lightning flash. On the bare ground I will pick violets and bind them together and offer them to Percival, something given him by me. Look now at what Percival has given me. Look at the street now that Percival is dead. The houses are lightly founded to be puffed over by a breath of air. Reckless and random the cars race and roar and hunt us to death like bloodhounds. I am alone in a hostile world. The human face is hideous. This is to my liking. I want publicity and violence and to be dashed like a stone on the rocks. I like factory chimneys and cranes and lorries. I like the passing of face and face and face, deformed, indifferent. I am sick of prettiness; I am sick of privacy. I ride rough waters and shall sink with no one to save me.

"Percival, by his death, has made me this present, has revealed this terror, has left me to undergo this humiliation—faces and faces, served out like soup-plates by scullions; coarse, greedy, casual; looking in at shop-windows with pendent parcels; ogling, brushing, destroying everything, leaving even our love impure, now touched by their dirty fingers.

"Here is the shop where they sell stockings. And I could believe that beauty is once more set flowing. Its whisper comes down these aisles, through these laces, breathing among baskets of coloured ribbons. There are then warm hollows grooved in the heart of the uproar; alcoves of silence where we can shelter under the wing of beauty from truth which I desire. Pain is suspended as a girl silently slides open a drawer. And then, she speaks; her voice wakes me. I shoot to the bottom among the weeds and see envy, jealousy, hatred and spite scuttle like crabs over the sand as she speaks. These are our companions. I will pay my bill and take my parcel.

"This is Oxford Street. Here are hate, jealousy, hurry, and indifference frothed into the wild semblance of life. These are our
companions. Consider the friends with whom we sit and eat. I
think of Louis, reading the sporting column of an evening newspaper, afraid of ridicule; a snob. He says, looking at the people
passing, he will shepherd us if we will follow. If we submit he
will reduce us to order. Thus he will smooth out the death of
Percival to his satisfaction, looking fixedly over the cruet, past
the houses at the sky. Bernard, meanwhile, flops red-eyed into
some arm-chair. He will have out his notebook; under D, he will
enter 'Phrases to be used on the deaths of friends.' Jinny, pirouetting across the room, will perch on the arm of his chair and
ask, 'Did he love me?' 'More than he loved Susan?' Susan, engaged to her farmer in the country, will stand for a second with
the telegram before her, holding a plate; and then, with a kick
of her heel, slam to the oven door. Neville, after staring at the
window through his tears will see through his tears, and ask,
'Who passes the window?'—'What lovely boy?' This is my trib-
ute to Percival; withered violets, blackened violets.

"Where shall I go then? To some museum, where they keep
rings under glass cases, where there are cabinets, and the dresses
that queens have worn? Or shall I go to Hampton Court and
look at the red walls and courtyards and the seemliness of herded
yew trees making black pyramids symmetrically on the grass
among flowers? There shall I recover beauty, and impose order
upon my raked, my dishevelled soul? But what can one make in
loneliness? Alone I should stand on the empty grass and say,
Rooks fly; somebody passes with a bag; there is a gardener with
a wheelbarrow. I should stand in a queue and smell sweat, and
scent as horrible as sweat; and be hung with other people like a
joint of meat among other joints of meat.

"Here is a hall where one pays money and goes in, where one
hears music among somnolent people who have come here after
lunch on a hot afternoon. We have eaten beef and pudding
enough to live for a week without tasting food. Therefore we

cluster like maggots on the back of something that will carry us on. Decorous, portly—we have white hair waved under our hats; slim shoes; little bags; clean-shaven cheeks; here and there a military moustache, not a speck of dust has been allowed to settle anywhere on our broadcloth. Swaying and opening programmes, with a few words of greeting to friends, we settle down, like walruses stranded on rocks, like heavy bodies incapable of waddling to the sea, hoping for a wave to lift us, but we are too heavy, and too much dry shingle lies between us and the sea. We lie gorged with food, torpid in the heat. Then, swollen but contained in slippery satin, the sea-green woman comes to our rescue. She sucks in her lips, assumes an air of intensity, inflates herself and hurls herself precisely at the right moment as if she saw an apple and her voice was the arrow into the note, 'Ah!'

"An axe has split a tree to the core; the core is warm; sound quivers within the bark. 'Ah,' cried a woman to her lover, leaning from her window in Venice, 'Ah, Ah!' she cried, and again she cries 'Ah!' She has provided us with a cry. But only a cry. And what is a cry? Then the beetle-shaped men come with their violins; wait; count; nod; down come their bows. And there is ripple and laughter like the dance of olive trees and their myriad-tongued grey leaves when a seafarer, biting a twig between his lips where the many-backed steep hills come down, leaps on shore.

" 'Like' and 'like' and 'like'—but what is the thing that lies beneath the semblance of the thing? Now that lightning has gashed the tree and the flowering branch has fallen and Percival, by his death, has made me this gift, let me see the thing. There is a square; there is an oblong. The players take the square and place it upon the oblong. They place it very accurately; they make a perfect dwelling-place. Very little is left outside. The structure is now visible; what is inchoate is here stated; we are not so various or so mean; we have made oblongs and stood them upon squares. This is our triumph; this is our consolation.

"The sweetness of this content overflowing runs down the walls of my mind, and liberates understanding. Wander no more, I say; this is the end. The oblong has been set upon the square; the spiral is on top. We have been hauled over the shingle, down to the sea. The players come again. But they are mopping their faces. They are no longer so spruce or so debonair. I will go. I will set aside this afternoon. I will make a pilgrimage. I will go to Greenwich. I will fling myself fearlessly into trams, into omnibuses. As we lurch down Regent Street, and I am flung upon this woman, upon this man, I am not injured, I am not outraged by the collision. A square stands upon an oblong. Here are mean streets where chaffering goes on in street markets, and every sort of iron rod, bolt and screw is laid out, and people swarm off the pavement, pinching raw meat with thick fingers. The structure is visible. We have made a dwelling-place.

"These then are the flowers that grow among the rough grasses of the field which the cows trample, wind-bitten, almost deformed, without fruit or blossom. These are what I bring, torn up by the roots from the pavement of Oxford Street, my penny bunch, my penny bunch of violets. Now from the window of the tram I see masts among chimneys; there is the river; there are ships that sail to India. I will walk by the river. I will pace this embankment, where an old man reads a newspaper in a glass shelter. I will pace this terrace and watch the ships bowling down the tide. A woman walks on deck, with a dog barking round her. Her skirts are blown; her hair is blown; they are going out to sea; they are leaving us; they are vanishing this summer evening. Now I will relinquish; now I will let loose. Now I will at last free the checked, the jerked back desire to be spent, to be consumed. We will gallop together over desert hills where the swallow dips her wings in dark pools and the pillars stand entire. Into the wave that dashes upon the shore, into the wave that flings its white foam to the uttermost corners of the earth I throw my violets, my offering to Percival."

he sun no longer stood in the middle of the sky. Its light slanted, falling obliquely. Here it caught on the edge of a cloud and burnt it into a slice of light, a blazing island on which no foot could rest. Then another cloud was caught in the light and another and another, so that the waves beneath were arrow-struck with fiery feathered darts that shot erratically across the quivering blue.

The topmost leaves of the tree were crisped in the sun. They rustled stiffly in the random breeze. The birds sat still save that they flicked their heads sharply from side to side. Now they paused in their song as if glutted with sound, as if the fullness of midday had gorged them. The dragon-fly poised motionless over a reed then shot its blue stitch further through the air. The far hum in the distance seemed made of the broken tremor of fine wings dancing up and down on the horizon. The river water held the reeds now fixed as if glass had hardened round them; and then the glass wavered and the reeds swept low. Pondering, sunken headed the cattle stood in the fields and cumbrously moved one foot and then another. In the bucket near the house the tap stopped dripping, as if the bucket were full, and then the tap dripped one, two, three separate drops in succession.

The windows showed erratically spots of burning fire, the elbow of one branch, and then some tranquil space of pure clarity. The blind hung red at the window's edge and within the room daggers of light fell upon chairs and tables making cracks across their lacquer and polish. The green pot bulged enormously, with its white window elongated in its side. Light driving darkness before it spilt itself profusely upon the corners and bosses; and yet heaped up darkness in mounds of unmoulded shape.

The waves massed themselves, curved their backs and crashed.

Up spurted stones and shingle. They swept round the rocks, and
the spray, leaping high, spattered the walls of a cave that had
been dry before, and left pools inland, where some fish, stranded,
lashed its tail as the wave drew back.

"I have signed my name," said Louis, "already twenty times. I,
and again I, and again I. Clear, firm, unequivocal, there it stands,
my name. Clear-cut and unequivocal am I too. Yet a vast inheritance of experience is packed in me. I have lived thousands of
years. I am like a worm that has eaten its way through the wood
of a very old oak beam. But now I am compact; now I am gathered together this fine morning.

"The sun shines from a clear sky. But twelve o'clock brings
neither rain nor sunshine. It is the hour when Miss Johnson
brings me my letters in a wire tray. Upon these white sheets I
indent my name. The whisper of leaves, water running down
gutters, green depths flecked with dahlias or zinnias; I, now a
duke, now Plato, companion of Socrates; the tramp of dark men
and yellow men migrating east, west, north and south; the eternal procession, women going with attaché cases down the Strand
as they went once with pitchers to the Nile; all the furled and
close-packed leaves of my many-folded life are now summed in
my name; incised cleanly and barely on the sheet. Now a full-
grown man; now upright standing in sun or rain, I must drop
heavy as a hatchet and cut the oak with my sheer weight, for if I
deviate, glancing this way, or that way, I shall fall like snow and
be wasted.

"I am half in love with the typewriter and the telephone. With
letters and cables and brief but courteous commands on the telephone to Paris, Berlin, New York I have fused my many lives
into one; I have helped by my assiduity and decision to score
those lines on the map there by which the different parts of the
world are laced together. I love punctually at ten to come into
my room; I love the purple glow of the dark mahogany; I love

the table and its sharp edge; and the smooth-running drawers. I love the telephone with its lip stretched to my whisper, and the date on the wall; and the engagement book. Mr. Prentice at four; Mr. Eyres sharp at four-thirty.

"I like to be asked to come to Mr. Burchard's private room and report on our commitments to China. I hope to inherit an arm-chair and a Turkey carpet. My shoulder is to the wheel; I roll the dark before me, spreading commerce where there was chaos in the far parts of the world. If I press on, from chaos making or-der, I shall find myself where Chatham stood, and Pitt, Burke, and Sir Robert Peel. Thus I expunge certain stains, and erase old defilements; the woman who gave me a flag from the top of the Christmas tree; my accent; beatings and other tortures; the boasting boys; my father, a banker at Brisbane.

"I have read my poet in an eating-house, and, stirring my cof-fee, listened to the clerks making bets at the little tables, watched the women hesitating at the counter. I said that nothing should be irrelevant, like a piece of brown paper dropped casually on the floor. I said their journeys should have an end in view; they should earn their two pound ten a week at the command of an august master; some hand, some robe, should fold us about in the evening. When I have healed these fractures and compre-hended these monstrosities so that they need neither excuse nor apology which both waste our strength, I shall give back to the street and the eating-shop what they lost when they fell on these hard times and broke on these stony beaches. I shall assemble a few words and forge round us a hammered ring of beaten steel.

"But now I have not a moment to spare. There is no respite here, no shadow made of quivering leaves, or alcove to which one can retreat from the sun, to sit, with a lover, in the cool of the evening. The weight of the world is on our shoulders; its vision is through our eyes; if we blink or look aside, or turn back to finger what Plato said or remember Napoleon and his conquests, we inflict on the world the injury of some obliquity. This is life; Mr. Prentice at four; Mr. Eyres at four-thirty. I like to hear the soft rush of the lift and the thud with which it stops on my landing and the heavy male tread of responsible feet down the corridors. So by dint of our united exertions we send ships to the remotest parts of the globe; replete with lavatories and gymnasiums. The weight of the world is on our shoulders. This is life. If I press on, I shall inherit a chair and a rug; a place in Surrey with glass houses, and some rare conifer, melon, or flowering tree which other merchants will envy.

"Yet I still keep my attic room. There I open the usual little book; there I watch the rain glisten on the tiles till they shine like a policeman's waterproof; there I see the broken windows in poor people's houses; the lean cats; some slattern squinting in a cracked looking-glass as she arranges her face for the street corner; there Rhoda sometimes comes. For we are lovers.

"Percival has died; (he died in Egypt; he died in Greece; all deaths are one death). Susan has children; Neville mounts rapidly to the conspicuous heights. Life passes. The clouds change perpetually over our houses. I do this, do that, and again do this and then that. Meeting and parting, we assemble different forms, make different patterns. But if I do not nail these impressions to the board and out of the many men in me make one; exist here and now and not in streaks and patches, like scattered snow wreaths on far mountains; and ask Miss Johnson as I pass through the office about the movies and take my cup of tea and accept also my favourite biscuit, then I shall fall like snow and be wasted.

"Yet when six o'clock comes and I touch my hat to the commissionaire, being always too effusive in ceremony since I desire so much to be accepted; and struggle, leaning against the wind, buttoned up, with my jaws blue and my eyes running water, I wish that a little typist would cuddle on my knees; I think that my favourite dish is liver and bacon; and so am apt to wander to the river, to the narrow streets where there are frequent public-houses, and the shadows of ships passing at the end of the street, and women fighting. But I say to myself, recovering my sanity, Mr. Prentice at four; Mr. Eyres at four-thirty. The hatchet must fall on the block; the oak must be cleft to the centre. The weight of the world is on my shoulders. Here is the pen and the paper; on the letters in the wire basket I sign my name, I, I, and again I."

"Summer comes, and winter," said Susan. "The seasons pass. The pear fills itself and drops from the tree. The dead leaf rests on its edge. But steam has obscured the window. I sit by the fire watching the kettle boil. I see the pear tree through the streaked steam on the window-pane.

"Sleep, sleep, I croon, whether it is summer or winter, May or November. Sleep I sing—I, who am unmelodious and hear no music save rustic music when a dog barks, a bell tinkles, or wheels crunch upon the gravel. I sing my song by the fire like an old shell murmuring on the beach. Sleep, sleep, I say, warning off with my voice all who rattle milk-cans, fire at rooks, shoot rabbits, or in any way bring the shock of destruction near this wicker cradle, laden with soft limbs, curled under a pink coverlet.

"I have lost my indifference, my blank eyes, my pear-shaped eyes that saw to the root. I am no longer January, May or any other season, but am all spun to a fine thread round the cradle, wrapping in a cocoon made of my own blood the delicate limbs of my baby. Sleep, I say, and feel within me uprush some wilder, darker violence, so that I would fell down with one blow any intruder, any snatcher, who should break into this room and wake the sleeper.

"I pad about the house all day long in apron and slippers, like my mother who died of cancer. Whether it is summer, whether it is winter, I no longer know by the moor grass, and the heath flower; only by the steam on the window-pane, or the frost on the window-pane. When the lark peels high his ring of sound and it falls through the air like an apple paring, I stoop; I feed my baby. I, who used to walk through beech woods noting the jay's feather turning blue as it falls, past the shepherd and the tramp, who stared at the woman squatted beside a tilted cart in a ditch, go from room to room with a duster. Sleep, I say, desiring sleep to fall like a blanket of down and cover these weak limbs; demanding that life shall sheathe its claws and gird its lightning and pass by, making of my own body a hollow, a warm shelter for my child to sleep in. Sleep, I say, sleep. Or I go to the window, I look at the rook's high nest; and the pear tree. 'His eyes will see when mine are shut,' I think. 'I shall go mixed with them beyond my body and shall see India. He will come home, bringing me trophies to be laid at my feet. He will increase my possessions.'

"But I never rise at dawn and see the purple drops in the cabbage leaves; the red drops in the roses. I do not watch the setter nose in a circle, or lie at night watching the leaves hide the stars and the stars move and the leaves hang still. The butcher calls; the milk has to be stood under a shade lest it should sour.

"Sleep, I say, sleep, as the kettle boils and its breath comes thicker and thicker issuing in one jet from the spout. So life fills my veins. So life pours through my limbs. So I am driven forward, till I could cry, as I move from dawn to dusk opening and shutting, 'No more. I am glutted with natural happiness.' Yet more will come, more children; more cradles, more baskets in the kitchen and hams ripening; and onions glistening; and more beds of lettuce and potatoes. I am blown like a leaf by the gale; now brushing the wet grass, now whirled up. I am glutted with natural happiness; and wish sometimes that the fullness would pass from me and the weight of the sleeping house rise, when we sit reading, and I stay the thread at the eye of my needle. The lamp kindles a fire in the dark pane. A fire burns in the heart of the ivy. I see a lit-up street in the evergreens. I hear traffic in the brush of the wind down the lane, and broken voices, and laughter, and Jinny who cries as the door opens, 'Come, Come!'

"But no sound breaks the silence of our house, where the fields sigh close to the door. The wind washes through the elm trees;

a moth hits the lamp; a cow lows; a crack of sound starts in the rafter, and I push my thread through the needle and murmur, 'Sleep.'"

"Now is the moment," said Jinny. "Now we have met, and have come together. Now let us talk, let us tell stories. Who is he? Who is she? I am infinitely curious and do not know what is to come. If you, whom I meet for the first time, were to say to me, 'The coach starts at four from Piccadilly,' I would not stay to fling a few necessaries in a bandbox, but would come at once.

"Let us sit here under the cut flowers, on the sofa by the picture. Let us decorate our Christmas tree with facts and again with facts. People are so soon gone; let us catch them. That man there, by the cabinet; he lives, you say, surrounded by china pots. Break one and you shatter a thousand pounds. And he loved a girl in Rome and she left him. Hence the pots, old junk found in lodging-houses or dug from the desert sands. And since beauty must be broken daily to remain beautiful, and he is static, his life stagnates in a china sea. It is strange though; for once as a young man, he sat on damp ground and drank rum with soldiers.

"One must be quick and add facts deftly, like toys to a tree, fixing them with a twist of the fingers. He stoops, how he stoops, even over an azalea. He stoops over the old woman even, because she wears diamonds in her ears, and, bundling about her estate in a pony carriage, directs who is to be helped, what tree felled, and who turned out tomorrow. (I have lived my life I must tell you all these years and I am now past thirty, perilously, like a mountain goat leaping from crag to crag; I do not settle long anywhere; I do not attach myself to one person in particular; but you will find that if I raise my arm, some figure at once breaks off and will come.) And that man is a judge; and that man is a millionaire, and that man, with the eyeglass, shot his governess through the heart with an arrow when he was ten years old. Afterwards he rode through deserts with dispatches, took part in revolutions and now collects materials for a history of his mother's family, long settled in Norfolk. That little man with a blue chin has a right hand that is withered. But why? We do not know. That woman, you whisper discreetly, with the pearl pagodas hanging from her ears, was the pure flame who lit the life of one of our statesmen; now since his death she sees ghosts, tells fortunes, and has adopted a coffee-coloured youth whom she calls the Messiah. That man with the drooping moustache, like a cavalry officer, lived a life of the utmost debauchery (it is all in some memoir) until one day he met a stranger in a train who converted him between Edinburgh and Carlisle by reading the Bible.

"Thus, in a few seconds, deftly, adroitly, we decipher the hieroglyphs written on other people's faces. Here, in this room, are the abraded and battered shells cast on the shore. The door goes on opening. The room fills and fills with knowledge, anguish, many kinds of ambition, much indifference, some despair. Between us, you say, we could build cathedrals, dictate policies, condemn men to death, and administer the affairs of several public offices. The common fund of experience is very deep. We have between us scores of children of both sexes, whom we are educating, going to see at school with the measles, and bringing up to inherit our houses. In one way or another we make this day, this Friday, some by going to the Law Courts; others to the city; others to the nursery; others by marching and forming fours. A million hands stitch, raise hods with bricks. The activity is endless. And tomorrow it begins again; tomorrow we make Saturday. Some take train for France; others ship for India. Some will never come into this room again. One may die tonight. Another will beget a child. From us every sort of building, policy, venture, picture, poem, child, factory, will spring. Life comes; life goes; we make life. So you say.

"But we who live in the body see with the body's imagination things in outline. I see rocks in bright sunshine. I cannot take these facts into some cave and, shading my eyes, grade their yellows, blues, umbers into one substance. I cannot remain seated for long. I must jump up and go. The coach may start from Piccadilly. I drop all these facts—diamonds, withered hands, china pots and the rest of it, as a monkey drops nuts from its naked paws. I cannot tell you if life is this or that. I am going to push out into the heterogeneous crowd. I am going to be buffeted; to be flung up, and flung down, among men, like a ship on the sea.

"For now my body, my companion, which is always sending its signals, the rough black 'No,' the golden 'Come' in rapid running arrows of sensation, beckons. Some one moves. Did I raise my arm? Did I look? Did my yellow scarf with the strawberry spots float and signal? He has broken from the wall. He follows. I am pursued through the forest. All is rapt, all is nocturnal and the parrots go screaming through the branches. All my senses stand erect. Now I feel the roughness of the fibre of the curtain through which I push; now I feel the cold iron railing and its blistered paint beneath my palm. Now the cool tide of darkness breaks its waters over me. We are out of doors. Night opens; night traversed by wandering moths; night hiding lovers roaming to adventure. I smell roses; I smell violets; I see red and blue just hidden. Now gravel is under my shoes; now grass. Up reel the tall backs of houses guilty with lights. All London is uneasy with flashing lights. Now let us sing our love song— Come, come, come. Now my gold signal is like a dragon-fly flying taut. Jug, jug, jug, I sing like the nightingale whose melody is crowded in the too narrow passage of her throat. Now I hear crash and rending of boughs and the crack of antlers as if the beasts of the forest were all hunting, all rearing high and plunging down among the thorns. One has pierced me. One is driven deep within me. And velvet flowers and leaves whose coolness has been stood in water wash me round, and sheathe me, embalming me."

"Why, look," said Neville, "at the clock ticking on the mantelpiece? Time passes, yes. And we grow old. But to sit with you, alone with you, here in London, in this firelit room, you there, I here, is all. The world ransacked to its uttermost ends, and all its heights stripped and gathered of their flowers holds no more. Look at the firelight running up and down the gold thread in the curtain. The fruit it circles droops heavy. It falls on the toe of your boot, it gives your face a red rim—I think it is the firelight and not your face; I think those are books against the wall, and that a curtain, and that perhaps an arm-chair. But when you come everything changes. The cups and saucers changed when you came in this morning. There can be no doubt, I thought, pushing aside the newspaper, that our mean lives, unsightly as they are, put on splendour and have meaning only under the eyes of love.

"I rose. I had done my breakfast. There was the whole day before us, and as it was fine, tender, noncommittal, we walked through the Park to the Embankment, along the Strand to St. Paul's, then to the shop where I bought an umbrella, always talking, and now and then stopping to look. But can this last? I said to myself, by a lion in Trafalgar Square, by the lion seen once and for ever;—so I revisit my past life, scene by scene, there is an elm tree, and there lies Percival. For ever and ever, I swore. Then darted in the usual doubt. I clutched your hand. You left me. The descent into the Tube was like death. We were cut up, we were dissevered by all those faces and the hollow wind that seemed to roar down there over desert boulders. I sat staring in my own room. By five I knew that you were faithless. I snatched the telephone and the buzz, buzz, buzz of its stupid voice in your empty room battered my heart down, when the door opened and there you stood. That was the most perfect of our meetings. But these meetings, these partings, finally destroy us.

"Now this room seems to me central, something scooped out of the eternal night. Outside lines twist and intersect, but round us, wrapping us about. Here we are centred. Here we can be silent, or speak without raising our voices. Did you notice that and then that? we say. He said that, meaning. . . . She hesitated, and I believe suspected. Anyhow, I heard voices, a sob on the stair late at night. It is the end of their relationship. Thus we spin round us infinitely fine filaments and construct a system. Plato and Shakespeare are included, also quite obscure people, people of no importance whatsoever. I hate men who wear crucifixes on the left side of their waistcoats. I hate ceremonies and lamentations and the sad figure of Christ trembling beside another trembling and sad figure. Also the pomp and the indifference and the emphasis, always on the wrong place, of people holding forth under chandeliers in full evening dress, wearing stars and decorations. Some spray in a hedge, though, or a sunset over a flat winter field, or again the way some old woman sits, arms akimbo, in an omnibus with a basket—those we point at for the other to look at. It is so vast an alleviation to be able to point for another to look at. And then not to talk. To follow the dark paths of the mind and enter the past, to visit books, to brush aside their branches and break off some fruit. And you take it and marvel, as I take the careless movements of your body and marvel at its ease, its power—how you fling open windows and are dexterous with your hands. For alas! my mind is a little impeded, it soon tires; I fall damp, perhaps disgusting, at the goal.

"Alas! I could not ride about India in a sun-helmet and return to a bungalow. I cannot tumble, as you do, like half-naked boys on the deck of a ship, squirting each other with hose-pipes. I want this fire, I want this chair. I want some one to sit beside after the day's pursuit and all its anguish, after its listenings, and its waitings, and its suspicions. After quarrelling and reconciliation I need privacy—to be alone with you, to set this hubbub in order. For I am as neat as a cat in my habits. We must oppose the waste and deformity of the world, its crowds eddying round and round disgorged and trampling. One must slip paper-knives, even, exactly through the pages of novels, and tie up packets of letters neatly with green silk, and brush up the cinders with a hearth broom. Everything must be done to rebuke the horror of deformity. Let us read writers of Roman severity and virtue; let us seek perfection through the sand. Yes, but I love to slip the virtue and severity of the noble Romans under the grey light of your eyes, and dancing grasses and summer breezes and the laughter and shouts of boys at play—of naked cabin-boys squirting each other with hose-pipes on the decks of ships. Hence I am not a disinterested seeker, like Louis, after perfection through the sand. Colours always stain the page; clouds pass over it. And the poem, I think, is only your voice speaking. Alcibiades, Ajax, Hector and Percival are also you. They loved riding, they risked their lives wantonly, they were not great readers either. But you are not Ajax or Percival. They did not wrinkle their noses and scratch their foreheads with your precise gesture. You are you. That is what consoles me for the lack of many things—I am ugly, I am weak—and the depravity of the world, and the flight of youth and Percival's death, and bitterness and rancour and envies innumerable.

"But if one day you do not come after breakfast, if one day I see you in some looking-glass perhaps looking after another, if the telephone buzzes and buzzes in your empty room, I shall then, after unspeakable anguish, I shall then—for there is no end to the folly of the human heart—seek another, find another, you. Meanwhile, let us abolish the ticking of time's clock with one blow. Come closer."

The sun had now sunk lower in the sky. The islands of cloud had gained in density and drew themselves across the sun so that the rocks went suddenly black, and the trembling sea holly lost its blue and turned silver, and shadows were blown like grey cloths over the sea. The waves no longer visited the further pools or reached the dotted black line which lay irregularly marked upon the beach. The sand was pearl white, smoothed and shining.

Birds swooped and circled high up in the air. Some raced in the furrows of the wind and turned and sliced through them as if they were one body cut into a thousand shreds. Birds fell like a net descending on the tree-tops. Here one bird taking its way alone made wing for the marsh and sat solitary on a white stake, opening its wings and shutting them.

Some petals had fallen in the garden. They lay shell-shaped on the earth. The dead leaf no longer stood upon its edge, but had been blown, now running, now pausing, against some stalk. Through all the flowers the same wave of light passed in a sudden flaunt and flash as if a fin cut the green glass of a lake. Now and again some level and masterly blast blew the multitudinous leaves up and down and then, as the wind flagged, each blade regained its identity. The flowers, burning their bright discs in the sun, flung aside the sunlight as the wind tossed them, and then some heads too heavy to rise again drooped slightly.

The afternoon sun warmed the fields, poured blue into the shadows and reddened the corn. A deep varnish was laid like a lacquer over the fields. A cart, a horse, a flock of rooks—whatever moved in it was rolled round in gold. If a cow moved a leg it stirred ripples of red gold, and its horns seemed lined with light. Sprays of flaxen-haired corn lay on the hedges, brushed from the shaggy carts that came up from the meadows short

*legged and primeval looking. The round-headed clouds never
dwindled as they bowled along, but kept every atom of their
rotundity. Now, as they passed, they caught a whole village in
the fling of their net and, passing, let it fly free again. Far away
on the horizon, among the million grains of blue grey dust,
burnt one pane, or stood the single line of one steeple or one
tree.*

*The red curtains and the white blinds blew in and out, flap-
ping against the edge of the window, and the light which entered
by flaps and breadths unequally had in it some brown tinge, and
some abandonment as it blew through the blowing curtains in
gusts. Here it browned a cabinet, there reddened a chair, here it
made the window waver in the side of the green jar.*

*All for a moment wavered and bent in uncertainty and am-
biguity, as if a great moth sailing through the room had shadowed the immense solidity of chairs and tables with floating
wings.*

"And time," said Bernard, "lets fall its drop. The drop that has
formed on the roof of the soul falls. On the roof of my mind
time, forming, lets fall its drop. Last week, as I stood shaving,
the drop fell. I, standing with my razor in my hand, became
suddenly aware of the merely habitual nature of my action (this
is the drop forming) and congratulated my hands, ironically, for
keeping at it. Shave, shave, shave, I said. Go on shaving. The
drop fell. All through the day's work, at intervals, my mind went
to an empty place, saying, 'What is lost? What is over?' And
'Over and done with,' I muttered, 'over and done with,' solacing
myself with words. People noticed the vacuity of my face and
the aimlessness of my conversation. The last words of my sentence tailed away. And as I buttoned on my coat to go home I
said more dramatically, 'I have lost my youth.'

"It is curious how, at every crisis, some phrase which does not
fit insists upon coming to the rescue—the penalty of living in

an old civilisation with a notebook. This drop falling has nothing to do with losing my youth. This drop falling is time tapering to a point. Time, which is a sunny pasture covered with a dancing light, time, which is widespread as a field at midday, becomes pendent. Time tapers to a point. As a drop falls from a glass heavy with some sediment, time falls. These are the true cycles, these are the true events. Then as if all the luminosity of the atmosphere were withdrawn I see to the bare bottom. I see what habit covers. I lie sluggish in bed for days. I dine out and gape like a codfish. I do not trouble to finish my sentences, and my actions, usually so uncertain, acquire a mechanical precision. On this occasion, passing an office, I went in and bought, with all the composure of a mechanical figure, a ticket for Rome.

"Now I sit on a stone seat in these gardens surveying the eternal city, and the little man who was shaving in London five days ago looks already like a heap of old clothes. London has also crumbled. London consists of fallen factories and a few gasometers. At the same time I am not involved in this pageantry. I see the violet-sashed priests and the picturesque nursemaids; I notice externals only. I sit here like a convalescent, like a very simple man who knows only words of one syllable. 'The sun is hot,' I say. 'The wind is cold.' I feel myself carried round like an insect on top of the earth and could swear that, sitting here, I feel its hardness, its turning movement. I have no desire to go the opposite way from the earth. Could I prolong this sense another six inches I have a foreboding that I should touch some queer territory. But I have a very limited proboscis. I never wish to prolong these states of detachment; I dislike them; I also despise them. I do not wish to be a man who sits for fifty years on the same spot thinking of his navel. I wish to be harnessed to a cart, a vegetable-cart that rattles over the cobbles.

"The truth is that I am not one of those who find their satisfaction in one person, or in infinity. The private room bores me, also the sky. My being only glitters when all its facets are exposed to many people. Let them fail and I am full of holes, dwindling like burnt paper. Oh, Mrs. Moffat, Mrs. Moffat, I say, come and sweep it all up. Things have dropped from me. I have outlived certain desires; I have lost friends, some by death—Percival—others through sheer inability to cross the street. I am not so gifted as at one time seemed likely. Certain things lie beyond my scope. I shall never understand the harder problems of philosophy. Rome is the limit of my travelling. As I drop asleep at night it strikes me sometimes with a pang that I shall never see savages in Tahiti spearing fish by the light of a blazing cresset, or a lion spring in the jungle, or a naked man eating raw flesh. Nor shall I learn Russian or read the Vedas. I shall never again walk bang into the pillar-box. (But still a few stars fall through my night, beautifully, from the violence of that concussion.) But as I think, truth has come nearer. For many years I crooned complacently, 'My children ... my wife ... my house ... my dog.' As I let myself in with my latch-key I would go through that familiar ritual and wrap myself in those warm coverings. Now that lovely veil has fallen. I do not want possessions now. (Note: an Italian washerwoman stands on the same rung of physical refinement as the daughter of an English duke.)

"But let me consider. The drop falls; another stage has been reached. Stage upon stage. And why should there be an end of stages? and where do they lead? To what conclusion? For they come wearing robes of solemnity. In these dilemmas the devout consult those violet-sashed and sensual-looking gentry who are trooping past me. But for ourselves, we resent teachers. Let a man get up and say, 'Behold, this is the truth,' and instantly I perceive a sandy cat filching a piece of fish in the background. Look, you have forgotten the cat, I say. So Neville, at school, in the dim chapel, raged at the sight of the doctor's crucifix. I, who am always distracted, whether by a cat or by a bee buzzing round the bouquet that Lady Hampden keeps so diligently pressed to her nose, at once make up a story and so obliterate the angles of the crucifix. I have made up thousands of stories; I have filled innumerable notebooks with phrases to be used when I have found the true story, the one story to which all these phrases refer. But I have never yet found that story. And I begin to ask, Are there stories?

"Look now from this terrace at the swarming population beneath. Look at the general activity and clamour. That man is in difficulties with his mule. Half a dozen good-natured loafers offer their services. Others pass by without looking. They have as many interests as there are threads in a skein. Look at the sweep of the sky, bowled over by round white clouds. Imagine the leagues of level land and the aqueducts and the broken Roman pavement and the tombstones in the Campagna, and beyond the Campagna, the sea, then again more land, then the sea. I could break off any detail in all that prospect—say the mule-cart —and describe it with the greatest ease. But why describe a man in trouble with his mule? Again, I could invent stories about that girl coming up the steps. 'She met him under the dark archway. . . . "It is over," he said, turning from the cage where the china parrot hangs.' Or simply, 'That was all.' But why impose my arbitrary design? Why stress this and shape that and twist up little figures like the toys men sell in trays in the street? Why select this, out of all that,—one detail?

"Here am I shedding one of my life-skins, and all they will say is, 'Bernard is spending ten days in Rome.' Here am I marching up and down this terrace alone, unoriented. But observe how dots and dashes are beginning, as I walk, to run themselves into continuous lines, how things are losing the bald, the separate identity that they had as I walked up those steps. The great red pot is now a reddish streak in a wave of yellowish green. The world is beginning to move past me like the banks of a hedge when the train starts, like the waves of the sea when a steamer moves. I am moving too, am becoming involved in the general sequence when one thing follows another and it seems inevitable that the tree should come, then the telegraph-pole, then the break in the hedge. And as I move, surrounded, included and taking part, the usual phrases begin to bubble up, and I wish to free these bubbles from the trap-door in my head, and direct my steps therefore towards that man, the back of whose head is half familiar to me. We were together at school. We shall undoubtedly meet. We shall certainly lunch together. We shall talk. But wait, one moment wait.

"These moments of escape are not to be despised. They come too seldom. Tahiti becomes possible. Leaning over this parapet I see far out a waste of water. A fin turns. This bare visual impression is unattached to any line of reason, it springs up as one might see the fin of a porpoise on the horizon. Visual impressions often communicate thus briefly statements that we shall in time to come uncover and coax into words. I note under F., therefore, 'Fin in a waste of waters.' I, who am perpetually making notes in the margin of my mind for some final statement, make this mark, waiting for some winter's evening.

"Now I shall go and lunch somewhere, I shall hold my glass up, I shall look through the wine, I shall observe with more than my usual detachment, and when a pretty woman enters the restaurant and comes down the room between the tables I shall say to myself, Look where she comes against a waste of waters. A meaningless observation, but to me, solemn, slate-coloured, with a fatal sound of ruining worlds and waters falling to destruction.

"So, Bernard (I recall you, you the usual partner in my enterprises), let us begin this new chapter, and observe the formation of this new, this unknown, strange, altogether unidentified and terrifying experience—the new drop—which is about to shape itself. Larpent is that man's name."

"In this hot afternoon," said Susan, "here in this garden, here in this field where I walk with my son, I have reached the summit of my desires. The hinge of the gate is rusty; he heaves it open. The violent passions of childhood, my tears in the garden when Jinny kissed Louis, my rage in the schoolroom, which smelt of pine, my loneliness in foreign places, when the mules came clattering in on their pointed hoofs and the Italian women chattered at the fountain, shawled, with carnations twisted in their hair, are rewarded by security, possession, familiarity. I have had peaceful, productive years. I possess all I see. I have grown trees from the seed. I have made ponds in which goldfish hide under the broad-leaved lilies. I have netted over strawberry beds and lettuce beds, and stitched the pears and the plums into white bags to keep them safe from the wasps. I have seen my sons and daughters, once netted over like fruit in their cots, break the meshes and walk with me, taller than I am, casting shadows on the grass.

"I am fenced in, planted here like one of my own trees. I say, 'My son,' I say, 'My daughter,' and even the ironmonger looking up from his counter strewn with nails, paint and wire-fencing respects the shabby car at the door with its butterfly nets, pads and beehives. We hang mistletoe over the clock at Christmas, weigh our blackberries and mushrooms, count out jampots, and stand year by year to be measured against the shutter in the drawing-room window. I also make wreaths of white flowers, twisting silver-leaved plants among them for the dead, attaching my card with sorrow for the dead shepherd, with sympathy for the wife of the dead carter; and sit by the beds of dying women, who murmur their last terrors, who clutch my hand; frequenting rooms intolerable except to one born as I was and early acquainted with the farmyard and the dung-heap and the hens straying in and out, and the mother with two rooms and growing children. I have seen the windows run with heat, I have smelt the sink.

"I ask now, standing with my scissors among my flowers, Where can the shadow enter? What shock can loosen my laboriously gathered, relentlessly pressed-down life? Yet sometimes I am sick of natural happiness, and fruit growing, and children scattering the house with oars, guns, skulls, books won for prizes and other trophies. I am sick of the body, I am sick of my own craft, industry and cunning, of the unscrupulous ways of the mother who protects, who collects under her jealous eyes at one long table her own children, always her own.

"It is when spring comes, cold, showery, with sudden yellow flowers—then as I look at the meat under the blue shade and press the heavy silver bags of tea, of sultanas, I remember how the sun rose, and the swallows skimmed the grass, and phrases that Bernard made when we were children, and the leaves shook over us, many-folded, very light, breaking the blue of the sky, scattering wandering lights upon the skeleton roots of the beech trees where I sat, sobbing. The pigeon rose. I jumped up and ran after the words that trailed like the dangling string from an air ball, up and up, from branch to branch escaping. Then like a cracked bowl the fixity of my morning broke, and putting down the bag of flour I thought, Life stands round me like glass round the imprisoned reed.

"I hold scissors and snip off hollyhocks, who went to Elvedon and trod on rotten oak-apples, and saw the lady writing and the gardeners with their great brooms. We ran back panting lest we should be shot and nailed like stoats to the wall. Now I measure, I preserve. At night I sit in the arm-chair and stretch my arm for my sewing; and hear my husband snore; and look up when the light from a passing car dazzles the windows and feel the waves of my life tossed, broken, round me who am rooted; and hear cries, and see others' lives eddying like straws round the piers of a bridge while I push my needle in and out and draw my thread through the calico.

"I think sometimes of Percival who loved me. He rode and fell in India. I think sometimes of Rhoda. Uneasy cries wake me at dead of night. But for the most part I walk content with my sons. I cut the dead petals from hollyhocks. Rather squat, grey before my time, but with clear eyes, pear-shaped eyes, I pace my fields."

"Here I stand," said Jinny, "in the Tube station where everything that is desirable meets—Piccadilly South Side, Piccadilly

North Side, Regent Street and the Haymarket. I stand for a moment under the pavement in the heart of London. Innumerable wheels rush and feet press just over my head. The great avenues of civilisation meet here and strike this way and that. I am in the heart of life. But look—there is my body in that looking glass. How solitary, how shrunk, how aged! I am no longer young. I am no longer part of the procession. Millions descend those stairs in a terrible descent. Great wheels churn inexorably urging them downwards. Millions have died. Percival died. I still move. I still live. But who will come if I signal?

"Little animal that I am, sucking my flanks in and out with fear, I stand here, palpitating, trembling. But I will not be afraid. I will bring the whip down on my flanks. I am not a whimpering little animal making for the shadow. It was only for a moment, catching sight of myself before I had time to prepare myself as I always prepare myself for the sight of myself, that I quailed. It is true; I am not young—I shall soon raise my arm in vain and my scarf will fall to my side without having signalled. I shall not hear the sudden sigh in the night and feel through the dark some one coming. There will be no reflections in window-panes in dark tunnels. I shall look into faces, and I shall see them seek some other face. I admit, for one moment the soundless flight of upright bodies down the moving stairs like the pinioned and terrible descent of some army of the dead downwards and the churning of the great engines remorselessly forwarding us, all of us, onwards made me cower and run for shelter.

"But now I swear, making deliberately in front of the glass those slight preparations that equip me, I will not be afraid. Think of the superb omnibuses, red and yellow, stopping and starting, punctually in order. Think of the powerful and beautiful cars that now slow to a foot's pace and now shoot forward; think of men, think of women, equipped, prepared, driving onward. This is the triumphant procession; this is the army of victory with banners and brass eagles and heads crowned with laurel-leaves won in battle. They are better than savages in loin-cloths, and women whose hair is dank, whose long breasts sag, with children tugging at their long breasts. These broad thoroughfares—Piccadilly South, Piccadilly North, Regent Street and the Haymarket—are sanded paths of victory driven through the jungle. I too, with my little patent-leather shoes, my handkerchief that is but a film of gauze, my reddened lips and my finely pencilled eyebrows march to victory with the band.

"Look how they show off clothes here even under ground in a perpetual radiance. They will not let the earth even lie wormy and sodden. There are gauzes and silks illumined in glass cases and underclothes trimmed with a million close stitches of fine embroidery. Crimson, green, violet, they are dyed all colours. Think how they organise, roll out, smooth, dip in dyes, and drive tunnels blasting the rock. Lifts rise and fall; trains stop, trains start as regularly as the waves of the sea. This is what has my adhesion. I am a native of this world, I follow its banners. How could I run for shelter when they are so magnificently adventurous, daring, curious, too, and strong enough in the midst of effort to pause and scrawl with a free hand a joke upon the wall? Therefore I will powder my face and redden my lips. I will make the angle of my eyebrows sharper than usual. I will rise to the surface, standing erect with the others in Piccadilly Circus. I will sign with a sharp gesture to a cab whose driver will signify by some indescribable alacrity his understanding of my signals. For I still excite eagerness. I still feel the bowing of men in the street like the silent stoop of the corn when the light wind blows, ruffling it red.

"I will drive to my own house. I will fill the vases with lavish, with luxurious, with extravagant flowers nodding in great bunches. I will place one chair there, another here. I will put ready cigarettes, glasses and some gaily covered new unread book in case Bernard comes, or Neville or Louis. But perhaps it will not be Bernard, Neville or Louis, but somebody new, somebody unknown, somebody I passed on a staircase and, just turning as we passed, I murmured, 'Come.' He will come this afternoon;

somebody I do not know, somebody new. Let the silent army of the dead descend. I march forward."

"I no longer need a room now," said Neville, "or walls and firelight. I am no longer young. I pass Jinny's house without envy, and smile at the young man who arranges his tie a little nervously on the doorstep. Let the dapper young man ring the bell; let him find her. I shall find her if I want her, if not, I pass on. The old corrosion has lost its bite—envy, intrigue and bitterness have been washed out. We have lost our glory too. When we were young we sat anywhere, on bare benches in draughty halls with the doors always banging. We tumbled about half naked like boys on the deck of a ship squirting each other with hose-pipes. Now I could swear that I like people pouring profusely out of the Tube when the day's work is done, unanimous, indiscriminate, uncounted. I have picked my own fruit. I look dispassionately.

"After all, we are not responsible. We are not judges. We are not called upon to torture our fellows with thumbscrews and irons; we are not called upon to mount pulpits and lecture them on pale Sunday afternoons. It is better to look at a rose, or to read Shakespeare as I read him here in Shaftesbury Avenue. Here's the fool, here's the villain, here in a car comes Cleopatra, burning on her barge. Here are figures of the damned too, noseless men by the police-court wall, standing with their feet in fire, howling. This is poetry if we do not write it. They act their parts infallibly, and almost before they open their lips I know what they are going to say, and wait the divine moment when they speak the word that must have been written. If it were only for the sake of the play, I could walk Shaftesbury Avenue for ever.

"Then coming from the street, entering some room, there are people talking, or hardly troubling to talk. He says, she says, somebody else says things have been said so often that one word is now enough to lift a whole weight. Argument, laughter, old grievances—they fall through the air, thickening it. I take a book and read half a page of anything. They have not mended the spout of the teapot yet. The child dances, dressed in her mother's clothes.

"But then Rhoda, or it may be Louis, some fasting and anguished spirit, passes through and out again. They want a plot, do they? They want a reason? It is not enough for them, this ordinary scene. It is not enough to wait for the thing to be said as if it were written; to see the sentence lay its dab of clay precisely on the right place, making character; to perceive, suddenly some group in outline against the sky. Yet if they want violence, I have seen death and murder and suicide all in one room. One comes in, one goes out. There are sobs on the staircase. I have heard threads broken and knots tied and the quiet stitching of white cambric going on and on on the knees of a woman. Why ask, like Louis, for a reason, or fly like Rhoda to some far grove and part the leaves of the laurels and look for statues? They say that one must beat one's wings against the storm in the belief that beyond this welter the sun shines; the sun falls sheer into pools that are fledged with willows. (Here it is November; the poor hold out matchboxes in wind-bitten fingers.) They say truth is to be found there entire, and virtue, that shuffles along here, down blind alleys, is to be had there perfect. Rhoda flies with her neck outstretched and blind fanatic eyes, past us. Louis, now so opulent, goes to his attic window among the blistered roofs and gazes where she has vanished, but must sit down in his office among the typewriters and the telephone and work it all out for our instruction, for our regeneration, and the reform of an unborn world.

"But now in this room, which I enter without knocking, things are said as if they had been written. I go to the book-case. If I choose, I read half a page of anything. I need not speak. But I listen. I am marvellously on the alert. Certainly, one cannot read this poem without effort. The page is often corrupt and mud-stained, and torn and stuck together with faded leaves, with scraps of verbena or geranium. To read this poem one must have myriad eyes, like one of those lamps that turn on slabs of racing water at midnight in the Atlantic, when perhaps only a spray of seaweed pricks the surface, or suddenly the waves gape and up shoulders a monster. One must put aside antipathies and jealousies and not interrupt. One must have patience and infinite care and let the light sound, whether of spiders' delicate feet on a leaf or the chuckle of water in some irrelevant drainpipe, unfold too. Nothing is to be rejected in fear or horror. The poet who has written this page (what I read with people talking) has withdrawn. There are no commas or semicolons. The lines do not run in convenient lengths. Much is sheer nonsense. One must be sceptical, but throw caution to the winds and when the door opens accept absolutely. Also sometimes weep; also cut away ruthlessly with a slice of the blade soot, bark, hard accretions of all sorts. And so (while they talk) let down one's net deeper and deeper and gently draw in and bring to the surface what he said and she said and make poetry.

"Now I have listened to them talking. They have gone now. I am alone. I could be content to watch the fire burn for ever, like a dome, like a furnace; now some spike of wood takes the look of a scaffold, or pit, or happy valley; now it is a serpent curled crimson with white scales. The fruit on the curtain swells beneath the parrot's beak. Cheep, cheep, creaks the fire, like the cheep of insects in the middle of a forest. Cheep, cheep, it clicks while out there the branches thrash the air, and now, like a volley of shot, a tree falls. These are the sounds of a London night. Then I hear the one sound I wait for. Up and up it comes, approaches, hesitates, stops at my door. I cry, 'Come in. Sit by me. Sit on the edge of the chair.' Swept away by the old hallucination, I cry, 'Come closer, closer.'"

"I come back from the office," said Louis. "I hang my coat here, place my stick there—I like to fancy that Richelieu walked with such a cane. Thus I divest myself of my authority. I have been sitting at the right hand of a director at a varnished table. The maps of our successful undertakings confront us on the wall. We have laced the world together with our ships. The globe is strung with our lines. I am immensely respectable. All the young ladies in the office acknowledge my entrance. I can dine where I like now, and without vanity may suppose that I shall soon acquire a house in Surrey, two cars, a conservatory and some rare species of melon. But I still return, I still come back to my attic, hang up my hat and resume in solitude that curious attempt which I have made since I brought down my fist on my master's grained oak door. I open a little book. I read one poem. One poem is enough.

O western wind . . .

O western wind, you are at enmity with my mahogany table and spats, and also, alas, with the vulgarity of my mistress, the little actress, who has never been able to speak English correctly—

O western wind, when wilt thou blow . . .

Rhoda, with her intense abstraction, with her unseeing eyes the colour of snail's flesh, does not destroy you, western wind, whether she comes at midnight when the stars blaze or at the most prosaic hour of midday. She stands at the window and looks at the chimney pots and the broken windows in the houses of poor people—

O western wind, when wilt thou blow . . .

"My task, my burden, has always been greater than other people's. A pyramid has been set on my shoulders. I have tried to do a colossal labour. I have driven a violent, an unruly, a vicious team. With my Australian accent I have sat in eating shops and tried to make the clerks accept me, yet never forgotten my solemn and severe convictions and the discrepancies and incoherences that must be resolved. As a boy I dreamt of the Nile, was reluctant to awake, yet brought down my fist on the grained oak door. It would have been happier to have been born without a destiny, like Susan, like Percival, whom I most admire.

> O western wind, when wilt thou blow,
> That the small rain down can rain?

"Life has been a terrible affair for me. I am like some vast sucker, some glutinous, some adhesive, some insatiable mouth. I have tried to draw from the living flesh the stone lodged at the centre. I have known little natural happiness, though I chose my mistress in order that, with her cockney accent, she might make me feel at my ease. But she only tumbled the floor with dirty under linen, and the charwoman and the shop boys called after me a dozen times a day, mocking my prim and supercilious gait.

> O western wind, when wilt thou blow,
> That the small rain down can rain?

"What has my destiny been, the sharp-pointed pyramid that has pressed on my ribs all these years? That I remember the Nile and the women carrying pitchers on their heads; that I feel myself woven in and out of the long summers and winters that have made the corn flow and have frozen the streams. I am not a single and passing being. My life is not a moment's bright spark like that on the surface of a diamond. I go beneath ground torturously, as if a warder carried a lamp from cell to cell. My destiny has been that I remember and must weave together, must plait into one cable the many threads, the thin, the thick, the broken, the enduring of our long history, of our tumultuous and varied day. There is always more to be understood; a discord to be listened for; a falsity to be reprimanded. Broken and soot-stained are these roofs with their chimney cowls, their loose slates, their slinking cats and attic windows. I pick my way over broken glass, among blistered tiles, and see only vile and famished faces.

"Let us suppose that I make reason of it all—one poem on a page, and then die. I can assure you it will not be unwillingly. Percival died. Rhoda left me. But I shall live to be gaunt and sere, to tap my way, much respected, with my gold-headed cane along the pavements of the city. Perhaps I shall never die, shall never attain even that continuity and permanence—

> O western wind, when wilt thou blow,
> That the small rain down can rain?

"Percival was flowering with green leaves and was laid in the earth with all his branches still sighing in the summer wind. Rhoda, with whom I shared silence when the others spoke, she who hung back and turned aside when the herd assembled and galloped with orderly, sleek backs over the rich pastures, has gone now like the desert heat. When the sun blisters the roofs of the city I think of her; when the dry leaves patter to the ground; when the old men come with pointed sticks and pierce little bits of paper as we pierced her—

> O western wind, when wilt thou blow,
> That the small rain down can rain?
> Christ! that my love were in my arms,
> And I in my bed again!

I return now to my book; I return now to my attempt."

"Life, how I have dreaded you," said Rhoda, "oh, human beings, how I have hated you! How you have nudged, how you have interrupted, how hideous you have looked in Oxford Street, how squalid sitting opposite each other staring in the Tube! Now as I climb this mountain, from the top of which I shall see Africa, my mind is printed with brown-paper parcels and your faces. I have been stained by you and corrupted. You smelt so unpleasant, too, lining up outside doors to buy tickets. All were dressed in indeterminate shades of grey and brown, never even a blue feather pinned to a hat. None had the courage to be one thing rather than another. What dissolution of the soul you demanded in order to get through one day, what lies, bowings, scrapings, fluency and servility! How you chained me to one spot, one hour, one chair, and sat yourselves down opposite! How you snatched from me the white spaces that lie between hour and hour and rolled them into dirty pellets and tossed them into the wastepaper basket with your greasy paws. Yet those were my life.

"But I yielded. Sneers and yawns were covered with my hand. I did not go out into the street and break a bottle in the gutter as a sign of rage. Trembling with ardour, I pretended that I was not surprised. What you did, I did. If Susan and Jinny pulled up their stockings like that, I pulled mine up like that also. So terrible was life that I held up shade after shade. Look at life through this, look at life through that; let there be rose leaves, let there be vine leaves—I covered the whole street, Oxford Street, Piccadilly Circus, with the blaze and ripple of my mind, with vine leaves and rose leaves. There were boxes, too, standing in the passage when the school broke up. I stole secretly to read the labels and dream of names and faces. Harrogate, perhaps, Edinburgh, perhaps, was ruffled with golden glory where some girl whose name I forgot stood on the pavement. But it was the name only. I left Louis; I feared embraces. With fleeces, with vestments I have tried to cover the blue-black blade. I implored day to break into night. I have longed to see the cupboard dwindle, to feel the bed soften, to float suspended, to perceive lengthened trees, lengthened faces, a green bank on a moor and two figures in distress saying good-bye. I flung words in fans like those the sower throws over the ploughed fields when the earth is bare. I desired always to stretch the night and fill it fuller and fuller with dreams.

"Then in some hall I parted the boughs of music and saw the house we have made; the square stood upon the oblong. 'The house which contains us all,' I said, lurching against people's shoulders in an omnibus after Percival died; yet I went to Greenwich. Walking on the embankment, I prayed that I might thunder for ever on the verge of the world where there is no vegetation, but here and there a marble pillar. I threw my bunch into the spreading wave. I said, 'Consume me, carry me to the furthest limit.' The wave has broken; the bunch is withered. I seldom think of Percival now.

"Now I climb this Spanish hill; and I will suppose that this mule back is my bed and that I lie dying. There is only a thin sheet between me now and the infinite depths. The lumps in the mattress soften beneath me. We stumble up—we stumble on. My path has been up and up, towards some solitary tree with a pool beside it on the very top. I have sliced the waters of beauty in the evening when the hills close themselves like birds' wings folded. I have picked sometimes a red carnation, and wisps of hay. I have sunk alone on the turf and fingered some old bone and thought: When the wind stoops to brush this height, may there be nothing found but a pinch of dust.

"The mule stumbles up and on. The ridge of the hill rises like mist, but from the top I shall see Africa. Now the bed gives under me. The sheets spotted with yellow holes let me fall through. The good woman with a face like a white horse at the end of the bed makes a valedictory movement and turns to go. Who then comes with me? Flowers only, the cowbind and the moonlight coloured may. Gathering them loosely in a sheaf I made of them a garland and gave them— Oh, to whom? We launch out now over the precipice. Beneath us lie the lights of the herring fleet. The cliffs vanish. Rippling small, rippling grey, innumerable waves spread beneath us. I touch nothing. I see nothing. We may sink and settle on the waves. The sea will drum in my ears. The white petals will be darkened with sea water. They will float for a moment and then sink. Rolling me over the waves will shoulder me under. Everything falls in a tremendous shower, dissolving me.

"Yet that tree has bristling branches; that is the hard line of a cottage roof. Those bladder shapes painted red and yellow are faces. Putting my foot to the ground I step gingerly and press my hand against the hard door of a Spanish inn."

he sun was sinking. The hard stone of the day was cracked and light poured through its splinters. Red and gold shot through the waves, in rapid running arrows, feathered with darkness. Erratically rays of light flashed and wandered, like signals from sunken islands, or darts shot through laurel groves by shameless, laughing boys. But the waves, as they neared the shore, were robbed of light, and fell in one long concussion, like a wall falling, a wall of grey stone, un-pierced by any chink of light.

A breeze rose; a shiver ran through the leaves; and thus stirred they lost their brown density and became grey or white as the tree shifted its mass, winked and lost its domed uniform-ity. The hawk poised on the topmost branch flicked its eyelids and rose and sailed and soared far away. The wild plover cried in the marshes, evading circling, and crying further off in lone-liness. The smoke of trains and chimneys was stretched and torn and became part of the fleecy canopy that hung over the sea and the fields.

Now the corn was cut. Now only a brisk stubble was left of all its flowing and waving. Slowly a great owl launched itself from the elm tree and swung and rose, as if on a line that dipped, to the height of the cedar. On the hills the slow shadows now broadened, now shrank, as they passed over. The pool on the top of the moor lay blank. No furry face looked there, or hoof splashed, or hot muzzle seethed in the water. A bird, perched on an ash-coloured twig, sipped a beakful of cold water. There was no sound of cropping, and no sound of wheels, but only the sudden roar of the wind letting its sails fill and brushing the tops of the grasses. One bone lay rain-pocked and sun-bleached till it shone like a twig that the sea has polished. The tree, that

*had burnt foxy red in spring and in midsummer, bent pliant
leaves to the south wind, was now black as iron, and as bare.*

*The land was so distant that no shining roof or glittering
window could be any longer seen. The tremendous weight of the
shadowed earth had engulfed such frail fetters, such snail-shell
encumbrances. Now there was only the liquid shadow of the
cloud, the buffeting of the rain, a single darting spear of sunshine, or the sudden bruise of the rainstorm. Solitary trees
marked distant hills like obelisks.*

*The evening sun, whose heat had gone out of it and whose
burning spot of intensity had been diffused, made chairs and
tables mellower and inlaid them with lozenges of brown and
yellow. Lined with shadows their weight seemed more ponderous as if colour, tilted, had run to one side. Here lay knife, fork
and glass, but lengthened, swollen, and made portentous.
Rimmed in a gold circle the looking-glass held the scene immobile as if everlasting in its eye.*

*Meanwhile the shadows lengthened on the beach; the black-
ness deepened. The iron black boot became a pool of deep blue.
The rocks lost their hardness. The water that stood round the
old boat was dark as if mussels had been steeped in it. The foam
had turned livid and left here and there a white gleam of pearl
on the misty sand.*

"Hampton Court," said Bernard. "Hampton Court. This is our
meeting-place. Behold the red chimneys, the square battlements
of Hampton Court. The tone of my voice as I say 'Hampton
Court' proves that I am middle-aged. Ten years, fifteen years
ago, I should have said 'Hampton Court?' with interrogation--
what will it be like? Will there be lakes, mazes? Or with anticipation, What is going to happen to me here? Whom shall I
meet? Now, Hampton Court—Hampton Court—the words beat
a gong in the space which I have so laboriously cleared with half

a dozen telephone messages and post cards, give off ring after ring of sound, booming, sonorous: and pictures rise—summer afternoons, boats, old ladies holding their skirts up, one urn in winter, some daffodils in March—these all float to the top of the waters that now lie deep on every scene.

"There at the door by the Inn, our meeting-place, they are already standing—Susan, Louis, Rhoda, Jinny and Neville. They have come together already. In a moment, when I have joined them, another arrangement will form, another pattern. What now runs to waste, forming scenes profusely, will be checked, stated. I am reluctant to suffer that compulsion. Already at fifty yards' distance I feel the order of my being changed. The tug of the magnet of their society tells upon me. I come nearer. They do not see me. Now Rhoda sees me, but she pretends, with her horror of the shock of meeting, that I am a stranger. Now Neville turns. Suddenly, raising my hand, saluting Neville I cry, 'I too have pressed flowers between the pages of Shakespeare's sonnets,' and am churned up. My little boat bobs unsteadily upon the chopped and tossing waves. There is no panacea (let me note) against the shock of meeting.

"It is uncomfortable too, joining ragged edges, raw edges; only gradually, as we shuffle and trample into the Inn, taking coats and hats off, does meeting become agreeable. Now we assemble in the long, bare dining-room that overlooks some park, some green space still fantastically lit by the setting sun so that there is a gold bar between the trees, and sit ourselves down."

"Now sitting side by side," said Neville, "at this narrow table, now before the first emotion is worn smooth, what do we feel? Honestly now, openly and directly as befits old friends meeting with difficulty, what do we feel on meeting? Sorrow. The door will not open; he will not come. And we are laden. Being now all of us middle-aged, loads are on us. Let us put down our loads. What have you made of life, we ask, and I? You, Bernard; you, Susan; you, Jinny; and Rhoda and Louis? The lists have been posted on the doors. Before we break these rolls, and help ourselves to fish and salad, I feel in my private pocket and find my credentials—what I carry to prove my superiority. I have passed. I have papers in my private pocket that prove it. But your eyes, Susan, full of turnips and cornfields, disturb me. These papers in my private pocket—the clamour that proves that I have passed—make a faint sound like that of a man clapping in an empty field to scare away rooks. Now it has died down altogether, under Susan's stare (the clapping, the reverberation that I have made), and I hear only the wind sweeping over the ploughed land and some bird singing—perhaps some intoxicated lark. Has the waiter heard of me, or those furtive everlasting couples, now loitering, now holding back and looking at the trees which are not yet dark enough to shelter their prostrate bodies? No; the sound of clapping has failed.

"What then remains, when I cannot pull out my papers and make you believe by reading aloud my credentials that I have passed? What remains is what Susan brings to light under the acid of her green eyes, her crystal, pear-shaped eyes. There is always somebody, when we come together, and the edges of meeting are still sharp, who refuses to be submerged; whose identity therefore one wishes to make crouch beneath one's own. For me now, it is Susan. I talk to impress Susan. Listen to me, Susan.

"When some one comes in at breakfast, even the embroidered fruit on my curtain swells so that parrots can peck it; one can break it off between one's thumb and finger. The thin, skimmed milk of early morning turns opal, blue, rose. At that hour your husband—the man who slapped his gaiters, pointing with his whip at the barren cow—grumbles. You say nothing. You see nothing. Custom blinds your eyes. At that hour your relationship is mute, null, dun-coloured. Mine at that hour is warm and various. There is no repetition for me. Each day is dangerous. Smooth on the surface, we are all bone beneath like snakes coiling. Suppose we read the *Times*; suppose we argue. It is an experience. Suppose it is winter. The snow falling loads down the roof and seals us together in a red cave. The pipes have burst. We stand a yellow tin bath in the middle of the room. We rush helter-skelter for basins. Look there—it has burst again over the bookcase. We shout with laughter at the sight of ruin. Let solidity be destroyed. Let us have no possessions. Or is it summer? We may wander to a lake and watch Chinese geese waddling flat-footed to the water's edge, or see a bone—like a city church with young green trembling before it. (I choose at random; I choose the obvious.) Each sight is an arabesque scrawled suddenly to illustrate some hazard and marvel of intimacy. The snow, the burst pipe, the tin bath, the Chinese goose—these are signs swung high aloft upon which, looking back, I read the character of each love; how each was different.

"You meanwhile—for I want to diminish your hostility, your green eyes fixed on mine, and your shabby dress, your rough hands, and all the other emblems of your maternal splendour— have stuck like a limpet to the same rock. Yet it is true, I do not want to hurt you; only to refresh and furbish up my belief in myself that failed at your entry. Change is no longer possible. We are committed. Before, when we met in a restaurant in London with Percival, all simmered and shook; we could have been anything. We have chosen now, or sometimes it seems the choice was made for us—a pair of tongs pinched us between the shoulders. I chose. I took the print of life not outwardly, but inwardly upon the raw, the white, the unprotected fibre. I am clouded and bruised with the print of minds and faces and things so subtle that they have smell, colour, texture, substance, but no name. I am merely 'Neville' to you, who see the narrow limits of my life and the line it cannot pass. But to myself I am immeasurable; a net whose fibres pass imperceptibly beneath the world. My net is almost indistinguishable from that which it surrounds. It lifts whales—huge leviathans and white jellies, what is amorphous and wandering; I detect, I perceive. Beneath my eyes opens—a book; I see to the bottom; the heart—I see to the depths. I know what loves are trembling into fire; how jealousy shoots its green flashes hither and thither; how intricately love crosses love; love makes knots; love brutally tears them apart. I have been knotted; I have been torn apart.

"But there was another glory once, when we watched for the door to open, and Percival came; when we flung ourselves unattached on the edge of a hard bench in a public room."

"There was the beech wood," said Susan, "Elvedon, and the gilt hands of the clock sparkling among the trees. The pigeons broke the leaves. The changing travelling lights wandered over me. They escaped me. Yet look, Neville, whom I discredit in order to be myself, at my hand on the table. Look at the gradations of healthy colour here on the knuckles, here on the palm. My body has been used daily, rightly, like a tool by a good workman, all over. The blade is clean, sharp, worn in the centre. (We battle together like beasts fighting in a field, like stags making their horns clash.) Seen through your pale and yielding flesh, even apples and bunches of fruit must have a filmed look as if they stood under glass. Lying deep in a chair with one person, one person only, but one person who changes, you see one inch of flesh only; its nerves, fibres, the sullen or quick flow of blood on it; but nothing entire. You do not see a house in a garden; a horse in a field; a town laid out, as you bend like an old woman straining her eyes over her darning. But I have seen life in blocks, substantial, huge; its battlements and towers, factories and gasometers; a dwelling place made from time immemorial after an hereditary pattern. These things remain square, prominent, undissolved in my mind. I am not sinuous or suave; I sit among you abrading your softness with my hardness, quenching the silver-grey flickering moth-wing quiver of words with the green spurt of my clear eyes.

"Now we have clashed our antlers. This is the necessary prelude; the salute of old friends."

"The gold has faded between the trees," said Rhoda, "and a slice of green lies behind them, elongated like the blade of a knife seen in dreams, or some tapering island on which nobody sets foot. Now the cars begin to wink and flicker, coming down the avenue. Lovers can draw into the darkness now; the boles of the trees are swollen, are obscene with lovers."

"It was different once," said Bernard. "Once we could break the current as we chose. How many telephone calls, how many post cards, are now needed to cut this hole through which we come together, united, at Hampton Court? How swift life runs from January to December! We are all swept on by the torrent of things grown so familiar that they cast no shade; we make no comparisons; think scarcely ever of I or of you; and in this unconsciousness attain the utmost freedom from friction and part the weeds that grow over the mouths of sunken channels. We have to leap like fish, high in the air, in order to catch the train from Waterloo. And however high we leap we fall back again into the stream. I shall never now take ship for the South Sea Islands. A journey to Rome is the limit of my travelling. I have sons and daughters. I am wedged into my place in the puzzle.

"But it is only my body—this elderly man here whom you call Bernard—that is fixed irrevocably—so I desire to believe. I think more disinterestedly than I could when I was young and must dig furiously like a child rummaging in a bran-pie to discover my self. 'Look, what is this? And this? Is this going to be a fine present? Is that all?' and so on. Now I know what the parcels hold; and do not care much. I throw my mind out in the air as a man throws seeds in great fan-flights, falling through the purple sunset, falling on the pressed and shining ploughland which is bare.

"A phrase. An imperfect phrase. And what are phrases? They have left me very little to lay on the table, beside Susan's hand; to take from my pocket, with Neville's credentials. I am not an authority on law, or medicine, or finance. I am wrapped round with phrases, like damp straw; I glow, phosphorescent. And each of you feels when I speak, 'I am lit up. I am glowing.' The little boys used to feel, 'That's a good one, that's a good one,' as the phrases bubbled up from my lips under the elm trees in the playing-fields. They too bubbled up; they also escaped with my phrases. But I pine in solitude. Solitude is my undoing.

"I pass from house to house like the friars in the Middle Ages who cozened the wives and girls with beads and ballads. I am a traveller, a pedlar, paying for my lodging with a ballad; I am an indiscriminate, an easily pleased guest; often putting up in the best room in a four-poster; then lying in a barn on a haystack. I don't mind the fleas and find no fault with silk either. I am very tolerant. I am not a moralist. I have too great a sense of the shortness of life and its temptations to rule red lines. Yet I am not so indiscriminate as you think, judging me—as you judge me—from my fluency. I have a little dagger of contempt and severity hidden up my sleeve. But I am apt to be deflected. I make stories. I twist up toys out of anything. A girl sits at a cottage door; she is waiting; for whom? Seduced, or not seduced? The headmaster sees the hole in the carpet. He sighs. His wife, drawing her fingers through the waves of her still abundant hair reflects—et cetera. Waves of hands, hesitations at street corners, some one dropping a cigarette into the gutter—all are stories. But which is the true story? That I do not know. Hence I keep my phrases hung like clothes in a cupboard, waiting for some one to wear them. Thus waiting, thus speculating, making this note and then another I do not cling to life. I shall be brushed like a bee from a sunflower. My philosophy, always accumulating, welling up moment by moment, runs like quicksilver a dozen ways at once. But Louis, wild-eyed but severe, in his attic, in his office, has formed unalterable conclusions upon the true nature of what is to be known."

"It breaks," said Louis, "the thread I try to spin; your laughter breaks it, your indifference, also your beauty. Jinny broke the thread when she kissed me in the garden years ago. The boasting boys mocked me at school for my Australian accent and broke it. 'This is the meaning,' I say; and then start with a pang —vanity. 'Listen,' I say, 'to the nightingale, who sings among the trampling feet; the conquests and migrations. Believe—' and then am twitched asunder. Over broken tiles and splinters of glass I pick my way. Different lights fall, making the ordinary leopard-spotted and strange. This moment of reconciliation, when we meet together united, this evening moment, with its wine and shaking leaves, and youth coming up from the river in white flannels, carrying cushions, is to me black with the shadows of dungeons and the tortures and infamies practised by man upon man. So imperfect are my senses that they never blot out with one purple the serious charge that my reason adds and adds against us, even as we sit here. What is the solution, I ask myself, and the bridge? How can I reduce these dazzling, these dancing apparitions to one line capable of linking all in one? So I ponder; and you meanwhile observe maliciously my pursed lips, my sallow cheeks and my invariable frown.

"But I beg you also to notice my cane and my waistcoat. I have inherited a desk of solid mahogany in a room hung with maps. Our steamers have won an enviable reputation for their cabins replete with luxury. We supply swimming-baths and gymnasiums. I wear a white waistcoat now and consult a little book before I make an engagement.

"This is the arch and ironical manner in which I hope to distract you from my shivering, my tender, and infinitely young and unprotected soul. For I am always the youngest; the most naïvely surprised; the one who runs in advance in apprehension and sympathy with discomfort or ridicule—should there be a smut on a nose, or a button undone. I suffer for all humiliations. Yet I am also ruthless, marmoreal. I do not see how you can say that it is fortunate to have lived. Your little excitements, your childish transports, when a kettle boils, when the soft air lifts Jinny's spotted scarf and it floats weblike, are to me like silk streamers thrown in the eyes of the charging bull. I condemn you. Yet my heart yearns towards you. I would go with you through the fires of death. Yet am happiest alone. I luxuriate in gold and purple vestments. Yet I prefer a view over chimney-pots; cats scraping

their mangy sides upon blistered chimney-stacks; broken windows; and the hoarse clangour of bells from the steeple of some
brick chapel."

"I see what is before me," said Jinny. "This scarf, these wine-
coloured spots. This glass. This mustard pot. This flower. I like
what one touches, what one tastes. I like rain when it has turned
to snow and become palpable. And being rash, and much more
courageous than you are, I do not temper my beauty with mean-
ness lest it should scorch me. I gulped down entire. It is made of
flesh; it is made of stuff. My imagination is the body's. Its visions
are not fine spun and white with purity like Louis's. I do not
like your lean cats and your blistered chimney-pots. The scrannel
beauties of your roof-tops repel me. Men and women, in uni-
forms, wigs and gowns, bowler hats and tennis shirts beautifully
open at the neck, the infinite variety of women's dresses (I note
all clothes always) delight me. I eddy with them, in and out, in
and out, into rooms, into halls, here, there, everywhere, wherever they go. This man lifts the hoof of a horse. This man shoves
in and out the drawers of his private collection. I am never alone.
I am attended by a regiment of my fellows. My mother must
have followed the drum, my father the sea. I am like a little dog
that trots down the road after the regimental band, but stops to
snuff a tree-trunk, to sniff some brown stain, and suddenly careers across the street after some mongrel cur and then holds one
paw up while it sniffs an entrancing whiff of meat from the
butcher's shop. My traffics have led me into strange places. Men,
how many, have broken from the wall and come to me. I have
only to hold my hand up. Straight as a dart they have come to
the place of assignation—perhaps a chair on a balcony, perhaps
a shop at a street corner. The torments, the divisions of your lives
have been solved for me night after night, sometimes only by the
touch of a finger under the tablecloth as we sat dining—so fluid
has my body become, forming even at the touch of a finger into
one full drop, which fills itself, which quivers, which flashes,
which falls in ecstasy.

"I have sat before a looking-glass as you sit writing, adding up figures at desks. So, before the looking-glass in the temple of my bedroom, I have judged my nose, and my chin; my lips that open too wide and show too much gum. I have looked. I have noted. I have chosen what yellow or white, what shine or dullness, what loop or straightness suits. I am volatile for one, rigid for another, angular as an icicle in silver, or voluptuous as a candle flame in gold. I have run violently like a whip flung out to the extreme end of my tether. His shirt front, there in the corner, has been white; then purple; smoke and flame have wrapped us about; after a furious conflagration—yet we scarcely raised our voices, sitting on the hearth-rug, as we murmured all the secrets of our hearts as into shells so that nobody might hear in the sleeping-house, but I heard the cook stir once, and once we thought the ticking of the clock was a footfall—we have sunk to ashes, leaving no relics, no unburnt bones, no wisps of hair to be kept in lockets such as your intimacies leave behind them. Now I turn grey; now I turn gaunt; but I look at my face at midday sitting in front of the looking-glass in broad daylight, and note precisely my nose, my chin, my lips that open too wide and show too much gum. But I am not afraid."

"There were lamp-posts," said Rhoda, "and trees that had not yet shed their leaves on the way from the station. The leaves might have hidden me still. But I did not hide behind them. I walked straight up to you instead of circling round to avoid the shock of sensation as I used. But it is only that I have taught my body to do a certain trick. Inwardly I am not taught; I fear, I hate, I love, I envy and despise you, but I never join you happily. Coming up from the station refusing to accept the shadow of the trees and the pillar-boxes, I perceived, from your coats and umbrellas, even at a distance, how you stand embedded in a substance made of repeated moments run together; are committed, have an attitude, with children, authority, fame, love, society; where I have nothing. I have no face.

"Here in this dining-room you see the antlers and the tum-

blers; the salt-cellars; the yellow stains on the table-cloth.
'Waiter!' says Bernard. 'Bread!' says Susan. And the waiter
comes; he brings bread. But I see the side of a cup like a mountain and only parts of antlers, and the brightness on the side of
that jug like a crack in darkness with wonder and terror. Your
voices sound like trees creaking in a forest. So with your faces
and their prominences and hollows. How beautiful, standing at
a distance immobile at midnight against the railings of some
square! Behind you is a white crescent of foam, and fishermen
on the verge of the world are drawing in nets and casting them.
A wind ruffles the topmost leaves of primeval trees. (Yet here
we sit at Hampton Court.) Parrots shrieking break the intense
stillness of the jungle. (Here the trams start.) The swallow dips
her wings in midnight pools. (Here we talk.) That is the cir-
cumference that I try to grasp as we sit together. Thus I must
undergo the penance of Hampton Court at seven-thirty precisely.

"But since these rolls of bread and wine bottles are needed by
me, and your faces with their hollows and prominences are beautiful, and the table-cloth and its yellow stains, far from being
allowed to spread in wider and wider circles of understanding
that may at last (so I dream, falling off the edge of the earth at
night when my bed floats suspended) embrace the entire world,
I must go through the antics of the individual. I must start when
you pluck at me with your children, your poems, your chilblains
or whatever it is that you do and suffer. But I am not deluded.
After all these callings hither and thither, these pluckings and
searchings, I shall fall alone through this thin sheet into gulfs
of fire. And you will not help me. More cruel than the old tor-
turers you will let me fall, and will tear me to pieces when I am
fallen. Yet there are moments when the walls of the mind grow
thin; when nothing is unabsorbed, and I could fancy that we
might blow so vast a bubble that the sun might set and rise in
it and we might take the blue of midday and the black of midnight and be cast off and escape from here and now."

"Drop upon drop," said Bernard, "silence falls. It forms on the roof of the mind and falls into pools beneath. For ever alone, alone, alone,—hear silence fall and sweep its rings to the farthest edges. Gorged and replete, solid with middle-aged content, I, whom loneliness destroys, let silence fall, drop by drop.

"But now silence falling pits my face, wastes my nose like a snowman stood out in a yard in the rain. As silence falls I am dissolved utterly and become featureless and scarcely to be distinguished from another. It does not matter. What matters? We have dined well. The fish, the veal cutlets, the wine have blunted the sharp tooth of egotism. Anxiety is at rest. The vainest of us, Louis perhaps, does not care what people think. Neville's tortures are at rest. Let others prosper—that is what he thinks. Susan hears the breathing of all her children safe asleep. Sleep, sleep, she murmurs. Rhoda has rocked her ships to shore. Whether they have foundered, whether they have anchored, she cares no longer. We are ready to consider any suggestion that the world may offer quite impartially. I reflect now that the earth is only a pebble flicked off accidentally from the face of the sun and that there is no life anywhere in the abysses of space."

"In this silence," said Susan, "it seems as if no leaf would ever fall, or bird fly."

"As if the miracle had happened," said Jinny, "and life were stayed here and now."

"And," said Rhoda, "we had no more to live."

"But listen," said Louis, "to the world moving through abysses of infinite space. It roars; the lighted strip of history is past and our Kings and Queens; we are gone; our civilisation; the Nile; and all life. Our separate drops are dissolved; we are extinct, lost in the abysses of time, in the darkness."

"Silence falls; silence falls," said Bernard. "But now listen, tick, tick; hoot, hoot; the world has hailed us back to it. I heard for one moment the howling winds of darkness as we passed beyond life. Then tick, tick (the clock); then hoot, hoot (the cars). We are landed; we are on shore; we are sitting, six of us, at a table. It is the memory of my nose that recalls me. I rise; 'Fight,' I cry, 'fight!' remembering the shape of my own nose and strike with this spoon upon this table pugnaciously."

"Oppose ourselves to this illimitable chaos," said Neville, "this formless imbecility. Making love to a nursemaid behind a tree, that soldier is more admirable than all the stars. Yet sometimes one trembling star comes in the clear sky and makes me think the world beautiful and we maggots deforming even the trees with our lust."

("Yet, Louis," said Rhoda, "how short a time silence lasts. Already they are beginning to smooth their napkins by the side of their plates. 'Who comes?' says Jinny; and Neville sighs, remembering that Percival comes no more. Jinny has taken out her looking-glass. Surveying her face like an artist, she draws a powder-puff down her nose, and after one moment of deliberation, has given precisely that red to the lips that the lips need. Susan, who feels scorn and fear at the sight of these preparations, fastens the top button of her coat, and unfastens it. What is she making ready for? For something, but something different."

"They are saying to themselves," said Louis, " 'it is time. I am still vigorous,' they are saying, 'My face shall be cut against the black of infinite space.' They do not finish their sentences. 'It is time,' they keep saying. 'The gardens will be shut.' And going with them, Rhoda, swept into their current, we shall perhaps drop a little behind."

"Like conspirators who have something to whisper," said Rhoda.)

"It is true, and I know for a fact," said Bernard, "as we walk down this avenue, that a King, riding, fell over a molehill here. But how strange it seems to set against the whirling abysses of infinite space a little figure with a golden teapot on his head. Soon one recovers a belief in figures: but not at once in what they put on their heads. Our English past—one inch of light. Then people put teapots on their heads and say, 'I am a King!'

No, I try to recover, as we walk, the sense of time, but with that streaming darkness in my eyes I have lost my grip. This Palace seems light as a cloud set for a moment on the sky. It is a trick of the mind—to put Kings on their thrones, one following another, with crowns on their heads. And we ourselves, walking six abreast, what do we oppose, with this random flicker of light in us that we call brain and feeling, how can we do battle against this flood; what has permanence? Our lives too stream away, down the unlighted avenues, past the strip of time, unidentified. Once Neville threw a poem at my head. Feeling a sudden conviction of immortality I said, 'I too know what Shakespeare knew.' But that has gone."

"Unreasonably, ridiculously," said Neville, "as we walk, time comes back. A dog does it, prancing. The machine works. Age makes hoary that gateway. Three hundred years now seem more than a moment vanished against that dog. King William mounts his horse wearing a wig, and the court ladies sweep the turf with their embroidered panniers. I am beginning to be convinced, as we walk, that the fate of Europe is of immense importance, and, ridiculous as it still seems, that all depends upon the battle of Blenheim. Yes; I declare, as we pass through this gateway, it is the present moment; I am become a subject of King George."

"While we advance down this avenue," said Louis, "I leaning slightly upon Jinny, Bernard arm-in-arm with Neville, and Susan with her hand in mine, it is difficult not to weep, calling ourselves little children, praying that God may keep us safe while we sleep. It is sweet to sing together, clasping hands, afraid of the dark, while Miss Curry plays the harmonium."

"The iron gates have rolled back," said Jinny. "Time's fangs have ceased their devouring. We have triumphed over the abysses of space, with rouge, with powder, with flimsy pocket-handkerchiefs."

"I grasp, I hold fast," said Susan. "I hold firmly to this hand, any one's, with love, with hatred; it does not matter which."

"The still mood, the disembodied mood is on us," said Rhoda, "and we enjoy this momentary alleviation (it is not often that one has no anxiety) when the walls of the mind become transparent. Wren's palace, like the quartet played to the dry and stranded people in the stalls, makes an oblong. A square is stood upon the oblong and we say, 'This is our dwelling-place. The structure is now visible. Very little is left outside.'"

"The flower," said Bernard, "the red carnation that stood in the vase on the table of the restaurant when we dined together with Percival is become a six-sided flower; made of six lives."

"A mysterious illumination," said Louis, "visible against those yew trees."

"Built up with much pain, many strokes," said Jinny.

"Marriage, death, travel, friendship," said Bernard; "town, and country; children and all that; a many-sided substance cut out of this dark; a many-faceted flower. Let us stop for a moment; let us behold what we have made. Let it blaze against the yew trees. One life. There. It is over. Gone out."

"Now they vanish," said Louis. "Susan with Bernard. Neville with Jinny. You and I, Rhoda, stop for a moment by this stone urn. What song shall we hear now that these couples have sought the groves and Jinny, pointing with her gloved hand, pretends to notice the water-lilies, and Susan, who has always loved Bernard, says to him, 'My ruined life, my wasted life.' And Neville, taking Jinny's little hand, with the cherry-coloured finger-nails, by the lake by the moonlit water, cries, 'Love, love,' and she answers, imitating the bird, 'Love, love?' What song do we hear?"

"They vanish, towards the lake," said Rhoda. "They slink away over the grass furtively, yet with assurance as if they asked of our pity their ancient privilege—not to be disturbed. The tide in the soul, tipped, flows that way; they cannot help deserting us. The dark has closed over their bodies. What song do we hear, the owl's, the nightingale's, the wren's? The steamer hoots; the light on the electric rails flashes; the trees gravely bow and bend.

The flare hangs over London. Here is an old woman, quietly returning, and a man, a late fisherman comes down the terrace with his rod. Not a sound, not a movement must escape us."

"A bird flies homeward," said Louis. "Evening opens her eyes and gives one quick glance among the bushes before she sleeps. How shall we put it together, the confused and composite message, that they send back to us, and not they only, but many dead, boys and girls, grown men and women, who have wandered here, under one king or another?"

"A weight has dropped into the night," said Rhoda, "dragging it down. Every tree is big with a shadow that is not the shadow of the tree behind it. We hear a drumming on the roofs of a fasting city when the Turks are hungry and uncertain tempered. We hear them crying with sharp, stag-like barks, 'Open, open.' Listen to the trams squealing and to the flashes from the electric rails. We hear the beech trees and the birch trees raise their branches as if the bride had let her silken nightdress fall and come to the doorway saying, 'Open, open.'"

"All seems alive," said Louis. "I cannot hear death anywhere tonight. Stupidity, on that man's face, age, on that woman's, would be strong enough, one would think, to resist the incantation, and bring in death. But where is death tonight? All the crudity, odds and ends, this and that, have been crushed like glass splinters into the blue, the red-fringed tide, which, drawing into the shore, fertile with innumerable fish, breaks at our feet."

"If we could mount together, if we could perceive from a sufficient height," said Rhoda, "if we could remain untouched without any support—but you, disturbed by faint clapping sounds of praise and laughter, and I, resenting compromise and right and wrong on human lips, trust only in solitude and the violence of death and thus are divided."

"For ever," said Louis, "divided. We have sacrificed the embrace among the ferns, and love, love, love by the lake, standing, like conspirators who have drawn apart to share some secret, by the urn. But now look, as we stand here, a ripple breaks on the horizon. The net is raised higher and higher. It comes to the top of the water. The water is broken by silver, by quivering little fish. Now leaping, now lashing, they are laid on shore. Life tumbles its catch upon the grass. There are figures coming towards us. Are they men or are they women? They still wear the ambiguous draperies of the flowing tide in which they have been immersed."

"Now," said Rhoda, "as they pass that tree, they regain their natural size. They are only men, only women. Wonder and awe change as they put off the draperies of the flowing tide. Pity returns, as they emerge into the moonlight, like the relics of an army, our representatives, going every night (here or in Greece) to battle, and coming back every night with their wounds, their ravaged faces. Now light falls on them again. They have faces. They become Susan and Bernard, Jinny and Neville, people we know. Now what a shrinkage takes place! Now what a shrivelling, what an humiliation! The old shivers run through me, hatred and terror, as I feel myself grappled to one spot by these hooks they cast on us; these greetings, recognitions, pluckings of the finger and searchings of the eyes. Yet they have only to speak, and their first words, with the remembered tone and the perpetual deviation from what one expects and their hands moving and making a thousand past days rise again in the darkness, shake my purpose."

"Something flickers and dances," said Louis. "Illusion returns as they approach down the avenue. Rippling and questioning begin. What do I think of you—what do you think of me? Who are you? Who am I?—that quivers again its uneasy air over us, and the pulse quickens and the eye brightens and all the insanity of personal existence without which life would fall flat and die, begins again. They are on us. The southern sun flickers over this urn; we pust off into the tide of the violent and cruel sea. Lord help us to act our parts as we greet them returning—Susan and Bernard, Neville and Jinny."

"We have destroyed something by our presence," said Bernard, "a world perhaps."

"Yet we scarcely breathe," said Neville, "spent as we are. We are in that passive and exhausted frame of mind when we only wish to rejoin the body of our mother from whom we have been severed. All else is distasteful, forced and fatiguing. Jinny's yellow scarf is moth-coloured in this light; Susan's eyes are quenched. We are scarcely to be distinguished from the river. One cigarette end is the only point of emphasis among us. And sadness tinges our content, that we should have left you, torn the fabric; yielded to the desire to press out, alone, some bitterer, some blacker juice, which was sweet too. But now we are worn out."

"After our fire," said Jinny, "there is nothing left to put in lockets."

"Still I gape," said Susan, "like a young bird, unsatisfied, for something that has escaped me."

"Let us stay for a moment," said Bernard, "before we go. Let us pace the terrace by the river almost alone. It is nearly bedtime. People have gone home. Now how comforting it is to watch the lights coming out in the bedrooms of small shopkeepers on the other side of the river. There is one—there is another. What do you think their takings have been today? Only just enough to pay for the rent, for light and food and the children's clothing. But just enough. What a sense of the tolerableness of life the lights in the bedrooms of small shopkeepers give us! Saturday comes, and there is just enough to pay perhaps for seats at the Pictures. Perhaps before they put out the light they go into the little garden and look at the giant rabbit couched in its wooden hut. That is the rabbit they will have for Sunday dinner. Then they put out the light. Then they sleep. And for thousands of people sleep is nothing but warmth and silence and one moment's sport with some fantastic dream. I have posted my letter, the green-grocer thinks, to the Sunday newspaper. Suppose I win five hundred pounds in the football competition? And we shall kill the rabbit. Life is pleasant. Life is good. I have posted the letter. We shall kill the rabbit. And he sleeps.

"That goes on. Listen. There is a sound like the knocking of railway trucks in a siding. That is the happy concatenation of one event following another in our lives. Knock, knock, knock. Must, must, must. Must go, must sleep, must wake, must get up —sober, merciful word which we pretend to revile, which we press tight to our hearts, without which we should be undone. How we worship that sound like the knocking together of trucks in a siding!

"Now far off down the river I hear the chorus; the song of the boasting boys, who are coming back in large charabancs from a day's outing on the decks of crowded steamers. Still they are singing as they used to sing, across the court, on winters' nights, or with the windows open in summer, getting drunk, breaking the furniture, wearing little striped caps, all turning their heads the same way as the brake rounded the corner; and I wished to be with them.

"What with the chorus, and the spinning water and the just perceptible murmur of the breeze we are slipping away. Little bits of ourselves are crumbling. There! Something very important fell then. I cannot keep myself together. I shall sleep. But we must go; must catch our train; must walk back to the station—must, must, must. We are only bodies jogging along side by side. I exist only in the soles of my feet and in the tired muscles of my thighs. We have been walking for hours it seems. But where? I cannot remember. I am like a log slipping smoothly over some waterfall. I am not a judge. I am not called upon to give my opinion. Houses and trees are all the same in this grey light. Is that a post? Is that a woman walking? Here is the station, and if the train were to cut me in two, I should come together on the further side, being one, being indivisible. But what is odd is that I still clasp the return half of my ticket to Waterloo firmly between the fingers of my right hand, even now, even sleeping."

*N*ow the sun had sunk. Sky
and sea were indistinguishable. The waves breaking spread their
white fans far out over the shore, sent white shadows into the
recesses of sonorous caves and then rolled back sighing over the
shingle.

The tree shook its branches and a scattering of leaves fell to
the ground. There they settled with perfect composure on the
precise spot where they would await dissolution. Black and grey
were shot into the garden from the broken vessel that had once
held red light. Dark shadows blackened the tunnels between the
stalks. The thrush was silent and the worm sucked itself back
into its narrow hole. Now and again a whitened and hollow
straw was blown from an old nest and fell into the dark grasses
among the rotten apples. The light had faded from the tool-
house wall and the adder's skin hung from the nail empty. All
colours in the room had overflown their banks. The precise
brush stroke was swollen and lopsided; cupboards and chairs
melted their brown masses into one huge obscurity. The height
from floor to ceiling was hung with vast curtains of darkness.
The looking-glass was pale as the mouth of a cave shadowed by
hanging creepers.

The substance had gone from the solidity of the hills. Travel-
ling lights drove a plumy wedge among unseen and sunken
roads, but no lights opened among the folded wings of the hills,
and there was no sound save the cry of a bird seeking some lone-
lier tree. At the cliff's edge there was an equal murmur of air
that had been brushed through forests, of water that had been
cooled in a thousand glassy hollows of mid-ocean.

As if there were waves of darkness in the air, darkness moved
on, covering houses, hills, trees, as waves of water wash round
the sides of some sunken ship. Darkness washed down streets ed-

dying round single figures, engulfing them; blotting out couples clasped under the showery darkness of elm trees in full summer foliage. Darkness rolled its waves along grassy rides and over the wrinkled skin of the turf, enveloping the solitary thorn tree and the empty snail shells at its foot. Mounting higher, darkness blew along the bare upland slopes, and met the fretted and abraded pinnacles of the mountain where the snow lodges for ever on the hard rock even when the valleys are full of running streams and yellow vine leaves, and girls, sitting on verandahs, look up at the snow, shading their faces with their fans. Them, too, darkness covered.

"Now to sum up," said Bernard. "Now to explain to you the meaning of my life. Since we do not know each other (though I met you once I think on board a ship going to Africa) we can talk freely. The illusion is upon me that something adheres for a moment, has roundness, weight, depth, is completed. This, for the moment, seems to be my life. If it were possible, I would hand it you entire. I would break it off as one breaks off a bunch of grapes. I would say, 'Take it. This is my life.'

"But unfortunately, what I see (this globe, full of figures) you do not see. You see me, sitting at a table opposite you, a rather heavy, elderly man, grey at the temples. You see me take my napkin and unfold it. You see me pour myself out a glass of wine. And you see behind me the door opening, and people passing. But in order to make you understand, to give you my life, I must tell you a story—and there are so many, and so many—stories of childhood, stories of school, love, marriage, death, and so on; and none of them are true. Yet like children we tell each other stories, and to decorate them we make up these ridiculous, flamboyant, beautiful phrases. How tired I am of stories, how tired I am of phrases that come down beautifully with all their feet on the ground! Also, how I distrust neat designs of life that are drawn upon half sheets of notepaper. I begin to long for some little language such as lovers use, broken words, inarticulate words, like the shuffling of feet on the pavement. I begin to seek some design more in accordance with those moments of humiliation and triumph that come now and then undeniably. Lying in a ditch on a stormy day, when it has been raining, then enormous clouds come marching over the sky, tattered clouds, wisps of cloud. What delights me then is the confusion, the height, the indifference and the fury. Great clouds always changing, and movement; something sulphurous and sinister, bowled up, helter-skelter; towering, trailing, broken off, lost, and I forgotten, minute, in a ditch. Of story, of design I do not see a trace then.

"But meanwhile, while we eat, let us turn over these scenes as children turn over the pages of a picture-book and the nurse says, pointing: 'That's a cow. That's a boat.' Let us turn over the pages, and I will add, for your amusement, a comment in the margin.

"In the beginning, there was the nursery, with windows opening on to a garden, and beyond that the sea. I saw something brighten—no doubt the brass handle of a cupboard. Then Mrs. Constable raised the sponge above her head, squeezed it, and out shot, right, left, all down the spine, arrows of sensation. And so, as long as we draw breath, for the rest of time, if we knock against a chair, a table, or a woman, we are pierced with arrows of sensation—if we walk in a garden, if we drink this wine. Sometimes indeed, when I pass a cottage with a light in the window where a child has been born, I could implore them not to squeeze the sponge over that new body. Then, there was the garden and the canopy of the currant leaves which seemed to enclose everything; flowers, burning like sparks upon the depths of green; a rat wreathing with maggots under a rhubarb leaf; the fly going buzz, buzz, buzz upon the nursery ceiling, and plates upon plates of innocent bread and butter. All these things happen in one second and last for ever. Faces loom. Dashing round the corner, 'Hullo,' one says, 'there's Jinny. That's Neville. That's Louis in grey flannel with a snake belt. That's Rhoda.' She had a basin in which she sailed petals of white flowers. It was Susan who cried, that day when I was in the tool-house with Neville; and I felt my indifference melt. Neville did not melt. 'Therefore,' I said, 'I am myself, not Neville,' a wonderful discovery. Susan cried and I followed her. Her wet pocket-handkerchief, and the sight of her little back heaving up and down like a pump-han-dle, sobbing for what was denied her, screwed my nerves up. 'This is not to be borne,' I said, as I sat beside her on the roots that were hard as skeletons. I then first became aware of the presence of those enemies who change, but are always there; the forces we fight against. To let oneself be carried on passively is unthinkable. 'That's your course, world,' one says, 'mine is this.' 'So let's explore,' I cried, and jumped up, and ran downhill with Susan and saw the stableboy clattering about the yard in great boots. Down below, through the depths of the leaves, the gardeners swept the lawns with great brooms. The lady sat writing. Transfixed, stopped dead, I thought, 'I cannot interfere with a single stroke of those brooms. They sweep and they sweep. Nor with the fixity of that woman writing.' It is strange that one cannot stop gardeners sweeping nor dislodge a woman. There they have remained all my life. It is as if one had woken in Stonehenge surrounded by a circle of great stones, these enemies, these presences. Then a wood-pigeon flew out of the trees. And being in love for the first time, I made a phrase—a poem about a wood-pigeon—a single phrase, for a hole had been knocked in my mind, one of those sudden transparences through which one sees everything. Then more bread and butter and more flies droning round the nursery ceiling on which quivered islands of light, ruffled, opalescent, while the pointed fingers of the lustre dripped blue pools on the corner of the mantelpiece. Day after day as we sat at tea we observed these sights.

"But we were all different. The wax—the virginal wax that coats the spine melted in different patches for each of us. The growl of the boot-boy making love to the tweeny among the gooseberry bushes; the clothes blown out hard on the line; the dead man in the gutter; the apple tree, stark in the moonlight; the rat swarming with maggots; the lustre dripping blue—our white wax was streaked and stained by each of these differently. Louis was disgusted by the nature of human flesh; Rhoda by our cruelty; Susan could not share; Neville wanted order; Jinny love; and so on. We suffered terribly as we became separate bodies.

"Yet I was preserved from these excesses and have survived many of my friends, am a little stout, grey, rubbed on the thorax as it were, because it is the panorama of life, seen not from the roof, but from the third story window that delights me, not what one woman says to one man, even if that man is myself. How could I be bullied at school therefore? How could they make things hot for me? There was the Doctor lurching into chapel, as if he trod a battleship in a gale of wind, shouting out his commands through a megaphone, since people in authority always become melodramatic—I did not hate him like Neville, or revere him like Louis. I took notes as we sat together in chapel. There were pillars, shadows, memorial brasses, boys scuffling and swopping stamps behind Prayer Books; the sound of a rusty pump; the Doctor booming, about immortality and quitting ourselves like men; and Percival scratching his thigh. I made notes for stories; drew portraits in the margin of my pocket-book and thus became still more separate. Here are one or two of the figures I saw.

"Percival sat staring straight ahead of him that day in chapel. He also had a way of flicking his hand to the back of his neck. His movements were always remarkable. We all flicked our hands to the backs of our heads—unsuccessfully. He had the kind of beauty which defends itself from any caress. As he was not in the least precocious, he read whatever was written up for our edification without any comment, and thought with that magnificent equanimity (Latin words come naturally) that was to preserve him from so many meannesses and humiliations, that Lucy's flaxen pigtails and pink cheeks were the height of female beauty. Thus preserved, his taste later was of extreme fineness. But there should be music, some wild carol. Through the window should come a hunting-song from some rapid un-apprehended life—a sound that shouts among the hills and dies away. What is startling, what is unexpected, what we cannot account for, what turns symmetry to nonsense—that comes suddenly to my mind, thinking of him. The little apparatus of observation is unhinged. Pillars go down; the Doctor floats off; some sudden exaltation possesses me. He was thrown, riding in a race, and when I came along Shaftesbury Avenue tonight, those insignificant and scarcely formulated faces that bubble up out of the doors of the Tube, and many obscure Indians, and people dying of famine and disease, and women who have been cheated, and whipped dogs and crying children—all these seemed to me bereft. He would have done justice. He would have protected. About the age of forty he would have shocked the authorities. No lullaby has ever occurred to me capable of singing him to rest.

"But let me dip again and bring up in my spoon another of these minute objects which we call optimistically, 'characters of our friends'—Louis. He sat staring at the preacher. His being seemed conglobulated in his brow, his lips were pressed; his eyes were fixed, but suddenly they flashed with laughter. Also he suffered from chilblains, the penalty of an imperfect circulation. Unhappy, unfriended, in exile he would sometimes, in moments of confidence, describe how the surf swept over the beaches of his home. The remorseless eye of youth fixed itself upon his swollen joints. Yes, but we were also quick to perceive how cutting, how apt, how severe he was, how naturally, when we lay under the elm trees pretending to watch cricket, we waited his approval, seldom given. His ascendancy was resented, as Percival's was adored. Prim, suspicious, lifting his feet like a crane, there was yet a legend that he had smashed a door with his naked fist. But his peak was too bare, too stony for that kind of mist to cling to it. He was without those simple attachments by which one is connected with another. He remained aloof; enigmatic; a scholar capable of that inspired accuracy which has something formidable about it. My phrases (how to describe the moon) did not meet with his approval. On the other hand, he envied me to the point of desperation for being at my ease with servants. Not that the sense of his own deserts failed him. That was commensurate with his respect for discipline. Hence his success, finally. His life, though, was not happy. But look—his eye turns white as he lies in the palm of my hand. Suddenly the sense of what people are leaves one. I return him to the pool where he will acquire lustre.

"Neville next—lying on his back staring up at the summer sky. He floated among us like a piece of thistle-down, indolently haunting the sunny corner of the playing-field, not listening, yet not remote. It was through him that I have nosed round without ever precisely touching the Latin classics and have also derived some of those persistent habits of thought which make us irredeemably lopsided—for instance about crucifixes, that they are the mark of the devil. Our half-loves and half-hates and ambiguities on these points were to him indefensible treacheries. The swaying and sonorous Doctor, whom I made to sit swinging his braces over a gas-fire, was to him nothing but an instrument of the inquisition. So he turned with a passion that made up for his indolence upon Catullus, Horace, Lucretius, lying lazily dormant, yes, but regardant, noticing, with rapture, cricketers, while with a mind like the tongue of an ant-eater, rapid, dexterous, glutinous, he searched out every curl and twist of those Roman sentences, and sought out one person, always one person to sit beside.

"And the long skirts of the masters' wives would come swishing by, mountainous, menacing; and our hands would fly to our caps. And immense dullness would descend unbroken, monotonous. Nothing, nothing, nothing broke with its fin that leaden waste of waters. Nothing would happen to lift that weight of intolerable boredom. The terms went on. We grew; we changed; for, of course, we are animals. We are not always aware by any means; we breathe, eat, sleep automatically. We exist not only separately but in undifferentiated blobs of matter. With one scoop a whole brakeful of boys is swept up and goes cricketing, footballing. An army marches across Europe. We assemble in parks and halls and sedulously oppose any renegade (Neville, Louis, Rhoda), who sets up a separate existence. And I am so made, that, while I hear one or two distinct melodies, such as Louis sings, or Neville, I am also drawn irresistibly to the sound of the chorus chanting its old, chanting its almost wordless, almost senseless song that comes across courts at night; which we hear now booming round us as cars and omnibuses take people to theatres. (Listen; the cars rush past this restaurant; now and then, down the river, a siren hoots, as a steamer makes for the sea.) If a bagman offers me snuff in a train I accept. I like the copious, shapeless, warm, not so very clever, but extremely easy and rather coarse aspect of things; the talk of men in clubs and public-houses, of miners half naked in drawers—the forthright, perfectly unassuming, and without end in view except dinner, love, money and getting along tolerably; that which is without great hopes, ideals, or anything of that kind; what is unassuming except to make a tolerably good job of it. I like all that. So I joined them, when Neville sulked or Louis, as I quite agree sublimely, turned on his heel.

"Thus, not equally by any means or with order, but in great streaks my waxen waistcoat melted, here one drop, there another. Now through this transparency became visible those wondrous pastures, at first so moonwhite, radiant, where no foot has been; meadows of the rose, the crocus, of the rock and the snake too; of the spotted and swart; the embarrassing, the binding and tripping up. One leaps out of bed, throws up the window; with what a whirr the birds rise! You know that sudden rush of wings, that exclamation, carol, and confusion; the riot and babble of voices; and all the drops are sparkling, trembling, as if the garden were a splintered mosaic, vanishing, twinkling, not yet formed into one whole; and a bird sings close to the window. I heard those songs. I followed those phantoms. I saw Joans, Dorothys, Miriams, I forget their names, passing down avenues, stopping on the crest of bridges to look down into the river. And from among them rise one or two distinct figures, birds who sang with the rapt egotism of youth by the window; broke their snails on stones, dipped their beaks in sticky, viscous matter; hard, avid, remorseless; Jinny, Susan, Rhoda. They had been educated on the east coast or on the south coast. They had grown long pigtails and acquired the look of startled foals, which is the mark of adolescence.

"Jinny was the first to come sidling up to the gate to eat sugar. She nipped it off the palms of one's hands very cleverly, but her ears were laid back as if she might bite. Rhoda was wild—Rhoda one never could catch. She was both frightened and clumsy. It was Susan who first became wholly woman, purely feminine. It was she who dropped on my face those scalding tears which are terrible, beautiful; both, neither. She was born to be the adored of poets, since poets require safety; some one who sits sewing, who says, 'I hate, I love,' who is neither comfortable nor prosperous, but has some quality in accordance with the high but unemphatic beauty of pure style which those who create poetry so particularly admire. Her father trailed from room to room and down flagged corridors in his flapping dressing-gown and worn slippers. On still nights a wall of water fell with a roar a mile off. The ancient dog could scarcely heave himself up on to his chair. And some witless servant could be heard laughing at the top of the house as she whirred the wheel of the sewing-machine round and round.

"That I observed even in the midst of my anguish when, twisting her pocket-handkerchief, Susan cried, 'I hate; I love.' 'A worthless servant,' I observed, 'laughs upstairs in the attic,' and that little piece of dramatisation shows how incompletely we are merged in our own experiences. On the outskirts of every agony sits some observant fellow who points; who whispers as he whispered to me that summer morning in the house where the corn comes up to the window, 'The willow grows on the turf by the river. The gardeners sweep with great brooms and the lady sits writing.' Thus he directed me to that which is beyond and outside our own predicament; to that which is symbolic, and thus perhaps permanent, if there is any permanence in our sleeping, eating, breathing, so animal, so spiritual and tumultuous lives.

"The willow tree grew by the river. I sat on the smooth turf with Neville, with Larpent, with Baker, Romsey, Hughes, Percival and Jinny. Through its fine plumes specked with little pricked ears of green in spring, of orange in autumn, I saw boats; buildings; I saw hurrying, decrepit women. I buried match after match in the turf decidedly to mark this or that stage in the process of understanding (it might be philosophy; science; it might be myself) while the fringe of my intelligence floating unattached caught those distant sensations which after a time the mind draws in and works upon; the chime of bells; general murmurs; vanishing figures; one girl on a bicycle who, as she rode, seemed to lift the corner of a curtain concealing the populous undifferentiated chaos of life which surged behind the outlines of my friends and the willow tree.

"The tree alone resisted our eternal flux. For I changed and changed; was Hamlet, was Shelley, was the hero, whose name I now forget, of a novel by Dostoevsky; was for a whole term, incredibly, Napoleon; but was Byron chiefly. For many weeks at a time it was my part to stride into rooms and fling gloves and coat on the back of chairs, scowling slightly. I was always going to the bookcase for another sip of the divine specific. Therefore, I let fly my tremendous battery of phrases upon somebody quite inappropriate—a girl now married, now buried; every book, every window-seat was littered with the sheets of my unfinished letters to the woman who made me Byron. For it is difficult to finish a letter in somebody else's style. I arrived all in a lather at her house; exchanged tokens but did not marry her being no doubt unripe for that intensity.

"Here again there should be music. Not that wild hunting-song, Percival's music; but a painful, guttural, visceral, also soaring, lark-like, pealing song to replace these flagging, foolish transcripts—how much too deliberate! how much too reasonable!—which attempt to describe the flying moment of first love. A purple slide is slipped over the day. Look at a room before she comes and after. Look at the innocents outside pursuing their way. They neither see nor hear; yet on they go. Moving oneself in this radiant yet gummy atmosphere, how conscious one is of every movement—something adheres, something sticks to one's hands, taking up a newspaper even. Then there is the being eviscerated—drawn out, spun like a spider's web and twisted in agony round a thorn. Then a thunder-clap of complete indifference; the light blown out; then the return of measureless irresponsible joy; certain fields seem to glow green for ever, and innocent landscapes appear as if in the light of the first dawn—one patch of green, for example, up at Hampstead; and all faces are lit up, all conspire in a hush of tender joy; and then the mystic sense of completion and then that rasping, dog-fish skin-like roughness—those black arrows of shivering sensation, when she misses the post, when she does not come. Out rush a bristle of horned suspicions, horror, horror, horror— but what is the use of painfully elaborating these consecutive sentences when what one needs is nothing consecutive but a bark, a groan? And years later to see a middle-aged woman in a restaurant taking off her cloak.

"But to return. Let us again pretend that life is a solid substance, shaped like a globe, which we turn about in our fingers. Let us pretend that we can make out a plain and logical story, so that when one matter is despatched—love for instance—we go on, in an orderly manner, to the next. I was saying there was a willow tree. Its shower of falling branches, its creased and crooked bark had the effect of what remains outside our illusions yet cannot stay them, is changed by them for the moment, yet shows through stable, still, and with a sternness that our lives lack. Hence the comment it makes; the standard it supplies, and the reason why, as we flow and change, it seems to measure. Neville, for example, sat with me on the turf. But can anything be as clear as all that, I would say, following his gaze, through the branches, to a punt on the river, and a young man eating bananas from a paper bag? The scene was cut out with such intensity and so permeated with the quality of his vision that for a moment I could see it too; the punt, the bananas, the young man, through the branches of the willow tree. Then it faded.

"Rhoda came wandering vaguely. She would take advantage of any scholar in a blowing gown, or donkey rolling the turf with slippered feet to hide behind. What fear wavered and hid itself and blew to a flame in the depths of her grey, her startled, her dreaming eyes? Cruel and vindictive as we are, we are not bad to that extent. We have our fundamental goodness surely or to talk as I talk freely to some one I hardly know would be impossible—we should cease. The willow as she saw it grew on the verge of a grey desert where no bird sang. The leaves shrivelled as she looked at them, tossed in agony as she passed them. The trams and omnibuses roared hoarse in the street, ran over rocks and sped foaming away. Perhaps one pillar, sunlit, stood in her desert by a pool where wild beasts come down stealthily to drink.

"Then Jinny came. She flashed her fire over the tree. She was like a crinkled poppy, febrile, thirsty with the desire to drink dry dust. Darting, angular, not in the least impulsive, she came prepared. So little flames zigzag over the cracks in the dry earth. She made the willows dance, but not with illusion; for she saw nothing that was not there. It was a tree; there was the river; it was afternoon; here we were; I in my serge suit; she in green. There was no past, no future; merely the moment in its ring of light, and our bodies; and the inevitable climax, the ecstasy.

"Louis, when he let himself down on the grass, cautiously spreading (I do not exaggerate) a mackintosh square, made one acknowledge his presence. It was formidable. I had the intelligence to salute his integrity; his research with bony fingers wrapped in rags because of chilblains for some diamond of indissoluble veracity. I buried boxes of burnt matches in holes in the turf at his feet. His grim and caustic tongue reproved my indolence. He fascinated me with his sordid imagination. His heroes wore bowler-hats and talked about selling pianos for tenners. Through his landscape the tram squealed; the factory poured its acrid fumes. He haunted mean streets and towns where women lay drunk, naked, on counterpanes on Christmas day. His words falling from a shot tower hit the water and up it spurted. He found one word, one only for the moon. Then he got up and went; we all got up; we all went. But I, pausing, looked at the tree, and as I looked in autumn at the fiery and yellow branches, some sediment formed; I formed; a drop fell; I fell—that is from some completed experience I had emerged.

"I rose and walked away—I, I, I; not Byron, Shelley, Dostoevsky, but I, Bernard. I even repeated my own name once or twice. I went, swinging my stick, into a shop, and bought—not that I love music—a picture of Beethoven in a silver frame. Not that I love music, but because the whole of life, its masters, its adventurers then appeared in long ranks of magnificent human beings behind me; and I was the inheritor; I, the continuer; I, the person miraculously appointed to carry it on. So, swinging my stick, with my eyes filmed, not with pride but with humility rather, I walked down the street. The first whirr of wings had gone up, the carol, the exclamation; and now one enters; one goes into the house, the dry, uncompromising, inhabited house, the place with all its traditions, its objects, its accumulations of rubbish, and treasures displayed upon tables. I visited the family tailor, who remembered my uncle. People turned up in great quantities, not cut out, like the first faces (Neville, Louis,

Jinny, Susan, Rhoda), but confused, featureless, or changed their features so fast that they seemed to have none. And blushing yet scornful, in the oddest condition of raw rapture and scepticism, I took the blow; the mixed sensations; the complex and disturbing and utterly unprepared-for impacts of life all over, in all places at the same time. How upsetting! How humiliating never to be sure what to say next, and those painful silences, glaring as dry deserts, with every pebble apparent; and then to say what one ought not to have said, and then to be conscious of a ramrod of incorruptible sincerity which one would willingly exchange for a shower of smooth pence, but could not, there at that party, where Jinny sat quite at her ease, rayed out on a gilt chair.

"Then says some lady with an impressive gesture, 'Come with me.' She leads one into a private alcove and admits one to the honour of her intimacy. Surnames change to Christian names; Christian names to nicknames. What is to be done about India, Ireland or Morocco? Old gentlemen answer the question standing decorated under chandeliers. One finds oneself surprisingly supplied with information. Outside the undifferentiated forces roar; inside we are very private, very explicit, have a sense indeed, that it is here, in this little room, that we make whatever day of the week it may be. Friday or Saturday. A shell forms upon the soft soul, nacreous, shiny, upon which sensations tap their beaks in vain. On me it formed earlier than on most. Soon I could carve my pear when other people had done dessert. I could bring my sentence to a close in a hush of complete silence. It is at that season too that perfection has a lure. One can learn Spanish, one thinks, by tying a string to the right toe and waking early. One fills up the little compartments of one's engagement book with dinner at eight; luncheon at one-thirty. One has shirts, socks, ties laid out on one's bed.

"But it is a mistake, this extreme precision, this orderly and military progress; a convenience, a lie. There is always deep below it, even when we arrive punctually at the appointed time with our white waistcoats and polite formalities, a rushing stream of broken dreams, nursery rhymes, street cries, half-finished sentences and sights—elm trees, willow trees, gardeners sweeping, women writing—that rise and sink even as we hand a lady down to dinner. While one straightens the fork so precisely on the table-cloth, a thousand faces mop and mow. There is nothing one can fish up in a spoon; nothing one can call an event. Yet it is alive too and deep, this stream. Immersed in it I would stop between one mouthful and the next, and look intently at a vase, perhaps with one red flower, while a reason struck me, a sudden revelation. Or I would say, walking along the Strand, 'That's the phrase I want,' as some beautiful, fabulous phantom bird, fish or cloud with fiery edges swam up to enclose once and for all some notion haunting me, after which on I trotted taking stock with renewed delight of ties and things in shop-windows.

"The crystal, the globe of life as one calls it, far from being hard and cold to the touch, has walls of thinnest air. If I press them all will burst. Whatever sentence I extract whole and entire from this cauldron is only a string of six little fish that let themselves be caught while a million others leap and sizzle, making the cauldron bubble like boiling silver, and slip through my fingers. Faces recur, faces and faces—they press their beauty to the walls of my bubble—Neville, Susan, Louis, Jinny, Rhoda and a thousand others. How impossible to order them rightly; to detach one separately, or to give the effect of the whole—again like music. What a symphony, with its concord and its discord and its tunes on top and its complicated bass beneath, then grew up! Each played his own tune, fiddle, flute, trumpet, drum or whatever the instrument might be. With Neville, 'Let's discuss Hamlet.' With Louis, science. With Jinny, love. Then suddenly, in a moment of exasperation, off to Cumberland with a quiet man for a whole week in an inn, with the rain running down the window-panes and nothing but mutton and mutton and again mutton for dinner. Yet that week remains a solid

stone in the welter of unrecorded sensation. It was then we
played dominoes; then we quarrelled about tough mutton. Then
we walked on the fell. And a little girl, peeping round the door,
gave me that letter, written on blue paper, in which I learnt that
the girl who had made me Byron was to marry a squire. A man
in gaiters, a man with a whip, a man who made speeches about
fat oxen at dinner—I exclaimed derisively and looked at the racing clouds, and felt my own failure; my desire to be free; to escape; to be bound; to make an end; to continue; to be Louis; to
be myself; and walked out in my mackintosh alone, and felt
grumpy under the eternal hills and not in the least sublime; and
came home and blamed the meat and packed and so back again
to the welter; to the torture.

"Nevertheless, life is pleasant, life is tolerable. Tuesday follows Monday; then comes Wednesday. The mind grows rings;
the identity becomes robust; pain is absorbed in growth. Opening and shutting, shutting and opening, with an increasing hum
and sturdiness, the haste and fever of youth are drawn into service until the whole being seems to expand in and out like the
mainspring of a clock. How fast the stream flows from January
to December! We are swept on by the torrent of things grown so
familiar that they cast no shadow. We float, we float. . . .

"However, since one must leap (to tell you this story) I
leap, here, at this point, and alight now upon some perfectly commonplace object—say the poker and tongs, as I saw
them sometime later, after that lady who had made me Byron
had married, under the light of one whom I will call the third
Miss Jones. She is the girl who wears a certain dress expecting
one at dinner, who picks a certain rose, who makes one feel
'Steady, steady, this is a matter of some importance,' as one
shaves. Then one asks, 'How does she behave to children?' One
observes that she is a little clumsy with her umbrella; but minded
when the mole was caught in the trap; and finally, would not
make the loaf at breakfast (I was thinking of the interminable
breakfasts of married life as I shaved) altogether prosaic—it

would not surprise one sitting opposite this girl to see a dragon-fly perched on the loaf at breakfast. Also she inspired me with a desire to rise in the world; also she made me look with curiosity at the hitherto repulsive faces of new-born babies. And the little fierce beat—tick-tack, tick-tack—of the pulse of one's mind took on a more majestic rhythm. I roamed down Oxford Street. We are the continuers, we are the inheritors, I said, thinking of my sons and daughters; and if the feeling is so grandiose as to be absurd and one conceals it by jumping on to a bus or buying the evening paper, it is still a curious element in the ardour with which one laces up one's boots, with which one now addresses old friends committed to different careers. Louis, the attic dwel-ler; Rhoda, the nymph of the fountain always wet, both con-tradicted what was then so positive to me; both gave the other side of what seemed to me so evident (that we marry, that we domesticate); for which I loved them, pitied them, and also deeply envied them their different lot.

"Once I had a biographer, dead long since, but if he still fol-lowed my footsteps with his old flattering intensity he would here say, 'About this time Bernard married and bought a house. . . . His friends observed in him a growing tendency to domes-ticity. . . . The birth of children made it highly desirable that he should augment his income.' That is the biographic style, and it does to tack together torn bits of stuff, stuff with raw edges. After all, one cannot find fault with the biographic style if one begins letters 'Dear Sir,' ends them 'yours faithfully'; one cannot despise these phrases laid like Roman roads across the tumult of our lives, since they compel us to walk in step like civilised people with the slow and measured tread of policemen though one may be humming any nonsense under one's breath at the same time—'Hark, hark, the dogs do bark,' 'Come away, come away, death,' 'Let me not to the marriage of true minds,' and so on. 'He attained some success in his profession. . . . He in-herited a small sum of money from an uncle'—that is how the biographer continues and if one wears trousers and hitches them

up with braces, one has to say that though it is tempting now
and then to go blackberrying; tempting to play ducks and drakes
with all these phrases. But one has to say that.

"I became, I mean, a certain kind of man, scoring my path
across life as one treads a path across the fields. My boots became
worn a little on the left side. When I came in, certain rearrange-
ments took place. 'Here's Bernard!' How differently different
people say that! There are many rooms—many Bernards. There
was the charming, but weak; the strong, but supercilious; the
brilliant, but remorseless; the very good fellow, but, I make no
doubt, the awful bore; the sympathetic, but cold; the shabby, but
—go into the next room—the foppish, worldly, and too well
dressed. What I was to myself was different; was none of these.
I am inclined to pin myself down most firmly there before the
loaf at breakfast with my wife, who being now entirely my wife
and not at all the girl who wore when she hoped to meet me a
certain rose, gave me that feeling of existing in the midst of unconsciousness such as the tree-frog must have couched on the
right shade of green leaf. 'Pass' . . . I would say. 'Milk' . . . she
might answer, or 'Mary's coming' . . . —simple words for those
who have inherited the spoils of all the ages but not as said then,
day after day, in the full tide of life, when one feels complete,
entire, at breakfast. Muscles, nerves, intestines, blood-vessels, all
that makes the coil and spring of our being, the unconscious
hum of the engine, as well as the dark and flicker of the tongue,
functioned superbly. Opening, shutting; shutting, opening; eating, drinking; sometimes speaking—the whole mechanism
seemed to expand, to contract, like the mainspring of a clock.
Toast and butter, coffee and bacon, the *Times* and letters—suddenly the telephone rang with urgency and I rose deliberately
and went to the telephone. I took up the black mouth. I marked
the ease with which my mind adjusted itself to assimilate the
message—it might be (one has these fancies) to assume command of the British Empire; I observed my composure; I remarked with what magnificent vitality the atoms of my atten-

tion dispersed, swarmed round the interruption, assimilated the message, adapted themselves to a new state of affairs and had created, by the time I put back the receiver, a richer, a stronger, a more complicated world in which I was called upon to act my part and had no doubt whatever that I could do it. Clapping my hat on my head, I strode into a world inhabited by vast numbers of men who had also clapped their hats on their heads, and as we jostled and encountered in trains and tubes we exchanged the knowing wink of competitors and comrades braced with a thousand snares and dodges to achieve the same end—to earn our livings.

"Life is pleasant. Life is good. The mere process of life is satisfactory. Take the ordinary man in good health. He likes eating and sleeping. He likes the snuff of fresh air and walking at a brisk pace down the Strand. Or in the country there's a cock crowing on a gate; there's a foal galloping round a field. Something always has to be done next. Tuesday follows Monday; Wednesday Tuesday. Each spreads the same ripple of well-being, repeats the same curve of rhythm; covers fresh sand with a chill or ebbs a little slackly without. So the being grows rings; identity becomes robust. What was fiery and furtive like a fling of grain cast into the air and blown hither and thither by wild gusts of life from every quarter is now methodical and orderly and flung with a purpose—so it seems.

"Lord, how pleasant! Lord, how good! How tolerable is the life of little shopkeepers, I would say, as the train drew through the suburbs and one saw lights in bedroom windows. Active, energetic as a swarm of ants, I said, as I stood at the window and watched workers, bag in hand, stream into town. What hardness, what energy and violence of limb, I thought, seeing men in white drawers scouring after a football on a patch of snow in January. Now being grumpy about some small matter—it might be the meat—it seemed luxurious to disturb with a little ripple the enormous stability, whose quiver, for our child was about to be born, increased its joy, of our married life. I snapped at dinner. I spoke unreasonably as if, being a millionaire, I could throw away five shillings; or, being a perfect steeple-jack, stumbled over a footstool on purpose. Going up to bed we settled our quarrel on the stairs, and standing by the window looking at a sky clear like the inside of a blue stone, 'Heaven be praised,' I said, 'we need not whip this prose into poetry. The little language is enough.' For the space of the prospect and its clarity seemed to offer no impediment whatsoever, but to allow our lives to spread out and out beyond all bristling of roofs and chimneys to the flawless verge.

"Into this crashed death—Percival's. 'Which is happiness?' I said (our child had been born), 'which pain?' referring to the two sides of my body, as I came downstairs, making a purely physical statement. Also I made note of the state of the house; the curtain blowing; the cook singing; the wardrobe showing through the half-opened door. I said, 'Give him (myself) another moment's respite,' as I went downstairs. 'Now in this drawing-room he is going to suffer. There is no escape.' But for pain words are lacking. There should be cries, cracks, fissures, whiteness passing over chintz covers, interference with the sense of time, of space; the sense also of extreme fixity in passing objects; and sounds very remote and then very close; flesh being gashed and blood spurting, a joint suddenly twisted—beneath all of which appears something very important, yet remote, to be just held in solitude. So I went out. I saw the first morning he would never see—the sparrows were like toys dangled from a string by a child. To see things without attachment, from the outside, and to realise their beauty in itself—how strange! And then the sense that a burden has been removed; pretence and make-believe and unreality are gone, and lightness has come with a kind of transparency, making oneself invisible and things seen through as one walks—how strange. 'And now what other discovery will there be?' I said, and in order to hold it tight ignored newspaper placards and went and looked at pictures. Madonnas and pillars, arches and orange trees, still as on the first day of creation, but acquainted with grief, there they hung, and I gazed at them. 'Here,' I said, 'we are together without interruption.' This freedom, this immunity, seemed then a conquest, and stirred in me such exaltation that I sometimes go there, even now, to bring back exaltation and Percival. But it did not last. What torments one is the horrible activity of the mind's eye— how he fell, how he looked, where they carried him; men in loin-cloths, pulling ropes; the bandages and the mud. Then comes the terrible pounce of memory, not to be foretold, not to be warded off—that I did not go with him to Hampton Court. That claw scratched; that fang tore; I did not go. In spite of his impatiently protesting that it did not matter; why interrupt, why spoil our moment of uninterrupted community?—Still, I repeated sullenly, I did not go, and so, driven out of the sanctuary by these officious devils, went to Jinny because she had a room; a room with little tables, with little ornaments scattered on little tables. There I confessed, with tears—I had not gone to Hampton Court. And she, remembering other things, to me trifles but torturing to her, showed me how life withers when there are things we cannot share. Soon, too, a maid came in with a note and as she turned to answer it and I felt my own curiosity to know what she was writing and to whom, I saw the first leaf fall on his grave. I saw us push beyond this moment, and leave it behind us for ever. And then sitting side by side on the sofa we remembered inevitably what had been said by others; 'the lily of the day is fairer far in May'; we compared Percival to a lily—Percival whom I wanted to lose his hair, to shock the authorities, to grow old with me; he was already covered over with the lilies.

"So the sincerity of the moment passed; so it became symbolical; and that I could not stand. Let us commit any blasphemy of laughter and criticism rather than exude this lily-sweet glue; and cover him with phrases, I cried. Therefore I broke off, and Jinny, who was without future, or speculation, but respected the moment with complete integrity, gave her body a flick with the whip, powdered her face (for which I loved her), and waved to

me as she stood on the doorstep, pressing her hand to her hair so
that the wind might not disorder it, a gesture for which I honoured her, as if it confirmed our determination—not to let lilies
grow.

"I observed with disillusioned clarity the despicable nonentity
of the street; its porches; its window curtains; the drab clothes,
the cupidity and complacency of shopping women; and old men
taking the air in comforters; the caution of people crossing; the
universal determination to go on living, when really, fools and
gulls that you are, I said, any slate may fly from a roof, any car
may swerve, for there is neither rhyme nor reason when a drunk
man staggers about with a club in his hand—that is all. I was like
one admitted behind the scenes: like one shown how the effects
are produced. I returned, however, to my own snug home and
was warned by the parlourmaid to creep upstairs in my stockings. The child was asleep. I went to my room.

"Was there no sword, nothing with which to batter down
these walls, this protection, this begetting of children and living behind curtains, and becoming daily more involved and committed, with books and pictures? Better burn one's life out like
Louis, desiring perfection; or like Rhoda leave us, flying past us,
to the desert; or choose one out of millions and one only like
Neville; better be like Susan and love and hate the heat of the
sun or the frost-bitten grass; or be like Jinny, honest, an animal.
All had their rapture; their common feeling with death; something that stood them in stead. Thus I visited each of my friends
in turn, trying with fumbling fingers to prise open their locked
caskets. I went from one to the other holding my sorrow—no,
not my sorrow but the incomprehensible nature of this our life
for their inspection. Some people go to priests; others to poetry;
I to my friends, I to my own heart, I to seek among phrases and
fragments something unbroken—I to whom there is not beauty
enough in moon or tree; to whom the touch of one person with
another is all, yet who cannot grasp even that, who am so imperfect, so weak, so unspeakably lonely. There I sat.

"Should this be the end of the story? a kind of sigh? a last ripple of the wave? A trickle of water to some gutter where, burbling, it dies away? Let me touch the table—so—and thus recover my sense of the moment. A sideboard covered with cruets; a basket full of rolls; a plate of bananas—these are comfortable sights. But if there are no stories, what end can there be, or what beginning? Life is not susceptible perhaps to the treatment we give it when we try to tell it. Sitting up late at night it seems strange not to have more control. Pigeon-holes are not then very useful. It is strange how force ebbs away and away into some dry creek. Sitting alone, it seems we are spent; our waters can only just surround feebly that spike of sea-holly; we cannot reach that further pebble so as to wet it. It is over, we are ended. But wait— I sat all night waiting—an impulse again runs through us; we rise, we toss back a mane of white spray; we pound on the shore; we are not to be confined. That is, I shaved and washed; did not wake my wife, and had breakfast; put on my hat, and went out to earn my living. After Monday, Tuesday comes.

"Yet some doubt remained, some note of interrogation. I was surprised, opening a door, to find people thus occupied; I hesitated, taking a cup of tea, whether one said milk or sugar. And the light of the stars falling, as it falls now, on my hand after travelling for millions upon millions of years—I could get a cold shock from that for a moment—not more, my imagination is too feeble. But some doubt remained. A shadow flitted through my mind like moths' wings among chairs and tables in a room in the evening. When, for example, I went to Lincolnshire that summer to see Susan and she advanced towards me across the garden with the lazy movement of a half-filled sail, with the swaying movement of a woman with child, I thought, 'It goes on; but why?' We sat in the garden; the farm carts came up dripping with hay; there was the usual country gabble of rooks and doves; fruit was netted and covered over; the gardener dug. Bees boomed down the purple tunnels of flowers; bees embedded themselves on the golden shields of sunflowers. Little twigs were blown across the grass. How rhythmical, and half conscious and like something wrapped in mist it was; but to me hateful, like a net folding one's limbs in its meshes, cramping. She who had refused Percival lent herself to this, to this covering over.

"Sitting down on a bank to wait for my train I thought then how we surrender, how we submit to the stupidity of nature. Woods covered in thick green leafage lay in front of me. And by some flick of a scent or a sound on a nerve, the old image—the gardeners sweeping, the lady writing—returned. I saw the figures beneath the beech trees at Elvedon. The gardeners swept; the lady at the table sat writing. But I now made the contribution of maturity to childhood's intuitions—satiety and doom; the sense of what is unescapable in our lot; death; the knowledge of limitations; how life is more obdurate than one had thought it. Then, when I was a child, the presence of an enemy had asserted itself; the need for opposition had stung me. I had jumped up and cried, 'Let's explore.' The horror of the situation was ended.

"Now what situation was there to end? Dullness and doom. And what to explore? The leaves and the wood concealed nothing. If a bird rose I should no longer make a poem—I should repeat what I had said before. Thus if I had a stick with which to point to indentations in the curve of being, this is the lowest; here it coils useless on the mud where no tide comes—here, where I sat with my back to a hedge, and my hat over my eyes, while the sheep advanced remorselessly in that wooden way of theirs, step by step on stiff, pointed legs. But if you hold a blunt blade to a grindstone long enough, something spurts—a jagged edge of fire; so held to lack of reason, aimlessness, the usual, all massed together, out spurted in one flame hatred, contempt. I took my mind, my being, the old dejected, almost inanimate object and lashed it about among these odds and ends, sticks and straws, detestable little bits of wreckage, flotsam and jetsam, floating on the oily surface. I jumped up, I said, 'Fight.' 'Fight,' I repeated. It is the effort and the struggle, it is the perpetual warfare, it is the shattering and piecing together—this is the daily

battle, defeat or victory, the absorbing pursuit. The trees, scattered, put on order; the thick green of the leaves thinned itself
to a dancing light. I netted them under with a sudden phrase. I
retrieved them from formlessness with words.

"The train came in. Lengthening down the platform, the
train came to a stop. I caught my train. And so back to London
in the evening. How satisfactory, the atmosphere of common
sense and tobacco; old women clambering into the third-class
carriage with their baskets; the sucking at pipes; the good nights
and see you tomorrows of friends parting at wayside stations,
and then the lights of London—not the flaring ecstasy of youth,
not that tattered violet banner, but still the lights of London all
the same; hard, electric lights, high up in offices; street lamps
laced along dry pavements; flares roaring above street markets. I
like all this when I have dispatched the enemy for a moment.

"Also I like to find the pageant of existence roaring, in a
theatre for instance. The clay-coloured, earthy nondescript animal of the field here erects himself and with infinite ingenuity
and effort puts up a fight against the green woods and green
fields and sheep advancing with measured tread, munching.
And, of course, windows in the long grey streets were lit up;
strips of carpet cut the pavement; there were swept and gar-
nished rooms, fire, food, wine, talk. Men with withered hands,
women with pearl pagodas hanging from their ears came in
and went out. I saw old men's faces carved into wrinkles and
sneers by the work of the world; beauty cherished so that it
seemed newly sprung even in age; and youth, so apt for pleasure that pleasure, one thought, must exist; it seemed that grass-
lands must roll for it; and the sea be chopped up into little
waves; and the woods rustle with bright-coloured birds for
youth, for youth expectant. There one met Jinny and Hal,
Tom, and Betty; there we had our jokes and shared our secrets;
and never parted in the doorway without arranging to meet
again in some other room as the occasion, as the time of the year,

suggested. Life is pleasant; life is good; after Monday comes Tuesday, and Wednesday follows Tuesday.

"Yes, but after a time with a difference. It may be that something in the look of the room one night, in the arrangement of the chairs, suggests it. It seems comfortable to sink down on a sofa in a corner, to look, to listen. Then it happens that two figures standing with their backs to the window appear against the branches of a spreading tree. With a shock of emotion one feels, 'There are figures without features robed in beauty, doomed yet eternal.' In the pause that follows, while the ripples spread, the girl to whom one should be talking says to herself, 'He is old.' But she is wrong. It is not age; it is that a drop has fallen; another drop. Time has given the arrangement another shake. Out we creep from the arch of the currant leaves, out into a wider world. The true order of things—this is our perpetual illusion—is now apparent. Thus in a moment, in a drawing-room, our life adjusts itself to the majestic march of day across the sky.

"It was for this reason that instead of pulling on my patent-leather shoes and finding a tolerable tie, I sought Neville. I sought my oldest friend, who had known me when I was Byron; when I was Meredith's young man, and also that hero in a book by Dostoevsky whose name I have forgotten. I found him alone, reading. A perfectly neat table; a curtain pulled methodically straight; a paper-knife dividing a French volume—nobody, I thought, ever changes the attitude in which we saw them first, or the clothes. Here he has sat in this chair, in these clothes, ever since we first met. Here was freedom; here was intimacy, the firelight broke off some round apple on the curtain. There we talked; sat talking; sauntered down that avenue, the avenue which runs under the trees, under the thick-leaved murmuring trees, the trees that hung with fruit, which we have trodden so often together, so that now the turf is bare round some of those trees, round certain plays and poems, certain favourites of ours —the turf is trodden bare by our incessant unmethodical pacing.

If I have to wait, I read; if I wake in the night, I feel along the shelf for a book. Swelling perpetually augmented, there is a vast accumulation of unrecorded matter in my head. Now and then I break off a lump, Shakespeare it may be, it may be some old woman called Peck; and say to myself, smoking a cigarette in bed, 'That's Shakespeare. That's Peck'—with a certainty of recognition and a shock of knowledge which is endlessly delightful, though not to be imparted. So we shared our Pecks, our Shakespeares; compared each other's versions; allowed each other's insight to set our own Peck or Shakespeare in a better light; and then sank into one of those silences which are now and again broken by a few words, as if a fin rose in the wastes of silence; and then the fin, the thought, sinks back into the depths spreading round it a little ripple of satisfaction, content.

"Yes, but suddenly one hears a clock tick. We who had been immersed in this world became aware of another. It is painful. It was Neville who changed our time. He who had been thinking with the unlimited time of the mind, which stretches in a flash from Shakespeare to ourselves, poked the fire and began to live by that other clock which marks the approach of a particular person. The wide and dignified sweep of his mind contracted. He became on the alert. I could feel him listening to sounds in the street. I noted how he touched a cushion. From the myriads of mankind and all time past he had chosen one person, one moment in particular. A sound was heard in the hall. What he was saying wavered in the air like an uneasy flame. I watched him disentangle one footstep from other footsteps; wait for some particular mark of identification and glance with the swiftness of a snake at the handle of the door. (Hence the astonishing acuteness of his perceptions; he has been trained always by one person.) So concentrated a passion shot out others like foreign matter from a still, sparkling fluid. I became aware of my own vague and cloudy nature full of sediment, full of doubt, full of phrases and notes to be made in pocket-books. The folds of the curtain became still, statuesque; the paper-weight on the table hardened; the threads on the curtain sparkled; everything became definite, external, a scene in which I had no part. I rose, therefore; I left him.

"Heavens! how they caught me as I left the room, the fangs of that old pain! the desire for some one not there. For whom? I did not know at first; then remembered Percival. I had not thought of him for months. Now to laugh with him, to laugh with him at Neville—that was what I wanted, to walk off arm-in-arm together laughing. But he was not there. The place was empty.

"It is strange how the dead leap out on us at street corners, or in dreams.

"This fitful gust blowing so sharp and cold upon me sent me that night across London to visit other friends, Rhoda and Louis, desiring company, certainty, contact. I wondered, as I mounted the stairs, what was their relationship? What did they say alone? I figured her awkward with the tea-kettle. She gazed over the slate roofs—the nymph of the fountain always wet, obsessed with visions, dreaming. She parted the curtain to look at the night. 'Away!' she said. 'The moor is dark beneath the moon' (I rang, I waited). Louis perhaps poured out milk in a saucer for the cat; Louis, whose bony hands shut like the sides of a dock closing themselves with a slow anguish of effort upon an enormous tumult of waters, who knew what has been said by the Egyptian, the Indian, by men with high cheek-bones and solitaries in hair shirts. I knocked: I waited; there was no answer. I tramped down the stone stairs again. Our friends—how distant, how mute, how seldom visited and little known. And I, too, am dim to my friends and unknown; a phantom, sometimes seen, often not. Life is a dream surely. Our flame, the will-o'-the-wisp that dances in a few eyes is soon to be blown out and all will fade. I recalled my friends. I thought of Susan. She had bought fields; cucumbers and tomatoes ripened in her hothouses. The vine that had been killed by last year's frost was putting out a leaf or two. She walked heavily with her sons across her meadows. She went about the land attended by men in gaiters, pointing with her stick at a roof, at hedges, at walls fallen into disrepair. The pigeons followed her, waddling, for the grain that she let fall from her capable, earthy fingers. 'But I no longer rise at dawn,' she said. Then Jinny—entertaining, no doubt, some new young man. They reached the crisis of the usual conversation. The room would be darkened; chairs arranged. For she still sought the moment. Without illusions, hard and clear as crystal, she rode at the day with her breast bared. She let its spikes pierce her. When the lock whitened on her forehead she twisted it fearlessly among the rest. So when they come to bury her nothing will be out of order. Bits of ribbons will be found curled up. But still the door opens. Who is coming in? she asks, and rises to meet him, prepared, as on those first spring nights when the tree under the big London houses where respectable citizens were going soberly to bed scarcely sheltered her love; and the squeak of trams mixed with her cry of delight and the rippling of leaves had to shade her languor, her delicious lassitude as she sank down cooled by all the sweetness of nature satisfied. Our friends, how seldom visited, how little known—it is true; and yet, when I meet an unknown person, and try to break off, here at this table, what I call 'my life,' it is not one life that I look back upon; I am not one person; I am many people; I do not altogether know who I am—Jinny, Susan, Neville, Rhoda, or Louis: or how to distinguish my life from theirs.

"So I thought that night in early autumn when we came together and dined once more at Hampton Court. Our discomfort was at first considerable, for each by that time was committed to a statement, and the other person coming along the road to the meeting-place dressed like this or that, with a stick or without seemed to contradict it. I saw Jinny look at Susan's earthy fingers and then hide her own; I, considering Neville, so neat and exact, felt the nebulosity of my own life blurred with all these phrases. He then boasted, because he was ashamed of one room and one person and his own success. Louis and Rhoda, the conspirators, the spies at table, who take notes, felt 'After all, Bernard can make the waiter fetch us rolls—a contact denied us.' We saw for a moment laid out among us the body of the complete human being whom we have failed to be, but at the same time, cannot forget. All that we might have been we saw; all that we had missed, and we grudged for a moment the other's claim, as children when the cake is cut, the one cake, the only cake, watch their slice diminishing.

"However, we had our bottle of wine, and under that seduction lost our enmity, and stopped comparing. And, half-way through dinner, we felt enlarge itself round us the huge blackness of what is outside us, of what we are not. The wind, the rush of wheels became the roar of time, and we rushed—where? And who were we? We were extinguished for a moment, went out like sparks in burnt paper and the blackness roared. Past time, past history we went. For me this lasts but one second. It is ended by my own pugnacity. I strike the table with a spoon. If I could measure things with compasses I would, but since my only measure is a phrase, I make phrases—I forget what, on this occasion. We became six people at a table in Hampton Court. We rose and walked together down the avenue. In the thin, the unreal twilight, fitfully like the echo of voices laughing down some alley, geniality returned to me and flesh. Against the gateway, against some cedar tree I saw blaze bright, Neville, Jinny, Rhoda, Louis, Susan and myself, our life, our identity. Still King William seemed an unreal monarch and his crown mere tinsel. But we—against the brick, against the branches, we six, out of how many million millions, for one moment out of what measureless abundance of past time and time to come, burnt there triumphant. The moment was all; the moment was enough. And then Neville, Jinny, Susan and I as a wave breaks, burst asunder, surrendered—to the next leaf, to the precise bird, to a child with a hoop, to a prancing dog, to the warmth that is hoarded in woods after a hot day, to the lights twisted like white ribbon on rippled waters. We drew apart; we were consumed in the dark-

ness of the trees leaving Rhoda and Louis to stand on the terrace
by the urn.

"When we returned from that immersion—how sweet, how
deep!—and came to the surface and saw the conspirators still
standing there it was with some compunction. We had lost what
they had kept. We interrupted. But we were tired, and whether
it had been good or bad, accomplished or left undone, the dusky
veil was falling upon our endeavours; the lights were sinking as
we paused for a moment upon the terrace that overlooks the
river. The steamers were landing their trippers on the bank;
there was a distant cheering, the sound of singing, as if people waved their hats and joined in some last song. The sound
of the chorus came across the water and I felt leap up that old
impulse, which has moved me all my life, to be thrown up and
down on the roar of other people's voices, singing the same song;
to be tossed up and down on the roar of almost senseless merri-
ment, sentiment, triumph, desire. But not now. No! I could not
collect myself; I could not distinguish myself; I could not help
letting fall the things that had made me a minute ago eager,
amused, jealous, vigilant and hosts of other things into the
water. I could not recover myself from that endless throwing
away, dissipation, flooding forth without our willing it and
rushing soundlessly away out there under the arches of the
bridge, round some clump of trees or an island, out where
seabirds sit on stakes, over the roughened water to become
waves in the sea—I could not recover myself from that dissipation. So we parted.

"Was this then, this streaming away mixed with Susan,
Jinny, Neville, Rhoda, Louis, a sort of death? A new assembly of
elements? Some hint of what was to come? The note was scribbled, the book shut, for I am an intermittent student. I do not
say my lessons by any means at the stated hour. Later, walking
down Fleet Street at the rush hour, I recalled that moment; I
continued it. 'Must I for ever,' I said, 'beat my spoon on the table-
cloth? Shall I not, too, consent?' The omnibuses were clogged;

one came up behind another and stopped with a click, like a link added to a stone chain. People passed.

"Multitudinous, carrying attaché-cases, dodging with incredible celerity in and out, they went past like a river in spate. They went past roaring like a train in a tunnel. Seizing my chance I crossed; dived down a dark passage and entered the shop where they cut my hair. I leant my head back and was swathed in a sheet. Looking-glasses confronted me in which I could see my pinioned body and people passing; stopping, looking, and going on indifferent. The hairdresser began to move his scissors to and fro. I felt myself powerless to stop the oscillations of the cold steel. So we are cut and laid in swathes, I said; so we lie side by side on the damp meadows, withered branches and flowering. We have no more to expose ourselves on the bare hedges to the wind and snow; no more to carry ourselves erect when the gale sweeps, to bear our burden upheld; or stay, unmurmuring, on those pallid noondays when the bird creeps close to the bough and the damp whitens the leaf. We are cut, we are fallen. We are become part of that unfeeling universe that sleeps when we are at our quickest and burns red when we lie asleep. We have renounced our station and lie now flat, withered and how soon forgotten! Upon which I saw an expression in the tail of the eye of the hairdresser as if something interested him in the street.

"What interested the hairdresser? What did the hairdresser see in the street? It is thus that I am recalled. (For I am no mystic; something always plucks at me—curiosity, envy, admiration, interest in hairdressers and the like bring me to the surface.) While he brushed the fluff from my coat I took pains to assure myself of his identity and then, swinging my stick, I went into the Strand, and evoked to serve as opposite to myself the figure of Rhoda always so furtive, always with fear in her eyes, always seeking some pillar in the desert, to find which she had gone; she had killed herself. 'Wait,' I said, putting my arm in imagination (thus we consort with our friends) through her arm. 'Wait until these omnibuses have gone by. Do not cross so dangerously. These men are your brothers.' In persuading her I was also persuading my own soul. For this is not one life; nor do I always know if I am man or woman, Bernard or Neville, Louis, Susan, Jinny or Rhoda—so strange is the contact of one with another.

"Swinging my stick, with my hair newly cut and the nape of my neck tingling, I went past all those trays of penny toys imported from Germany that men hold out in the street by St. Paul's—St. Paul's, the brooding hen with spread wings from whose shelter run omnibuses and streams of men and women at the rush hour. I thought how Louis would mount those steps in his neat suit with his cane in his hand and his angular, rather detached gait. With his Australian accent ('My father, a banker at Brisbane') he would come, I thought, with greater respect to these old ceremonies than I do, who have heard the same lullabies for a thousand years. I am always impressed, as I enter, by the rubbed noses; the polished brasses; the flapping and the chanting, while one boy's voice wails round the dome like some lost and wandering dove. The recumbency and the peace of the dead impress me—warriors at rest under their old banners. Then I scoff at the floridity and absurdity of some scrolloping tomb; and the trumpets and the victories and the coats of arms and the certainty, so sonorously repeated, of resurrection, of eternal life. My wandering and inquisitive eye then shows me an awe-stricken child; a shuffling pensioner; or the obeisances of tired shop-girls burdened with heaven knows what strife in their poor thin breasts come to solace themselves in the rush hour. I stray and look and wonder and sometimes, rather furtively, try to rise on the shaft of somebody else's prayer into the dome, out, beyond, wherever they go. But then like the lost and wailing dove, I find myself failing, fluttering, descending and perching upon some curious gargoyle, some battered nose or absurd tombstone, with humour, with wonder, and so again watch the sightseers with their Baedekers shuffling past, while the boy's voice soars in the dome and the organ now and then indulges in a moment of elephantine triumph. How then, I asked, would Louis roof us all in? How would he confine us, make us one, with his red ink, with his very fine nib? The voice petered out in the dome, wailing.

"So into the street again, swinging my stick, looking at wire trays in stationers' shop-windows, at baskets of fruit grown in the colonies, murmuring Pillicock sat on Pillicock's Hill, or Hark, hark, the dogs do bark, or The World's great age begins anew, or Come away, come away, death—mingling nonsense and poetry, floating in the stream. Something always has to be done next. Tuesday follows Monday; Wednesday, Tuesday. Each spreads the same ripple. The being grows rings, like a tree. Like a tree, leaves fall.

"For one day as I leant over a gate that led into a field, the rhythm stopped: the rhymes and the hummings, the nonsense and the poetry. A space was cleared in my mind. I saw through the thick leaves of habit. Leaning over the gate I regretted so much litter, so much unaccomplishment and separation, for one cannot cross London to see a friend, life being so full of engagements; nor take ship to India and see a naked man spearing fish in blue water. I said life had been imperfect, an unfinished phrase. It had been impossible for me, taking snuff as I do from any bagman met in a train, to keep coherency—that sense of the generations, of women carrying red pitchers to the Nile, of the nightingale who sings among conquests and migrations. It had been too vast an undertaking, I said, and how can I go on lifting my foot perpetually to climb the stair? I addressed my self as one would speak to a companion with whom one is voyaging to the North Pole.

"I spoke to that self who has been with me in many tremendous adventures; the faithful man who sits over the fire when everybody has gone to bed, stirring the cinders with a poker; the man who has been so mysteriously and with sudden accretions of being built up, in a beech wood, sitting by a willow tree on a bank, leaning over a parapet at Hampton Court; the man who has collected himself in moments of emergency and banged his spoon on the table, saying, 'I will not consent.'

"This self now as I leant over the gate looking down over fields rolling in waves of colour beneath me made no answer. He threw up no opposition. He attempted no phrase. His fist did not form. I waited. I listened. Nothing came, nothing. I cried then with a sudden conviction of complete desertion, Now there is nothing. No fin breaks the waste of this immeasurable sea. Life has destroyed me. No echo comes when I speak, no varied words. This is more truly death than the death of friends, than the death of youth. I am the swathed figure in the hairdresser's shop taking up only so much space.

"The scene beneath me withered. It was like the eclipse when the sun went out and left the earth, flourishing in full summer foliage, withered, brittle, false. Also I saw on a winding road in a dust dance the groups we had made, how they came together, how they ate together, how they met in this room or that. I saw my own indefatigable busyness—how I had rushed from one to the other, fetched and carried, travelled and returned, joined this group and that, here kissed, here withdrawn; always kept hard at it by some extraordinary purpose with my nose to the ground like a dog on the scent; with an occasional toss of the head, an occasional cry of amazement, despair and then back again with my nose to the scent. What a litter—what a confusion; with here birth, here death; succulence and sweetness; effort and anguish; and myself always running hither and thither. Now it was done with. I had no more appetites to glut; no more stings in me with which to poison people; no more sharp teeth and clutching hands or desire to feel the pear and the grape and the sun beating down from the orchard wall.

"The woods had vanished; the earth was a waste of shadow. No sound broke the silence of the wintry landscape. No cock crowed; no smoke rose; no train moved. A man without a self, I said. A heavy body leaning on a gate. A dead man. With dispassionate despair, with entire disillusionment I surveyed the dust dance; my life, my friends' lives, and those fabulous presences, men with brooms, women writing, the willow tree by the river—clouds and phantoms made of dust too, of dust that changed, as clouds lose and gain and take gold or red and lose their summits and billow this way and that, mutable, vain. I, carrying a notebook, making phrases, had recorded merely changes; a shadow, I had been sedulous to take note of shadows. How can I proceed now, I said, without a self, weightless and visionless, through a world weightless, without illusion?

"The heaviness of my despondency thrust open the gate I leant on and pushed me, an elderly man, a heavy man with gray hair, through the colourless field, the empty field. No more to hear echoes, no more to see phantoms, to conjure up no opposition, but to walk always unshadowed making no impress upon the dead earth. If even there had been sheep munching, pushing one foot after another, or a bird, or a man driving a spade into the earth, had there been a bramble to trip me, or a ditch, damp with soaked leaves, into which to fall—but no, the melancholy path led along the level, to more wintriness, and pallor and the equal and uninteresting view of the same landscape.

"How then does light return to the world after the eclipse of the sun? Miraculously. Frailly. In thin stripes. It hangs like a glass cage. It is a hoop to be fractured by a tiny jar. There is a spark there. Next moment a flush of dun. Then a vapour as if earth were breathing in and out, once, twice, for the first time. Then under the dullness some one walks with a green light. Then off twists a white wraith. The woods throb blue and green, and gradually the fields drink in red, gold, brown. Suddenly a river snatches a blue light. The earth absorbs colour like a sponge, slowly drinking water. It puts on weight; rounds itself; hangs pendent; settles and swings beneath our feet.

"So the landscape returned to me; so I saw fields rolling in waves of colour beneath me, but now with this difference; I saw but was not seen. I walked unshadowed; I came unheralded. From me had dropped the old cloak, the old response; the hollowed hand that beats back sounds. Thin, as a ghost, leaving no trace where I trod, perceiving merely, I walked alone in a new world, never trodden; brushing new flowers, unable to speak save in a child's words of one syllable; without shelter from phrases—I who have made so many; unattended, I who have always gone with my kind; solitary I who have always had some one to share the empty grate, or the cupboard with its hanging loop of gold.

"But how describe the world seen without a self? There are no words. Blue, red—even they distract, even they hide with thickness instead of letting the light through. How describe or say anything in articulate words again?—save that it fades, save that it undergoes a gradual transformation, becomes, even in the course of one short walk, habitual—this scene also. Blindness returns as one moves and one leaf repeats another. Loveliness returns as one looks with all its train of phantom phrases. One breathes in and out substantial breath; down in the valley the train draws across the fields lop-eared with smoke.

"But for a moment I had sat on the turf somewhere high above the flow of the sea and the sounds of the woods, had seen the house, the garden, and the waves breaking. The old nurse who turns the pages of the picture-book had stopped and had said, 'Look. This is the truth.'

"So I was thinking as I came along Shaftesbury Avenue tonight. I was thinking of that picture in the picture-book. And when I met you in the place where one goes to hang up one's coat I said to myself, 'It does not matter whom I meet. All this little affair of "being" is over. Who this is I do not know; nor care; we will dine together.' So I hung up my coat, tapped you on the shoulder, and said, 'Sit with me.'

"Now the meal is finished; we are surrounded by peelings and bread-crumbs. I have tried to break off this bunch and hand it you; but whether there is substance or truth in it I do not know. Nor do I know exactly where we are. What city does that stretch of sky look down upon? Is it Paris, is it London where we sit or some southern city of pink-washed houses lying under cypresses, under high mountains, where eagles soar? I do not at this moment feel certain.

"I begin now to forget; I begin to doubt the fixity of tables, the reality of here and now, to tap my knuckles smartly upon the edges of apparently solid objects and say, 'Are you hard?' I have seen so many different things, have made so many different sentences. I have lost in the process of eating and drinking and rubbing my eyes along surfaces that thin, hard shell which cases the soul, which, in youth, shuts one in—hence the fierceness, and the tap, tap, tap of the remorseless beaks of the young. And now I ask, 'Who am I?' I have been talking of Bernard, Neville, Jinny, Susan, Rhoda and Louis. Am I all of them? Am I one and distinct? I do not know. We sat here together. But now Percival is dead, and Rhoda is dead; we are divided; we are not here. Yet I cannot find any obstacle separating us. There is no division between me and them. As I talked I felt, 'I am you.' This difference we make so much of, this identity we so feverishly cherish, was overcome. Yes, ever since old Mrs. Constable lifted her sponge and pouring warm water over me covered me with flesh I have been sensitive, percipient. Here on my brow is the blow I got when Percival fell. Here on the nape of my neck is the kiss Jinny gave Louis. My eyes fill with Susan's tears. I see far away, quivering like a gold thread, the pillar Rhoda saw, and feel the rush of the wind of her flight when she leapt.

"Thus when I come to shape here at this table between my hands the story of my life and set it before you as a complete thing, I have to recall things gone far, gone deep, sunk into this life or that and become part of it; dreams, too, things surrounding me, and the inmates, those old half-articulate ghosts who keep up their hauntings by day and night; who turn over in their sleep, who utter their confused cries, who put out their phantom fingers and clutch at me as I try to escape—shadows of people one might have been; unborn selves. There is the old brute, too, the savage, the hairy man who dabbles his fingers in ropes of entrails; and gobbles and belches; whose speech is guttural, visceral—well, he is here. He squats in me. Tonight he has been feasted on quails, salad, and sweetbread. He now holds a glass of fine old brandy in his paw. He brindles, purrs and shoots warm thrills all down my spine as I sip. It is true, he washes his hands before dinner, but they are still hairy. He buttons on trousers and waistcoats, but they contain the same organs. He jibs if I keep him waiting for dinner. He mops and mows perpetually pointing with his half-idiot gestures of greed and covetousness at what he desires. I assure you, I have great difficulty sometimes in controlling him. That man, the hairy, the ape-like, has contributed his part to my life. He has given a greener glow to green things, has held his torch with its red flames, its thick and smarting smoke, behind every leaf. He has lit up the cool garden even. He has brandished his torch in murky by-streets where girls suddenly seem to shine with a red and intoxicating translucency. Oh, he has tossed his torch high! He has led me wild dances!

"But no more. Now tonight, my body rises tier upon tier like some cool temple whose floor is strewn with carpets and murmurs rise and the altars stand smoking; but up above, here in my serene head, come only fine gusts of melody, waves of incense, while the lost dove wails, and the banners tremble above tombs, and the dark airs of midnight shake trees outside the open windows. When I look down from this transcendency, how beautiful are even the crumbled relics of bread! What shapely spirals the peelings of pears make—how thin, and mottled like some sea-bird's egg. Even the forks laid straight side by side appear lucid, logical, exact; and the horns of the rolls which we have left are glazed, yellow-plated, hard. I could worship my hand even, with its fan of bones laced by blue mysterious veins and its astonishing look of aptness, suppleness and ability to curl softly or suddenly crush—its infinite sensibility.

"Immeasurably receptive, holding everything, trembling with

fullness, yet clear, contained—so my being seems, now that desire urges it no more out and away; now that curiosity no longer dyes it a thousand colours. It lies deep, tideless, immune, now that he is dead, the man I called 'Bernard,' the man who kept a book in his pocket in which he made notes—phrases for the moon, notes of features; how people looked, turned, dropped their cigarette ends; under B, butterfly powder, under D, ways of naming death. But now let the door open, the glass door that is for ever turning on its hinges. Let a woman come, let a young man in evening-dress with a moustache sit down; is there anything that they can tell me? No! I know all that, too. And if she suddenly gets up and goes, 'My dear,' I say, 'you no longer make me look after you.' The shock of the falling wave which has sounded all my life, which woke me so that I saw the gold loop on the cupboard, no longer makes quiver what I hold.

"So now, taking upon me the mystery of things, I could go like a spy without leaving this place, without stirring from my chair. I can visit the remote verges of the desert lands where the savage sits by the campfire. Day rises; the girl lifts the watery fire-hearted jewels to her brow; the sun levels his beams straight at the sleeping house; the waves deepen their bars; they fling themselves on shore; back blows the spray; sweeping their waters they surround the boat and the sea-holly. The birds sing in chorus; deep tunnels run between the stalks of flowers; the house is whitened; the sleeper stretches; gradually all is astir. Light floods the room and drives shadow beyond shadow to where they hang in folds inscrutable. What does the central shadow hold? Something? Nothing? I do not know.

"Oh, but there is your face. I catch your eye. I, who had been thinking myself so vast, a temple, a church, a whole universe, unconfined and capable of being everywhere on the verge of things and here too, am now nothing but what you see—an elderly man, rather heavy, grey above the ears, who (I see myself in the glass) leans one elbow on the table, and holds in his left hand a glass of old brandy. That is the blow you have dealt me. I have walked bang into the pillar-box. I reel from side to side. I put my hands to my head. My hat is off—I have dropped my stick. I have made an awful ass of myself and am justly laughed at by any passer-by.

"Lord, how unutterably disgusting life is! What dirty tricks it plays us, one moment free; the next, this. Here we are among the breadcrumbs and the stained napkins again. That knife is already congealing with grease. Disorder, sordidity and corruption surround us. We have been taking into our mouths the bodies of dead birds. It is with these greasy crumbs, slobbered over napkins, and little corpses that we have to build. Always it begins again; always there is the enemy; eyes meeting ours; fingers twitching ours; the effort waiting. Call the waiter. Pay the bill. We must pull ourselves up out of our chairs. We must find our coats. We must go. Must, must, must—detestable word. Once more, I who had thought myself immune, who had said, 'Now I am rid of all that,' find that the wave has tumbled me over, head over heels, scattering my possessions, leaving me to collect, to assemble, to heap together, summon my forces, rise and confront the enemy.

"It is strange that we who are capable of so much suffering, should inflict so much suffering. Strange that the face of a person, whom I scarcely know save that I think we met once on the gangway of a ship bound for Africa—a mere adumbration of eyes, cheeks, nostrils—should have power to inflict this insult. You look, eat, smile, are bored, pleased, annoyed—that is all I know. Yet this shadow which has sat by me for an hour or two, this mask from which peep two eyes, has power to drive me back, to pinion me down among all those other faces, to shut me in a hot room; to send me dashing like a moth from candle to candle.

"But wait. While they add up the bill behind the screen wait one moment. Now that I have reviled you for the blow that sent me staggering among peelings and crumblings and old scraps of meat, I will record in words of one syllable how also under your gaze with that compulsion on me I begin to perceive this, that and the other. The clock ticks; the woman sneezes; the waiter comes—there is a gradual coming together, running into one, acceleration and unification. Listen: a whistle sounds, wheels rush, the door creaks on its hinges. I regain the sense of the complexity and the reality and the struggle, for which I thank you. And with some pity, some envy and much good will, take your hand and bid you good night.

"Heaven be praised for solitude! I am alone now. That almost unknown person has gone, to catch some train, to take some cab, to go to some place or person whom I do not know. The face looking at me has gone. The pressure is removed. Here are empty coffee-cups. Here are chairs turned but nobody sits on them. Here are empty tables and nobody any more coming to dine at them tonight.

"Let me now raise my song of glory. Heaven be praised for solitude. Let me be alone. Let me cast and throw away this veil of being, this cloud that changes with the least breath, night and day, and all night and all day. While I sat here I have been changing. I have watched the sky change. I have seen clouds cover the stars, then free the stars, then cover the stars again. Now I look at their changing no more. Now no one sees me and I change no more. Heaven be praised for solitude that has removed the pressure of the eye, the solicitation of the body, and all need of lies and phrases.

"My book, stuffed with phrases, has dropped to the floor. It lies under the table to be swept up by the charwoman when she comes wearily at dawn looking for scraps of paper, old tram tickets, and here and there a note screwed into a ball and left with the litter to be swept up. What is the phrase for the moon? And the phrase for love? By what name are we to call death? I do not know. I need a little language such as lovers use, words of one syllable such as children speak when they come into the room and find their mother sewing and pick up some scrap of bright wool, a feather, or a shred of chintz. I need a howl; a cry.

When the storm crosses the marsh and sweeps over me where I lie in the ditch unregarded I need no words. Nothing neat. Nothing that comes down with all its feet on the floor. None of those resonances and lovely echoes that break and chime from nerve to nerve in our breasts making wild music, false phrases. I have done with phrases.

"How much better is silence; the coffee-cup, the table. How much better to sit by myself like the solitary sea-bird that opens its wings on the stake. Let me sit here for ever with bare things, this coffee-cup, this knife, this fork, things in themselves, myself being myself. Do not come and worry me with your hints that it is time to shut the shop and be gone. I would willingly give all my money that you should not disturb me but let me sit on and on, silent, alone.

"But now the head waiter, who has finished his own meal, appears and frowns; he takes his muffler from his pocket and ostentatiously makes ready to go. They must go; must put up the shutters, must fold the tablecloths, and give one brush with a wet mop under the tables.

"Curse you then. However beat and done with it all I am, I must haul myself up, and find the particular coat that belongs to me; must push my arms into the sleeves; must muffle myself up against the night air and be off. I, I, I, tired as I am, spent as I am, and almost worn out with all this rubbing of my nose along the surfaces of things, even I, an elderly man who is getting rather heavy and dislikes exertion must take myself off and catch some last train.

"Again I see before me the usual street. The canopy of civilisation is burnt out. The sky is dark as polished whale-bone. But there is a kindling in the sky whether of lamplight or of dawn. There is a stir of some sort—sparrows on plane trees somewhere chirping. There is a sense of the break of day. I will not call it dawn. What is dawn in the city to an elderly man standing in the street looking up rather dizzily at the sky? Dawn is some sort of whitening of the sky; some sort of renewal. Another day; another Friday; another twentieth of March, January, or September. Another general awakening. The stars draw back and are extinguished. The bars deepen themselves between the waves. The film of mist thickens on the fields. A redness gathers on the roses, even on the pale rose that hangs by the bedroom window. A bird chirps. Cottagers light their early candles. Yes, this is the eternal renewal, the incessant rise and fall and fall and rise again.

"And in me too the wave rises. It swells; it arches its back. I am aware once more of a new desire, something rising beneath me like the proud horse whose rider first spurs and then pulls him back. What enemy do we now perceive advancing against us, you whom I ride now, as we stand pawing this stretch of pavement? It is death. Death is the enemy. It is death against whom I ride with my spear couched and my hair flying back like a young man's, like Percival's, when he galloped in India. I strike spurs into my horse. Against you I will fling myself, unvanquished and unyielding, O Death!"

The waves broke on the shore.

HARVEST BOOKS